DOWNS-LORD DOOMSDAY

GW00371088

Also by John Whitbourn from Earthlight

The Royal Changeling
Downs-Lord Dawn
Downs-Lord Day

DOWNS-LORD DOOMSDAY

JOHN WHITBOURN

Third Panel of the Downs-Lord Triptych

EARTHLIGHT

SIMON & SCHUSTER

London • New York • Sydney • Tokyo • Singapore • Toronto • Dublin

A VIACOM COMPANY

First published in Great Britain by Earthlight, 2002
An imprint of Simon & Schuster UK Ltd
A Viacom Company

1 3 5 7 9 10 8 6 4 2

Simon & Schuster UK Ltd
Africa House
64–78 Kingsway
London WC2B 6AH

Simon & Schuster Australia
Sydney

www.simonsays.co.uk

A CIP catalogue record for this book is available
from the British Library.

ISBN 0-671-03302-6

Typeset in Goudy by SX Composing DTP, Rayleigh, Essex
Printed and bound in the UK by Omnia Books Ltd, Glasgow

DEDICATION

This book (for all its imperfections) is dedicated to the memory of my beloved mother:

Joan Whitbourn (nee Jackson)

Born Newport, Isle of Wight, 1917.
Died Binscombe, Surrey, 2000.

'We kissed and parted. I humbly hope to meet again, and to part no more.'

Samuel Johnson, 18 October 1767

(AN EARLIER) DEDICATION

To: Liz and Lucy.

As Mick ('*Cold English blood runs hot!*') Jagger once said ('Brown Sugar', 1971):

'Mmmmmmmmmmmmm!'

'He cast upon them the fierceness of his anger, wrath and indignation, and trouble, by sending evil angels among them.'

Psalm 78. Verse 49.

'The gathering darkness makes it useless to be a troubadour. Songs are for joy, not sadness. I have come into the world too late.'

Guirut Riquier, 'Last of the Troubadours'. 1230–94.

PROLOGUE

Thomas Blades, a seventeenth-century curate, discovers a magical door to another world – or rather to an alternative Earth. But here, humanity is not the top of the food chain, as Blades finds when the poor, burrow-dwelling humans he stumbles over are hunted and eaten by the Null – mighty, ravening beasts whose intelligence and killing ability make them top predator.

Returning to our own world for weapons, Blades fulfils his vow to become humanity's saviour on this new Earth and, over the years, builds an empire of which he becomes the first god-king. Power shifts between humanity and Null but, as the humans grow in sophistication, so come treachery, jealousy and murder – and god-king Blades changes much from the timid cleric who first happened upon 'New-Wessex'.

Decades later, new enemies appear, worse and less natural than the Null, and merciless 'angels' usurp the realm. With confidence in his creation already shaken, Blades goes into chastened exile back on Earth, seeking solace in poverty and repentance.

However, life goes on and in New-Wessex the god-king is sorely missed. To his abandoned and oppressed children, even after the lapse of four centuries, the return of Blades 'Null-Bane' remains their only hope . . .

Blade's distant descendant, Guy, hereditary 'Ambassador', is commissioned to cross the void to find and fetch the living God back from Old Earth. After braving many dangers together with Nicolo, his brother, and devout devotee, Hunter, he discovers Blades in the sybarite isle of Capri, reduced to broken beggary, seeking pardon for his sins. Guy piously concludes that the people's faith is once again being put to the test.

Brought back at gun-point, the siren temptations of god-kingship slowly weaken Blades's resolve. Guy, together with his stange and sorcerous, but dearly beloved, young wife, Bathesheba (or '*Bathie*') of the Fruntierfolke tribe, rouses Blades from his slumber and sets him against the angels and evolved-Null. Null-Paris dies in flames, the yoke of slavery is thrown off, and yet avenging angels prove unable to harm Blades – or Guy . . .

At the cost of brother, father, friend and home, Guy reinstates Blades in New-Wessex to set the world aright. Great matters, beyond his understanding, are afoot and only Bathie and his faith sustain Guy through savage loss and tribulation.

Now, under curious protection, god-king Blades and Guy Ambassador oversee a new beginning for mankind . . .

The *Downs-Lord Triptych* offers three connected scenes from a baroque Empire in the making, dovetailing to create a portrait of eventful centuries. Here is an exotic saga of transformation and a hymn to the exuberance of unfettered life.

'Dead men tell no tales,' stated Guy Ambassador, a dry voice echoing in the emptiness. Despite all the stress, his stutter lay dormant. Just like the figure before him.

The man on the quay wouldn't confirm or deny the saying. In fact he said nothing – but at the same time said a great deal. Normal towns don't have corpses for doormen, nor leave cadavers to greet guests.

However, Yarmouth had never been a 'normal' town at the best of times, which was why they now approached it with such caution. The day was crystal clear and promising, the Isle of Wight's beauty never more enticing. Nevertheless, the *Lady Bridget* stood offshore for ages, gun ports and rigging aquiver, ready to fire or flee at the slightest sign of wizardry.

Then, when even the liveliest imagination failed to discern life, the longboat had made for land as if they never expected to arrive. The oars cut the waves with the strength of resignation, their wielders not the usual American slaves but Wessex freemen with lives to lose, capable of grasping their dreadful project.

Judging a book by its cover, an outsider would never guess that 'King' Guy (to give him his proper, hand-me-down, title) was in his rightful place. The old-fashioned wig and mere militia colonel's scarlet coat and cocked hat were a snare to the unwary. Snow on the roof, other than wig powder, needn't imply the fire had gone out. That this man of the world had gained around the equator signified nothing. He retained that world's measure and inner light still glittered from deceptively mild eyes. Guy was where he should be, at the boat's prow and leading the way, foremost in breeding and danger.

His companions begrudged him neither distinction, each knowing they wouldn't be there but for him – in more senses than one. Even hardened veterans of the seaways and Sicily gunpowder run deferred to a man who'd fought with angels – and prevailed; the same man who'd razed Null-Paris to the

1

ground! Likewise, a score of years might have passed since, but the return of Blades the Great remained daily acclaimed. The god-king's guide home fully merited the gift of kingship and pre-eminence in any vessel.

Therefore *he* had the privilege of meeting and greeting the quay's sole inhabitant. It was for him to assess and pass judgement. Guy's gratitude knew no start.

It wasn't a long-standing carcass. From a kindly distance you might even expect him to rise again. The eye-sockets were still occupied and the face he'd finally turned to the sun was tanned but not blackened. Hair on the head which lolled over the quay's edge played at the wind's behest, although its master no longer could.

The whim of the tide took them right past his unseeing gaze, giving every mariner the chance to wonder what sights he now saw and when they might share the same view. Every sensible calculation suggested quite soon.

'Make fast.'

Guy's words snapped them out of their spell and they pondered that mere singleton death no more. Given that Wight equalled wizardry, there were better things to worry about.

Bosun expertly got them into position and encircled the mooring. After a second's deference to the choppy sea, it was possible for Guy to disembark with dignity.

He could see properly now. A long *seax* knife, up and under the rib-cage had parted their friend from the world. An expert job, putting his starry gown only a few stitches short of perfect repair. Guy leaned down to close two sightless eyes – whilst simultaneously making sure. His pistol hovered ready to finish the job.

It proved completed hours or even days before. Those eyelids stubbornly resisted his compassion. Their tale was told; they saw no more. Which was a relief.

Then, for all – or maybe because – they'd served as life-windows for a wizard, Guy commended the late owner to God's mercy. He'd probably well need it.

But after that there was no escaping progression. Guy was free to look around and people were expecting him to. The opportunity was there and wide open to him, but for a space he stayed staring down, modest as a maiden.

Of course, it couldn't go on. Therefore he had to. Guy forced himself and surveyed the scene.

The place was so steeped in legend, he hardly expected the quay to be plain tar and timber just like any other. It bore his weight, then that of his team. It did just what any old quay would do and no more – bar cradle a dead man. At the very least Guy anticipated effigies and tendrils and a baroque slipway into wonder. Here though was simple sunshine and the slap of the tide against wood. Looking right up revealed just standard sky. If you stunned the imaginative faculties it could almost be normality.

Life doesn't like self-deception – Guy knew from experience. It *disapproved* of heads in the clouds. The stiff-necked stumbled and fell to their ruin. Wisely, he lowered his vision and beheld.

The fortifications could almost pass for normal: squat stone creations adapted to the cannon age and bristling with fine examples of same. They'd given the Imperial fleet a bloody nose and hulls awash with gore during the one and only reincorporation attempt. In conjunction with the horrible fate of the marines put ashore, it had been a purchase price and more to buy the centuries of solitude the Wizards of Wight apparently craved.

All the same, in its simple utility, Yarmouth castle might well have been something made by normal men – except, that is, for the layers upon layers of paint. Thick coats splashed or poured on, in vivid purple and yellow and blue and anything else that came to hand, saved the day for the cause of the uncanny.

The quay penetrated between twin bastions. Guy waved men towards the gap but led the way himself.

He walked alone, which felt highly novel. His generally inseparable 'huscarl' bodyguards, the two 'P's, so christened for

3

their names and alikeness, were today separate and sullen back aboard the *Lady Bridget*. Guy hadn't seen any sense in using them up in a foregone conclusion when his other body, no less precious than the one he lived in, required guarding. Lady Bathesheba Fruntierfolke-Ambassador was flesh of his flesh, as well as wife. Living on, she would still require protection. Her welfare justified the present strangeness of solitude.

Planks protested underfoot, as though they'd had a long holiday from boots. Other than that and a few spectator gulls, all was silence below the eternal breath of the wind. On Guy strode, expecting a cannonball or lightning-bolt any second.

You didn't need to be an antiquarian. First the functional: forts and quay and port, and then the earliest portions of four centuries ago. With an overly indulgent eye they could almost be conventional. Guy recognised places that were obviously houses: constructed in the New-Wessex rustic-baroque vernacular. However, after that it was anyone's guess. Given its head, Yarmouth stretched back and went wild: a mad architect's green and gold (his favourites apparently) daymare, plunging deep into the island's own greenery or brown mud of the Yar estuary.

There were gaps: whether paths or orifices Guy didn't care to say. For the moment he was just happy to be alive, without vain hopes of making sense of anything. Here was hardly the place for that.

Behind the quay and boat berths and harbour barrier was St James's Square, a sane survivor from the little space of years before the wizards turned in on themselves. It was expansive compared to the creations which hung over it and might have beckoned you in elsewhere. Here though was different.

Even Guy hesitated and lost half a pace, a blemish in his elegant, albeit gangly, gait. If he hadn't got a grip the sailors might have borrowed the tone and bottle-necked behind him: a prickly ganglion of rifle-armed suspicion. Undignified.

Sooner death than that. Guy told his legs to recall their status and follow instructions. He boldly walked into the naked light of Yarmouth town square.

The revolver was an affectation. He recognised that and let it hang upon its lanyard. Thinking last thoughts, he crossed to the very centre, alone.

First a graceful bow, then recovery and finally arms spread wide, to reveal a merely gold-brocade-waistcoat-protected breast. It was the traditional ambassadorial gesture of presentation. He was here and harmless, at their service, even to the extent of them killing him – if that was what they *really* wanted.

The windows like eyes and mouths and other less mentionables made no comment. There was a quality to the silence that made Guy suspect he actually *was* all alone, save for his drag-along company of nervy mariners.

Mad Yarmouth, home to magecraft and dark researches, self-isolated hermitage of mystery for centuries, looked back at the Ambassador and was speechless.

Guy had to suppress the little fountain of joy that sponsored. He was not here to talk to himself. On the other hand, if that was the only option . . . For the very first time, a vision of himself sailing back out of Wight, home to wife and home and years beyond, gained a sliver of credibility.

'Helloooooooooooo!'

There, he'd said it, out loud, causing the sailors to cringe against the walls, trying to merge with bricks and mortar.

The words played around the square, finding cosy corners in which to fade and die. The wizards' city swallowed them up. It had no reply, save for the gargoyles' echoes. The weirdness-in-stone was self-sufficient, hearing all but saying nothing. It had grown wise during the days of seclusion, learning many things. Apparently, now was the time to silently ponder them.

But to an Ambassador discourse was the very stuff of being: its circulating, driven-under-pressure, lifeblood. Guy couldn't be doing with taciturn opponents.

'I am here! Where are *you*?'

They wouldn't say. Assertion and question followed his other brave words into oblivion.

Beyond the few homely streets, eccentricity soon blossomed

5

into raving madness. One aperture, whether pathway or entrance, looked as good as another.

Guy took up his pistol again. He'd have them speak to him, even if it were only to moan.

Once! Twice! Thrice! Gunpowder expressed his wishes into the sky. Anywhere else it would have prompted a show of birds but here, beyond the carpet-edge of civilisation, the fusillade was lonely. In time, Guy even heard the distant clink of a returning cartridge against a tiled roof.

Now was the moment of greatest danger for an Ambassador: that of appearing ridiculous. He had to recover lost ground.

'They are scared of us!' he announced to deeply unconvinced colleagues. 'Therefore, we shall have to flush them out . . .'

Feeling as conspicuous as a pea on a drum and 10 feet tall besides – without the accompanying assurance – Guy headed for the nearest promising avenue. For a while he was all alone in the dark there, but in due course arriving company shed light on the matter with tinderbox and tar-torch.

It was a chamber of sorts, irregular but just about functional, set as if for a gathering that had turned violent. If you so chose, you could read a certain story into the upset chairs and wall gouges.

Again, to an Ambassador such loutishness was anathema. The very antithesis to diplomacy. Guy accordingly regarded it with disdain for the minimum possible period. A far door offered exit from the nonsense and Guy took it, his armed and wary friends trailing behind him like ducklings.

At the beginning they had a semblance of military order: a rearguard and Guy-vanguard, moving forward by sections, clinging on to the option of 'covering fire'. However, it soon became apparent that this was neither the time nor place. Amidst the sepulchral twists and turns, even a conventionally armed enemy could have taken them any time, let alone masters of the dimensions-beyond. So the group bunched together for mutual support and comfort and Guy did not have the cold heart to rebuke them. What would be would be, and there was little dignity in striking martial postures before an invincible foe. Nonchalance was the proper response to here and now, and Guy deepened his supercilious expression, even if there was no one to see it.

The door led to stairs which travelled up for ages, and then plunged straight back down, for no apparent reason and without arriving anywhere meaningful meanwhile. They took its route like a centipede: travelling but without sense or purpose. The landing midway was thick with dust, virgin before their trampling boots came violating through.

By rights they should have reappeared where they started, according to Guy's reckoning, but the stairs inexplicably descended to an entirely different place: a corridor seemingly snaking on for ever.

Guy wasn't having it. He'd left hide-and-seek behind long ago, in the brief space allotted him to serve as childhood. He called a halt, intending to say something pithy, but both inspiration and the moment were marred by those foremost bashing into him. His black hat was dislodged and wig pigtails jostled.

'Do *not*,' he instructed, once they disengaged, 'for one moment, think that we are lost or chase in vain. No indeed. We are conquerors, annexing what no – normal – man dared tread before.'

He didn't even believe it himself, but clever tutors had decades back dug out any danger of insincerity. An Ambassador could state that black was white and make it sound like his deepest belief. Usually that sufficed, but right now it required more than honey tones to convince some wide-eyed sacrificial lambs. They were in the dark and mislaid and yet supposedly conquering heroes. Each looked within to double check and received an instant negative.

Still, Guy had said it and God would have heard. If they should all die immediately, then at least his last words would be honourable and manly. The merciful Deity surely didn't insist that you *mean* them.

The only alternatives were forward or back. The former was

7

at least progress or novelty and that swung it. Guy strode on and everyone followed.

All along the walls, to either side, were portraits – or possibly landscapes, for it was hard to tell. They started off readily graspable, in rich detail and colour, but rapidly succumbed to a minimalist trend. Only a minute or two of marching sufficed to take the invaders past puzzled-looking wizards of yesteryear and the beauties of Wight nature, to opulent frames surrounding almost nothing. Finally, sketchy lines gave way to blank canvas and they were absolved from looking. Only meticulous Guy remained on duty to notice that even the white voids were proudly signed.

Far too long later, the stone lane terminated in a vault. Its sole – but more than sufficient – furnishing was a huge sculpture, rich in writhing life stilled into one bronze second. From its erotic depths an heroic figure tore free from the tangled orgy to study the heavens. The abstainer, with hips that could be either sex, was struggling from beseeching hands and offered parts to glimpse something beyond. One hand shaded its gaze to better see the heart's desire. It was well done but disturbing on a wealth of levels.

According to their varying tastes, Guy and the sailors studied different aspects of the work: the heaving loins or desperate escapee. Some simply admired the skill displayed, for all it seemed more a triumph of casting, poured from molten, rather than laborious carving.

Then Guy drew close and saw that the flow had been uneven. He observed a patch in which white flesh and bone peeked through.

He drew back before any other could follow his example.

'On!' Guy kept it level, so as not to alarm. They were jittery enough without learning what wizards considered 'art'.

There was a choice of routes, until choice became tedious and instinct led the way. They progressed up and down rampways, high over echoing halls and refectories, or squeezed through claustrophobic dorms and womb-like laboratories. The ways ranged from obstacle courses dripping with excess plaster like rainbow stalactites to passages royal-visit clean and bare. Others were distressingly intestinal-shaped and scented, plus hock-high in waste. One memorable corridor was a maze of spikes, thrusting out of every surface, requiring threading through like a giant shark's mouth. Every second they expected the walls to close and clench and then digest them. Rhyme or reason had never alighted there.

Guy was powerfully reminded of the termites' nest confines of Null-Paris, to the disruption of his innards and freezing of his spine. They also met no one, which, in one sense, was the worst of outcomes. In time, an enemy unseen is more formidable than a tangible foe at your throat. Any army can be defeated by its own imagination, before the firing of a single shot.

Then, without warning, they were back in the square, and even that watery sunlight was like a long-lost love. They tumbled into the open air like drunkards and drank it in.

Fortunately, Yarmouth's heart was empty. A platoon of determined toddlers might have routed them at that moment.

Guy scolded himself for his lack of direction. That he'd fully expected to be blasted away in short order was no excuse. A real Ambassador was always an arrow, a single-shot, not buckshot spread promiscuously. If the Grim Reaper failed to show then Guy should have a plan. The present lack was scandalous. What would his father have said? Perhaps it was just as well an angel had toasted Sir Tusker Ambassador to a crisp twenty years before.

St James's Church presented itself at the square's north-west corner, a survivor from Yarmouth's earliest days, prior to the falling of the curtain and birth of mystery. It still looked like a church, with proper spire and crown: a fit place to fall on your knees and thank the Almighty – even for sending you to God-forsaken places.

Guy suddenly longed for it like relief from long pain. Allegedly, there lurked in such places the one fine fact above all others. Granted, there was also the likelihood of Blades icons galore, but averted eyes and focused mind could maybe overlook those in the quest for refreshment. Certainly, at that moment, desire was easily up to marching over little difficulties like risk, fear and discretion. By comparison, false gods ought to be easy meat.

Dispensing with unwelcome prominence in the square, Guy led them on and in.

In the event, he need not have feared distraction. There was none of it to combat. The interior of St James's had been rendered utterly void and pitch black. Not a speck of furnishing or holy accoutrements remained. The overlapping layers of actual pitch on every surface swallowed any stray ray of light that might intrude. This was interstellar dark, a void: easy to fall into and be lost in eternal night.

Guy charitably wondered if that was the intention. Rather than a frenzy of desecration, it was possible the house of God had been cleared for pondering on the very *deepest* matters.

A brace of sailors were first to enter, pushing wide the already open doors, but neither felt inclined to linger. They could see nothing worth taking, nor pierce the dark corners where sitting tenants might skulk. Consequently, to their wisdom it held no appeal.

Guy, however, strode straight in and past his minions, intrigued by those self-same features – and to set an example. Cocked hat resolutely undoffed, he surveyed in awesome wonder.

Perversely enough, after the initial shock, he found the vacuum to be well stocked: packed with interest and strange attraction. With the total absence of anything to dwell upon, there came opportunity to contemplate *everything*, in the round, without cease. The hard world beneath his feet seemed less . . . undeniable. In time it might even leave you alone and slowly fade away . . .

As a pious man, Guy ought to have deplored the expulsion of all that was holy, but there in the dark and silence he again sensed the possibility of fine intentions behind the ransacking. This was, in its way, still a sacred place, undiminished – or perhaps even enhanced – by its lack of brazen Blades and other

fripperies of god-king worship. Like the still inkier darkness of
the spire and bell tower he now stared up at, there might be
such a thing, he supposed, as a search for *higher* truths.

For a second, the notion winked at him, luscious as a houri,
and he had to draw back. This was not for him, at least not
right now.

His unsophisticated friends proved less easily seduced. From
behind he heard them curse the place and wish it ill – and by
implication, his overlong stay there also. For the moment he
could not totally depart from the majority view: a distressing
dilemma for a New-Wessex aristocrat. He had perforce to go
along with the mob and pretend to value its opinions.

'Disgusting!' he said, emerging from St James's. 'Blasphemy
of blasphemies!'

They moved on, a rifle-hedgehog of prickly disapproval,
into the rest of a lengthy day.

Those they had so feared and yet now almost hoped for had
not been gone long. In hours of exploration into Yarmouth's
crazed depths, time and again they came upon the remnants
of recent meals – and other, less wholesome, indulgences.
Dried blood and dinners were frequent hallmarks of having
just missed their quarry. Yet, save for the lone token on the
quay, people, alive or dead, remained elusive, even if their
spoor grew strong enough for the toughest stomach. A field of
crucifixes proved thankfully unoccupied, though plainly
veterans of hard use. In one snug parlour it looked as though
an entire daisy-chain of people had slit each other's throats –
and then strolled elsewhere, leaving only lifeblood. In
another, scarlet, hall, a sizeable gathering seemed to have
gorged themselves to death on sweet pastries and then, alone
among the consequences, tidied their own bodies away. The
landing party looked and learned but were not detained.

If they'd been unnerved before it was as nothing to their
trepidation now. They jumped at every shadow even though
(or because) they were in amazing abundance. They trembled
at the Solent wind's caressing of the rooftops. The garish
colour schemes contrived to set nerve-endings and vision

11

atingle. The wizards had lived amongst starbursts of the most vivid orange and within walls of shocking pink, so that every glance left an afterglow burning in the eyes. There was no comfort to be seen and Guy knew he could not restrain his rabble much longer. Very soon one man-miming slice of shade would earn itself a bullet, provoking a suicidal firefight in a confined place.

He could hardly blame them or think the less of these normally valiant men. They had imbibed the fear along with their mother's milk. Centuries of legend had left their mark even on his refined sensibilities. Every New-Wessex child heard of the wizards who no longer talked to men and who'd taken their own island out of the busy, silly, world. They were co-opted as an ever present threat to keep infants in bed and urge them to sleep. To naughty children the wizards were always 'coming to get you'.

Adults were not immune either. The fate of the fleet that once sought to gatecrash Wight's reveries was well known. It was the prime material for winter fireside tales, better and more chilling than any ghost story. After that festival of drowning and horror, only madmen would dare to try and elbow in on the sorcerers' solitude. It was thus no great mystery if the sailors accordingly behaved as men mad. They were simply acting in role. Guy had to sympathise – even if only in invisible, undetectable form.

Finally, at midday, a noon only the wild optimists amongst them had expected to see, they found the stairway to the highest minaret in Yarmouth. From each successive landing window they beheld ever better views of the Solent and the *Lady Bridget* at anchor, far, far, below.

Further across the water, the decayed little port of New-Lymington beckoned like the best of places, more tempting at that moment than hearth or home or marital bed. *There* was New-Wessex, albeit its perilous edge. *Here* was beyond the pale. A few miles made a world of difference. As they filed past the windows every man lusted after Lymington, no matter what his previous opinion.

Nearer to, the island's green Downs rose up to meet the chalk cliffs and set of needle-like pinnacles which terminated them. Everything looked sunlit and innocent enough but reputation stole away all charm. Over such beauty, word had it, the wizards hunted their sacrificial victims, chasing men like foxes or hares to the place of holocaust at Mottistone. For the informed spectator, given the choice, the cruel sea was the unlikely sweeter prospect.

Bosun suggested showing the 'Long Man' banner from the uppermost window when they arrived, to inform the *Lady Bridget* they were still alive. Guy nodded approval, seeing little harm in it and the off-chance of eternal fame. *Someone* had to be the man who raised the New-Wessex flag over reconquered Yarmouth. It might as well be Guy Ambassador – even if he delegated the actual wagging.

It was not to be. A whiff of death, that discernible sweet meatiness of the air, alerted them they were drawing to some or other conclusion. And so it proved. What they sought was waiting for them at the top.

The last wizard of Yarmouth reclined on a lush divan, surrounded by rotting meals and bodies. Pale as bone, but starry-silk clad and still superior, he surveyed them as they emerged from the stairs.

It seemed both futile and pedestrian to raise weapon or voice. He was what they were after and here he was. The rest was up to him.

Sheepishly, the group coagulated in the sky-high chamber. They were divided whether to honestly gag on the stench or suppress their heaves for fear of giving offence. Maybe mage nostrils were more robust than mortals', or perhaps this one had been around long enough to acclimatise. His whey-face supplied no clues to assist them.

Similarly, the wizard wasn't minded – or possibly strong enough – to converse and the pregnant pause grew way overdue. Guy presumed to perform a caesarean and queried the mess.

Apparently it *was* a presumption. The wizard matched

13

Guy's raised eyebrow with one of his own. It carried infinitely greater weight.

All the same, the man deigned to oblige.

'Diversions,' he said of the piled-high plates and man-middens: assorted tattooed slaves interwoven in death. 'Diversions and companions. They wore out.'

Guy looked and nodded, as if he entirely understood. He did not. They were many but by no means an island's worth. Nor wizards. The larger mystery still remained.

'You were laggard,' the emaciated face continued. 'Timid, cautious, insects! So careful of what is not worth keeping! You have tried my patience. I was willing to wait but not *for ever*. *Not* at the price of boredom!'

He waved a skeletal hand at the offensive array.

'As even you may perceive, supplies have gotten low and I am too weak to gather more. The servants are gone, my brothers and sisters are gone. One way or another. I am left all alone. Except perhaps for Harbourmaster-mage? He said he might linger to guide you in . . .'

Guy made a bold guess and recalled the quay's custodian.

'Also gone. Self-removed I suspect.'

The wizard appeared to have expected little less.

'But still *in situ*?'

Guy confirmed and his interrogator smiled.

'He *said* he wouldn't wander – not in body, anyway. Even when the rest . . . went their own ways. He loved this place. Now he will always remain.'

To Guy's mind there was little merit in that. The man had deprived himself of all choice in the matter. Even so, the Ambassador was just glad he'd not given in to first thoughts and heaved the body overboard. It was the notion of a splash amongst the silence that had deterred him, rather than delicacy – but any old motive served so long as it did the trick. At least he hadn't compounded their desecration in coming here at all.

'His presence steeled you to land, didn't it?' It was more accusation than question, a last spittle-flecked flare of the embers. 'Otherwise you'd still be out there, peering and trembling, wouldn't you, you . . . dreary mundanes?'

Wise men never lightly dispute wizard opinion. Guy confirmed the falsehood with one of his stock of wry 'you've-got-me-there' expressions.

'Thought so. Therefore you should have kissed his feet as you passed. Even that spurned shell rendered great service by emboldening you. Though I pity enough to linger I should not have awaited you for ever. As it is, you are barely in time . . .'

He indicated his readily countable ribs.

Guy bowed thanks for the favour, if such it was, for something seemed expected.

The wizard's hair was waist-long-wild, his nails grown into milky twisted talons. One set of them flapped feebly, dismissively, at the sign of human gratitude.

'Do not thank me yet,' said the wizard. 'Not before you *know*.'

'Know what?' interrupted Bosun, in his eagerness, out of turn, in breech of all etiquette – thereby doubly earning a snub.

Even wizards know the proper way. The skeleton looked expectantly at Guy.

'Know w-what?' asked Guy, politely, as though he'd spoken first and the offence had never been.

The wizard gathered his remaining strength.

'Listen well!'

They were all agog.

'The dream,' he told them, his face suddenly rapt, 'is *over*!'

The mere humans looked from one to another, seeking enlightenment where there was none.

'The dream . . .' the wizard repeated, more to himself than them, for his own sweet pleasure, '. . . is *over*!'

He liberated a great breath, a long overdue exhalation. Then he plunged a slim dagger deep into his own heart. Then he vanished.

Strip naked and bathe in the sweetest and most pure rain or stream water that may be procured. Then pray a space, or, if literate, dwell upon an apposite passage from the latter portions of the Holy Blades-Bible. Repent of your sins, yea even the crafty, secret ones – for the All-Seeing eye sees all . . .

Then, having donned your finest raiment, fall upon one knee to give good ear and learn. The voice of the Universe is graciously pleased to address you.

'To the greater glory of G*d.

'A thought descends from the pinnacle of the Most High, and out of lovingkindness to my creation I shall recount it. Therefore attend! For I say unto you this day, and most solemnly so, the angel wars are not yet won! Nor are they at an end! Only an angel-friend speaks thus and such belly-crawling, verminous lickspittles may be dealt with by the pious as they – angrily – see fit, without fear of sanction or reproof. Their lives here shall be short and degrading. Their eternal fate is torment whilst sealed in boiling pits of their own filth! Like so-called "Blades XXIII", my negligent regent whilst I was away. He had to abdicate. His head still stars atop a spike over Traitor's Gate, I believe. Indeed.

'Whilst I think of it, I today decree that the blood-money for murder or manslaughter for such as are proved to be backsliders and milky-livered carbuncles upon mankind shall be reduced to payment of one half of a demi-*Tom* in respect of the full-grown and free, or a bucket of grain for infants and slaves. And the families of such disgraces should count themselves lucky to get that. I should say so!

'Where was I? Oh, yes. The long subjection may be gloriously overthrown, the capricious and humiliating tortures abated, but that is *not* an end of it. Oh no. Some may say the malice of our diabolic enemies has fizzled out in sulking and petulance. When they dare to lift their heads they find humanity's twin – or father and son – champions, there to smite them hip and brow, with many a grievous blow! The rich-in-faith say that when *I* am with you (and my dearly beloved King Guy obediently beside me) then what shall they fear from mere angels?

'Well, verily I answer you, look for the once fair city of New-Staleybridge. But look in vain! It is at one with Sodom and Gomorrah (concerning which you may have recounted to you from the Holy Blades-Bible). It is at one with the dead and gone. Equally, it is at one and flush with the ground, being razed and flattened. Horrible sight! The angels, in their mad rage, poured on fire and brimstone and even less pleasant things until poor Staleybridge was no more!

'Next, go, I urge you; go behold the beauty of Snowdonia! Drink in the greeny delights of the Isle of Anglesey! Go feast your eyes on snowy mountains and wild wonder, which are a foretaste and ghost of the glories that await the righteous in oneness with G*d!

'Then cease your preparations, unpack your pack, for your Lord countermands. He shall save you the trouble and vain journey. Our enemy did behead the high mountain and blast the valleys black. Anglesey is beneath the waves. Its church spires peek forth as remembrance and reproach: sad tokens of congregations drowned! The angels again! Such is the nature of their nature. Such is the limitless fiery wrathfulness of their wrath!

'True, they have suffered under our lashes for these iniquities. I summoned their captains and kings to answer for those and other atrocities and they could not refuse me. I called them and they came, shrinking, and – I most solemnly assure you – they took long indeed to die under the sword of my obedient lieutenant, King Guy. Their flayed skins whiten the broad doors of my Cathedral. They carpet the Holy of Holies! Am I speaking petty revenge? My oath, I am *not*!

17

'Lo, angels now harken to the words of man, like a hound who knows he has done wrong. Their tails are down (metaphorically). They give good ear to my meditations! Yea, sweet indeed is the shriek of an angel!

'They have learned now, learned bitter lessons, as did we under their long tutelage. They withhold their cruel hand and swallow again their bile that they would fain spew over us. Which is good news.

'Yet, dear children, I would have you ever remember what stands between *then* and *now*; that which interposes 'tween you and them. But for *my* strong right arm, this world would be cinders. Ponder that in your heart and in the stillnesses of the night and grow wise!

'Hear, oh Wessex and all the world, I am the Lord your G*d and the Lord your G*d is I!

'Visible to your privileged eyes, I, Blades the Great, returner and redemptor, am one with *Him* beyond and we are indivisible and eternal. Certainly.

'Therefore, whilst I may graciously devolve a portion of power and favour to my dearly beloved subordinate, King Guy Ambassador, I am displeased to hear of churches and shrines being raised to him. This practice will cease forthwith.

'Amen.'

Being a promulgation and emanation from his Divine-Holiness, Emperor Blades the Great, Downs-Lord and Lord of All.

Given at New-Godalming, Wessex, England, Humandom. As exactly recounted from the fountainhead, this eighth-day of August, in the season of Fall, in the 480th year After Blades (Praise be).

Printed under licence by the Resurgam Press, by permission of his serene reverence, David Morris-Carnivore, Cardinal of the Promulgation and Propagation Engines. Unauthorised reproduction forbidden under pain of death plus everlasting damnation.

'The day thou gavest, Lord, is ended . . .'

Sentiments sung in myriad current evensongs, from cathedral to church to chapel, right down to humble household shrine, were speedily coming true. Outside, leathery *'parliaments'* called it a day too and wheeled home to their rank, bone-stiffened nests. Dusk advanced from the east, threatening the scintillating starburst-centre of civilisation with obscurity. Night loomed – and also beckoned – in the fortress-metropolis of New-Godalming.

Therefore, all over the city lights were being born, the products of candle or oil or, in wealthy quarters, the gas system purloined from fallen 'America'. Darkness reeled back from their counter-spell to the point of defeat. Nowadays, people set their own schedule. Night was more than just a chance to quit the burrow without being eaten. That Null-dictated regime was mere shameful legend, increasingly mythical. The boot was on the other foot and purple monsters now fitted in with the *meat's* hours, taking long overdue turn at a spot of shyness and skulking. This was the modern world, no longer obligated by either Null or Nature's timetables. So, though the day might well be ended, mankind had no reason to be blind or kow-tow. The bustle barely slowed. Even 'Blades XXIII' in his long vigil atop Traitor's Gate could have seen, had he not been twenty years dead, beheaded and pickled. Had birds not long since had his eyes. A glow reached out into the countryside and clawed for the sky.

Beyond that aura's furthest reach (for the moment) a lesser beacon was born – and straight away received homage out of all proportion. One minor scintillation in the rural murk suddenly outranked all the urban glare. The tireless watchers found it no mystery. They knew who spoke and who was spoken to. Hascombe Hill, one of the nearby green hills not yet incorporated within Godalming's wider still and wider walls, was crowned with a signal-tower. More scrutinised than a plotter's palace, the humble pile of plank and bargate enjoyed eagle-eye attention both night and day.

Its flickering mirror-relayed message pierced humandom's heart and found warm welcome there. Clerks of high renown abandoned all to decipher the on/off blinking. A steady drizzle of holy water rained on them as they toiled, courtesy of an acolyte's libations, to inspire them in the sacred task. It matched and mixed with their perspiration – for it is no small thing to interpret for a god.

From hand to hand and form to form the message soared, in ever ascending precedence. Along the length of a corridor it leaped from clerk to bishop to cardinal of the *'Onefaith'*. Progressively transcribed from mere paper to parchment to vellum, and ultimately as characters hammered into sheet-gold, it was conveyed (as fast as piety permitted) finally in fit state to carry mere men's words before their creator.

The Cardinal of Converse entered into the throne room on his belly, ready to crawl all the way to the Infinite. However, since it was both a large room and lengthy trip, a rope-hauled moving trackway of marble slats had long ago been provided for everyone's convenience.

Powered by slaves bred to brawn and nothing but, the Cardinal sped face down towards the Almighty. Through subtle raisings of the intervening ninety-nine silk curtains he went, past envious petitioners and the most highly favoured come to worship. In his ears, above the rumbling of the track, arrived the eternal adoration of the Immortals, a thousand-strong corps of choristers, so-called since they sang in never-ending relay. Like the humbler faithful beyond the Cathedral-Palace walls, their efforts were funnelled from outside along sinuous voice-tubes and cunning amplification chambers. As a consequence, praise and pleas came from everywhere and nowhere. Rather like the recipient of all the their reverence, they were ubiquitous.

At the far end of what seemed a very long (and yet not long enough) way, the housing grew so tall and broad as to command its own weather system. Vapour hung in the higher reaches, combining to form embryonic clouds. The roof was lost to sight and gloom, and glowing angels, either carved or real, commanded the heights. The uninitiated could be excused for feeling that somehow, some way back, they had crossed the great abyss into whatever lay beyond.

The Cardinal *knew* what lay beyond – at least this far, he did. The job that had put years on him and greyed his hair required that he often tread – or ride – this route. Nevertheless, familiarity bred neither comfort nor contempt. The poor man's butterflies were just as lively as on his first visit.

Then the obeisance-conveyance slowed to a practised halt and the Cardinal had to raise his head to face facts.

A world-egg, taller than a dozen men and enamelled into cobalt perfection, soared above him. Around its solid silver mount stood the golden huscarls: shoulder to shoulder, an unbroken shieldwall of blue-eyed hostility, the bodyguard of the divine seething in an absolute fury of devotion. They had no small-talk, any more than they had mercy or imagination. Free from family or fancy, their every motion and notion was solely in the service of their Lord. Chosen at birth, lucky creatures, in lieu of wages they'd been led to an enviably single-minded outlook on life: something better than sordid mammon. All it cost was the little matter of childhood – a small price, surely, for seeing clearly. To a man they were duly grateful.

One of the lighter treated, an almost suave example by their standards, came forward at the Cardinal's urgent importuning. He took the sheaves of gold and read and judged. Then the Cardinal collapsed in relief when that judgement accorded with his own.

It never got any easier, never became any less of a strain. Upon *his* shoulders lay responsibility for disturbing a god-king's dreaming. And on his shoulders would fall the price – delivered via a huscarl's axe – for one too many false alarms.

There must have been some preagreed signal or device hidden to the Cardinal's eyes, for never yet had he seen initiation of the terrible next stage. Nevertheless, because of

21

something said or done, the egg began to crack, dividing down the long axis. Perfection parted to reveal a candle-blaze within.

Like life, it seemed a painfully slow business – but similarly a process to be meekly endured in fear and longing. Sounds like sheet-metal tearing and the lamentations of an oil-parched ratchet accompanied the gradual widening of the gap. Light fell from within – and that was not all. Surplus meals and concubines and other less identifiable stuff tumbled out and to the ground below. In its own sweet time, all was revealed.

The tenth decade of life saw Blades the Great ('Curate Thomas Blades', as was) desiccated down to shrunken minimum. Two eyes starring out from deep pits declared an anger their body could no longer express, nor cataracts allow to shine forth cleanly.

Through the swiftest of sidelong glances and facts gleaned from chance reflections, the Cardinal added to his meagre store of detail. The interior of the egg was a mural serpent swallowing its own tail; 360 degrees of facsimile green Downs below blue sky of Downs-country day. Therein, sunk into a rose-quartz throne cushioned to womb-like comfort, Blades spent his days and years in the little copy of the world he'd weaved, upholding the Universe from second to second.

The Cardinal's sense of privilege was long since gone and now he merely wished to be away. He writhed under the suspicion that the god-king's glare never left him for a second.

Again, by inscrutable arrangement, the courtier-huscarl reappeared at Blades's side. He read from the sheets of gold into the motionless ear and the Cardinal prayed – to the selfsame object of terror – that the apparent tightening of withered claws upon the throne was mere illusion: a bowel-churning fantasy written by the hazing of the moisty air.

The god-king's lips were generally above the angle of the Cardinal's lowered vision and so he was not privy to the whispering which ensued. His next material involvement was to hear the slap, slap, slap of slippers upon marble and find the huscarl's feet beside his pounding head.

He had to raise himself a smidgen to receive the intended

reply. His face dared lift to perceive his prize. The Cardinal's breath faltered.

It was not in the god-king's own hand, naturally, but that twist of paper and the scrawl it bore had been privy to the presence. The Cardinal accepted it with reverence and special tweezers of gold, secreting the treasure in a venerable pouch of Null skin: antique heirloom-hide peeled from one of the first monsters to fall to Blade's miraculous 'muskets'.

Then there was nothing more to do or say. Emperor and god-king, Blades I and last, Downs-Lord Paramount, Emperor of New-Wessex and its Dependencies, Protector of Assyria-in-Sussex, Despot of New Godalming and the Holy of Holies, Sultan of Mercia and the Marches, General of Hosts, Firer of Cannon, Musket-Master, Keeper of the Citadel Keys, Redemptor and Defender of the Faith and Bane of the Null, etc. etc. . . . had spoken.

A sonorous blow on a gong signalled to the distant slaves that the audience was done and their passenger was leaving. Slowly, amidst rumbling and much gladness, the Cardinal trundled feet-first away from the Almighty.

Distracted, the nonagenarian god-king failed to notice. His chesty cough was playing up again.

'Fire!'

Guy said the word and did the deed, just as he was asked.

Nothing happened. Silence continued like cacophony. The captain looked shamefaced.

'Perhaps this one as well, my lord . . .' he suggested, indicating an adjacent red circle. 'We're still learning, you see, and . . .'

Guy made nothing of it. He happily pushed that button too.

Though forewarned as a firework party, everyone jumped when the gun turret spoke. The whole ship shook and its iron deck cringed beneath them. Bright, beautiful day was briefly suspended.

Key

%/₀ gross moral turpitude

Murder

Treachery

Assassination

sordidness

atrocities

excesses: { cider
            wine

A Refreshment to the Memory
or
Cookpots of ill-will
or
Places it is as well not to go back to for a while

Extracted from the commonplace book of GUY PMBASSADOR

New-York %/₀

Liverpool - port (massacres)

Key (a busy Summer)

Llanarth !

Caer-di %/₀

Norfolk Utopias (rain, bleakness and rash promises)

Frontierfolke Reservation (in-laws)

New Godalming (Blades)

Kent (Levellers and Atheists)

Cymric slave-sinkings

Home (many reasons)

Wadebridge

Tonbridge

Dorchester

Wight (Wizards)

bad memories

Reprinted, under licence, by the
School of Ambassadorial Studies,
Ideology, Philosophy and Dogma Course. Level V.

People pretended not to be getting back into their skins whilst downing draughts of agitated air. Even Polly's and Prudence's white faces went whiter still as their long black locks rose to dance in the storm.

Guy graciously let himself be led outside, clear of the powder fug. He was just in time to see his creation arc high above the Isle of Wight, set fair to cross right over and into the beyond. Its vapour trail was the mightiest work of human hands he'd ever seen. And Guy had seen New-Godalming Cathedral!

The second mightiest was presently under his feet, awesomely afloat in New-Southampton harbour. Though still largely a carnival of rust and neglect on its upper decks, the Blades's Wessex Ship *Saucy Sailor*, a salvaged and rechristened American dreadnought, was the new pride of the Wessex fleet there assembled. It put all the other wood and sail and steam ships to shame. Desire for reassurance tempted people to keep checking she flew the friendly 'Long Man' pennant.

Birds fled and swooping *parliaments* cawed disapproval: Nature's lonely adverse review. Everyone else raved. Guy Ambassador could take no credit for either ship or show, but he politely accepted a round of applause from the invited audience. With such a great prize to report, rescued from rotting in what Wessex explorers believed was once Boston harbour, piety and etiquette dictated a spark from the Bladian bonfire should preside over playing with its solitary restored gun.

Ingenious New-Wessex artisans, a burgeoning social class on the up, had already 'back-engineered' the essential principles and risked life and limb experimenting on the trip over. In the discreet obscurity of the wide Atlantic, they'd had endless fun, shooting blameless clouds or pounding the capacious ocean, hopeful of raising a *wyrm* to practise on. Now, with the steel monster's secrets mostly theirs and a stock of shells cobbled together from scavenging, they felt free to show off their power and cleverness. Unfortunately, form decreed an aristocrat should proxy do it for them.

Somewhere beyond Wight, out in the English Channel, a distant boom heralded the dawn of a new age of warfare. All over the ship and throughout the fleet, gathered mariners cheered, though deeper thought might have rendered them less jubilant. These 'six-inch shells' would penetrate a ship – any ship – to explore and test its contents of flesh far better than 'modern' – but now instantly old-fashioned – cannonballs.

With equally small justification, the 'boys ashore' – the merchants and garrison and their families of Southampton-reborn – added distant acclamation. 'Long Man' flags were waved to greet the exciting spectacle. Only a few foreigners abstained from joy and a pair of Leveller galleys were suddenly all urgent to depart; a disturbed ants' nest of corsairs and awakening oars, desperate to be away and break the news back home.

Looking to the far end of the estuary, Guy saw the little black sweeper boats, prickly with swivel-guns, about their constant to and fro. Aside from keeping the anti-penile-wyrm nets in good repair, they also held the key to New-Wessex's newest port – for a further free gift from the *Saucy Sailor* had been the innovation of mines. Having laid them, only Wessex-men knew the way through and safe exit was by their kind indulgence. The Levellers would have to ask nicely to leave. A point would be doubly made.

Meanwhile, back in the midst of things, the dying down of cordite and clamour found the captain still labouring at excuses.

'. . . Not yet *totally* conversant,' he explained, a voice emerging from smoke and glimpses of gold braid, only occasionally prevailing over more raucous sounds. 'Not in *every* aspect of the operat—'

Guy's ears were still ringing and required no further workload. He politely signalled 'enough'.

In truth, it would take a sour disposition indeed to cavil at mere details of the marvel patched up and hauled back over perilous oceans. Novelty, if not charity, led everyone to overlook patchwork plating and inelegant repairs. They were details: mere weeds along the way. The fact was that she loomed yards and centuries over any other ship in the harbour. Compared to the dreadnought's towering sides, the rest looked like anachronisms: vessels from another age. Their pretty flags and pennants and dragon-faced gunports might be easier on the eye, but things had just moved on apace. Looks were no longer an issue and gave way to a greyer imperative. Blithely unaware, the *Lady Bridget* docked beside her own nemesis.

The same could be said of all Southampton port. An on-its-way tomorrow laughed at mere wooden stockades and Null-nets. Elegant minarets and baroque style had just become indulgences. The natives might well cheer today but in the bright new future they'd be seeing a lot less sunshine. Vital places would need to get underneath some serious concrete and Southampton-by-the-sea put on a heavy hat and veil, disguising every charm. Likewise, her hinterland of neat fields and hamlets no longer looked so immune or blessed.

However, all that belonged to futurity, weakest of all forces operating on the human mind. The present – 'Queen Here-and-now' – shouted louder and had you within clawing reach. Her shrieking recommenced, jostling everybody on.

Guy's ever-questing antenna instantly perceived he had become a nuisance. Once the wondrous shell had gone to kill fishes far away, once the desired impression was made, his hosts had other things to do: a million and one duties not made any easier by quasi-divine scrutiny. He was still welcome, but . . .

Despite all, Guy retained a kind heart. He obliged it and them by feigning an urgent appointment elsewhere. The *Lady Bridget* apparently beckoned – as she so often did when excuses were sought.

In truth he had nothing special to do nor any particular place to go – unless one counted home, which currently seemed an extravagant demand. He both had and hadn't solved the mystery of Yarmouth. He'd also selfishly failed to die in the doing. That left him in limbo whilst the Imperium learned and cursed and devised another suicide mission for him. He could just as well obediently await news of it anchored off Hampshire as anywhere. Guy was getting used to the 'welcome, but . . .' phenomenon: nowadays it met him every place he went. He didn't take offence.

Sailors of the Wessex fleet, peacocks by comparison, gawked at the novelty of Guy's bone-pale bodyguards before recalling themselves to pipe him off the grey metal colossus. A sandwich to Guy's filling, the brace of lady huscarls topped and tailed his progress down the rope and then sat, impassive to either side, in the rowboat. As ever, they noted all but revealed nothing, all the way back to their floating home. Guy felt safe and free to think.

He certainly deserved a space of mooching and nothing-much indulgence. In the busyness of that meat-grinding termed the Angel Wars, there'd been no time to ponder the luxury of *implications*. Between wake and sleep – and all too often during oblivion as well – life had felt like running screaming down a corridor. With no end in sight, no doors or windows presenting themselves as escape routes, the sole sure thing had been that return was not an option. Just the notion of trudging all the way back up the years was unendurable. So, set-faced, stiff-lipped, he'd gone on and events went with him. And then arrived a lull, as now. It was . . . nice – positively longed for once upon a time – but still unsettling, almost a betrayal. It brought the fresh worry of just what conclusions you might come to.

Recollection of those years had been an extra sprinkle of unease atop the Yarmouth holiday. Wizard architecture precisely matched in stone memory of days when it would have been sweeter not to wake. War, war, war, and not a moment for racing or love; that he could have faced – or be stiffened to it by Mrs Ambassador. But when struggle was subverted by the pain of disillusion, then every daybreak was unwelcome news. Whole years had slipped through his fingers that way and the waste didn't bear thinking about. Guy glimpsed unpleasant deductions grinning at him from mental journey's end and it was easier just to turn aside or dally. Trailing fingertips in the waves and admiring Polly's perfect moon-face were immensely preferable.

Despite residual guilt (that nerve being not quite burned out), Guy decided to be kind with himself. For if he wouldn't, who would? No one, he answered his own question, *that's* who.

Reason repeated (in its usual feeble voice) that Guy had no grounds for reproach. He and Blades had done their best, but they couldn't be everywhere at once. Well, maybe Blades could, being a god, but in his infinite wisdom he'd decided against ubiquity – as was his right. Together they'd held the line – more or less, with lapses. Blame had to be fairly pinned upon the aggressor, not the victim's imperfections.

So, sadly, humanity lost a city here, a treasured vista there. It became dangerous to form attachments to either place or person. As swift and equal thank you, the god-king or his vice-regent had mangled many an angelic invader. Eventually, Guy's revolverful into the rainbow general-angel of Windover Hill registered a defining blow; some unguessable savage bereavement to them. Thereafter the unpleasantness scaled down to sullen silence and covert vendetta. Wisdom or restraint or constraint prevented the angels from expressing their frank opinion of rough treatment.

That was a mercy and for most it sufficed. The present was incomparable improvement on what had gone before. They were no longer the playthings of higher beings or vermin trod underfoot. Lack of understanding only enhanced general gratitude to the two men (or more than men), paladins of humanity standing between Humandom and Armageddon. New temples to the god-king sprang up like exuberant fungi and old ones were refurbished to fresh glory. But for Blades's prohibition, there'd have been statues and shrines to Guy too. However, His Wonderfulness thought that adulation would be bad for a mere Ambassador, albeit one raised to sub-kingship, and Guy wisely, loyally, agreed. It also helped that he had no wish to be worshipped. All that fending off prayers and omnipotence. Too tiring, too twenty-four-hours-a-day. A man of simple tastes, Guy didn't fancy it.

What Guy fancied was well represented by the buxom figurehead of the *Lady Bridget*. A day at the races would have been nice as well. It wasn't much to ask for – except apparently it was. Alas, opportunity and, probably, ability alike were missing, the old pleasure-centres numbed or dead. Still, he could dream . . .

Desire for lost joys and lightness of being, rather than lofty thoughts, cheerfully occupied the brief passage. Prudence had to nudge him back to grim reality.

Arrival coincided with the return of the longboat from Yarmouth. Together they drew along the *Bridget*'s larboard flank.

'So soon?' queried Guy.

'Sooner, lord,' growled Bosun, 'if I'd had *my* way . . .'

It was surely every sailor's fantasy to have a whole town to ravish: doubly so if unopposed. Yet Yarmouth held no booty or women to take – only well-springs of fear and suspicious shadows. Bowel-churning and sterile stuff in short. So, for all that the town was their oyster they'd turned their noses up at it. The conquerors were returned jaw-droppingly early, clutching only a souvenir or two apiece.

Concern for dignity led Guy to prefer that the landing party tackle the rope ladder first. But iron-etiquette couldn't care less about mere men's little wishes. It rode roughshod over moments of weakness. An aristocrat of New-Wessex – and scion, however distant, of the Holy blood – was required to show omnicompetence in every field and facet of life. Even a man's huscarls – companions earned by force of will and fame – were not meant to help. Polly and Prudence were scanning elsewhere for other threats.

Luckily, limbs not really designed for the job passably conquered the air to maintain the deception. Then, when Guy was standing on comparatively solid wood, and his huscarls also aloft, the companions of the previous day had complete freedom to follow on as they pleased. Looking back, and not for the first time, the king-by-permission ruefully reflected that liberty was joined at the hip with lack of ambition.

'No rest for the wicked, my lord . . .'

Guy suppressed his sigh and turned.

'Oh . . . hello, Thirteen. Hello again . . .'

No rest indeed; no escape from the treadmill for Guy. Awaiting him was Viscount Sea-captain XIII, hereditary custodian of the *Lady Bridget* and venerated direct descendant of her very first captain (who'd come over with Blades from Paradise!). Not a figure to be lightly ignored.

The same was true in spades of the two letters he brandished. Glorified by plate-sized seals, they needed no other introduction.

The 'Hermes' mirror-relay system might flick news about, hitching on the speed of light, but discretion reserved a role for hoof and foot. Horse couriers wore ruts between fleet and capital carrying the personal stuff, spreading wealth as well as mud and dust. Teams stood by all the way, all day, ready to join the relay race – and meanwhile wanted bed and board. Blacksmiths, ostlers and innkeepers blessed each message, whether it thundered past or paused for fast food and reshoeing. If one went by the next might not.

Expensive? Yes. Wasteful? Perhaps. But taking the broad view, the system worked well – after a fashion. Gold trickled down from the throne; all sorts of people were made happy. The urgent men and mounts lived short lives, granted, but the word of Blades got delivered fresh.

It wasn't done to delay opening missives from the Almighty, even to seek privacy, so Sea-captain turned his back and all company melted away till Guy was the centre of a zone of solitude.

He knew his own priorities but also knew others were watching, whatever their pretence. The Imperial despatch must come first and word from a beloved await its turn.

A single sharp finger-thrust penetrated the scarlet seal's hymen. Then a great square of fine velum needed unfolding to reveal . . . not much.

31

Guy scanned. No greetings, thanks or fond concern. Just bludgeon-bluntness:

'*Wizards do **NOT** disappear into thin air.*'

But they *do* – and did and had, Guy reflected. Heaven knew (or ought to) that he above all people could vouch for vanishments. Men married to mages got used to them. They were a sorcerer's stock in trade.

'*The Wight corpses you recount are **INSUFFICIENT**. Yea, not one thousandth part of the harvest we might expect and bless. The great preponderance are unaccounted for. They have **NOT** sought our permission to quit our realm. They were **NOT** dismissed.*

'*Look **INTO** the matter. We wish to **ADMONISH** them. Such is our divine **WILL** and command.*

'*Then return. Soon. There is other work for you to do.*'

A spidery B verified the charmless rant.

Guy was more pleased than its sender ever intended. Here were orders he could bend to his desire, without ever breaking them. Ambiguous clauses winked suggestively at him, almost *demanding* to be seduced and tipped on their back. Any Ambassador worth his salt could have his way with these saucy wench-words as and when it suited him.

It was like the strange 'cricket' game Blades had suddenly ordained as a religious obligation throughout the land. Carelessness or contempt had led the Captain-of-Captains to bowl a delivery it was a *sin* not to strike for six. Though more a spinner of exquisite subtlety himself and thus low down the Ambassador XI's batting order, Guy was well up to slogging a 'dolly' ball right over the pavilion.

So he obediently took a 'look into' the distance, towards Wight, peering hard for several seconds. It was never going to solve the mystery but technically fulfilled his obligation. Mission accomplished, Guy hid both grin and letter away.

The seal of the Ambassadors was less grand but protected what lay beyond more fervidly. Fingers proved insufficient to end its stewardship and Guy finally had to deploy his stiletto blade.

Then he read and wished the seal had fought for ever.

Another stillbirth. Her fourth. A girl. '*Since G*d saw fit . . .*'

Guy's shoulders slumped once, as though someone had struck him. A solitary outward sign, followed by instant recovery. His face remained a commendable mask throughout.

The Ambassador laid the letter to rest as reverently as he would have his daughter. Then he crept down below to cry.

'W-why?'

'Hedonist incursion.' There wasn't going to be any argument. In the cause of Guy's safety Sea-captain's rough and ready piety emboldened him. 'The Great North Road? No, no, *no*. Nothing but eyes and feathers there for days yet.'

Involuntary visualisation of the savages' peculiar dress-sense illustrated the warning vividly. In their hunger and thirst for the elusive goal of 'inimitable living' the lewd fanatics appalled all decent conventions. They were well up to charging down the mouth of myriad muskets and ripping up a king when they got there – if it 'seemed like a good idea at the time'. They had no respect, for themselves or others. A gentleman could avoid such *hoi polloi* without loss of face – for fear of losing his actual face.

Therefore, Guy didn't quite know why he was querying a diversion to Pevensey-Assyria. It suited him perfectly well when there were only tears waiting back home. Even so, some oppositional spirit whipped him on.

'Couldn't the Southampton garrison clear the way?'

Sea-captain stretched his mouth out of its usual 'twenty past eight'. It made him look the absolute picture of his father to Guy's (broadly) affectionate memory. 'Twelve' had saved the day at New-Dieppe and brought Guy, Bathie and Blades – and hope – home. He was briefly here in spirit now, on a flying visit from his watery grave. *He* would have said what his son was about to.

Thirteenth-generation mariners inherit no high opinion of

land-soldiers. Just the thought of them chancing it against real wild humans amused 'Thirteen'.

'No.' he said again, this time definitively.

So, Guy had gone through the motions of protest and could now accept a few day's delay with good grace. His safe-conduct through the realm of Pevensey was of such rarity that it almost pleaded for use and perhaps that was a factor in Sea-captain's decision. Not many foreign ships got into Pevensey-Assyria nowadays – leastways, not under their own power planning to emerge again. To the current generation of mariners it was just a forbidding line of impaling stakes along the shoreline, the exact opposite of anything 'come-hither'.

Almost as bad, though more communicative, a few miles along that coast brought you to the tiresome pirates of Freeport Hastings with their lust for politics and prizes. Accordingly, the sea-lanes for legitimate traffic tended to thin and falter in those regions, and civilisation beyond, in Dover and the Anglian Utopias, had to pay premium rates for supply. It was only natural that sailors should be curious and seek updates on now ageing hand-me-down tales. They'd dine out for years on any fresh information, securing free ale in any tavern. An Ambassador aboard was joint licence and incitement to go voyaging. Guy recalled dear cousin Bacon Ambassador who'd been effectively kidnapped for a wild-goose chase round 'Scotland' when Blades came back and exploration started again. Admittedly, he'd returned a better man (or at least, Ambassador) for it, but white hair and trembling hands were a shame in one so young.

For a second Guy even wondered if Hedonists were actually rampaging anywhere beyond the realms of Sea-captain's imagination, but then rejected the unworthy thought. He'd seen the man's brown brow furrowed in daily prayer. The very thought of inconveniencing Blades the Great would pale that same weather-beaten face. More likely he wanted to convey Guy via somewhere not even the Hedonist hellbound-on-horseback would dare venture.

In the two decades since the god-king's return the city-state of Pevensey-Assyria had sequestered itself, turning into a prosaic version of the Wight wizards Guy had failed to find. The pious realm had not known how to greet Blades's long longed-for second coming, finding it not entirely up to expectations. In his own way, Guy could sympathise with that, but the Pevensey men's concerns were different. True, Blades had returned, they conceded, but where, oh where, was his first-born (their own patron sub-deity) Sennacherib?

When the messiah arrived in unexpected, deficient format and could not or would not answer their great question, it prompted Pevensey puzzlement, followed by morose seclusion. Ensuing years saw Sussex bathed in ample Imperial displeasure but its independence preserved by martial reputation. Pevensey's mail-clad legions and galley fleet were the stuff of legend: mankind's mainstay during the great Null wars. That the place was also a storm brewing, a boil fit to burst, Guy well perceived. An Ambassador could catch the blasphemy-tinged whiff of it from counties away. He half expected the lancing job to be high on Blades's list called 'Things for Guy to do'.

Then he realised there would be pleasure in pre-empting his Almightyness – and that settled it. Mistress Fun was a teasing filly of late and you mounted her when and where you could.

'Very well, my dear Thirteen,' Guy confirmed, 'Pevensey it shall be' – though he'd heard Sea-captain set the course a full five minutes past.

The sweeper-boats parted the wyrm-curtains for them and led the way through a mini maze of mines. The god-king's writ in all its majesty now fully extended here; the gainsay of the brooding island opposite was withdrawn. No ships might enter in or depart save with Blades's blessing. Guy knew full well that wasn't always so and felt a consequent lift in spirits.

There was a time when impudent Leveller ideologues and other unbelievers or couldn't-cares would sail in without so much as a by-your-leave. Even the miracle of a returned Blades and the chastening of angels and Null had failed to charm the hard core of the hardhearted. Levellers and

35

'Freeports' still persisted in their errors, and nests of atheists and the indifferent continued to abound – or so at least it seemed to Guy's dashed hopes. Until recently therefore, though by heart and founding part of the glorious Wessex Imperium, New-Southampton had been no stranger to visitors offering minimal respect. Now all that would change. Fresh armaments fetched back over the Atlantic, and the reviving of grand ambition, meant slights need no longer be overlooked. The charred remains of a Kernow quinquereme, just visible at low water, stood – or sank – as stark testimony of that.

No, Guy told himself in the privacy of reflection, studying their wake as the tugboats let slip and the *Lady Bridget* got underway, say what you like, but Blades-the-god *had* put the 'great' back into 'Greater Wessex'. It was wicked to dissent. The picture might not please in every detail and the frame seem a trifle . . . tight, but there was no denying it was a work of art. Things were better than they had been, following a terrible low. Guy remembered *then* well enough to want to count his blessings. What a shame, therefore, that curses were inextricably wrapped up with them.

Idle logic then led him to wonder what posterity would make of his own few brushstrokes upon the canvas of the present. What had *he* put back into New-Wessex after he put Blades back into it?

Nothing immediately sprang to mind. There was blood and gore and miscarriages and executions – but they were just the standard stuff of history. The intensely satisfying smell of burned angel feathers – *that* was his alone and maybe would count. Or maybe not. These were all *huge* things, but also somehow lightweight – and past. None of them really fitted the bill.

As to the future, well perhaps he had a few years left in which to salvage a good account of himself to render at Judgement. The trouble was, you couldn't rely on material turning up. Everything so far had been tried and found wanting. If there truly *was* a good reason for Guy Ambassador to tread the earth, then it didn't lie in swordplay or the occasional witty comment.

He looked around for inspiration but there was only the receding port or sea. Nearer to were Polly and Prudence, ever present – but they were blanker palettes than any of the empty pictures he had seen in Yarmouth.

His huscarls came as a pair, the sole arrangement about which they were inflexible, and he'd bought them as such. Whether they were sisters or not history didn't relate, though alikeness strongly hinted that way. Unfortunately, a previous owner had put them beyond helpful comment on the matter. Blades – or someone – had clipped their vocal chords. Their memories were likewise cauterised scar-tissue. They refused to be drawn on pre-Guy days.

Guy's compassion had rescued them from degrading Imperial servitude and zoo-like slavery – sad victims of the fall in Fruntierfolke clan fortunes. It had pleased him to spend lavishly to halt their dancing to Blades's senile passions: curing a tiny portion of life's cruelty with mere gold. Bathie's discovery of possible kinship and cousinhood only came later as strange coincidence, rendering the two doubly deserving of purchase. By then, though, the deed was done and Guy had already moulded their destinies, even as he healed their bruised humanity. Huscarls were treated differently from family. As prospective assets rather than relatives, Polly and Prudence had secured a far easier ride.

For once a good turn went unpunished. Even before there were suspicions of affinity, the whey-faced pair came to worship their actual redeemer rather than their supposed one. *He* made no demands on them other than what they loved to give. *He* gave them weapons to put some space between themselves and life. After all they'd seen that defended ditch was most welcome. A little kindness went a long way when it had rarity value, and they were duly grateful.

Next, the young veterans of outrageous fortune cultivated an other-worldly disconnection. They declined to train or trim their hair till it fell in great tumbling tides, dyed to

37

darkest night and a shocking contrast to face and apparel. It publicised the point quite nicely.

Guy humoured them and subtly fanned their devotion. He bought milk-white gowns and lethal implements enamelled to bone shade, the better to wed these rarest of bodyguards. Their education was finished by the best masters of manslaughter around. History had arranged that New-Wessex possessed them in profusion.

It was further expense but yet still a bargain. Fruntierfolke servants were novelties in the market and never came cheap. The nature of the merchandise meant that those susceptible to loyalty carried a hefty surcharge. One act of charity had bought Guy jewels of great value at a knock-down price. It only confirmed his belief that virtue was its own reward.

Normally, the two were as ubiquitous as air and just as little noticed. Sometimes only the absence of the kohl-eyed duo would rouse him to actually perceiving them. Now, deep ponderings forced him into recognition. What *had* he put back into life? What *was* his indispensable thread amidst the tapestry of New-Wessex?

Prudence was perhaps a shade taller than Polly, her chin the more challenging. These were the only signs that served to differentiate them. Elsewise they were each as alien and lovely as the other.

Sadly, Guy concluded there was only one thing he could still 'put in'. One joy he could both give and receive. The alternative was backgammon or shuffling his favourite pack of cards even shinier. Watery gruel in comparison . . .

So, Guy proposed an excursion to poor-man's paradise and his huscarls happily agreed. Arm in arm, questing hands already petitioning the pearly gates for entrance, the trio went below.

'I well recall a time', said Sea-captain, 'when all this coast was nothing but *Wild* and Null shaking their fists at you. Now look at it . . .'

Guy already was. He'd been privately lauding an absence of purple and orange and vomit-coloured Wild jungle. Inwardly he was applauding the arrival of fortified housing in neat array and the owners who must have shot those Null before building well back beyond range of their aquatic cousins. He'd been imagining beacon bonfires of dying Wild vegetation and pioneers braving poisonous fumes or predator plants up to one last gnash. It was stiffening just to think of it. In a world only recently returned to humanity's stewardship, straight lines and nature in a corset were still a joy to see.

'Good luck to them, I say!' Guy replied, meaning those unseen, perhaps shy, new natives.

His judgement, though uncontroversial, still shocked Sea-captain, for the silence had lasted long. The most senior mariner in New-Wessex had begun to fear he'd done something wrong.

'Amen!' he hurriedly agreed, hopeful of sparking conversational flame. 'If a man *must* live ashore, then let him conquer new land and clear it. "*Wider still and wider*" eh?'

Only Guy knew that now popular phrase and mission statement was lifted from a songbook found in the accursed Professor's American realm. Like many things from that tainted source, if the label was removed and the item exorcised, it was capable of conversion to the side of right. Of course, for propriety's sake, awareness had to be severely restricted. It required Blades himself to authorise a borrowing.

'"*May thy bounds be set*",' Guy completed the couplet – and wished he hadn't.

'"*Oh, Blades, who made us mighty*",' warbled Sea-captain, thinking his companion had come alive at last, '"*Make us mightier y- . . .*"'

'Yes, th-thank you,' Guy cut him off. 'I know the words.'

Sea-captain could overlook it if he chose. He saw beyond stock human mythology to view the actual ageing bundle of sadness and greatness beside him – and so held both in more subtle regard. For all his lieutenants reckoned him 'rougher than a bear's arse', Sea-captain had a conscience about ferrying this sad Ambassador from place to place he didn't want to go. He realised he had brought Guy nothing but bad news.

'My apologies, lord. I'm aware my voice is not of the best . . .'

Guy raised the flat of his hand to a troubled brow.

'No. It's I who must repent to you. It was the lack of melodious organ accompaniment that threw me. I've become unmannerly in my old age. Sing away, Sea-captain, if that's what you wish. This is your ship.'

Again, his companion was taken aback, more surprised than if he'd got a slap. Sea-captain spread blue and gold-braid sleeves.

'But your *world*, surely?' he queried, in cautious alarm.

Guy coolly looked at it as the shore passed by. If all this was indeed his, he failed to see why it gave him so little pleasure or return. Perhaps because he had no foundations on which anything pleasing could sit? Quite possibly. Granted, there were seats of pleasure and pleasurable seats (his huscarls and harem sprang to mind). There were also his racing stable, 'the sport of kings', and the dramas of the backgammon board – but these were all fleeting joys; temporary encampments, not fortresses from which to make a stand.

And there he went again with his double meanings. More and more they were will o' the wisps, misleading his thoughts from the . . . straight and narrow to . . . moister ways. Nevertheless, it was a thought . . . Although still sore, he probably could go again – if the two P's were gentle. A 'stand'. Why not? It might at least stun the inner debate – for a spell. Hopes and parts rose.

Too soon. Distractions had to be husbanded for use in emergency. Guy slapped temptation down and dealt likewise with the means of indulging it.

'Where were we?' he resumed, slightly soprano.

Sea-captain was still undermined and shocked. That took priority even over kings assaulting their own groins.

'Still with my puzzlement, lord. I asked you, if not *your* world, then whose?'

'Whose indeed?'

40

It was one of his vast stock of meaningless-but-adequate holding answers, a tactic taught in the nursery at Ambassador Hall. He could reel them off until the most determined inquisitor collapsed from exhaustion.

'Tell me, Thirteen, have you ever been to Pevensey?'

Guy knew that curiosity propelled them along the Sussex shore, just as much as wind and tide. A practised navigator through men's motivations, he found it embarrassingly easy to steer clear of awkward questions

His victim went with the sudden change of direction in a way that the *Bridget* never could. Sea-captain slowly reversed back down the theological gang-plank into comparative safety. With temporary flooring underfoot to protect him from his personal abyss, he could consider the more mundane.

'As a boy, a powder-monkey,' he answered at last. 'Father signed us up aboard all different ships, you see: to find out who was fit to rise. We docked there once in the privateer *Jolly Joyce*. They were a funny lot even then. We weren't allowed above deck, let alone ashore.'

'But you peeped through the gunports,' prompted Guy, 'didn't you?'

'Naturally. What boy of spirit wouldn't?'

'Then you know almost as much as I. One has wandered its streets on occasion, but each time my mind was distracted. The place unveils secrets solely to its own.'

'They *kill* foreigners, I hear . . .' Sea-captain was pumping as brazenly as he dare, motivated as though he were in the bilges of the *Bridget* herself.

'Foreigners,' confirmed Guy, 'suspected foreigners, people whose shoes they object to . . . The world is a grave disappointment to them and they are not obliged to visitors for any reminding. The grim *Levels* all around them have entered into their souls. Accordingly, our paths must soon part. I strongly suggest you anchor some way short and let me make my own way in.'

Part of Sea-captain's mind was always fixed upon posterity. He'd have liked to enter his clan's annals as the man who'd

41

elbowed into Pevensey. On the other hand, all accounts said the gunners of the hermit realm had grown proficient in ceaseless war with the sea-Null and other loathsome Levels-life. The *Lady Bridget* was as much a part of him as his rib-cage. He didn't want to risk either being peppered without good reason.

'Don't think I can oblige, lord,' he wavered. 'When *I* carry passengers I see 'em safe ashore.'

'Then do so through your strongest telescope. Or else the Great North Road would have been the safest option after all – Hedonists or no.'

It was a fair point, capable of confusing the sailor's guard. Then, when Guy saw the expendable troops of logic had entangled his friend, he sent the second wave in.

'And in truth, Master Sea-captain, you're more familiar with fabled Pevensey that you reveal. Are a few more morsels of knowledge worth the risk? You know how it is. I may – or may not – be inviolate, but you most certainly are not. This detour is sense to *me*, but you will do the impaling dance if they lay hands on you. All in all, I'd rather they didn't. Have you bred yet?'

In a world fixated upon the hereditary principle the abrupt question couldn't offend or take Sea-captain aback.

'Ten times, successfully!' he answered proudly. 'To date. Ten fruits of my loin! And the same number afloat in God's own navy, I'm proud to say. Baring mishaps and if Blades wills, there'll be Viscount Sea-captain XIV astride a *Lady Bridget*!'

'Then the risk is not so momentous as I imagined,' said Guy, after due consideration. 'In that case, I leave it up to you. I am not too proud to row a coracle ashore, but if you insist . . .'

That gave his companion food for thought even chewier than the normal shipboard rations. The only thing that could have extracted his teeth from it was an external threat. It propitiously arrived.

'Corsairs ahoy!' A cry fell from the crows-nest to meet with its identical twin rising from the fo'c's'le.

Guy's eyes were adapted to throne-rooms and bed-chambers

and it was some time before he saw. Long before that Sea-captain had acquired all the confirmation he needed and was altering reality to fit changed cases.

Even under full sail and with an compliant wind, the *Lady Bridget* could never hope to outrun the dart-like Leveller privateering ships. Conversely, if she struck sail the corsairs would follow suit and deploy oars with which to out-manoeuvre her. Therefore, story's end all came down to the brazen cannon presently rumbling out beneath Guy's feet. If the *Bridget* proved to have sharp teeth, then the corsairs – who were businessmen before they were fanatics – might make a commercial decision to leave well alone. It was a common enough calculation on the trade-lanes in present decadent days. Doubtless Sea-captain had been through the pantomime more times than he'd spawned successors.

However, there being a brace of corsairs tilted the odds heavily in their favour, even though the *Bridget* was one of the more feisty members of the pre-dreadnought fleet. Matters hinged upon precise assessments of profit. She *might* exact more than a bloody nose before she was had, maybe ending up as just a worthless prize, afire. Negotiation was therefore an eminently sensible first option and the Ambassador in Guy could only approve. And not only the ambassadorial component either . . .

He'd been present at a sea-fight once before, an innocent bystander-witness to mindless aggression between two Wessex noble houses with warships to waste at the bottom of the sea. Padraig-of-the-nine-hundred-books, Earl of Dublin, a scholarly and gilded youth with many golden years before him, had chanced to be beside Guy when a cannonball converted him a head shorter.

The suddenly even more gilded youth had walked on several paces, his silken sleeves still emphasising the point his missing mouth had fully intended to make, before the whole realised that things were badly wrong. Guy, meanwhile, was covered in slimy souvenirs of their brief acquaintance, requiring prolonged attention from Polly's flannel.

43

He often revisited that yukky episode in his dreams, especially after late suppers, and so now had good reason to warm to moderation. He wished any negotiations well.

The thing was, piracy and pirates were eternal, unless a state really went to town and dedicated expensive years to killing the lot. Otherwise, their numbers never seemed noticeably less and usually quite liveable-with. Generally speaking, they were reasonable men (when faced with stout opposition) and willing to strike reasonable deals. If you paid them they'd sometimes go away for ages, for weeks or even months on end.

Sea-captain, though too busy to pause and explain the finer points of strategy, seemed set on a less mellow course. He was bawling out his crew at close range, hauling down sail and preparing a robust response. It transpired that the *Lady Bridget* was as belligerent as she looked – and then some – and all her spiky parts were in earnest. Even the swarming powder-monkeys had acquired cutlasses from somewhere and Guy gathered the galley was turned over to production of red-hot shot instead of dinner.

If nothing else, the preceding years had accustomed him to stoic acceptance of disgusting events and he could hardly countermand those unfolding now. That would be embarrassing. Even cannonball surgery would be preferable. No: the manly response to unchangeable fate is to outface it. Guy told his girly alarm to do as it was told and stay indoors. For the moment, Sea-captain might proceed as he saw fit – even if it was distressing.

The corsairs had the measure of them, or so they thought. The sea-turquoise ships converged like pincers to welcome their prey's apparent acceptance of fate. Iron ram-spikes on each prow, teasingly fashioned to resemble monster male organs, peeped up from below the waterline. Only the late slamming open of the *Bridget*'s gunports prevented a closing in for the kill.

Then, as Guy's stomach was twisting into complicated knots, he perceived that Sea-captain's plan was double-barrelled, the same as some of his larger cannon. Alongside the sturdy preparations there was also incongruous activity around the main mast and a fiddling with lines. Like the corsairs, Guy was deceived.

It struck him as premature, even if surrender was intended all along, to strike the flag so soon. A civilised settlement wasn't yet out of the question. The Ambassador was so far deluded that he took pistol to hand to give Sea-captain a more lasting metal reward than thirty pieces of silver. As the 'Long Man' fluttered down Guy took aim.

But then the corsairs' throaty cheers were suddenly aborted. An even more imposing emblem headed aloft to occupy pole-place.

The 'Golden Long Man', holding swords instead of sticks, strong legs athwart the green Downs, was flown in just two rare circumstances. It signified that either the god-king or Guy was aboard. Both cases were party-killers it was risky to ignore.

A few decades back, non-believers couldn't have cared less. However, after Blades's return and the Angel Wars, even the most sceptical reflected anew. They might not understand or approve but needs must take note. All the 'out-humans', from Hedonists to Christians, recognised that *something* was keeping the brimstone rain away.

Like a suit of armour that didn't fit or flatter, you could still be thankful for its protection in time of need. Not even a Leveller fanatic would rush to kick away pit-props holding up the mine above his head.

It should have been an unanswerable trump card but misuse by cunning captains in the past had left a spark of hope burning in the corsairs' cold hearts. Weapons poised and grins still fixed, they came closer to confirm as the *Bridget* drifted for their pleasure.

Pirate-spokesman was as predatory and sleek as his galley. A sartorial sunburst in cloth-of-gold, blond forelock flopping across an unlined brow, he harangued them through a megaphone.

'It had better be true, o' men of dusty knees,' he shouted, 'or else it's no-prisoners time!'

45

That was a lie for a start. No prisoners equalled no ransoms equalled no profit. It was a rare businessman who could steel himself to making expensive *examples*.

'Bring out your gods then!' the amplified Leveller demanded. 'Show us that we might worship! Let us bathe in the blast of his beneficent beauty!'

Guy thought he was a past master but this was sarcasm you could slice and serve even with a blunt knife. Some anarchic part of him wanted to cry 'Bravo!'

Of course, silence was enforced by the majority 'responsible' elements within, but it was nevertheless a pleasant surprise to find members of the Guy-underground still operating.

Guy now saw the method in Sea-captain's madness. The man had a stone in his sling come what may. They could either go down fighting and gain a name perpetual, or else pass on their way, unhindered. It barely mattered now what Levellers and other such scum knew of Wessex whereabouts. They could talk but not act. Common sense whipped even the worst into best behaviour.

The corsairs looked at the men of Wessex and they in turn looked at Guy. There was nothing else for it.

He made his way to port and then starboard to display himself. Guy spread his arms, he did a twirl, he disported. During the performance, he saw corsair commanders race along the rails, lent wings by a possibility too awful to contemplate. Though their crews were men of every nation, from Sussex-aborigines to stray Sicilians, the officers spoke their language – and blows served when words would not. Every pirate bow or rifle had to be lowered. Swivel guns must droop on their mountings like disappointed lovers. Before a shot was fired they were disarmed, turned by Guy's mere presence into eunuch-pirates.

There was not much left to say in the circumstances. Some, the bolder or more stupid, consoled themselves with comments about those who bowed and prayed to figments of the imagination. Most fumed in silence. But Guy saw others grow thoughtful and a few (they got everywhere) even cross themselves, covering all bets.

Then, unless the pirates wished to go for eternal – but probably short – infamy by pulling the world down, they had no other option but to sail away. Long oars rattled back into rowlocks when every expectation had been for the rattle of gunfire. Green sails went back aloft to commence a fresh hunt.

Sea-captain had other ideas, not wishing these 'entrepreneurs' to go to such trouble and then leave empty-handed. At his word the *Lady Bridget* also raised sail, simultaneously speaking with all the eloquence at her disposal. Broadsides broke the false peace and, unable to retaliate, the corsairs departed in undignified haste, labouring under a lash of Wessex shot.

The sea air became nose-wrinklingly acrid with powder residue and fat with smoke, but Guy drank it in like fine wine, just as he did the sight of a diminishing enemy. Only the savage row and some grosser nearby views remained regrettable, but even there ears could be covered and sense blinkered against the one, if not the other. And he'd seen worse.

Loosened fragments of Leveller galley, as well as some occupants, were taking to the air in graceless flight, leaving a trail of splinters and limbs in their wake. Those aboard the *Bridget* not fully occupied raising canvas or dealing death, applauded or added insult to injury by mooning at the turn-tail foe. For all that the afflicted had more pressing things on their mind just then, that final indignity didn't go unnoticed – and in the long term hurt the most.

It was fun while it lasted – which wasn't long. Specialised design and strong incentives soon carried the ruffled quinqueremes beyond reproach. Once again Sea-captain looked ahead and put his ship about to deliver a final broadside, waiting for the up-roll of the waves to maximise its reach.

Fate – or *Wyrd*, as the Wessex-men were taught to term it – smiled on the farewell. A shower of lead definitively shredded one Leveller mainsail – and the sailors hauling it – into a caterpillar-visited collection of holes and ribbons.

The sight of corsair oars flapping to maintain distance birthed a rousing cheer from the now standing-down Wessex ship. Oars and sails were a dangerous mix – even the holey variety, even in dead-calm seas. There'd be a harvest of damaged oarsmen aboard as unlucky strokes met waves and Neptune won. That Levellers priggishly refused to power piracy with slave rowers only sweetened the dish. It would be 'democrat' backs that were broken – and maybe Christian spines to boot. The world would be the better for it.

Slow but sure, the corsairs drew away, out of range and, shortly, out of mind, off to spread the word and act as missionaries of safe-conduct. Eventually, the green sails merged with the horizon, departing with many a blessing.

After a quick resetting of course and tidy-up, the *Lady Bridget* gave way to festivity – in which Guy could not partake. Singled out by the rude pointing finger of fate and nudged away from normal relations, he was again living in a bubble of awe, inhibiting all who brushed against it. Every human interaction was a matter of lowered faces and kid-glove responses. He saw that he was spoiling the fun.

Guy had learned about awe at Ambassador School, along with all the other useful emotions. Awe, he was taught, soon shaded into suspicion and fear – and men invariably came to hate what they feared. '*It's a two-edged sword,*' his tutor, a deceptively cheerful little gnome, had summarised. '*So mind you don't cut yourself! And take the initiative. Never let the bastards come to their own conclusions! If you must be hated let it be for good reason. Shock 'em with cruelty straight away, and then go gentle. Never fails. They'll love you for it – be eating out of your hands ever after . . .*'

A frequent disappointment to his teachers, Guy took the lesson in but kept it there. He believed any fool could be cruel and harden their hearts. The clever trick lay in retaining a kind spirit despite everything. He still preferred his way – but wondered why it always withdrew his invitation to jollities. Instead, the hero of the day got averted eyes and genuflections – a poor substitute. Also, his tutor's spectre had risen from its little grave to tut and stamp around inside Guy's head. He was marking everything '2 out of 10 – see me'.

Guy felt hard done by and left out. Unspoken irritation was brewing up an inner turmoil. All in all, what sort of putrid thanks was this?

More than ever, he had no reason not to be nice to himself and tell duty he was out. At his prompting, Polly and Prudence took him down below again. There they played backgammon for pennies and Prudence won two whole shillings. Then he read *It Depends How You Define . . .*, the ambassadorial house-journal, until his low opinion of man was reaffirmed. That meant events need no longer disappoint. He could be *glossy* again.

Meanwhile, the *Lady Bridget*, a vessel similarly awash with renewed confidence, travelled on, tacking along the wild Sussex coast.

'Where's-the-*wizards*? Where's-the-*wizards*?'

What began as sporadic heckling had become a chant, threatening to drown out Guy's address. Each section of the natural amphitheatre took it up and thousands of throats gave the impudent query weight. The mob – or 'audience' to give them their formal title – were turning even more ugly.

All of a sudden, the drab Pevensey 'Levels' looked power-fully tempting. Even sea-air and sand blasted vegetation acquired a certain charm, matching Guy's current mood. Both were fairly sad and twisted.

He spread his arms wide, hoping honesty and a brocade waistcoat might impress. A mistake. Looking more like a rumbled market trader, his dignity flapped away to live with someone else.

'I've already t-told you,' he said, still feigning sincerity as only an Ambassador can. 'I don't *know*.'

He even repeated it through a jewelled megaphone but all his training went to waste. It served no purpose and soothed no suspicions. The Levellers and Christians, plus stray Pevensey-men and other flotsam and jetsam, were having none of it. They were used to being misled by elites. These people reckoned they knew when they were being lied to.

On this occasion they were wrong, even if all their instincts were right. Ambassadors always employed truth as the solid foot battalions of their argument-armies when possible. Lies and embellishments were only Guy's mercenary light-cavalry scouts who retreated to the main body of veracity when challenged. The policy was simple common sense. Forces raised from the flashy kingdom of falsehood might look pretty and march sprightly, but they were also notoriously flimsy, folding at the first enemy 'boo'. It took an uncannily cool general to pitch them against the pricking lances of truth or make them stay to meet the charge. Unless you were one of those perverse Ambassadors who liked to pick fights with fate, honesty was always the best policy. And simpler. You suffered less headaches that way. The New-Wessex Epicurean philosopher, Ap-Gruffyths, held that the good life was merely the minimisation of headaches. Right then, Guy would not have disputed his drearily basic thesis.

Everything else *was* being disputed. From disgruntlement over unanswered questions, the rabble moved on to more cosmic discontents. Presumably, they knew they shouldn't kill the Ambassador but there remained a rich variety of responses below that. Also you couldn't bank on their good sense and moderation. Mobs aren't the most rational of collectives. Verbal missiles were just the first rung of escalating hacked-offness.

Ever fair, Guy conceded they had a point. It *was* a bloody nerve for some aristocrat from an enemy empire which sought to extinguish Levellerdom to come and lecture them, them of *all* people, on the joys of slavery. Its abolition had been the first action of their founder, Lilburne the Great, when he seceded. His lunacy was accordingly hallowed by centuries and sentiment. The concordat Wessex had imposed on the freeports might decree an annual address, but it didn't excuse liberties.

Normally, there was no problem. The 'Hectoring', as Levellerdom termed it, attracted a thin crowd and even more famished response. A missionary-bishop of the Onefaith world would proselytise for a spell and have his parentage questioned by way of thanks. Abuse and dead cats were generally his only reward. Planted 'converts' sparked few imitators and the whole thing gradually assumed the character of ritual: lustily entered into for form's sake, but not over-burdened with meaning.

It was therefore a brainwave, depending on your viewpoint, for Blades to order Guy to the task. That way his diversion eastwards would not go to waste. Indeed, as the terse message said, *'The hope was that his presence should raise a lasting, yea, even permanent, harvest.'*

Just so. As anticipated, the star attraction had revived the flagging event, and the Imperial choice of topic doubly so. The old oxbow depression by New-Northeye, neutral ground between Wessex and Pevensey and Levellerdom, had never seen such a throng. Guy surveyed without gladness, estimating that Freeport Hastings must be deserted – and wished he'd ordered a raid to coincide.

And he'd gone on to shower honeyed words and reason all over them, casting pearls before swine. He'd even gone the extra mile and degraded himself by hinting at the universal debt owed him. Guy hadn't wanted to, naturally, but it was specifically commanded. In the event, a mutiny could have saved his blushes, for everything thrown – from his direction at least – failed to stick.

The root problem lay in a lack of conviction. An alternative Guy was saying to them: 'Who knows? You could be right!'

How could he, a man born free and preferring death to servitude, talk up slavery to an audience similarly comprised? It was a shameful business and Guy2 was getting stroppy, raising his voice to Messrs Reason and Discretion, calling them awful names. Pretty soon, he might be audible over Guy's official voice. The traditional allegation about Ambassadors being two-faced would gain credence.

Fortunately (in one sense), Polly and Prudence were before him, employing their axes to deflect incoming solids. At the same time, though, their ears were being treated to his insincere words. That loyalty still prevailed, making both frantic to go forth and retaliate, only increased Guy's guilt. For them, of all people, to hear him praise the yoke was deeply embarrassing. Suppose they *had* been convinced, unlike the riffraff in front? Then what might they make of his motives in acquiring them?

And so it required every dreg of ambassadorial skill to give his words legs, and even then they limped, advancing into combat with reluctance. The massed ranks of Levellerdom shrugged them off and hurled them back.

'Consider!' Guy tried opening a new front. 'Consider the freedom a bonded workforce brings. Ponder the creations only leisure hours permit. The operas, the sonnets and so on. If you have to cook your own dinner there's no ti—'

They howled right through, round and over him. No one wanted to hear about that *or* his next gambit: the new, more humane, lighter alloys now used for slave fetters. Degraded types, bottle fortified, were baring their bottoms at him.

Fortunately, some of them were almost passable. Guy could transcend the pink vistas. And, if *that* was the way their minds worked . . . Ambassadors were taught to give people what they wanted.

'All right, then, ladies and gentlemen. Consider slave *harems*! Consider better bedtimes!'

Presumably they didn't hear, megaphone or no. One or two looked thoughtful but the general chorus continued just as lusty.

'Where's the *wizards*?' was all anyone wanted to know: the hot news of the moment, requiring a nice fresh answer served now, not his reheated defence of the indefensible. Somehow the facts had seeped out, faster than Guy could convey them to an ungrateful godhead at New-Godalming. Some rapscallion had leaked the highest confidences. It might even have been him.

Even now, as the dead cats flew (proving some had come prepared with closed minds), Guy did not protest. Blades had a right to command him here. Blades had authority to dictate both sermon and creed. Guy had a duty to obey. So long as you didn't look down, it made life nice and simple.

Nor was it *total* humbug. Guy could see the – borrowed – reasoning. To some extent New-Wessex depended on slavery. Machines were coming, you didn't have to be a prophet to see that, but until they did and Blades stopped banning them, there must be reliance on the old ways, on muscle power and plenty of it, and unfortunates obliged to do tedious things. Therefore, come the glorious day when all humanity sheltered under the Wessex wing, it would help if people were already harmonised.

And actually, Levellerdom had already conceded the principle and then papered over the cracks with hypocrisy. They abstained from slavery at the price of abandoning scruple. Piracy – or 'redistribution' – was their solution to the shortfall in surplus value. Their vaunted idealism shone forth from burning boats and towns.

Perhaps because of this, or perhaps the moggy-missiles, King Guy suddenly despised the sea of smug, outraged, faces, all of them disputing his words of wisdom when they should be agreeing. Sympathy could only survive so much rudery.

Guy felt an uncharacteristic flare of anger. What these ungrateful sodomites needed was the angels back – and moving amongst them with a fiery flail. They'd sing a different song – a symphony for ground teeth and wails – on that day. Meanwhile he'd be entirely safe and smirking. That'd serve 'em . . .

It would serve them unjustly. Guy's sweet nature reasserted itself. If he was honest he knew where his irritation originated – and it wasn't from the hail of filth. He knew – but hesitated to say, even to himself.

Others weren't so squeamish. That inner anarchist who'd been quashed before was back supplying unsolicited opinions. Just as vociferous as the Leveller crowd, his opinions were far more telling.

'Blades. *Bloody* Blades! *Admit it!*' the seditious particle explained, foam-mouthed. '*You know I'm right, you twister.*

53

And *he wants you gone. What d'you mean "who"? Deaf as well as stupid, are you? Blades! He wants you dead! Disgraceful! You should—*'

Then the internal lynch mob arrived to put a noose round his neck – or tourniquet round the flow of honesty. The squeaking was suppressed.

However, there'd been a wealth of truth in there, whilst it lasted. It *was* a suicidal gesture to lecture the most insubordinate people alive about 'the shameful waste of time that is freedom'. Had he really said that? When he did had he sounded as though he was even convincing himself?

Guy should have been thankful it was only pussies and phlegm arcing over. Anyone less indispensable would have copped something fatal by now. The Levellers were all armed: it was their 'constitutional right'. They were famed for severity to the lackeys of servitude. The god-king Blades must have known how his suggested speech would go down. And as for ordering a day out in Yarmouth . . .

It was a big issue to think of – and so Guy didn't.

Then for a second he believed – and feared – his wishes were coming true. He'd desired an angel amongst them – and now there was one . . .

She/it glared at Guy from the front row. How had he failed to notice her? How come everyone else continued to?

An angel's gaze is all-absorbing. Their eyes hold nothing back and are oceans to fall into. Guy had never been so unreservedly hated before.

Twin jet ovals glared up at him from a face that made his huscarls look florid. A breeze not of this world stirred her golden locks and glorious wings. She condensed the corridor of air between them until it was almost solid.

The Levellers might not be able to see, but those nearest were privy to her powerful emotions. They shrank away from they knew not what, flapping arms and huffing at hands turned frigid. A space was cleared.

It matched the void cleared in Guy. He was shocked to be washed in such undilute venom. He felt diminished that even an enemy should loathe him so wholeheartedly.

They had cause, admittedly, but this was excessive. From abashment Guy passed to affront. Even in war men stepped back from absolute savagery. Forgiveness was always an option, even if it lay generations away. Not so with angels. They never felt that way, for all that their perspectives were longer. These were black and white creatures, dismissive of shades.

Which made things straightforward, after a fashion. You could return the compliment in good conscience. Guy drew his sword to do so.

The Leveller audience wasn't to know they weren't in danger. They only saw a speaker carried away by his own oratory. As Guy leaped armed from the dais they recalled other places to be.

In one sense he was lucky not to be gunned down. Polly and Prudence couldn't have prevented it amidst such a throng. However, the innate decency of the Levellers (another Lilburne legacy), arse-baring and cat-calling/throwing aside, made most realise there'd been provocation. Guy's charge could claim good cause. Combined with common sense, it made them stay their trigger-fingers.

The ambassadorial weapon of choice was a stiletto, which, rather like the clan, was discreet, elegant and left little trace. For more crass displays of temper though, there were always firearms and the archetype Wessex short-sword: both well suited to making views known. Guy selected both.

The angel was unimpressed. The Ambassador could have been waving a tinsel wand for all she cared. She waited for him.

Visually uninvited like all the rest, Polly and Prudence were reduced to spectators. They meanwhile calmed their fears with displacement activity, clearing some space for Guy's solo fencing display. Their faith was touching – as were their axes. They believed their beloved knew what he was doing – for all the evidence to the contrary.

For the first time that day, Guy now had the Levellers'

respectful, rapt, attention. Sadly, he was turned indifferent. All his concentration was lavished on the feathered emissary whom he alone could see.

Pistol and sword provoked zero reaction. She was lost, ecstatic, in her own private festival of malice, where Guy was guest of honour but also excluded. It was up to him to gatecrash and drag the conductor's baton down.

'You,' he admonished her, 'should n-not be here! You are b-barred from our affairs. Blades commands it! And if he commands, then y—'

Her head jerked upright as if he'd used a more than verbal point. The look abated not at all but now she was truly with him. It failed to please her on any level. Guy's words died on his lips in the spectacular fashion she wished for all of him.

To an Ambassador there is no state more appalling than nothing left to say between two parties. All avenues were closed: a horrific state of affairs to the habitually subtle.

Thus there seemed just one way forward. Some injunction prevented angels from harming Guy but he wore no such shackles. She was his to have if he wanted.

Curiously, he didn't want. There'd been enough death. To emulate her kind was to descend to the same absolute zero of feeling: a pit beyond reach of light. It would be to dive deeper than humans are designed to, and risk never returning.

So Guy withheld his steel and thus was higher than angels. If such a thing were possible, she despised him all the more.

It was excruciating to bestow even words on such as he. The black lips moved over perfect needle-teeth but time elapsed before sound emerged.

'After all we've done for you,' she spat. 'Saved you in the Wild. Sacrificed ourselves. Held your hand to Capri. And now this. Green-eyed monster Guy! Rank ingratitude!'

Not thinking to have his ethics questioned, Guy was taken aback – which pleased her slightly. Accordingly, she went to it again.

'The dream is over!'

That shook him and made her smile.

'Yes, *over*,' she continued, still boring holes with her eyes. 'For most. But not for you. For *you* the nightmare has *far* to go!'

Guy's sword was even swifter than her lust to leave. Its very tip scored the alabaster shoulder, sending up a spray of golden blood.

Then she was gone, leaving only her mark.

Each gilded globule hissed hostility at the outer air and froze the ground it fell on.

'Hello!'

Nothing. Guy persevered.

'I said hellooooooooo!'

Their silence was eloquence itself. They clearly saw, they surely heard. Nevertheless, Pevensey's own thoughts proved adequate to herself, requiring no verbalisation. Only far-off music, skulls and bells on chains tinkling against stone, convinced Guy he hadn't gone deaf.

Pevensey-men lined the mossy walls, a distant black crenellation of heads to match the flint-and-mortar version they lurked behind. Ever vigilant, Guy estimated away and concluded all Pevensey had come to greet him – in their own peculiar way.

Whether that sprang from desire or command he had no way of knowing. Instead of smiling faces before the city gates there were cannon emplacements and glowing tapers poised for action. Above them the pleading arms of the walled up, either agitated or stilled for ever, extended from involuntary hermitages in the ramparts. Neither was exactly an enticement. The anonymous High Priest of Pevensey had scoured away every trace of welcome as deliberate policy.

Not that Guy wished to stay or be ushered in with hosannas. What *would* have been nice though was some little recognition of his existence beyond a stare. In time, the need for proof of continued life became imperative. Guy fought it but

57

their long, silent scrutiny gradually got to him.

He *could* have gone in – probably – if he insisted, but he would have had to go alone. If 'Guy Gatherer', retriever of the god-king, inexplicably surrounded himself with infidels ignorant of the blessed Sennacherib Co-redemptor, son of Blades, then that was his business. However, even he ought not to presume overmuch. His companions were bereft in this world and damned in the next: mere unbelieving bags of blood and guts. Pevensey's marksmen would be only too happy to demonstrate.

Polly and Prudence were permitted him, just so long as they strictly adhered to the iron-peg-outlined and snake-narrow corridors reserved for foreigners in Holy Sussex. Meanwhile, the totally out of the question *Lady Bridget* waited offshore, behind one of the conical islets or 'eyes' that dotted Pevensey lagoon. And even there the Wessex crew weren't allowed to show their offensive heads and had to exercise all discretion, lighting fires and answering nature on the far side of the island, well out of sight.

Still smarting about the angel's reminder and escape, not to mention the Levellers' abuse, Guy felt a sudden urge to daub over this oppressive still-life. It stood in gasping need of some livelier brush-strokes than native artists could provide. Happily, he remained in the mood to pamper himself with a little creativity.

Therefore whilst Guy obediently trod the straight and narrow towards the beach he also unholstered his revolver. Then, unhurriedly, leisurely style, like confident raps upon a door, he emptied it into the sky.

Each retort was a slap to the landscape's face. Of course, you couldn't discern detail from such a distance, but Guy devoutly believed a shudder circled the decay-green walls.

His nominal excuse was the rousing of the *Bridget*, and in this at least he was successful. Matchstick Wessex-men appeared over the brow of Chilleye and the crow's nest just visible above awakened to life.

As did the brooding city. A single shot rang out. The

foremost sailor screamed. Some master gunner, or a plain man powerfully inspired, had spoken for all Pevensey.

Now racked by guilt in addition to all his other troubles, a chastened Guy Ambassador did not look back but went meekly to the shore.

'Sorry about that, Lord.'

Guy was suddenly convinced they'd had this conversation before. And they had – repeatedly. Several rehearsals of the words sprang to mind. The same place but earlier in the day. To be convivial however, he recited it all again

'No. The apology is mine,' he told Sea-captain, very deliberately, anxious to get his lines right. 'My fault. Absolutely. Self-indulgence. I lost you a man.'

Sea-captain shrugged and drank deep – again. He'd seen men come and go until they were all a blur. There was no point in going all moody about one particular flicker in life's magic-lantern show. Guy had meant well; which was all you could ask of anyone. He always *meant* well.

Alcoholic warming threatened an avalanche of affection towards Ambassadors and all the universe, requiring urgent containment. The tankard was tilted higher till the spasm passed.

When it was drained and could provide cover no more, Sea-captain slammed the dry vessel down. The face that emerged was brick-red and refreshed; back to uncharitable normal. He surveyed the tavern's other clientele, visible through the private bar entrance where Polly and Prudence sat like chalk statues to either side. The patrons' backs were turned, their every sense determinedly attuned elsewhere. Try as he might Sea-captain wouldn't find contradiction there. The required abrasion would have to come from nearer home.

'Not your fault, lord. *Not*, I say. Have to correct you. Bastard shouldn't have stuck his bonce up. What? No, I mean it. Taught the rest a valuable lesson. Can't muck about, not in this life. You tempt fate – fate bites y'head off. Nothing wrong with that. Ah – you can pull all the faces you like but it's true! Maybe I even owe you. Destupidising the crew – does me a favour, don't it? And anyhow, I still say the mistake's mine. It was me who banked on them letting us dock. Should have guessed they'd turn funny. Can't land a party? Balls! I won't have it. You carry your own baggage? Not on any voyage *I* run! God forbid!'

Actually, 'God' very probably would. Blades was touchy concerning etiquette and adequate respect. He'd crucified someone who'd left a very minor noble to pick up his own dropped pencil.

Guy graciously conceded Sea-captain's point – whatever it was. Right now, he had no argument with him or anyone. The Ambassador stood on the glorious verge of understanding – and thus forgiving – all. It was only slightly a shame that rising to greet the revelation was out of the question.

Mere moments before, Guy had realised that the secret of the universe was something to do with an dusty old barometer he could glimpse over Sea-captain's right shoulder. The exact details were just beyond reach for the moment, acting like a saucy minx, teasing him with giggles and flashes, but he was confident of consummation sooner or later.

'*I'll have you shortly, mark my words* . . .' Guy fairly warned the meaning of life. A few more gulps of inspiration and he'd find the legs to leap up and have his way with her. Very shortly, yes indeed.

Of course, the sea-style movement of the tavern hardly helped. Guy hadn't reckoned on that continuing once safely ashore. Even so, it didn't do to overstate the problem. The bar wasn't revolving or anything extreme like that. Its four corners were just less dogmatically fixed than normal, that's all. There were no grounds for alarm or an end to imbibing. Not for a nice while anyway. It was rare enough for life to feel like a snug blanket and thus all the less reason to cast it off because 'duty' was shouting at you. For once, that accountant-with-a-megaphone was easy to ignore. It ranted away from the far side of a widening void whilst Guy took up another bottle.

Guy Ambassador upended its dimpled bottom over his crystal goblet.

'Whoops . . .'

'"My *cup runneth over*,"' quoted Sea-captain, and obligingly mopped up the lap-threatening overspill with his sleeve. There was no harm done: it was scarlet already.

However, the mishap still vaguely troubled Guy, devaluing his rich insights. He swore that his glass had stood in need of a refill. Or was it his mouth he was thinking of?

The warm momentum of the tide within carried him past such cavils, leaving them behind whinging on the bank; soon out of sight and mind.

It was a *good* day. Tomorrow might be horrible; doubtless duty would catch up and deliver a cross lecture to Guy's brain. Almost certainly the headache would be monstrous, as monstrous as the amount of wine. Yet there remained today – which seemed longer and gentler than normal days. For hour upon hour he hadn't remembered the thing he didn't want to remember. No one could now take that away from him.

The trouble with drink, though, is that it paves the way for a flash-flood of emotion, unfastening any flood defences into the bargain. In recalling that which he hadn't recalled, Guy . . . recalled.

His eyes welled and life cast off its thin disguise, turning on him with a werewolf snarl.

They were going to call her Daisy, if it was a girl – which it was, briefly but also for ever. Daisy Ambassador, beloved daughter of Guy and Batsheba, 480 AB–480 AB. RIP.

Fortunately, Sea-captain was looking the other way. Otherwise he would have asked about waving farewell to someone invisible. And that would have been painful.

After Pevensey's concrete – or lead – rebuff, Sea-captain had ferried Guy further along the coast to New-New-Winchelsea (as Blades, in his infinite wisdom, insisted it be known). Though insufficiently worshipful, at least the welcome there wasn't bullet-borne. The freeport pocketed a berthing fee and, having already heard about the 'Hectoring' and the patch of New-Northeye grass that would never grow again, left them alone.

So Guy didn't have to carry his own trunks after all, and could now sit at ease in a harbour tavern with Sea-captain whilst the Hermes mirror system conveyed the change of plans. As things turned out, it was probably all for the best. Unless, of course, you chanced to be the Wessex sailor buried on Chilleye but currently dancing in the sea's rough company after swift exhumation by Pevensey-men.

It would take at least a day – a delicious day away from duty – before the waiting Imperial coach could skirt round Sussex and link up. Quite inadvertently, Guy had given the forces of tedium the slip.

Thus he could now drift to his heart's content, watching the world go by and drinking as much Winchelsea wine as he wanted – with no upper limits on wanting bar human tolerance. The vast cellars extending under the freeport's fortified villas held enough bottles to stun an army. A poet might construe them as the town's veins and their contents its lifeblood. Through shrewd trading (and judicious use of untraceable violence) New-New-Winchelsea had cornered the vinous market, blossoming from dour pirate port into an abode of gracious living – albeit one with sharp teeth. Guy had seen proof of it even in the short walk to the tavern. Faces like fists rested atop moderating silk and lace. Predatory natures now surveyed the world through gorgeous disguise. Their swords were elegant as well as practical. And that was just the women.

Meanwhile, all the vineyards in partially liberated 'France', beleaguered behind their anti-Null walls, were well advised to ship to Wessex solely in Winchelsea vessels. It made sound commercial sense. Other routes and means seemed awfully prone to sinking.

So the wine was plentiful and cheap, the context benign. Guy had found the right place and time in which to endure, for the umpteenth time, Sea-captain's theories about America.

Today it arrived as welcome distraction, like reinforcements on the skyline just as the white flag was being sought. In its comforting repetition there was power to dry his eyes.

It helped that for once there was no task snapping at Guy's heels, making him wish the tale told quicker. Whilst a purple tide worked its wonders, he lost the itch to always *contribute*. Sea-captain could have said the Americans all turned into turkeys after abandoning their civilisation and Guy wouldn't have protested. It was as pleasing an explanation for the mystery as any.

This was Sea-captain's obsession, other than preserving his ship and line; the thing he thought about when nothing else imposed. He'd stated repeatedly (occupying hours he might have used to actually *do* it) that one day he'd write a book and settle the question for ever. Always within there was an unspoken hint. Guy heard that bat-squeak but never bit. Each time, he politely said he'd buy a copy for his library, but couldn't possibly take on the task himself.

Guy would slur-say so again today. Sea-captain wouldn't be offended. He never minded, even when sober. It was the invariable response of the authorial classes. They didn't understand the sense of urgency which filled a man of action when he realised all his hard-won wisdom might be lost.

' . . . Mystery?' Sea-captain asked, returning to the trod-hard conversational rut. 'What mystery? Know what *I* think? I think it got like a *school*! A *bad* school – more fear than love or learning. I mean, he was a Professor, wasn't he? He founded it and what did he know but everyone sitting up straight and listening to pearls of wisdom? And he'd brought 'em rifles and those "maxim guns" – so they listened good. Only he wasn't a *good* master – not like the Lord Blades. It was more kicks than kindness with him. Of course, they took the education and the things to kill the Null with and thank you very much. Meanwhile they licked his boots like he wanted and maybe some got to like the taste. But – and here's what I'm saying – he goes off and Blades slays him and suddenly, back at school, it's liberty hall! No more nose-to-the-grindstone and sit-up-pay-attention! The same as if I let the *Lady Bridget* go or stopped hanging slackers. They'd sail off to some warm place and sun 'emselves. I know it, for all I love 'em!'

It was very basic stuff for Guy: page 1 of the ambassadorial *Man Motivation* textbook, and akin to hearing the two-times table recited. Today, though, there was a certain nostalgia value in there, filtering out the irritation factor. Guy settled back to drink it in.

'So,' Sea-captain was really warming to his subject, 'the Professor crossed over and got his just deserts from our Blades, and his people back home are wondering, "Is he coming? Is he coming?" Only he never does, and then they think, "This ain't so bad" and "Life's easier now" and "Do we really need to get up so early in the morning? So what if the Null are creeping back? We can always blast 'em away. There's whole warehouses of bullets; enough to last for, oh, ages . . ." Do'y get my drift?'

'I'm buried in it. Like a snow*drift*,' answered Guy, because, at the time it seemed a clever thing to say. Then, even as the quip clambered over his lips he realised it wasn't. The play on words wouldn't come out to play and for the first time all afternoon, Sea-Captain's brow furrowed. Guy was fleetingly glad he was who he was. Elsewise it might have been keelhauling time.

Instead his companion just shook his head and all the puzzlement must have fallen out. Face-thunder faded away.

'Thus, what I postulate,' Sea-captain rallied into literary mode now, since that was how he wished his sagacity immortalised, 'is *"liberation-shock"*. His people-cum-pupils get daring and think their own thoughts for the first time. "Is his wonderfulness ever coming back at all and, if not, what are we wearing his uniform for?" Geddit? Some brave soul must have got up off his knees – I'm speaking metaphorical, mind – and the sky doesn't fall on his head! Next thing you know, school's out for ever ! They're done with the Professor and all learning!'

Guy devoted a befuddled thought to his own education and failed to envy the Americans. As best he could presently recall, Ambassador training had been deliciously adaptive to human foibles. In fact, it had positively *preyed* on them.

'Therefore the first Wessex ships to hit his republic's shores didn't find much to meet 'em. Ruins. Ruins and wild-boys revering heirloom guns. Sometimes the firesticks'd go bang: sometimes not. Can't take that chance with a Null coming at you. Most had reverted to bow and spear. Not so deadly but *reliable*, see?'

Sea-captain chuckled over an amusement better than another drink.

'One long, violent play-time. That's what they'd had. Centuries long. Holidays indefinitely extended. All structures, be they of brick or state, in advanced decay. Wildcats, bear and the Null enthroned, save in places they don't fancy. *Terrible* state of affairs. You can't fault us putting it right. Any way we could. *Righteous* war!'

So Blades had said, but Guy wasn't so sure. Intoxication made him brave and honest, even if only to himself. Truth was, they'd run out of slaves gained the conventional way. The little wars of Wessex could never generate sufficient numbers to keep industry going. Whatever 'industry' was. What *was* it? Guy tried to think.

The image of a factory in Winchester surged to mind, smutty black and disgusting as the original. Into it ant-like American slaves and Wessex foremen slouched, brothers under the same cloud of misery.

Blades was all for industry and guns by the ton, but Guy recollected no grass grew round that establishment. The stream which powered it was poisoned and dogs that drank from there died. A 'satanic mill' indeed.

Unaware, Sea-captain chuntered on.

'It's a charity to take poor wretches out of such suffering. Like you said to the Levellers.'

Had he? Had he *really*? Guy boggled. How bizarre.

All this thinking quite exhausted him and he applied his forehead to the table.

Sea-captain stared and then blearily stroked the

Ambassador's presented rat's tail hair, having lulled his own children to sleep that way. He made allowances, knowing the long day – and life – Guy had had. Those thin shoulders were not broad enough for the tasks demanded of them, and Sea-captain hated to be the bearer of additional burdens. He'd not have wasted a day numbing his behind in a low tavern talking American history but for that itch of conscience. It was such a shame. People owed this man so much but fortune repaid him so little.

Polly and Prudence rose in a geyser of black and white and Sea-captain hurriedly drew his comforting hand away, not wishing to lose it. Wine had waylaid the notion that they might object to his familiarity. His nervous system now supplied a horse-dose of instant sobriety and the message arrived all urgent and out of breath. Sea-captain had heard about these girls. You couldn't reason with them. He pointedly held his hands aloft.

Which was a funny position for the Imperial Courier to find him in.

Sea-captain had misinterpreted events and not noticed a new arrival. It was he who'd sponsored the huscarl eruption. It was he who was now boggling over a senior mariner apparently surrendering to nothing, plus King Guy, in like condition, fast asleep in a quayside dive.

Then the Courier had better things to think about. Unsuspected up to that moment, Polly and Prudence closed on him from behind. In seconds he was relieved of sword, credentials and dignity.

The pale-faces held the newcomer at bay until they'd studied his chain of office and were satisfied. Only then were his possessions returned to him. Open-mouthed, he remained at a loss for words.

Sea-captain supplied them. He first mimed the motion, and then, finding the huscarls willing, repeated it for real, gently rocking Guy's shoulder.

'Come along, my lord, wakey wakey! No rest for the wicked!'

Polly and Prudence looked at him and Sea-captain wished he hadn't said that.

King Guy's fatigue was such that he seemed beyond stirring. The silence became awkward.

Courier appeared to have left the coathanger inside his greatcoat, so rigid was his bearing. That wasn't the case, but a witness could be excused for thinking it. The explanation lay not in absentmindedness but Wessex's wealth of hereditary callings. Courier's post was no mere 'job' but a calling inherited from the hazy past. The mantle had been assumed so long ago that all memory of another family name was lost. Now he was 'just' Courier, the same as his father before him, the same as his son would be. Whether he liked it or not.

Those more-than-one-lifetime years piling up behind showed – to the point of exposing themselves – in his bearing and disdain. On the plus side, they made it seem less of a presumption for him to seize the initiative. The man advanced further into the tavern like a fastidious tightrope-walker poised over a sea of sewage: fearful of the potential for contamination but not deigning to look down.

He also proved to have company, and plainly wished they'd been about during the rough handling. In strict status order a coachman and blunderbuss-guard trailed behind like burly ducklings. Then, with impressive synchronisation requiring no signal, each swept off their tricorns and paid Guy homage.

That he wasn't awake to receive it hardly mattered. It was the done thing. Polly and Prudence and Sea-captain approved.

'Ambassador,' said Courier to Guy's horizontal head. 'The divine Blades summons you. Your carriage awaits.'

Charitably assuming Guy to be overcome by the honour, they loaded him aboard feet first.

He slept through the first few statelets, and the hangover chewing over his brain saw him past several more.

Thus Guy was robbed of the charms of the 'Sublime Margravate of East Weald', New-New-Winchelsea's nearest neighbour. He missed out on the spectacle of that land's rainbow-clad border guards and famous chained Null watch-dogs. Their Moses-and-the-Red-Sea re-enactment before the Imperial coach-and-four was lost on him, and likewise the repeat performance at the Margravate's further side. Several other petty princedoms were similarly slighted.

Guy rode in one of the famous slate-grey 'Sealed Coaches', with which it was war or worse, and probably blasphemy, to tamper. The Sealed Coach fleet paid no tolls and stopped for no one. Nor was it anyone's business who or what comprised their cargo. To prove that point from the outset, those who interfered and poked their nose in had the exact same portion severed. For persistent curiosity it was not unknown for heads to roll. Happily, though, people soon got the message and enshrined it in a proverb. *'He'd stare at a Sealed Coach!'* was New-Wessex judgement on the terminally inquisitive.

All morning they travelled through deep forest, for East Weald was vast enough to be only nibbled at by ship building and the iron foundries. However, from being a haunt of Null and an every-day-an-adventure sort of place, it was now shading imperceptibly into hunting reserve and retirement country for those who'd climbed the greasy pole. Grand houses like islands dotted the sea of green, less fortified in design with each passing year.

Nevertheless, there remained core New-Wessex folk in the vicinity, despite gentrification, forming the backbone for each successive micro-kingdom. Villages suddenly loomed into sight atop defendable rises, and smoke arose from the obscure abodes of woodcutters and charcoal tribes. From them the Wessex forces traditionally drew its light infantry and sharpshooters. They tended to be quiet men, of thoughtful disposition; not easily trainable but usefully armed with poacher skills. Guy had had the honour of their command one long ago summer, back when the madness of the Null breeding season still merited a grand muster. Despite the lapse of time, he still recalled the foresters accurately – and their accuracy with affection.

Neither party would ever know, but some of those very

same old soldiers observed their former colonel roll by. They might have emerged from cover to greet him had they but known. However, since they didn't they didn't, and there was no regimental reunion that day. Sealed Coaches were different, operating in a separate, safer, universe. The nature of their intended prey made Guy's old colleagues and would-be ambushers abandon all plans, and they withdrew into the greenwood, apologising in prayer.

Guy finally stirred to life in the Dukedom of Bodiam and accepted some water; though he could have been in Jericho for all he knew. He took no cognisance of its village-capital or folk taking to their knees, preferring that kindly sleep should take him again and draw a shroud over reality. 'Reality'? The name rang a vague bell, but nothing specific. So, water yes, but reality: no thank you. Guy would skin that particular bear when he caught it – assuming it'd stand still and oblige.

Accordingly, his entrance to the frontier-bishopric of New-Hawkhurst troubled Guy not at all, for he wrestled with worse problems than mere roadblocks and rudely pointing cannon. Deep in even less welcoming Dreamland he was having to take an exam he'd failed to prepare for. Fur-faced invigilators stood over him as, outer eyes closed, Guy stared at the paper and panicked. In endless loop, like a poisonous serpent devouring its own tail, it provided absorbing diversion to last him right through the gargoyle gallery that comprised Hawkhurst's main road and claim to fame.

Likewise, the world-renowned 'Doomsday' sculpted atop Hawkhurst Cathedral quite passed him by, as he did it, in tortured sleep. And perhaps that was just as well, for the furry men had grown stern and the exam questions sadistic. Prince-Bishop Rawlinson IV had commissioned a masterpiece, without doubt, but sight of stone souls in torment could only have added to Guy's woes.

A change of horses in New-Tonbridge woke him sufficiently to be excused the examination room. In the courtyard of the Royal Oak there, surrounded by a hastily assembled honour-guard of halberdiers, Guy felt up to accepting a cutlet and 'hair of the dog' from a lively-looking serving-maid. Combined, the three were sufficient sweeteners to let him get a dose of facts down.

Peering round the window blind he condescended to note the surroundings and locate himself. Riding atop javelins of light there arrived painful recognition. He'd been here before. When New-Tunbridge Wells sought to secede from 'Greater Tonbridge' Blades had sent his foremost Ambassador to arbitrate. Not far from here, Guy recalled, was the 'Civic Citadel' where he'd been (passive) witness to the burghers of Tonbridge being sedated with assurances, promises even – and more importantly, drugged wine. The promises were soon broken, and similarly the Tonbridge men's heads. Imperial Tonbridge was slit open, caesarean-style, and from the womb of colonial servitude out slid New-Tunbridge Wells, howling to join the nations of Bladedom. In the event it had gone as smoothly as Guy planned – slick as the treacherous Tunbridge Wells knives that night.

Guy always evaluated betrayals by weighing up little sins against large ones. A town hall awash with gore was better than two whole towns so. It came down to matters of degree, with ambassadorial clarity of thought informing humane considerations. In this case, neither side seemed willing to compromise. Each apparently longed for a little war to inflame the Weald. So, rather than embroil blameless soldiers and peasants, it was clearly more moral to knife one set of hot-heads and smile falsely at the other. Such, Guy recalled, was his thinking at the time, and even now, when age interposed tiresome 'but . . . but's', it retained some comforting validity. Also, he'd only been obeying orders . . .

Like everything else, the painful matter stemmed from Blades's decree and another about-turn of policy now hallowed by time. All other things being equal, the god-king had informed his diplomats, 'A thousand flowers should bloom' – if they cared to – even at the price of rendering the garden chaotic. Overnight, from weeding out separatists Ambassadors turned to loosening soil round them so that new blossoms might grow. Sickly shoots fit to die had been anointed with metaphoric manure, and even poison plants encouraged. Such obedience had raised abundant fruit. Nowadays, Humandom held more petty princes, earls, margraves and bishop-despots than once there were mayors.

So, New-Tunbridge Wells joined the patchwork of statelets and, when he last checked, Guy was a hero there, immortalised in bronze in the City Square. At the same time his after-the-event look of shocked innocence had deceived Tonbridge out of due grievance. All was well that ended well and everything being for the best ought to have made him feel better – but it hadn't then and didn't now. Speaking for himself – a mere featherweight opinion compared to Blades's he knew, but an insistent, courteous, voice all the same – Guy had preferred it when you could travel right from Kent to Cornwall and it was all New-Wessex without quibble.

Whereas now, in present times, any energetic thug could crown himself 'king' over a glorified market garden, just so long as he gave a nod to Wessex sovereignty and made his twelve-men-and-a-dog army available in emergency. If it were quite convenient . . . and no other pressing matter called . . . and the weather was amenable . . .

The thought of some modern musters he'd seen, compared to New-Wessex glory at its height, soured Guy's stomach even more. Regiments with pitchforks! Home-made cannon and cart-horse cavalry! The acid input impelled Guy fully awake. That and Courier's hysterical fussing to be gone and arrive at Monday by Sunday.

Guy's discontent was becoming complete. His wig was skew-whiff and crazed, a disgrace even to Medusa, its pigtails crushed and priapic. Powder and pomade had oozed into places they had no business being. The pattern on the coach's upholstery had imprinted itself on one side of his face and the ambassadorial body beneath felt like nine-tenths straining bladder. Even so, it was still too much trouble to move.

Bile rising met meat in the mouth and turned it disgusting. Likewise, Guy's whimsy about placing meat in the maid. The cutlet went out the window and Guy croaked a command that the coach should roll.

For once, Courier's burning desire for haste was appeased. That he'd not had to nudge Guy to depart meant whole seconds were saved. Brief as it was, the economy lit a glow of pious virtue that lasted for hours.

Courier looked at it thus: swift answer to Blades's call was the same as crusading. He was past partaking in the real thing now, or going hand to hand with Christians or Null, but if he could make feet run swift about Blades's business, then surely that was almost as good as.

Confident he'd just inched nearer to Heaven, Courier smiled upon Guy Ambassador. Guy misinterpreted that swift flex of the stick apparently jammed across Courier's mouth. Assuming it to be indigestion he politely pretended not to notice.

And Courier thought, 'Well, if that's the way the cold fish wants it . . .' and resolved not to unbend again. From such misunderstandings are life-long friendships lost.

Above their heads came whip-cracks and orders, and a fresh team took up the strain, gradually persuading the dead weight behind to follow them. Picking up speed they left the yard and clattered away up the cobbled High Street. The spark of divinity was leaving New-Tonbridge.

The maid Guy had dishonoured in fantasy looked and longed after it, till the last fading hoof-clop and jangle. Then she stooped to retrieve the chewed cutlet her boot had hid under sheltering skirts. A cloth and fervent prayer were wrapped round it.

Many years later, as polished bone mounted on silver the family could ill afford, her grandchildren would inherit the revered souvenir.

The Episcopate of New-Horsham was an improvement – particularly after traversing the grim little Spartas of Forest

Row and New-East-Grinstead *en route*. Mere decades back, Horsham had been a frontier town, guaranteeing the military perimeter and the Great East Road behind. Now, with the dying away of the Wild, its famed wall-guns pivoted only for show and discharge on high and holy days. The fraternity who'd once trained them on Null and worse abominations emerging from the multi-coloured jungle had transmuted into a social club of fond memories and tall stories.

Also, now that the surrounding landscape didn't bite, a pleasing petticoat of villas and pleasure gardens spread ever wider from the redundant walls. Wits could no longer – honestly – say a charmless person or bit of bad luck was *'rougher than Horsham'*.

To aid evolution and kill the proverb, one far-sighted Bishop of Horsham had lifted all tax burdens from artists residing within his realm. Hearing that call a tide of the self-proclaimed gifted invaded like Null on heat and now you couldn't walk its streets without encountering people seeking to civilise or explain the world. In small doses – akin to wedding cake – it was very nice, a soothing contrast to coal-bunker-smooth conditions prevailing elsewhere. Guy and Bathie acquired a summer residence there and over the years stole some useable quotes from writers desperate to sing for their supper.

Horsham's roadside sculptures and shrines weren't the nightmare raw material of Hawkhurst, but rather an expression of a world view not *entirely* savage. Guy recognised a few depictions of himself, amidst all the 'Blades in Glory' and 'Anguished Null'. Some weren't half bad, capturing the sardonic smile and kindly revisiting a lost slimness. If Ambassador Hall hadn't already been chock-a-block with the like, Guy might have been minded to put hand in pocket for them. He found it much easier to motivate himself to pistol practice when there was something fun to aim at.

Though history had moved on Horsham's old habits died hard. Since the day was failing the gates were barred, the wall-guns manned. But bad light or no, even the most lulled-to-softness sentinel could distinguish between Imperial visitors and the children of the Wild. Unseen hands rushed to oblige and just managed to get oak and metal up in time for the coach to rattle through without impediment.

Machiavelli Lodge was at the heart of the old town, where huge houses huddled together and yet presented blank faces to each other. Once they'd been boxes for basic living and soldiers' home sweet homes, but peace had brought with it money for conversion work. High walls now ensured privacy whilst creating sheltered inner courtyards. The little passage-ways between were eminently defendable by the few against the many. In short, the area had all the qualities required to make a wasps' nest for the elite and was doing very well.

King Guy's arrival set the seal on that, though his residence looked little different from any other, save for the ambassadorial 'Helping (or maybe throttling) Hands' coat of arms above its door. However, unlike the majority which lay empty except in high summer, Guy kept the place running full pitch throughout the year, even though it might not see him or Bathie from one season to another. His immense wealth made it possible but love of providing employment of the type he would have enjoyed himself played a part too. Wisely, he paid way over the odds to keep good people – and made surprise inspections like Judgement Day to keep them so. The result was he could turn up unannounced any time and still be assured of a hot meal and non-musty bed, as well as a warm welcome.

So it proved now (and it had better). Watts the butler was at the door before they were, scoring lots of points by being in presentable full livery even for this unexpected pleasure.

Bowing (save to Blades) had been prohibited a few years back; a further whim-decree, impossible to enforce and speedily forgotten amidst the blizzard of other ordinances. Soon enough the god-king's fancy had lightly turned elsewhere, to banning steam trains (but not steam-pumps) and high heels (on women), and even with the best will in the world it was not possible to recall *every* veto. Things moved on

74

– as they do – and, save amongst the painfully pious, people gradually reverted to suiting themselves. Even a Bladian edict couldn't wipe out the tattooed-on practice of a lifetime, least of all down in frontier-Sussex. There the old ways of expressing respect were back, if they'd ever gone away. Guy stumbled down from the coach to find Watts at midriff level.

They knew each other of old. Watts was a huscarl with Guy when Null-York bit the dust. He had an unrivalled display of pickled Null ears nailed above his bedstead and deserved early, easy, retirement. Guy fondly caught hold of a strand of Watts's wig and tweaked the man up. The boxer in butler's clothing obeyed that little tug because he wished to.

One of the nice things about long acquaintance, better even than trust, was the telepathy which developed. The lack of need for words and lawyer-precise definitions all the time. Guy could clap a hand to his brow, feigning distress, and Watts knew just what to do. He arose and signalled understanding. Watts knew of (had perhaps invented) a sovereign cure for self-induced suffering. No one else could brew it but he. Guy admired that skill almost as much as he deplored Watts's poverty of ambition. There was a fortune awaiting its wider marketing but the huscarl-flunky appeared content with what he had. The opacity of the servitor classes never ceased to amaze.

Meanwhile, Watts-the-inscrutable hastened to his mission, turning away without further word or ceremony.

Courier gasped and then raised his – sheathed – swordstick above his head to reward such impudence.

Guy's frown was sufficient: the worth of a well-pondered epistle. Polly stayed Courier's hand and held it, expressionless but implacable. Courier turned the same shade of plum as Guy's shirt.

'Very relaxed here,' was the best even an Ambassador could manage when weariness was so in charge. '*Ever* so relaxed.'

Guy authorised their chauffeur's liberation and then ambled in.

A consensus grew on forgetfulness of the nasty moment.

Whilst Watts lingered to arrange accommodation for coach and crew, Courier composed himself and followed on with the huscarls.

Some things never change and didn't ought to, for fear of offending the past and all propriety. Ever since they first sat on furniture better than empty boxes, the Ambassador clan had expressed themselves partial to façades, becoming grand patrons of the art. Now, four centuries after crawling from the burrows and a low place in the food chain, barely a surface in their abodes was allowed to show its true face. Veneers and panels and japanned plaques hid the shocking nudity of almost every surface. Even table and chair legs came equipped with smart trousers.

Guy drank it in as he had a vat of Winchelsea wine. Here was home, here was homeliness, where all things wore a mask. Enamel and paint and delicate inlays said: 'Hello, Guy, and welcome . . .'

Already he felt better, even before the medicine arrived. The gallumping legionaries of hangover were thrown back in rout by mere light cavalry of Ambassador style.

'Beer. Bath. Bread. Bed,' Guy announced. 'And then . . .' he paused, struggling for another *b*, 'blessed oblivion! And lots of it!'

'I don't think so, lord.'

The sound itself surprised as much its content. The confident tone likewise.

Guy had quite forgotten Courier's presence. His unspoken but eloquent day-long adverse review of Guy's condition had become part of the landscape, to be ignored with all the other horrors. To hear that cold-eyed disdain given voice was as great a shock as one of the divans protesting Guy's collapse upon it.

Afflicted or no, the Ambassador was still combat-ready. Surprise, though often supreme, was *not* a deity the clan sacrificed to. In making his reply anyone would have thought Guy was speaking to an equal whose place it was to comment.

'What do you suggest, then?' he asked, as solicitous as could be. 'Change the order, eh? Bread first, maybe? No, that won't do. Sticky fingers, you see. *Traveller's* hands.' He spread the slim digits to demonstrate like a child in front of nanny. 'So, bath before beer, instead? No – don't think so. Need one before I can enjoy the other. Put oblivion first? Obviously not. Can you bathe a sleeping man? Who knows? Do you? No. And can't eat or drink asleep either. But surely you're not suggesting I go to bed hungry? That wouldn't be kind, would it?'

Polly and Prudence might not be able to speak but they could scowl. They did so. Courier looked anxiously round.

'So, all in all,' Guy continued affably, as though the atmosphere wasn't crackling, 'I think *my* plan's best. Don't you? Thought so.'

He knocked off his cocked hat and started to wrestle out of the scarlet soldier's coat. 'Of course, only if it's all the same to you . . .'

The trouble with servants is that after years of service they're apt to usurp their master's voice. Courier came from a long line of those who'd ferried the high and mighty round. Somewhere along that line the border between cargo and carrier had got blurred. He'd sailed through more border posts than the High-King of the Null (deceased) and was now invincibly convinced he had the right to stop at nothing – or no one – when about Blades's business. Quite commendably therefore, he felt no – or little – fear.

'What I *propose*,' said the man, 'is a change of horses and' – this as gracious concession – 'additional refreshments as you see fit before pressing on. The divine will has already been diverted by one whole day. It is not for us to compound Pevensey's sin. Blades *calls* you. Blades *awaits*! All hail Blades!'

The acclamation fell flatter than Bathie's chest. Polly and Prudence had once 'hailed' at close range and bore the scars. Guy was making stately progress to similar opinions. Therefore, Courier's words flung themselves from the trapeze, fully expecting to be caught – only to meet empty air. After an agonising second they plunged towards sickening impact.

Still, privately, Guy thought it a fair point. From a certain perspective. And nicely put. He willed Pevensey-men's souls to Heaven as much as any pious man – but on the other hand they owed him a life. Surely that bought him a comfortable night between clean sheets in his own bed?

Through the mêlée of brain pains and confusion Guy was surprised to suddenly recall some apposite words from scripture.

Was it not St Paul – in so many ways a precursor and herald of Blades – who'd said: '*I want no trouble from anyone after this . . .*'?

Guy agreed with the apostle. *He* could have written that tonight. No more trouble, thank you. The cupboards of his mind couldn't shut for sheer quantity of the stuff as it was. He'd felt proud that so far, employing subtle sign language, he'd prevented Polly or Prudence or Watts from making a factory's worth of 'trouble' about Courier's presumption.

Guy nodded thoughtfully – a bad sign to those who knew Ambassadors well.

'Your case is full of merit,' he told Courier, 'and replete with telling points. I shall certainly consider it.'

Courier was an adult. He should have been aware that 'consideration' can last less than a second and give birth to no as well as yes. Nevertheless, he exhaled as though victorious.

'Meanwhile,' Guy raised his eyebrows like a hopeful suitor, 'time for a change of boots and linen? Then whoosh! Away. Most certainly. *Trust* me . . .'

Strangely, Courier – a wise man in all other respects – did. He signalled agreement and allowed the returned Watts to guide him off.

'Our guest, lord,' enquired the servant, over his shoulder, 'the Lobsterpot Suite?'

'Absolutely,' agreed Guy, grunting as Polly assisted with shedding the second skin of his cavalry boots. 'That sounds ideal.'

'An unusual name . . .' commented Courier, lulled into content now that he was actually moving again.

'Unusual place,' answered Watts, as he ushered the man through a door.

Every ambassadorial residence had portions where progress

could only flow in one direction. Those within found that doors opened before them but never the contrary. Thus, unless they cared to linger till Doomsday in soundproofed passages, they found their feet inexorably directed to snug accommodation (often as sumptuous as an honoured guest's room) to await collection – or not – at ambassadorial convenience. Skeletons in the cupboard were therefore no idle metaphor in many Ambassador homes, where forgetfulness or malice might cause them to permanently neglect their houseguests. Generally, though, Guy was more merciful and attentive. When circumstances permitted. All other things being equal.

More persistent or stupid than most, Courier failed to accept fate for ages, hammering on the disobliging door back in whilst speaking curses it was fortunate went unheard. Sadly, he laboured and lamented in vain, for those beyond never knew, spared any distress by thick oak and quilted panels which easily muffled his drumbeats to death.

In the end, Courier's keen sense of dignity dissuaded him from continuing and jellying his hands. Like many a tiresome predecessor, he plodded off down the one-way route, feeling like a hog on its final trip up the garden path, away to his overnight (or maybe longer) accommodation.

'Now, where were we?' said Guy simultaneously, and then breathed a sigh of joy as the second constricting boot came away. 'Ah, yes: beer. What do you have for us today?'

In his mind's eye, Watts was walking the fat-barrel-lined cellar beneath the length of the house.

'Well, lord, there's the house brew,' he offered. 'Nut brown and nicely mature. Or we've got a fair bit of Horsham Hop-magic that's ready. Else there's some Binscombe Old-ale left over from Yule – that grabs you like a buxom embrace. I could put my life-saver mixture in it and you'd never notice.'

Guy was wiggling his toes to celebrate their liberation from dark constraining caves, wordlessly savouring the moment. He gave a 'go-for-it' thumbs-up signal and Watts replied in kind, heading off on his mission of mercy.

Guy abruptly realised he genuinely *was* at fault, over

something well within his remit to control. No master worth serving, no general who aspired to inspire a charge, ate or drank before the very last of his troops did. What was he playing at? What kind of shit-abed godling had he turned into?

Years before, campaigning against yet another Christian catacomb-fortress in the Mendips, Guy had gone ten days without so much as a crumb crossing his lips, as they zigzagged the hills time and again, starving on the scorched earth that was all the heretics left behind for orthodoxy to conquer. It earned him inordinate credit amongst the rank and file – at the price, alas, of inexplicably reviving his old stutter.

Guy hurriedly shoved the thought away, not wishing to wake the slumbering encumbrance. He would wait a few moments before he tempted fate and spoke again.

That cheerfully coincided with his intentions anyway, and it wasn't as though he was at Court, where silence would seem rude. Here was just the time and place for some refreshing 'cat-got-your-tongue?'-ness.

Because it was useful and pleased them, Guy often conversed with his twin hench-ladies in a sign language they'd jointly evolved. There was no strict need for it, since their hearing was unimpaired, but it did mean he entered their world a shade and walked in their shoes. In short, it showed willing. And, as far as impassive masks can express, his possible cousins-in-law apparently appreciated the gesture.

'Are you happy?' he signed. 'Is there anything you wish?'

Together they indicated the departed Courier and then a slapped wrist. Guy did them the honour of pretending to give it serious thought.

'He means well,' Guy conveyed, inadvertently applying the same test of human actions as Sea-captain. 'Forgive him this time. Like all of us, he'll be sweeter for a night's rest.'

In fact, to honour his lineage and prove a point, Courier would be wasting the sleeping hours by trying to tunnel out of his luxurious cell. A full set of broken nails and one blunted sword later (not to mention some tears), he would discover that the heart of Machiavelli Lodge was iron-shod, just like its owner. His howl of anger which greeted the dawn only bounced off the steel he'd revealed and disturbed no one but himself.

'*Are you sure?*' Guy enquired again, using face and fingers. '*Very well then: ease and please yourselves. Be happy!*'

Quite possibly they would – being easily pleased. Guy knew that whatever he urged, they'd take sustenance in turn, joint vigilance unceasing, before lying down to sleep in relay before his threshold. Careless of draughts or hard flagstones, their joy lay in interposing themselves between him and harm.

They were wonderful girls and Guy loved Polly and Prudence with a pure affection. That remained true even when their companionship occasionally shimmied into the sexual (which was only another facet of friendship in easy-going New-Wessex and no skin off Lady Bathie's nose). They were twin solace and consolation, precursors for the purer-still parental love awaiting the daughters God hadn't 'seen fit' to permit.

However, since their idea of happiness wasn't his, Guy was forced to consider what he should do next. What was there for *him* to dress up in contentment's clothing?

Well, there were any number of song and dance acts willing to spring on stage to entertain, all of which did the trick, for a space – for a declining space. He really oughtn't to be ungrateful and turn his nose up at their well-meaning antics. What was so bad about Watts's beer-and-remedy cocktails? Was life such a hardship when it contained beef dripping and bread baked that morning, as well as mustard imported all the way from the yellow prairies of the Norfolk Latifundia? What was the big problem with a huge feather bed in the same room where he and Bathie had slept and probably conceived several of their heart-wounds? Nothing. The problem was himself – and the swine just wouldn't go away.

King Guy dined like a king and then retired.

Amidst such pleasures and reminders it was a mercy to slip into the little death of sleep, and Guy eagerly grasped it, relishing every non-moment.

'His Sublime Reverence, **CALIGULA**, Bishop of New-Horsham and New-Haslemere, by grace of **G*d** and permission of the Most High **BLADES** (who needs not our blessing) **REQUESTS** the pleasure and honour of the company of:

KING GUY AMBASSADOR, son of Tusker Ambassador, son of Tamburlane Ambassador etc. etc. Escort of the Almighty.

FOR: Throughout the course of the morrow, Thursday, the twenty-third day of March, more properly known as FIRSTMETMASS, the year of our Salvation 480 AB

FOR: The occasion of Bishop's Gold Medal Handicap **HORSE RACE**.

FOLLOWED BY: refreshments.

FOLLOWED BY: a **BATTLE** against the forces of evil.
10.00 for 10.30.

That changed everything. Guy had seen enough battles to last ten lifetimes. See one and you'd seen them all. The noise! The company! Yuks!

But a day at the races, though; that was different. The 'sport of kings', as Blades insisted it be called although he never indulged, was one of the few abiding passions in Guy's life. Just the thought of it supplied a spark to the driest of days – or leastways it always *had*.

Guy gloated over the prospect when the invitation arrived that morning, expecting expectation to flare into life. Only it didn't. However, he stoutly put that down to spiritual dampness caused by *events*. Miseries, like hangovers, often go away if they're ignored. Guy continued with preparations.

They were few. A cravat in his own racing colours, a replenished purse, a perspective-glass and hip flask stowed into his coat and everything was ready – as far as Guy was concerned. He got as far as the waiting coach, poised on the very cusp of a day out, about to outline the change of plans. Then poise turned into pause.

'You should never point a g-gun,' said Guy, at his most paternal and yet disinterested, 'unless you're prepared to use it. And I don't think you're prepared to use it. Are you?'

The blunderbuss wavered not an inch. Though an aperture not 3 inches wide it seemed somehow to swallow up the courtyard.

'On you, lord, no,' said Coachguard, whom Guy had hitherto lightly assumed to be yet another of the community of mutes. 'Never. Heaven forfend! But on such as *these* . . .,' the gun barrel traversed ever so slightly Polly and Prudence-wards, 'happily . . .'

He nodded at the alabaster bodyguards standing by Guy like statues. The Ambassador declined to flare. It was par for the course for Polly and Prudence to meet unreasoning prejudice. With the great change of circumstances consequent upon Blades's return, Fruntierfolke family fortunes were at a low ebb. From being the rough-diamond 'characters' of humanity, holding the Wild's sicker jokes at bay, they were now relegated to mercenary traffic and police duties – and loved accordingly. Thanks to mankind's ungrateful nature, whatever collective gratitude was owed them proved to be an unenforceable debt.

No longer so needed, their remaining strongholds be-leaguered by jealousy and disdain, the Fruntierfolke were either in reservations or scattered to the winds and a hand-to-mouth – and sword-to-head – existence. The guard-dog once admired for its ferocity was now suspected of rabies. Polly and Prudence had lived with it all their short lives.

Coachman evidently went with mainstream opinion. From inside his capacious coat out came a 'pepper-box' revolver; a hexagonal honeycomb of chambers atop a buckshot barrel. 'Wheel Greasers' was their colloquial name in the trade, specially designed for spreading a thin layer of highwayman over the road.

To gild the lily Coachman also flicked a catch and a jagged

83

little bayonet sprang erect to the fore of his mini-arsenal. Guy politely applauded – since it seemed expected he be impressed.

Coachguard's frown tightened.

'Where's Courier, my lord? What have *they* done with him? Are they thwarting the will of Blades?'

It was a common, if dishonest, subterfuge (since Guy's name and person were inviolable) to attribute his naughtiness to bad counsel by underlings. In principle there was some selfish appeal in that – until Blades purged several of Guy's friends (insofar as Ambassadors had them) to punish a wrongdoing entirely Guy's own. Like owning whipping-boys you hadn't requested – only with more capital consequences – it was another irritation to a tender conscience.

'Look at *me*,' he told the two mutinous minions. 'No, not at them: look at *me*. Courier is not harmed. He's just otherwise engaged.'

It was the plain truth. The Bishop's invitation, plus the prospect of a day's racing, had simply amended the grand plan a little, that was all. Instead of liberation, Courier had awoken to breakfast and a nice long book to keep him going through the postponement. Guy had personally scoured Machiavelli Lodge's library to find Courier something pious and turgid to improve and calm his day. If that wasn't consideration above and beyond the call of compassion then Guy didn't know what was.

'Blades calls! Blades awaits!' said Coachguard, half of a fanatic double-act with a limited repertoire. 'We go!'

Far away and within, locked in a padded room where he could not be heard or hurt himself, an irresponsible, splinter-Guy was grinding his teeth at the likes of *these* bandying words with the like of *him*. You'd never have guessed it to observe the outer shell.

'That's right,' replied Guy, with the patience of the saint he wasn't. 'We "go" to the races. Then a spot of dinner. Show our faces at the battle. *Then* we "go" to Blades. Tomorrow. Chop-chop! Like a rocket!'

With one hand peeking forth from a frill of lace, he imitated the dramatic motion of the army's latest toy, demonstrated to the cream of New-Wessex society up on Epsom Downs a few weeks before. Naturally, he restricted himself to mimicking those few which left the racks cleanly and headed broadly towards the target. To himself though, he retained more affection for the greater many which had gone their own sweet way.

Coachguard and Coachman didn't even need to consult.

'Blades calls!' they said, unintentionally in unison. 'Blades comes first!'

Blunderbuss and pepper-box made motion towards the waiting coach. These were committed men, worthy of respect. They'd no idea of how things might end but Guy recognised their collective will had signed a blank cheque to go all the way.

In the game of who-blinks-first the Ambassador could readily match them stake for stake. He wished he'd ordered up his own gilded coach from the stables, but there was no turning back now. Words tripped from his lips easy as 'um' or 'er'. He didn't even stutter.

'Yes, Blades comes first – eventually. Meanwhile Blades can bloody *wait!*'

It was like vomiting in a cathedral, or drunken song during a minute's silence. That Guy's voice, of all voices, should do the spewing/singing exploded outrage everywhere . . .

Coachguard's and Coachman's eyes were converted to saucers. Even Polly and Prudence flicked a look from one to the other. Then they employed their axes in similar manner.

Guy hadn't needed to give the word, nor was there time. In the deep blue sea of blasphemy he'd just launched upon, nothing was true and everything was permissible. Even a 'saviour' such as he might not be immune to gunpowder scouring and the lasting reform a bullet can provide.

His huscarls did the right thing unbidden. No serious blood. Polly's flashing figure-of-eight with a great-axe first took Coachman's pepper-box away and then his senses. A deft last minute turning of Sussex steel ensured its flat met his chin so that he was stunned but not slit like his fingers.

Happily, Coachman would recall none of it, save a ghost in a gown before him and a waft of air like a wall. Some fingertips were gone, granted, but there'd be no lasting harm, except perhaps to self-esteem.

Meanwhile, Coachguard, the cannier of the two, was spry enough to take a step back, and Prudence's iron missile failed to sedate him, for all she spoilt his aim. The blunderbuss discharged and punched in the face of a Null-gargoyle atop the house. Architecturally, it was no great loss, having appeared uninvited in numerous Guy nightmares. Now it could stand unrepaired as memorial to a worm's turning.

A second sweep sent the beloved blunderbuss flying after its contents but Coachguard wasn't yet disarmed. Guy suspected back-up weaponry, perhaps concealed behind the man's belt, sponsoring the mad zeal to continue. Nevertheless, even a split second of fumbling was too high a price to ask for retrieving it. The two Ps were on him well before the slightest hope of success.

As an Ambassador, as a person, Guy disapproved of fisticuffs. They were slow, they were undignified; they took a long time to come to a conclusion unless one party folded. The injection of metal, whether by gunpowder or by hand, was both quicker and cleaner and thus a more seemly method of resolving disputes. It dispensed with undignified scrambling in the dirt.

So Guy tut-tutted over this particular dust-raising ruck even as he restrained the great sortie of armed servants issuing from Machiavelli Lodge. A single shot had brought them forth at lightning speed, armed with everything from carving knives to curling tongs. Some had actually found time to armour up and load *en route* – which showed the calibre of the people in his employ. Guy had to commend that even as he deplored the disruption. A skirmish in the yard was nothing to get excited about and certainly no cause to delay dinner. His dark suspicion was they'd seized the chance to escape boring duties.

However, he hadn't the heart to rebuke anyone involved in the . . . misunderstanding – save perhaps himself. Everyone, in either camp had acted for the best, according to their own lights. You couldn't fairly fault them.

A martyr to always seeing both sides, Guy returned his attention to the gravel-storm in front.

By then Polly and Prudence had felled Coachguard, though not before he'd blacked Polly's eye and ripped her dress to reveal a shapely marble shoulder. The maturing coloration contrast between these Polly portions was highly noticeable and destined to be a hot topic of conversation in days in come. Fortunately, the Wessex joking classes were ignorant of the existence of pandas.

Polly had her revenge, not to mention her knees around Coachguard's neck. In a position highly enviable at any other time, she sat athwart his face and two strong thighs slowly squeezed him out of consciousness.

Less touched by events, Prudence rode the balance of the stallion whilst rifling through his pockets, in pursuit of weaponry and profit. Between them it was not long before a final convulsion of riding boots signalled an end to the little civil war.

Guy was as magnanimous in victory as he could never be in defeat. He personally stooped down to check Coachguard was still with them.

'Repair. Care. Be solicitous to them,' he told the impromptu but handy mass gathering of servitors. 'Especially soothe their wounded pride, which will be pained more than any other part. These are brave men, and pious. True, they may presently lack a certain vivacity, but treat them as our honoured guests!'

Watts was there, inconspicuous considering his brick-outhouse build, but always where he should be.

'And "honoured" in the Lobsterpot Suite?' he asked, service personified.

Guy exaggeratedly pretended to ponder a thing already decided.

'Yes, I think so,' he replied, sounding like a liberal tutor rewarding borderline pupils. 'It's their kind of place . . .'

87

"SEQUENCE OF THE PICT'S LANCE PROVINCE CONFLICT TO A.B. 475" — FROM: 'A DISQUISITION FOR STRATEGIC STUDIES STUDENTS AND THE MORE INTELLIGENT TYPE OF WOMEN AND CHILDREN AND CONNOISSEURS OF HUMANE FOLLY AND FUTILITY' BY LADY AVONABATTY, or THE HASTINGAS-PYGOPSICA PRESS A.D.477

1
New Haslemere
North Downs
New Horsham
Pict's Lane
Bladian Imperial Newdau circa 13.B.20- A.B. 420
South Downs
Pevensey Assyria
New Brighton

2
North Downs
New Horsham
Imperial Bishopric New Haslemere
Pict's Lane
New Horsham
Brighthaven Exploratory Incursions
South Downs
Pevensey Assyria
New Brighton
A.B. 420-425

3
New Haslemere
North Downs
New Horsham
Battle of Boleus A.D. 466
Demilitarised military province of Glass Lane
Squared State of Pevensey
South Downs
New Brighton
A.D. 465-8 The Great Invasion

4
New Haslemere
North Downs
New Horsham
Second Battle of Boleus A.D. 469
Pict's Lane
Hedonistic sea raids A.D. 470-471
South Downs
The Great Lamb Roast A.B. 475
Seagoing State of Pevensey Resurgent
New Brighton
A.B. 469-475

Polly's borrowed tricorn looked good on her, especially at that rakish angle. Coachman wouldn't be needing his hat for a space and it made her look the part. The rest of his uniform, however, though readily available whilst the captive guest was stripped and scrubbed, went unclaimed. Guy hadn't even bothered suggesting the intriguing transvestism. It was unthinkable that either Polly or Prudence should appear in anything but purest black or white, to match their view of the universe.

Nevertheless, in all other respects Polly was a perfect fit in her new role and the team obeyed her whip and commands as though they'd been together for years. Prudence sat alongside, complete with liberated blunderbuss, and from a distance you'd almost believe a proper Sealed Coach was bowling up for a day at the races.

That would have been frightening novelty in itself, but when proximity revealed the unorthodox manning Guy was guaranteed undying publicity for his truant holiday. *Not* what he wanted. He realised he hadn't thought this through – and, strange delight, didn't care.

New-Horsham's finest and lowest alike pretended not to look, such was the taboo on the grey conveyances, but an impulse even greater than self-preservation drew every eye to check Guy out. When there were no repercussions many gawked.

Polly and Prudence were glowing and magnificent in the aftermath of a little victory over Blades. They leaped down from the coach and, since it was enemy property and not their responsibility, flung the reins and a nominal demi-Tom at just any old ostler. *Their* place was with Guy the Redeemer, not as horse-holders for him who'd made them mutes.

God and/or Blades, plus a long-ago glacier no one there had the slightest inkling about, had ground out a scoop from the Downs just right for a race course. Some slightly smaller siblings sat nearby, ideal for athletics and archery or post-race entertainments, as intended today. Guy knew the place well, had raced his stable there and took its existence, along with wine and breasts, as further proof of the Deity's essential benevolence. He was happy just to be there – or so he kept telling himself.

Airborne horseflesh aroma, tinged with leather, money and excitement, was the spicy seasoning to a temperate day. Even an Ambassador could not be immune. Through long conditioning, Guy only had to see loose horse-boxes and a circle of rails to shed aloofness and dive into the comforting common stream. Just that in itself was a wonderful release from high position, let alone the winning and losing and pitting of wits. Today, though, he was left wondering where the familiar feeling had got to. It was certainly taking its time and lateness was tantamount to rudeness in Guy Ambassador's book.

In desperation he plumped for a double dosage, saying gracious nothings to the Bishop's entourage who'd rushed up to meet him, whilst pressing on to actually lay hands on the paddock and starting wire.

His face almost unfroze when he realised he'd been stood up. The pleasure wasn't coming and couldn't even be bothered to send apologies.

Unless . . . Perhaps some saboteur had removed the plug and drained all pleasure away. Guy knew he was grasping at straws but that was forgivable when even a lifted skirt no longer electrified. He felt in the grip of a terrifying revelation, a teetering on the brink when he'd thought the staircase continued. Near to panic and so far forgetting himself as to show his feelings, Guy looked about in accusation.

Who'd done it? He wanted to know, and know now! He wanted their names and someone to blame, but each blazing gaze bounced off uncomprehending faces.

Reason, that old ambassadorial weapon and pitfall for the foolish, reasserted itself. The culprit, if such there be, wasn't here, and there was nothing to gain in frightening these poor flunkies. Guy's amiable mask went back on.

However, the fact remained that he *had* been robbed of something. By somebody. And not of any old shan't-miss-it bauble, but an item of great prize. Therefore, even if he eventually had to reconcile himself to the loss and gap in his life, there still ought to be an accounting.

Guy carefully stowed the red hot grievance away.

He pretended first to seek and then to find a sharp stone within his shoe. The meeters and greeters were yearning for an innocent explanation of all the black looks. Anything would do. Sure enough, it worked perfectly and some spectators were so far deluded as to *see* the non-existent object and frown at it.

So, that was one hurdle crossed – the first and last Guy intended to jump today. He was here to watch others exert themselves for his pleasure and profit, not to put on a display of Ambassador acrobatics.

'I always examine the *going*,' he said, to further explain his behaviour, 'before I get going . . .'

And my, how all the sycophants laughed, as though he'd made the wittiest play on words ever. For the thousandth time, Guy reflected that society shouldn't really criticise Ambassadors for their two- – or more- – faced behaviour when it was such a willing accomplice. If people went around naked, with a mattress strapped to their back and a sign saying *'Take me! Take me!'*, it was a bit rich for them to protest when their kind offer was accepted.

Guy allowed himself to be guided back to where he should have gone in the first place, although their destination was as plain (and large) as the nose on his face. New-Wessex etiquette dictated that from dawn to dusk, or even in between if awake, the Blades-descended do nothing alone. The reasoning was that needs might arise unexpectedly, however trivial, and it was theologically unacceptable that a spark from the divine bonfire should have to deal with the tedious facts of life themselves.

Guy had had to put his foot down – and keep it there – just to get away with only Polly and Prudence. Before he'd mustered enough years and intransigence, plus full Ambassador-status to back both up, 'etiquette' had sicked helping hands on him every second of the day. On campaign, two gentlemen had allegedly even considered it an honour to accompany him to the latrine. They'd been the first to go.

So, with those battle honours behind him, Guy well recalled the drill for letting a cloud of the well-meaning and ambitious guide him a short space between *here* and *there*. He tried to look suitably lost and grateful.

His Sublimity, the Bishop of New-Horsham and New-Haslemere, did nothing by halves. If he wanted a golden pavilion to house himself and his guests, then it would *be* like a house and *extremely* golden. It would have a spine of cupolas along the top and mock battlements along each edge. It must grab the onlooker by the lapels and defy him not to notice, growling in a voice that brooked no dissent, that this was no pleasure dome of a jumped-up vicar, no best effort of the ruler, spiritual and temporal, of two glorified villages. No indeed. Rather, it said (to pillage a line from that incomparable collection, *The Golden Treasury* compiled by the otherwise satanic Professor) that the mighty should look upon the Bishop's works and despair.

Guy did – despair, that is. He saw this sort of spendthrift aggrandisement all the time as he flitted across the patchwork of handkerchief statelets, sewing here, unstitching there, and generally sticking the needle in. Their kinglets were all of a kind: unable to quite believe their luck and thus absurdly competitive. If a neighbouring despot had a black cat, then they straight away must have a blacker one. It was like dealing with spoilt children and no wonder Blades cuffed their ears so often – sometimes so hard their heads came off.

When they breasted the rise to the noisy tent the Bishop waddled out to meet them – as was meet and probably stipulated somewhere in Haddad's multi-volume *Right Action and Seemly Living*, which aspiring courtiers had to copy out ten times as their 'apprentice piece'. He also carried meat: a hunk already well worked over for himself, and a suspiciously large drumstick for Guy.

A jigsaw took delivery of its last piece. The Ambassador recalled Wessex countryfolk petitioning Blades about the great bustard bird's increasing rarity and the deprivation that entailed for their little festivities and marriage feasts. Here then was where it was going: into exalted gullets and, soon enough, extinction.

Guy politely declined, not wishing to be part of the sad process. Also, there looked enough grease on it to keep a laundry working overtime. He didn't want to burden Machiavelli Lodge with cleaning his militia coat twice in two days.

Rather than let such succulence go to waste, the Bishop employed it like a club to doff his mitre. Then he bowed with the fluidity of a dancer half his age and weight. The bowing prohibition clearly hadn't stuck here either, or else his grace thought himself above it.

'*Dear* Guy,' he said, words slipping in a whisper from between perfect white teeth, once the spine that bore them was righted. 'You are *gorgeously* welcome! Come in, come in, and whatever little we have is yours . . .'

There was genuine haste to overwhelm Guy with hospitality, but ulterior motives also. The Bishop had his eyes (and saliva) on that spurned drumstick. It wasn't the done thing to gnash it here in the open, before an unrefreshed guest. Yet temptation was mounting, almost high enough to provide a leg over the wall of manners. The dead bustard's moments were numbered.

When he could Guy liked to put things and people out of their misery. He was an incorrigible provider of lovers for otherwise doomed marriages, or euthanasia for city-states whose day was done. In short, he liked to show life up, by being far kinder that it was.

So Guy retrieved the toppled mitre himself and replaced it on the pink head. He smiled and signalled permission for a return to devouring.

As they crossed the canvas-of-gold threshold, the throng within arose (albeit some unsteadily) as one and rendered praise to Him who gave the day, plus side-thanks to his distant relative joining them. Guy economically employed the same smile on them as had reassured the Bishop.

Immediately they reached the age of understanding, Ambassador children were taken outside to note the weather-vanes which adorned each ambassadorial dwelling. They were then entrusted with the knowledge that here was their *actual* but secret heraldic symbol, not the ambivalent hands which adorned the gate.

'*For that is the way people are,*' they were told, in an anciently prescribed form of words. '*It and they conform to the strongest wind blowing - regardless of what went before. Every time you see one of these: recall!*'

The Bishop's golden boast didn't need to go over the top and sport a weather-vane for Guy to 'recall' right then. The lesson was burned deep into him and reinforced all the time. This lot would just as cheerfully see him sat on an impaling stake as play the glad hosts. Fortunately, any sting had long gone out of that realisation. There was a consolation of sorts in abysmally low expectations. For all its many defects, an ambassadorial education could at least be a very moderating thing.

So Guy returned their greetings in generous spirit. It was also the kindest thing to do, for he happened to know Blades was minded to let New-Haslemere aspire to independent statehood soon. On that day many of those here would be . . . inconvenient. Their faces might not fit into the rearranged mosaic and the great artist's palette knife would descend to chip them out.

For today, though, Guy kept his knowledge to himself and let everyone enjoy life's all too fleeting happy hours. With his Imperial nursemaids enjoying the hospitality of the Lobster-pot Suite, he could even join in, liberating a little holiday from being himself.

Whilst Polly and Prudence eyed up their Horsham counter-parts – huscarls of more conventional, male, beauty – the Bishop was so far ahead in his cups as to absent-mindedly drape a familiar arm round Guy's shoulders.

'Dear Guy . . .' he repeated, expansively, indicating with the other podgy hand a veritable horn-of-fortune feast spread before them, barely scratched by the mob's feeding frenzy. 'Dear Guy, I wish you *joy* . . .'

It was Guy's favourite salutation too, and thus stolen goods in the Bishop's mouth, depriving the Ambassador of valued vocabulary for the duration. Nevertheless, he felt a moment of most un-ambassadorial warmth towards this jolly, portly, prelate. With quickened pulse and keen anticipation, Guy thought he spied a shady avenue of off-duty moments to stroll along, one long enough to last all afternoon and maybe more. He was raring to set out on it, even at the price of having company – just so long as his grace was off duty too.

Then he could have kicked himself, rather than promenade and pound the ground. He'd been deceived; an Ambassador ambassadored. The false path proved to be just two strides long, leading straight into the office.

'By the way,' said the Bishop, suddenly all butter-wouldn't-melt innocence as he tore the crisp skin off the drumstick, 'Where's the wizards?'

'*Where's the wizards?*'

Second time around didn't diminish the shock of the proposition. Number one assault had been brushed off readily enough but predictably turned into a storm brewing over the rest of the day. Repetition had been threatening for hours but still arrived like a bucket of water: more shocking than reviving. He might pretend otherwise so long as it suited, seeming smooth as the silk he wore, but self-interest turned the Bishop of New-Horsham and New-Haslemere as blunt as buggery.

'I've r-really no idea.' Guy concealed any true reaction by continuing to quiz the race through his spy-glass. 'They gave me the slip in Yarmouth.'

Bishop Caligula also had a horse in this race but found the

subject to hand more intriguing. Even with a bevy of equine beauty throbbing towards them like poetry in motion, the man could avert his eyes to study the mundane. It was extraordinary.

'As do my own mages,' he said. 'Many's the one I've lost the same way.'

Oh yes, Guy could imagine. A grand empire of, what – 20 miles across? – might justify three, at most four, of that tiny minority of mankind able to make their wishes real. Anything more would involve Imperial permission and suspicion, and bleed the realm dry into the bargain.

'First they go dreamy,' the Bishop's lament continued, 'then lazy. Next thing is you wake to find the swine gone: not a farewell, not a trace. Even the bloodhound-Null can't find 'em. It's the wizard way. They feel the call of Wight like moths to a flame! Their own homeland, exclusive to the brethren. The yearning's too much for the poor things. A bishop's service no longer satisfies.'

His grace wouldn't get any argument from Guy. He'd read the secret reports detailing a similar bleeding away of the Imperial mages. If even they, indoctrinated since youth, couldn't be persuaded or compelled to stay and serve normal humanity, then what chance the luck-assembled band of second-rates and 'periodics' that Horsham could assemble?

'I mean,' the Bishop persisted, still toying with a bowl of chicken blancmange he'd carried out of the pavilion and wouldn't give up on, 'I pay them enough to make me weep and then they thank me by deserting! In ones and twos they go without a word: not a cheerio or even "damn y'eyes!" Of course, the question is what *greater* call have they heard, eh? An empty Yarmouth, yes, all right, well and good. But that merely betokens, does it not – mmmmmm, delicious stuff, this, but can't manage another bite' – (and yet he did) '. . . it betokens, I say, somewhere *else* wedged full of wizardry. Alarming notion, no? Better the devil you know: aware of his address, you see. Now all we've got is a double puzzle . . .'

It was cleverly done: a question dressed up as a theory: an

innocent thesis it would be rude not to ponder. And you'd never have guessed that they'd just been bypassed by a gallop of jockeys, the foremost in episcopal colours. The Bishop took not a blind bit of notice. The man was a barbarian.

Guy delayed reply till he saw his own fancy take the lead, as he'd been sure it would. They were on the home straight now: his forecast taking on flesh to realise itself in the real world. At least that much remained dependable.

Life-long study (inspired by a fateful precocious win) rendered a middle-aged Guy capable of prophecy – in one focused field. He could study a horse and predict its future, if only for the next half hour, accurately enough to earn gold and fame. To Guy it meant a great deal but he hugged it close, this mastery of one tiny skein of fate, knowing others were less impressed. Some begrudged the success, others the frivolity. For example, the Bishop's impatience for non-horsey progress was palpable. He was running in another race entirely.

Guy made a mighty effort and had mercy.

'Well, your mages aren't in Yarmouth, Bishop, I can tell you that much. Leastways, not any more. Unless they've turned hermit – and invisible. All I found was corpses.'

'Really?' The flare of interest was unashamed. Dead wizards were news, merchantable commodities in the marketplace for information. 'But surely—'

Enough. Enough. Enough. Guy had been harried and pumped enough when all he wanted to do was go racing. Time for the rose to show its thorns.

'It r-represents a multifaceted quandary,' he interrupted, 'none of whose *f-f-fascinating* facets should overly concern you, your grace. What the wizards did in Wight and where – and *if* – they still do it, is not the stuff of sleepless nights for a . . .,' – he let the search for an apt description go on slightingly long, whilst the word he wanted lay to hand throughout – '. . . *m-m-model* realm like your own . . .'

He gestured with his hand as if he might encompass its four none too remote corners by stretching.

The Bishop could have had another career as an Ambassador.

He just kept eating and the dunes of his face glistened and undulated exactly as before.

'I am the shepherd of a flock,' he corrected Guy in between chews, though not one iota offended to the outward eye. 'A bishop of the universal Church. A custodian of truth. All humanity is my business. One's concern does not falter at the bounds of this . . . "model" – thank you – realm.'

Guy let the perspective glass fall – and his face along with it. The moment was spoilt beyond any steward's enquiry. His horse had just come in (at 11-2 !) but the implacable prelate thought he had a winner too.

Guy sighed. An Ambassador's last resort and equivalent to a knee in the groin. It was wasted.

'Now,' the Bishop went on, as sensitive to nuance as a prize-fighter, 'if I were to know where all the errant wizards were gone, then I would have a head start in retrieving my own naughty rascals, would I not? *And* could maybe recruit a few more!'

The Bishop's face wore that shrewd 'I'm so sharp I might cut myself' expression Guy so loathed in the commercial (be it souls or sausages) classes.

'One *means*,' the breathy torrent continued unabated, 'you have the ear of the divine Emperor, as well as his – and our – love. If you were to ask him, on my behalf, as a *favour* . . .'

In some respects it was all very polished, a much thought-upon onslaught which left Guy high and dry with just one avenue of escape – which led straight back into the Bishop's maw. On the other hand, bad luck and timing decreed it should be the critical straw dumped upon an Ambassador-camel's back. Like pandas, those beasts were also as yet beyond New-Wessex cognisance, but the underlying principle applied.

For an instant, Guy felt like the sole person in the amphitheatre, the focus of every man's attention – and all of them *wanting* something. The whole universe seemed desirous of a piece of him, not caring if there was anything left at the end of the mad scramble. He was being *mucked about*.

Deep breathing and another cleansing sigh didn't sort things or himself out. On the plus side, though, Guy no longer gave a damn about passion-inspired stammering. People could either get the sense of it or go hang. He didn't care. A spectator beside his own rumbling volcano, he found that he *wanted* to watch its eruption, not witness some do-gooder cap it for the greater good. For however long it took, Guy Ambassador resigned from his surname-cum-calling.

Nevertheless, he hung on to the uniform – the face that went with the job. A bystander (and there were many, covert or otherwise, who'd hang on every misfiring word) would never have guessed anything had changed.

In reality, alteration was complete. Not just one cannon, but the whole ship's armament was loose, slip-sliding round the deck, wild and free.

Only Polly and Prudence picked up on it. They saw there was much amiss but couldn't figure out what or how come. Regardless, they closed in.

Too late, the Bishop sensed it. His tone turned more humble, though the facial sand dunes only hardened into ramparts.

'Your highness, I merely wanted to kn—'

Guy leaned down to his level.

'Do *not*,' he stated, 'for one *moment*, think I tire of your company! Oh no. I get your *point*. It's been well *put* . . .'

He let the image behind his eyes be that of an entirely different type of 'point', made of sharp steel and 'put' to good use. By virtue of the telepathy available to all in extremity, the Bishop shared his vision – or perhaps that was just Polly and Prudence's '*what do you want done with him?*' gaze.

His grace was both taken aback and affronted, the two sensations cancelling each other out to produce only repose. The net effect was as though he was undaunted.

'I see . . .' said the Bishop. Only he didn't.

'In fact,' Guy interrupted, leaning closer, and Polly and Prudence with him, 'I could go on chatting with you *all day long*. But then I m-might end up just as mad as you are – and that wouldn't do, would it? How would that take us f-f-forward, eh? No, what I think I'll do, if it's *all* the same, is flick my b-b-bloody fingers at the lot of you! And then I'll start the battle!'

And Guy turned his back on the Bishop, as he would a flunky, and departed.

Left behind, the charitable constructed some fig-leaves of justification. Starting and ending conflicts *was* ambassadorial business. Perhaps King Guy felt it was his duty to oblige, just as the Bishop was always called upon to say grace . . .

All the same, it *was* rude. Here in this midget realm the Bishop was the paramount ruler, arbiter of life and death and with more than a hand in what followed beyond as well. Also, this was his own little war, provoked and choreographed by him. It was a bit . . . daring to snatch the baton from his hand and start the music before the conductor gave the word. In plain speech, according to the best books and consensus, this was an outrage, only slightly muzzled by Guy's quasi-divinity.

Meanwhile, the man exulted in his offence. Guy felt shock waves impacting against his back, and a downpour of disapproval descending besides. Combined, the bracing social storm quite put a spring back in his steps.

The winning jockey, still mud-dappled from the chase, rushed up for Guy's blessing but was brushed aside. Females of former intimate acquaintance, ladies and lackeys alike, were cruelly snubbed by a transformed, tigerish Guy. Anyone too slow or dense to take the visual hints were slammed out of the way by Polly and Prudence – who were loving every minute and yet prey to growing alarm.

Guy knew the hurt he was doing, to feelings and fond memories, not to mention his hard-earned reputation, but he was done with 'caring'. Normally, he'd never *ever* have taken a short cut across a course, regardless of whether a race was in progress or no. Usually, the principle of the thing decided: principles whose gossamer weight he now trod lighter for shedding. Guy felt as free as a – bad-tempered, pecky – bird. The ground trembling under his feet at the approach of thoroughbred hoofs still didn't hasten his pace. Someone else could handle that and any other problems. Polly and Prudence most probably. They'd gleefully welcome a chance to apply great-axe to horse head, as revenge for the long hours they'd had to spend watching them.

Man and mount alike perceived it whilst still way off, pulling up well short. All bets were off.

So, the aborters of one race and postponers of those following, the triple tantrum crossed the course's centre circle and issued out the other side. By now the message had got through and they were in inglorious isolation.

Ordinarily, self-righteousness is a fizzy brew but not effervescent for long. Guy's self-distilled cordial, however, kept him going sprightly across the glacial gift and right to its outer rim, up to where the war was waiting.

Guy looked – and saw that it was *good*. 'Couldn't be better!' he told himself and all creation – but mostly himself.

The sun was bright, the birds were singing, all was well with the world – if you liked that sort of thing. Guy stood on the rim of the bowl and announced that '*Today is a good day to die!*' (or '*d-die!*')

It was a phrase prescribed by Blades for those high in his favour who might be tempted to let sinful self-preservation get in the way of duty. Guy had said it many times on the eve of battle, often with intellectual assent, but never before with whole heart.

Fortunately, he'd only muttered the words of defiance and surrender, or else Polly and Prudence would have bundled him away to spend a day in a sack until the mood passed. They might have got him there; doubtless he would have forgiven them after. But they wouldn't have changed his mind. Some inner decisions are irrevocable.

Even so, Polly and Prudence retained good grounds for concern, though the ghost masks remained pristine. Their Guy, master, lover, friend and solid reason for continuing, the gradual eraser of bad memories, *never* mumbled through gritted teeth – except today. He was *never* lit from within by dismay – except today. His were the kindest words and gentlest of touches – even when he was obliged to be cruel. His was the mildness and forgiving shrug of a usually harsh world. Therefore, if he of all people should turn feral and conform, everything they'd painstakingly built back up again went with him.

Pale faces looked from one to the other, confirming the worst. There'd not been fear like this since the glowing larynx-shears approached. Both had fondly thought themselves absolved from ever feeling the like again.

They found morsels of comfort though, after scratching around. The – now wobbly – fixed point in their universe had gone strange but not, thank the Creator, stark raving. His anger might be boiling but etiquette still held some reins on him when all others were bitten through. There remained that finger-grip on propriety and, praise be, his sense of honour.

Thus, when Guy descended from the rim into the sister saucer-depression beyond, he joined the army of his host, not the invader. Minimal standards were maintained. The same as if a house in which you were a guest was attacked by robbers, common decency dictated you lend a hand in repelling boarders.

Sighs of relief from behind rewarded him instead of applause. Polly and Prudence rushed to catch up, not stun.

King Guy *was* expected – only not so soon, and most certainly *not* as a participant. Things were far from ready. The one-foot-regiment-each grand armies of Horsham and Haslemere were at their firing points but otherwise in slack order. Aside from a few whey-faced novices most were chatting away to each other like Downs farmers on a market day. The mighty 'Crossed Crosiers' banner wasn't even unfurled yet. Wise in the ways of the world, Guy headed for the finest display of lace and brocade and, sure enough got what he wanted.

The Colonel of the Haslemere regiment had been studying a volume of saucy prints and was thrown into greater confusion by sanctified King Guy's arrival than an onslaught of Null.

'Er . . .' was all he could muster.

By now, though, the murder was gone from Guy's visage, hidden behind one of his finest false smiles. Even the stutter was back on its lead.

'Quite . . .' Guy agreed. 'I've read that one. *The School Maam's Oral Examination* – couldn't put it down. A book to be perused one-handed, eh?'

In fact it was already gone as if it had never existed, removed by sleight of hand from higher to ever lower ranks amongst the Colonel's well-trained staff.

Doubly on the back foot, the Colonel could only use his exonerated hands to doff his tricorn and bow brow to ground, signifying '*whatever you say . . .*'

'I have a notion,' explained Guy, 'to join you, because . . . because I so enjoyed my dinner. A sort of thank you. Therefore, refresh my memory, what's it all about?'

That *was* something at the Colonel's fingertips.

'Picts Lane province, lord,' he said, parroting words as though he believed them. 'The maps are unambiguous. It has been Horsham land since time immemorial! The sons of Brighton must be cured of their dreams and delusions!'

Having suffered grievously himself, Guy didn't like to deprive anyone of their dreams. However, his gatecrashing presence obliged him to concur.

'My oath, they must!' he said, also sounding like it was his dearest held belief. 'And so they shall!'

He turned to address a wider audience, raising his voice to include the black-and-oyster-coated rank and file – who were simultaneously shy and yet all ears.

'Today,' he said, 'we shall firmly inform these pathetic, bum-stroking Brighton Highlanders that – Polly, the seduction stick, if you please . . .'

From its protective sheath came the little onyx baton, so called because of the countless conversations and then assignations its fly-trapped-in-amber head provoked. Otherwise

Guy used it out of style and joy, for emphasising points particularly close to his heart.

'I say, gentlemen,' he went on, once armed, 'that we shall convince these' – one jab at the innocent air – 'savage southerners. We shall kindly put them beyond all the agonies of doubt!' A triple stab. 'We shall establish to their entire satisfaction and for all eternity that the veritable second Eden of Picts Lane is' – two vicious slashes across an invisible enemy – '*RIGHT OUT!*'

It got a cheer as well as some tricorns into the air. Even the Horsham 'Lobster' cavalry, iron-clad men on caparisoned horses away on one flank, who reckoned themselves gentlemen and declined to eavesdrop, got the gist. They politely applauded: a curious clanking of metallic hands.

In fact, although states and courts had proliferated such that even no-hoper and half-mad Ambassadors got a look-in, not even the least busy of that clan-cum-conspiracy had so far taken notice of this petty dispute. Guy now recalled a fleeting reference in *It Depends How You Define* . . . : a two-line sarcastic summary which he'd read, digested and ranked alongside such weighty matters as a puzzling pair of odd socks. Save for the great Blades himself delivering its inexplicable – but of course unquestionable – naming, Picts Lane was a few roads and farms of such surpassing obscurity as to make a dovecote look like the hub of the universe.

Nevertheless, Guy was really into it now, wound up and winding up, driven on by some inner demon. He raised hands and seduction stick to the insouciant sky.

'I call upon Blades,' he roared – itself an un-ambassadorial act – 'to witness just how happy I am to be preserved and here this day to grind the very notion of a Brightonian Picts Lane into the dirt and mud from which it should never have emerged! Too right I do!'

He'd been taught how to work a crowd early on, by market traders arrested on trumped-up charges for that very purpose. Those amongst them who proved to be open-handed, talented teachers got to leave – eventually – with both their liberty and ears. Some even got gold. For all his bluster and messy marriages, Guy's (fairly) dear departed father had run a quite liberal regime.

It helped that the young Guy had been an attentive pupil (though not given much choice in the matter), and he found all the long-ago-learned skills came flooding back. Combined with all the associated gurning and '*just look at my in-no-cent face, missus*' patter, plus a perfect slightly south of mainstream New-Wessex accent, the act went down a storm. Within minutes, the silly creatures were his for the asking.

He had an easy conscience about it. They'd been going to do what he wanted in any case, so this was an almost victimless crime. He'd done worse. Much worse.

At present the battleground looked forlorn and one-sided. However, all Guy had to do was turn in that empty direction and look vaguely hurt in order to make things happen.

'Strictly speaking,' pleaded the Colonel, in the tones of an underling who's absolutely right but not free to say so, 'commencement isn't until the third watch . . .'

Another of Blades's vetoes – this one vigorously enforced – was on any telling of time more precise than candles or sundials. For his part and for once, far from chafing under the weight of that yoke, Guy wholeheartedly approved. Whereas Levellers and the other sundry damned went burdened and frazzled by timepieces, having dabbled in the forbidden science of horology, Wessex life proceeded at a more stately pace, free of the sharp defining edges of 'late' or 'early'. In consequence, fewer Wessex-folk went mad or blew their brains out. It was a fact: Guy had seen the figures. Imperial philosophers drew the conclusion that thanks to clocks the hellbound were even in a hurry to arrive *there*.

Meanwhile, New-Wessex muddled along very nicely, thank you, with rough and ready measures and a loose terminology borrowed from naval parlance. The day was divided into 'watches' and 'bells' no one could be too dogmatic about.

That imprecision doubly served Guy now when he wanted to pinch Time's bottom and hurry it along a bit. He went through the motions of noting the sun's declension and quality of light. If he'd been a yokel he would have chewed upon his straw.

'Soon enough, I reckon,' he said. And that nonsense sufficed.

No one could accuse Guy of precious pride or trading upon rank. Since it was he who'd put the 'ever glorious array' of New-Horsham and New-Haslemere in a spot, he condescended to help get them in the right spot. For a space, whilst emissaries of the Bishop put the contrary case and received the rough edge of King Guy's tongue (backed by the edge of King Guy's huscarl's axes), that same sparkle from Blades's effulgent blaze embraced demotion down to drill-sergeant.

However, most unlike one of that breed, Guy was courteous towards those – possibly – about to die, his worse rebuke a tap upon the tricorn with an onyx wand. The far-flung had to crane to hear his courtly instructions. It seemed strange at first – and then strangely addictive.

The daring policy, never previously attempted with crude and licentious soldiery, proved surprisingly effective. That combination of the carrot of kindliness and feeble stick had the rustic army ready in record time.

His toy soldiers prepared, Guy moved to the front and looked left and right. Everyone – bar the enemy and thus someone to fight – was present and correct. This was as good as it was going to get.

Out on the wings, the Horsham Lobster cavalry and flamboyant Haslemere Hussars paraded as neatly as equine opinion permitted. Plumes and visors nodded, inspired to sprightly dance by the steeds beneath. Civilised conflicts accorded these aristocrats of the battlefield pride of place, plus considerable latitude, and it took a good general with a good excuse not to let them commence play. Man and mount, metaphorically or otherwise, were champing at the bit.

Linking them with the plebeian foot were clumps of artists' units, grouped according to clique and medium, today wielding pole-mounted scythe blades in sobering contrast to usual pen, brush, and chisel. Technically, they were all volunteers, inspired by patriotic love of their adopted home. In reality, the Bishop's no-nonsense recruitment officers had gone from studio to studio soliciting 'gratitude' for the holiday from taxation. Even louder than the voice of their muse, the artists heard the stern call of duty.

In turn, these should have abutted – but being sensible, shrank from – the episcopal artillery. In symmetrical divisions of sakers and wolf-headed culverins, the brazen engines of war were pointing the right way and ready. Their custodians – men of all nations and none – were almost the only professional military present that day, going about their technical business with seen-it-all-before coolness under admiring artistic eyes. Guy didn't have to worry about *them*.

Nearer in stood the army's core, twin two-tone line regiments drawn from the Bishop's brace of towns. They were a brave enough show, brightened by taller, brawnier, grenadier companies starring in each. These last's high mitre hats, vague reminders of their master's headgear, glorified with gold thread, raised them above their comrades in more than just height. Like the gunners, they seemed a shade happier within the here and now than most, stiffened by their status as chosen men. They were amiably killing time in checking their strings of grenades or incautiously smoking a final pipe.

So that was another mystery solved. In previous visits Guy had noticed an absence of tall peasants in Horsham and surrounds, and, with weightier things on his mind, put it down to diet or inbreeding. Now he saw the true explanation before – and looming above – him. Press-gangs presumably roamed Horsham's fields and taverns for grenadiers until extra inches were only a curse in the Bishop's realm. They represented not a head start in life but sure condemnation into the military – and maybe radical shortening courtesy of a cannon ball.

Be that as it may, the brick-outhouse elite looked cheerful enough. Maybe combating aggression wherever the Bishop wanted it was still preferable to a lifetime as a plough-jockey, starring up an ox's bottom. Guy decided to think so. It was charitable to ascribe higher motives to the lower classes – and not his problem in any case.

More importantly, he mustn't give anyone – including himself – the opportunity to grow thoughtful. That can prove fatal amongst waiting troops with only one life to live and perhaps less faith in the next one than they ought. Guy's little black stick drew out a cloud of skirmishers through the ranks.

These were the sole troop type permitted to stroll, duck, shamble, and generally behave like individuals. They now advanced and scattered in a pattern apparent only to themselves, drilled as a flock of rifle-armed sheep. Some even took licence so far as to lie down on the job, enhancing the scorched turf with their bottle-green uniforms. Charity said that they weren't having a rest but peering – in vain – for someone to employ sniper skills on.

Even more than normal, Guy was bursting to oblige them and all people. He killed two birds with one stone, urging things on and getting shot of nanny, by sending Polly and Prudence rearwards. They were to order the pair of 'cook-pot' mortars behind the lines to start the day's play.

These squat little innovations and their servitors proved wide awake and willing. Soon enough, twin trajectories arced high over the hill and out of sight beyond. The *crack*, *crack*, of their retort and a whiff of brimstone on the air finally roused some widespread response. Along the skyline spectators were rushing to the picnic tables provided. Guy even spotted the Bishop puffing away, pretending not to hasten, off to 'son-of-pavilion' facing the halfway line.

With his grace was a contingent of actual New-Wessex troops, colonels and above, whose presence made the battle legal and supposedly ensured 'fair play'. Just as importantly, they offered hope of an unbiased report back, lest any despot covertly nibble away at his neighbours and accumulate a Blades-challenging domain. It was an undemanding but *responsible* job, allocated to in-favour, in sight of retirement, types, and, notwithstanding the many perks and embarrassment of applicants, deserving of *respect*. Right now they weren't getting it. Perspective-glass views revealed aggrieved faces, unhappy about being hurried.

Sad to report, Guy relished seeing them scamper over the Downs; a sight seasoned by thought of red-faced redcoats dying to tell him off but lacking the authority. They'd be cross, they'd set pen to parchment, but the Ambassador's indifference knew no bounds. A little inconvenience would be good for their souls – though maybe less beneficial for episcopal ears and composure.

Ordinarily, New-Wessex monitors were chaperoned by a troop or three of Grand Army cavalry, who could make manifest any wrath and set 'errors' right on the spot. Alas, they'd not been thought necessary today. The Bishop was – well, a *bishop* – and as high as anyone in Blades's capricious favours. It was hardly to be expected he'd condone a collapse in standards. That over-confidence was now much repented of.

How, Guy correctly mused (with lamentably little sympathy) those high-ups must now be wishing they'd brought the mailed fist – even if it couldn't be used. Dinner had been disrupted. Someone to order about and shout at might at least have eased their indigestion.

The elderly Colonel of the Haslemeres joined Guy again and made an exquisite bow. Rerighted, he then took the air as if leaving the house for the first time that day.

'*Sweet*,' he said, in declamatory fashion, '*is the smell of gunpowder in the cause that is righteous!*'

It was nice, but not his. Guy suspected something purchased from one of Horsham's poetry peddlers. Or wasn't it a saying of the mysterious 'Saint Guy Fawkes' Blades was once mad keen to laud and make everyone venerate? Apparently, he'd blown up an alien tyrant – or deserved to have done, or something like that. The details were sketchy in Guy's mind as the story was much less emphasised nowadays. God-king Blades seemed to have gone off his former hero.

It didn't matter. So few things did. It wasn't necessary, and perhaps even cruel, to track the quote down to its lair. Let the poor part-time soldier have his moment of profundity.

'Sweet indeed,' Guy agreed, and amiably sent his nostrils aloft too. 'But not sweet enough. More mortaring, if you please. Then a general advance. Gentlemen: forward and *present arms*! Sing lustily and with good courage! Sound the fife and drum!'

Actually, the former were the tall, baroque, wind-pipes Blades's people had been wedded to since earliest days. Unable to convert them to less eerie-sounding instruments, the god-king had compromised – something not unknown in the beginning – and settled for a renaming. Blades's 'fife' looked nothing like those he'd known back home but only he knew any different and confusion was confined to him. With divinity offering so many distractions in those early days, it had been easy to be easygoing and overlook a few weeds along the way. A 10-foot-tall 'fife', carved and coloured weird, that sounded like torture? Why not?

Why not indeed? Guy's incitement was hardly needed. Wessex folk loved to make a noise, whether in merriment or mayhem. In next to no time each company's musicians were expressing martial themes. Kettle drums provided a back bass to the wind-pipes' unearthly throbbing, massaging the air for miles. Brought up on it, Guy's blood chilled and boiled at the same time.

Nor were his the only spirits raised. Stray Brightonian heads appeared over the green bowl's lip, summoned by shells put amongst them and the ululation of the Bishop's music. They were met by mocking cheers and catcalls from the home crowd, only gradually countered by hurriedly arriving rival supporters.

Formal opposition wasn't long in appearing to back up their chants in person. Over in waves came South Downs Highlanders, each clan clustered around their chieftain and horse-skull banner, fronted by a crust of their 'best men', owning armour *and* pistol *and* sword. Cultured circles said harsh things about their . . . foibles, but in clots and in the flesh they looked very convincing.

Next, dragged like dogs to a bath and always tucked

securely between heaving Highlander masses, arrived the town militias. Despised both for their habits and their habitations but tolerated for their industry, armed only with seax knives thrust into shrinking hands, Brightonian military theory reckoned them worthy of absorbing bullets destined for better men.

Brighton traditionally disdained to field skirmishers or other skittish types, preferring instead a prologue of pony lancers and horse archers. They and the Bishop's marksmen now passed the time with an unamusing game of chase-and-run in the midfield whilst more substantial units manoeuvred. Saddles were skilfully emptied from a distance and then the slower green-jackets got skewered as recompense. The crowd were kept from grumbling until serious play could commence.

Guy observed a shudder of pause and recognition as each unit strode over the hill and saw him. His costume was too distinctive, a generations-ago military fashion only clung to by nostalgics like himself. They hadn't been expecting him here, there were no contingency plans to deal with it. It would never do. His presence was blighting the day.

Polly and Prudence finally found Guy back in the obscurity of the ranks. He was exchanging clothes with the youngest and most obviously frightened soldier around.

King Guy adjusted the near-fit cocked hat atop the straw-headed youth and spruced up the hang of the scarlet coat to make a plough-boy look regal.

'Now,' he instructed, 'back up the hill you go, nice and slow, like no one's ever, *ever*, told you to hurry. And wave like this,' he demonstrated a languid spiral of the wrist, 'to anyone of colonel status and above – not below, mind, or you'll give the game away. And tell everyone *I* told you to do it. Then go and sit beside the Bishop and don't you move until I come back. Geddit? Are the words of my mouth and meditations of my heart finding a home in you?'

Supping at alternate cups of terror and relief, the young soldier almost nodded his head off.

'Sound lad. Now, did I leave a purse of gold Toms in my

pocket?' Guy frowned in fake concentration. 'Maybe I did. Maybe I didn't. Probably not. Anyhow, don't suppose they'll be there when I return. *Very* much doubt it. Get my drift?'

For humbler homes a gold Tom, the fist-sized ornate coinage of the realm, represented at least a calf or a hog. Two Toms represented the lap of luxury. Three and above were any laps you fancied plus a year off work. The soldier got Guy's drift before he even finished casting it.

The boy had missed his vocation as an actor. He deserted the ranks under the baleful but impotent eyes of his sergeants and promenaded up the slope like Lord Muck. A Lobster captain encountered en route got the royal wave and made tinny protests from inside his metal prison. Guy growled but there was no harm done. Even the nearby had barely heard. Unable to read it at such range, the enemy would be judging this book by its cover. From a distance the impostor looked the part and they would be deceived. The astoundingly promoted 'oyster-coat' went off to have dinner with the Bishop.

'You too,' Guy told Polly and Prudence. 'Else they won't believe it.'

Tough. The huscarls' synapses spoke as one, causing their heads to shake. They had a certain type of signing symbol reserved for rare questions like *'Do you mind if I stick needles in your eyes?'* or *'Don't you agree Blades is a kind deity?'* They demonstrated it to Guy's face now.

Legally speaking, mutiny by an oath-bound huscarl merited the impaling stake and no New-Wessex court would deny Guy redress. Happily, he hadn't the heart or inclination. Polly and Prudence had sat on enough things they didn't want to in their previous career and a soft heart like Guy's would never add to that total.

Instead, he waggled the seduction stick at them reprovingly. They cringed under his wrath but still wouldn't shift. Then Guy sighed and smiled at the same time.

'Right. Have it your way, oh bodyguards of no-bloody-good . . . But at least put on a tricorn and an oyster-coat .'

Those items were easier arranged than obedience and

obtainable at the snap of a finger. To make amends for their wickedness the pair dressed up without demure. True, they still looked odd: midnight locks and silvery dresses tumbling out from beneath military hat and coat, but like most deceits it only had to serve the passing moment. 'Long-term' could look after its tedious self.

With that life-and-death issue now settled, the pair could move on to merely urgent matters. Both signalled at the rear echelons, conversing with Guy about boxes, large boxes – on wheels, covertly sneaked up.

Guy's face and fingers were dismissive. The Bishop's secret weapon, employed promiscuously until familiar, had dwindled down into mere party piece status. The jaded Ambassador would be happy to watch but with no great expectations.

He signed the term that doubled up as both an obscenity and a curse between them. They divined the correct usage and their eyes alone said 'Oh, is that all?', requiring no amplification.

By now the Brighton array was joined by its own ever-changing box of tricks: the toys and hobby-horses of clan chieftains with excess time on their hands and money to burn. It was these that always made war with Sussex such a spectacle and pleasure. Say what you like about their haircuts and after-dark habits, but they had style. What started out ages ago as experiment had long since frozen into custom and was looked for without fail. If, Blades forbid, a Brighton army ever did turn up without a rag-tag of mercenaries and exotica, it would be booed all the way in and willed to lose even by core supporters.

No such danger today. They had brought along a unit of black-armoured 'Reiters', pistol-festooned riders all the way from Mercia: a king's ransom worth and a wonderful novelty so far south. Then, to gild the lily, there was a rabble of uncontrollable – but temporarily pointable – Hedonists rambling on behind, presumably happenstance recruits from the major incursion reported earlier.

Utterly indifferent to their provenance, the Bishop's men curled their lips at the Hedonists and the inadequate kilts they

113

were almost wearing, and at the 'lidless eye' motif painted on flesh and leather alike. They deplored the effeminate feather decorations no less than the two-handed swords juggled out of sheer pleasure in life – and the taking of it. The bulbous scarlet cod-pieces were too scandalous to even merit comment. Same side or no, many Brighton men agreed.

They must have come as a job-lot, for amongst them there were even some of the sober-suited variety; the Janus-face of that strange bipolar culture. Those Hedonists taking their turn at 'sensible' years, with one wife and children they knew the father of, those who kept the books and home fires burning, were rarely seen abroad. They stayed at home and bore a yoke willingly, knowing that the day would come when they might don 'eyes and feathers' again, swapping grey garb with their fellows returning from the razzle.

Perhaps these sports had got the itch early and begged the current Mrs Hedonist for a boys' night out. Or maybe the world was so turned upside down not even the Hedonists' weather-house act could be relied on any more. Either way it scarcely mattered, save as a spoiling of the Hedonistic fashion parade. Grey as the grave or peacock proud, they all fought just the same.

A Hedonist presence guaranteed a good show but also introduced a wild card into play. Like their swords, they were double-edged weapons, hazardous to both friend and foe, a cocktail of fear and jealousy making them equally unpopular enemies or allies. It was noticeable how rarely there were Hedonist prisoners taken – which was rough really, considering how they always took *their* prisoners . . .

Nervous behind these might-as-well-be-naked men and their suits-of-eyes, was the ramshackle Brighton artillery train. Diminutive 'falcons' and 'falconets' and even 'leather-guns' trundled along on squeaky wheels, desirous of getting where the action was before the armament of more civilised nations blatted them. They got a warm-hearted round of applause all round, as plucky underdogs always up for it and good for a laugh.

Magnified through the good offices of a spy-glass, many Brighton faces were pictures of indignation at the 'done thing' not being done. The burning Picts Lane province issue was to have been settled in a civilised manner, at a set hour, after lunch and upon sober reflection. Now the soft Wealden dirt-dwellers' impatience threatened to turn a thing of style and elegance into just another sordid brawl for land.

South Downs prejudice had long suspected that Wealden folk kept secret timepieces and jumped to their commands. That was not the Brighton or Sussex way and they emphasised the point by really ambling into position.

Guy sympathised, but still gave them a little jog with the artillery. Airbursts sprinkled some urgency. The cook-pot mortars also began to find their distance. Clumps of South Downers were discovering – briefly, before night fell for ever – that they could fly.

It wasn't exactly deadly stuff – not from a whole-army perspective – but a gall and provocation all the same, like a wasp at a picnic. It served to make the majority fall into line with Guy's schedule. Happily, it also drowned out a choral work of boos from the all-round audience, inspired by such boorish haste.

Guy's gratitude for that good fortune knew no start. Ordinarily, he would have been mortified, and less fearful of sharp swords than such social suicide. Today, though, all worries bar one tooted a stuffed trumpet and thumped a punctured drum. He had an overriding concern. It raised goosebumps which cannonballs overhead singularly failed to.

The Ambassador stood all alone amongst thousands and pondered an awful possibility. What if, somewhere along the line, cheerful, cheeky-chappie Guy, good company to himself and others, had quietly shut up shop, packed his bags and slipped away without so much as a cheerio? In middle age, when all things ought to be getting clearer, there'd come a day when Guy needed to know if the button marked 'pleasure' remained connected, or if the Guy Ambassador he'd known and rubbed along with was any longer at home. If not, then he might as well set off after him.

These seemed important questions, even if only to Guy, and well worth the breach of manners and a few tons of power fetched all the way from Sicily. In present no-messing mood, Guy felt entirely justified in basting the Brighton men with round-shot in order to get things moving.

Of course, it didn't help that he'd been spotted. A quick quiz through the glasses showed eyes seeking his sacred presence as the rumour did the rounds. It was only after the pseudo Guy-for-a-day was clearly observed dining at the Bishop's table that the Picts Lane contenders felt at ease about restating their claim. Once that false fact was established and conveyed, the zeal for combat and passion for incomparable Picts Lane returned. The South Downers banged their outsize seax choppers against iron shield bosses and their chieftains pushed forward the battle hors d'oeuvres.

Brighton's horse archers, shepherds all and custodians of mighty flocks that turned the Downs pearly, had skills acquired in protecting sheep from wolves and worse. It was their pleasure – and a pleasure to see if not afflicted yourself – to form a ring within bow-shot and then canter round and round, no hands, lobbing death from on high at each nearest approach.

'The "Cantabrian Circle",' said the Haslemere Colonel, once it was formed and doing its stuff in their face, thereby revealing himself as a student of classical terms as well as erotica. 'A pestilence speedily dealt with.'

If so, the remedy oughtn't to be withheld. The line regiments' muskets were no more accurate or deadly than the Downsmen's spiteful little horn-and-sinew-enhanced, rounded W composite-bows. In fact, the roaring shepherd boys were having the better of it.

It wasn't really Guy's place to give commands, and in contemporary warfare there was hardly a need for it. Matters proceeded according to custom and precedents, not needing a fussy hand upon the wheel. Even as he pondered the pressing need for reply, Guy saw the mysterious 'boxes' being wheeled up along gaps between the companies of foot. Each little horse-box-like wagon was preceded by youths bearing canvas screens painted with oyster-coat effigies. Time for time-hallowed phase two.

The jerky advance of these one-dimensional troops might have deceived on the first few occasions, but no longer. The whirling circle directed its venom that way, flicking specialist arrows with splayed tips. Along the line the delusional reinforcements were torn or went down, revealing the enigmatic truth behind.

It didn't matter (which seemed to be theme for the day). Simultaneously, the cabin doors crashed wide, heaved open by a rope and pulley system to let the contents surge forth.

These were not the crushed in spirit Null used as novelty bloodhounds by the Margrave of East Weald. The Bishop's menagerie retained their teeth and claws and lust for meat. Separated from their mountainous monster-mothers at birth, they were less socialised and cunning than wild types, but in their opinion of mankind and other presumptuous eatables you couldn't insert a wafer between the two. It was – just – possible to take a Null out of the feeding frenzy, but not the feeding frenzy out of the Null.

Encased in a steel crinoline on wheels, open only at the front, these specimens remained alive because of their value in the wars between man. No one forgot that they were top-dog once, for untold ages, until God sent Blades (or he sent himself – the theology was obscure) to amend things.

The up to twice man-sized creatures trundled forward, kept in that direction by handles and human drivers at the back. The Null were purple and beautiful, perfect marriages of muscle and appetite, fed to sleekness with live delicacies when not serving the Bishop in the field. Compared to them, their owners looked like sickly children.

Released from dark captivity they took the air. Almond eyes widened and slit nostrils flared. In their torment and humiliation they saw and smelt great larders of meat all around but opportunities for solace lay in just one direction. There was no question about questioning the call. Null

117

couldn't help themselves when hungry and angry. Like swift snails dragging their homes behind them they set off that way.

Even wearing heavy iron carapaces the creatures caught up. Shrieking ponies reared under raking claws, delivering the required rider for dinner. An arrow or two apiece didn't worry the Null, not while the red mist took them. It required a pincushion's worth, or luck, or a musket ball delivered handshake distant, to revise their plans. Some of the handlemen were deprived of earthly reward, a few purple mercenaries succumbed to eye shots or weight of numbers, but in essence the prickly shepherd circle was shoo'ed away, the one sure refuge lying in speedy flight.

Well spurred to it, Downs ponies could put distance between themselves and burdened Null – though the unencumbered variety would have given a race of interest to a betting man like Guy. The bulk of horse archers survived to flow like water round and through the clan formations.

Thwarted and outrun, the little Null tanks ought to have given pause for thought – and would have, had they been men. But they weren't, and proved it, showing the stupidity and mettle which once made them masters. All pressed on at speed, entirely of one – furious – mind. Long since abandoned by their handlers, each crashed into the Brighton ranks and were swallowed up – as they ventured a little swallowing themselves.

Too late, there emerged the specialist teams designated to deal with the Null threat. Knots of men wielding specially lengthened pikes and custodians of pitch and oil-coated hogs, ready to ignite once they'd tickled a Null palate, waited in vain. To show willing, they skewered or barbecued a few cripples and latecomers but otherwise wasted their winter of training. The laggard elite stood around embarrassed and trying to look useful, until joined by a clan chieftain and presumed employer. He said a few words – and then doled out headaches-as-wages with the flat of his blade.

The Bishop's ranks roared with amusement at the comic pay-day. They were doubly delighted by the exit of a few Null

118

from the world and the blushing of Brighton faces besides. The abrasive horse circle was gone, the sun was shining and they'd had a laugh. Things were going well. Then the question of 'going' rang all Guy's alarms. His agitated face looked either way along the line.

Not a moment too soon. The cavalry weren't going to wait much longer, King Guy or no, and their burning glances in his direction were no less impassioned than Guy's own. Horses pawed at the turf and amateur generals muttered. Etiquette dictated he or someone give the nod but there were limits. Very shortly, some wag would ventriloquise the word and they'd be away anyway of their own accord, to everyone's shared shame. Happily, Guy just beat them to it.

The Lobsters and Hussars set off at their wildly different paces against the pony lancers ranged against them and were gamely met in midfield. Respectively over- or under-armoured for the job, they made a meal of it in varying ways although the outcome was never in doubt. Downs cavalry weren't designed to meet a charge, especially if not in the mood to tempt fate that day. After all, Picts Lane was only Picts Lane – doubtless spoilt by decades of episcopal misrule. Back home there were Downs-bleaching flocks requiring love and attention. With that noble aim in mind, and only after a creditable struggle, the lancers set off to be reunited with their fleecy friends.

Guy saw that the Haslemere Hussars, flushed by victory, also seemed minded to give the South Downs a visit – thus conforming to every low expectation. The lace and scarlet soldiers were caught up in the savage joys of pursuit and nothing but a direct command from Almighty God would call them back – and maybe not even that. They did it every time and no one was the least bit surprised.

The Horsham Lobster horse, being comprised of the 'quality' and laden with crosses to bear no less heavy than the recently deceased Null, were better bets to return and lend a metal hand. It was (just) within the bounds of possibility for aristocrats and wealthy merchants to assist lesser breeds for free – so long as people didn't *expect*, or make it an obligation.

Spurred by fear of this aberration from the fringes of human behaviour, a Brighton elder committed the Reiters against them. Just as heavily protected as the Lobsters, with even their horses metal-shielded against incoming harm, they were a fair match, in style if not numbers, to Horsham's finest. Their polished practice, honed against the still uppity Null of the north, was the 'caracole'. Arrayed a dozen deep, the ebony cavalrymen would trot their mounts to within pistol shot of the foe and then fire, retreat and reload rank by rank, maintaining, in theory, a stationary position and constant fusillade.

Against Null sleeping-piles, protective of the mother cowering within, or versus irresolute savages, it worked a treat and earned them a good living all over Wessex. They'd even served abroad, persecuting other people's enemies as varied as snow-Null besieging the sulphur works in Iceland, or remnant Professorial regimes in the Americas. However, the one flaw in their military system, the maggot in the Reiters' jam, was an enemy prepared to absorb that first volley and then get stuck in at speed. They didn't like such unsporting types. Those tactics caught them wrong-footed, stationary and swordless. Empty pistols failed to frighten intrepid foes who took the Reiters' worst and then delivered sabres at the gallop.

The Lobsters were candidates for that exacting role, though neither professional nor fanatic. They had a local reputation to maintain and for future business and marriage prospects couldn't afford to turn tail too promptly. Thus, after the fleeting – if fierce – exchange of views and metal with the lancers, they were still up to wheeling about in moderate good order, to face the oncoming caracole.

Supposedly, Lobster armour was bullet-proof, as proven by the 'proof mark' on each, an indentation driven in but not through by the armourer's double-charged pistol at point blank range. The relevant guild was very vigilant. No set would be purchased without it.

All the same, it was a lot of faith to invest in any artisan's skill and diligence. You heard dark stories about proof marks made with a hammer and punch, not the overloaded real thing. Many a Lobster that day, as they jogged along as fast as over-burdened mounts could manage, was travelling back in his mind to a day of purchase and thoughts about refunds. Fortunately, their sluggish pace meant any pause was imperceptible. The most embittered of their Horsham vassals couldn't have said that the charge of the Lobsters was anything other than creditable.

Then both they and the Reiters were swallowed into a fluffy cloud of white and sparks, muffling all of the metallic clangs and cries. Mutually absorbed in each other's company, they were no longer a danger to anyone but themselves, leaving Guy free to ponder new thoughts.

With sideshows and fripperies all out of the way, the artillery trains were able to converse. The Brighton tiddlers had run in as close as they dared and found a place from which to do some good – or harm.

The Bishop's cannons found that an irresistible tease and soon had the measure of them, initiating a bravura, if unbalanced, duel. Wheels and men were whipped away from the gallant little Brighton falcons. Wicked splinters scoured the surrounds and a powder barrel exploded. It was almost worthy of disloyal applause to see a Horsham saker get a dose of the same medicine. One minute it was a fully manned and vocal piece, the epicentre of mad activity; the next a lonely display item, dappled red.

Paradoxically, it was Guy who saved the Brighton train, rather than their own efforts or sensible retreat. As someone who'd mixed with the military when occasion demanded, he knew the allure an artillery duel presented to two sets of professionals. It gave them something to talk about in days to come, when the two sides (or survivors thereof) mixed socially – which was all very nice but didn't necessarily help today. Again, an Ambassador was up against the myopia of the particularists, the clinging of sailors to a buoy.

From his hidey-hole within the ranks, he sent Polly to tell the artillerists to sing a new song. There was the minor matter of several thousand South Downers not a quarter mile away, many of them anxious for glory and every man-jack keen to be home in time to fold their flocks. It would do the Bishop's cause no harm to knock a few down whilst they waited.

The proud professional gunners harkened to Guy (via Polly) where they might have disdained advice from lesser men. Guy checked and saw that spikes were being applied, trunnions wheeled and new elevations accommodated to. Shortly after, the clan clumps got to feel the earth move under their feet. From time to time new corridors were torn through living walls of men by particularly smiled-upon shots.

In his new humble persona, Guy could do just what he wanted – which was, he supposed, the whole idea of the exercise. He was free, along with the two foot Colonels, to progress along the line smiling and exhorting and defying the South Down snipers. It was an act of bravado, at least on his part, for he was neither obliged nor bullet-proof. Lady Luck stepped in to remind him. The Colonel of the Horshams had his ankle clipped by a lucky – for some – shot. Of course, the man had to pretend otherwise.

'I think,' he said, as colour fled from face to foot and then leaked into the sward, 'if it's all the same to you, that I'll stay here.'

And naturally, Guy and the Haslemere Colonel went along with the charade, pretending that this was an eminently sensible suggestion and one they'd been just about to make themselves.

They then hurriedly – in leisurely manner – moved on to save the poor man's embarrassment. It was clear he wanted to swear and surrender to powerful emotions, plus perhaps a period of cosseting.

'To your right! To your *right*!' the two remaining commanders commanded, accompanied by broad, confident, smiles as though they were commending something as easy and beneficial as breathing. 'Only the man to your *right*!'

It was the newish drill for combating backward peoples and had apparently worked wonders against savages from Kent.

One flash of insight from an illiterate bayonet-drill sergeant called Degg, and suddenly the New-Wessex frontiers were less permeable than hitherto. Guy took it as further proof of the essential simplicity of all things worthy – bar diplomacy, of course.

Meanwhile, junior officers were attending to fine detail. By dint of stick and shouting, alternate companies were drawn back so as to present a chequerboard formation. Left exposed in the gaps in between, the artist units waited to fulfil their role with a nonchalance they didn't feel. Theirs was a glorious assignment, well worthy of a poem or painting or song-cycle. Doubtless it was the composing of same that caused all the whitened knuckles and cold sweat.

Guy realised that despite the premature start Horsham had dallied and delayed right-action until everything was nick of time again. He almost had to run to ensure the furthest extremities got the 'right' message before everything started in earnest.

The 'Golden Horde' of Brighton had got tired of standing still under the lead lash and their own wind-pipes struck up an air packed with pugnacious notes. The whole assembly moved like an awoken carpet in Guy's direction.

Horsham's artillery had opportunity to clear its throat a few times more, before wisdom suggested a sharpish scampering away. To celebrate that last chance they brought out the new-fangled 'canister' shells whose myriad little pellets, once liberated from parental container home, barged their way through the oncoming like obstreperous youths, without so much as an 'Excuse . . .' or 'Pardon me . . .' Subtle and discriminating as a rabid elephant about the same job, they carved instant avenues through the tight-packed clans, allowing sunshine and horizon – pink-tinged sunshine and horizon – to peep through. The innovation was judged a great success by those not on the receiving end.

However, all good things must come to an end. The cunning artillerists always deputised a man to do nothing much but stand and stare, calculating the enemy's approach as a function of the time needed to reload. Pioneers of the dismal science of computation, they'd reduced it to a fine art in judging the point where R (reload), or time required for another pot-shot, was equal to or less than AD (approaching death), over NS (nearest safety).

Therefore, Guy felt a guilt-inducing stab of gladness when a few of them descended from perfection and felt a real stab, delivered by fleeter than expected South Downers. Perfection should be reserved for God alone, and wasn't a fit, pretty or healthy ambition for humans.

The sacrificial town militias were sent on first, advancing cringing, two steps forward, one step back. They made a show and waved their weapons; took a volley in the mush and then went away to think about it. No one tutted. They'd served their purpose, masking the prickly millipede of Downs warriors behind.

Guy and the Colonels (the walking-wounded gentleman now back in the reins with gargantuan bandaged foot, like a comic gout sufferer) were too canny to fall for that. They'd ordered only grenadier company fire: sufficient to send Brighton's accountants et al back to their duties, but not a crippling diminishment of firepower. The mitred men might even have reloaded before the grand arrival, but if not, they still had their little glass-globe grenades. Either way, it cleared the air. Metaphorically.

Guy swept one languid spiral of powder smoke from before his eyes. He didn't really need to see when he could hear and count the footfalls, but it was an additional comfort. Loosely speaking.

Native South Downers tended towards the woolly in appearance, and in many aspects, bar mildness, resembled the flocks they owned. Their clothes were fleecy, their faces hirsute. A Brightonian with no moustache in charge of his features was deemed no man at all. Likewise, flock style, they sang from the same songbook as well. An aggressive bleating preceded their charge.

Guy was not deluded, knowing the parallels were only

fleece deep. All the same, it constituted some mud he could throw.

'They drill like sheep,' he observed, suddenly giving his thoughts voice, to everyone and no one. 'Therefore, gentlemen, let us "baaaa" back!'

It was overly rich for the oyster-coats; a metaphor too far. They tried their best but refused the jump. The Colonels had to interpret.

'Pre-*sent*!'

For a wonderful moment they thought that alone had done the job. Picts Lane was theirs with barely a shot, and the taste of celebratory toasts (wine for the higher types and ale for the plebs) shimmied on many a lip. Of course, it was way too soon and way out. Any ejaculations of joy – and there were some – were premature. The multiple musket erections all along the line had given the South Downers pause – but only for a purpose. Their 'best men' slowed only to discharge carbines and heirloom pistols and then charged on as before. Those not so blessed copied with huge lead darts, racked behind their shields. These last cartwheeled across the intervening space and smoke, drawing Horsham eyes aloft when they should have stayed squinting front.

And that was entirely as intended – for the Brightonians might be savage but not stupid. Pause or no, they'd gained paces and a reduction in the inevitable lead rain. The darts arrived with thuds and 'aaaarg's, and Guy had to strain his vocal chords to be heard – which didn't improve his mood.

'*Take aim*!'

Now it was eyes down and straight, not needing much urging. The hairy horde filled the scene, demanding undivided attention.

'Brighton boasters!' announced a nearby captain – and to his credit sounded almost convinced. 'Nothing to it!'

Polly and Prudence snuggled in close to Guy, though otherwise looking miles away. They disdained to tote a footslogger's musket, for all they wore the right gear. If their axes were to hand then they were happy – and Heaven alone

125

knew what firepower lay concealed beneath those dresses in any case.

'Front rank, *fire!*'

The universe exploded and Guy's eardrums felt like joining in. Instantly everyone was in a world of their own, called smoke-cosmos. It even dampened down the sounds of agony and anger. Guy knew of old, from his very first Null skirmish, that you now just had to take things on faith. Faith was a tricky thing, granted, but restricted purely to musketry, you were on sound ground.

'Second rank, *fire!*'

It got worse and thicker, but a bold man might have dared say he saw faces approaching through the gloom.

So: they hadn't wiped them out, or reasoned Picts Lane free.

'Third rank, *fire!*'

To jab him in the ribs for all the nonsense about 'faith', the fog deceived Guy. The third and last line had barely relaxed trigger-fingers before shaggy men leaped in from nowhere. Ranks one and two had bayonets at the ready, but number three were going to be out of luck. The nail-studded heels of their musket butts would have to substitute.

The South Downers hit like a rabid horse and cart. Nevertheless, it transpired they had a drill to act out too, although not one taught by any civilised state. Shields backed up by a shoulder swept the first encounter away, maybe even putting him out of the fight thanks to the stubby spike to front. Raised seaxes then descended like Doomsday on encounter two and freestyle ensued – assuming life remained.

The Bishop's men weren't without their own plans to spoil the show, even if it felt like the sky had just fallen in. The bayonet drill drummed into them came back to most, and many had the faith (that word again) to thrust out and up, not at the nemesis before them, but the version to their right.

The Achilles' heel of a chopping weapon is that you must lift to deliver. For a second the armpits flashed as snug home for a length of steel. Any shield is hugging the front and redundant. Degg had spotted it fighting against Mancunian raiders and lived to tell the tale, gaining fame and promotion in a torrid moment. Born on that fleeting field, his new creed was passed on and up until it made conversions amidst the exalted. They issued orders and amended the manuals and that was that. Naturally though, doubts remained, especially down amongst those who'd have to live or die thereby. It wasn't until today that many there truly saw the light and believed. It was a heady – or armpitty – revelation.

The faith or trust came into it insofar as you needed to neglect your own problems and selflessly attend to the next man's. If your leftward colleague let you down, then you were baring an unprotected bonce to a 'Brighton knighthood' and would never make the same mistake again. Not everyone had the fibre to make that leap of faith, but enough did – a surprising amount.

A likewise surprising horde of South Downers kissed the light goodbye at once, and fell impaled. A madcap dash ended against a wall. The fatal jar juddered right along the front.

There wasn't space for axe-work in such an intimate – if clothed – orgy and so Polly and Prudence plied the stiletto to protect Guy and, should chance arise, themselves. Little guessing the great danger and opportunity combined within spitting and seax distance, the South Downers persuaded themselves to give the tasty trio room and wide berth. Alas, that kind gesture went without reward. It only meant the great-axes could come out to play.

More in keeping with past fixtures, some Horsham companies were still cut to ribbons, the survivors left shuddering or nursing severed extremities. The time-engraved pattern was then for them to be mopped up by an arriving South Downs second line. Here and there, that was the case today. Grenadiers *never* gave up, of course, sooner igniting all their grenades at once and taking some shaggies with them rather than be the mockery of a Brighton alehouse, but ample rank and file reckoned too much was asked of them and showed a clean pair of heels. These the howling wolves-in-sheep's-clothing caught up with to visibly demonstrate the runners *did* have guts after all. They even had enough impetus left over to crump against Horsham's second echelon.

That arrival was keenly awaited, other than by a few faintheart formations who turned and fled, having died horribly in imagination already. However, those overactive minds were in the minority. The rest stood fast, even though their muskets had already said all they were going to. The guns were now plugged with prickly bayonets keen for sheathing in meat. Smokescreens notwithstanding, line two had seen the check delivered by the front ranks with the 'Degg method'. A lot thought they could do at least as well.

For sure enough, and overall, the new drill had prevailed. The Brighton charge was stopped dead in many places, as though speeding on to a spike. Sergeant Degg wasn't around that day to see it, but he'd just become a colonel and won a harem.

Those South Downers who'd broken through found the second line hard going and no fun to play with. In a change of plans they shrank back and instead picked on artists' units cowering between the caustic chequer pieces.

Scythe blades are fine for harvest and, once adapted, passable for reaping men too. Even so, they need to be brandished with resolution. Those brandishing them must act as a team. Otherwise, they just look like tools waggled by fools.

The rebuffed Brightonians certainly thought so and tucked in. Any number of novels and great works were thrust into the realm of now-never-will-be as things were thrust into their begetters.

The Bishop's tax men may have been laughing, but not so the beard-twisting Brighton generals back up on the rim. Afflicting the gifted might be amusing but right now it was also nothing but indulgence: mere 'displacement activity'. All the while the Horsham second line was plucking out bayonets and reloading.

Shepherd commanders shrieked and screamed and had the wind-tubes bellow rebuke – but no one who ought to be was listening. As individualistic (in their way) as the artists in their way, most Brightonians were neglecting reality in favour of more amenable fantasy. Doubtless that was consoling, whilst it lasted, but there fast approached a time when reality would tap them on the shoulder, too hard to ignore, and say 'Oi!'

When it came, the resounding volley blasted away savage and surviving artist alike. Point blank, even smooth-bore muskets had their work cut out to miss. Smirks as well as powder sent each lead ball off. Second row knew they were on to a winner.

As smoke and groans lingered over twitching piles of men, the focus of play moved elsewhere. Survivors from the front line were more jubilant than people in dire straits have a right to be. The repulsed clans were only withdrawn a score of paces, even if hostilities were reduced to abuse and the odd dart pinning tricorns to Horsham heads. They remained just a hop and a skip away from each other's throats. Things still looked lively – but 'things' were deceptive. To all intents and purposes the match was nigh complete.

The men of the South Downs wanted to leave with dignity and discuss the subtleties of bayonet drill in more congenial company. Picts Lane province must await liberation another day. Likewise, Horsham and Haslemere men were envisaging hearth and home as returning heroes. Even the victorious Hussars and Lobsters, now trickling back, weren't inclined to mix it any more. Anxious to live and revisit the day in memory, both sides were panting for a final whistle and someone to supply the excuse to go.

Generally, it was given by the New-Wessex invigilators. Perhaps the only point of these pointless little Blades-sanctioned wars between Blades-sanctioned statelets was that very absence of *point* and passion. They served to tap the reservoir of bad blood in men and polities alike; they gave the chance for those who liked such things to shine, but truly they were much ado about nothing. Save against the Null, modern war wasn't waged to the bitter end and unalterable conclusions.

Burned towns and dead civilians were features of the bad old days. It was one of those areas where Blades was – inadvertently, perhaps – a civilising influence, domesticating the beast in man.

Coincidentally, some of the Bishop's men chose then to take up the traditional call of 'Blades is great! Blades is great!' – which was both bold statement of something or other and prayer rolled into one.

The Brightonians could rightfully say it too, without fear of contradiction – and did so, with gusto. After the carnage and waste it was something both sides felt able to assert in unison. Like handshakes at the end of a fiercely contested cricket match, the affirmation and twin counter-affirmation acted as a calming coda to committed play.

Only Guy could not be glad. Actually, he didn't think Blades *was* all that great, even though he should do. And, *no*, he didn't feel overwhelmed about continued existence. Things hadn't gone the way he wanted. He was still around and would have to go up and on into tomorrow. There remained the nagging necessity to think it all through.

To universal shock and horror, he stepped forward, the lone *nay* amongst thousands of *ayes* – and twice that number of eyes tracked his every move. *En route* he snatched the Bishop's personal silken banner. It had gained some extra ventilation during proceedings but remained a highly potent talisman.

Not understanding but never doubting, Polly and Prudence went with him.

'Play on!' he said, to everyone his voice might assault. 'Play on! For I call on Almighty G-G-God to witness how much I want Picts Lane province to remain Horsham's – *f-f-forever!*'

And armed only with his seduction stick, Guy set off into the clans who might dispute that.

Amidst all the smoke and excitement, he remained unrecognised, the focus of burning hatred from both sides for being so blasted *keen*. Save to those few in the know, his unprotected back was as threatened as his breast. Polly and Prudence looked one to another, thought-exchanging whether now was the right time for laying non-loving hands upon the beloved.

Only one section of the audience applauded Guy's zeal. Brighton's auxiliary Hedonists had had a limited day out so far, simply dispersing the Bishop's skirmishers. True, they'd also caught and tortured a few laggard artillerists, and creased themselves with laughter whilst pretending to rape the captured cannons. After that, though, their needs had been woefully neglected. The South Downers always reserved the main charge for themselves, and their eye-clad mercenaries were left with nothing to do but sprawl on the grass, re-dressing their long locks and experimenting with prisoners.

Guy's brave show brought them to their feet again, to shout approval. Unlike almost all who said it, Hedonists actually *believed* today might be a good day to die.

Then they erupted through the shocked Brighton ranks like the bursting of a boil – so the blame for resumed hostilities lifted a little from Guy's shoulders. Their two-handed swords made hypnotic figures-of-eight in the process of clearing a way before them.

Polly and Prudence hated Hedonists. Back in former slave days, they'd been loaned to one of their phantasmagoric castles, and what time they'd not been on their backs or knees had been lost in a surreal nightmare, punctuated only by sleep and screams. It was a pleasure to hack the first few of these old acquaintances and put axes in eyes, either real or painted.

One medusa-coiffeured head rolled, and, captainless, its ship careered on to bump into the Bishop's ranks, only there acknowledging no more orders would descend. Polly smiled and, had there been time, would have taken a bow.

Meanwhile, Prudence defused a hearty blow with the haft of her axe and, pirouetting gracefully, used that spiral momentum to flick the guilty sword away. Aghast at being unmanned, the weapon's former owner fell on her in a haze of hair and teeth.

Accordingly, it was no longer an occasion for poise or style, but pragmatism time. Polly whipped her revolver from its shoulder holster and dealt with Prudence's would-be murderer, plus five other applicants.

All that was all very well and a joy to be savoured later. In the interval Guy had got away and was actively courting his end of days. The two Ps couldn't afford any prettiness but had to cut their way after him, dispensing with aplomb in favour of speed.

The underdressed and overpainted types were all over him, like adolescents swarming a 'friendly' girl. It was only purest fortune that he and his silly stick hadn't already been anatomised into an apprentice-butcher's lesson.

Twin aspects of the grim reaper they might be, but Polly and Prudence could only do so much. It was thus a blessing that the more aware amongst the Bishop's men came forward to assist. In the process of wading in, some of those who might otherwise have survived the day and gone home to friends and family thereby fell at the last. Either way, living or dying, his self-sacrificing supporters weren't even acknowledged, let alone thanked. In more normal frame of mind, Guy would have suffered agonies of guilt for his selfishness.

Now, though, he experienced only a great nothingness – and frustration. It was getting so that if he tried to throw himself at the ground he'd miss. He'd heard before that those who actually sought death found her elusive, but Guy had never credited it till today. Yet the tide of battle was washing round him like a rock in a stream, leaving him be. It was a nuisance. Surely swords and pistols were unknowing things, not susceptible to irony or paradox? He mulishly persisted with his experiment.

Passing Hedonists presented no barrier to his cleaving through. They either gave him funny looks and passed on by, or else were felled before any harm was done. Guy came to see it would take a bloody-minded march deep into the Brighton ranks to find what he was looking for.

Plain as the balls on a Hedonist, his salvation lay in the fact that the South Downers couldn't believe it. An oyster-coat with no visible instrument of malice was strolling up to them

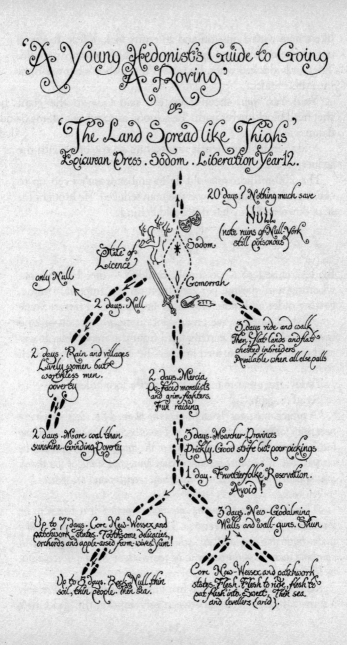

'A Young Hedonist's Guide to Going A Roving'

or

'The Land Spread like Thighs'

Epicurean Press . Sodom . Liberation Year 12.

20 days? Nothing much save NULL (note ruins of Null York still poisonous)

Sodom

State of Licence

only Null

2 days. Null

Gomorrah

2 days. Rain and villages. Lively women but worthless men. poverty

3 days ride and walk. Then, flat lands and flat chested inbreeders. Available when all else palls

2 days. Mercia. Po-faced moralists and grim flakters. Fun raiding

2 days. More coal than swishine. Grinding Poverty

3 days. Marcher Provinces. Prickly. Good strife but poor pickings

1 day. Trunderfolke Reservation. Avoid!

Up to 7 days. Core New-Wessex and patchwork states. Toothsome delicacies, orchards and apple-arsed farm-wives! Yum!

3 days. New-Godalming. Walls and wall-guns. Shun

Up to 5 days. Rock. Null thin soil, thin people. Then sea.

Core New-Wessex and patchwork states. Flesh. Flesh to ride, flesh to eat. Flesh into Sweet. Then sea and levellers (arid).

like a man with a mission and an entire lack of fear. It was so out of the ordinary no one reacted as they ordinarily would. They only ducked when he hurled the Bishop's banner right into their midst.

'You! Yes, *you*, sheep-molester!' said Guy to the giant shepherd blocking his path. 'Be so good as to get out off my d-damn way!'

And then he impatiently tapped him on the brow with the seduction stick.

The 200-million-year-old fly-in-amber wasn't even up to causing a headache. Nor was the man seduced. He brought his seax down and Guy left the world behind.

Blades refused to – or simply couldn't – die. He just *sat*, wizening and glaring, perched high on the Imperial throne, getting older and older and more impotent and bitter. Some courtiers claimed to see an aura of divine protection around him, absolving their earthly Lord from the inevitable. It was as though he'd unfinished business he couldn't bring himself to face.

Today, the great man was looking for loopholes.

'Read it again.'

'*A prince must not flinch from being blamed for vices which are necessary for safeguarding the state. This is because, taking everything into account, he will find that some of the things which appear to be virtues will, if he practises them, ruin him, and some of the things that appear to be wicked will bring him security and prosperity.*'

'More.'

'*There arises the following question: whether it is better to be loved than feared, or the reverse. The answer is that one would like to be both the one and the other; but because it is difficult to combine them, it is far better to be feared than loved if you cannot be both.*'

Reader-huscarl looked up from under his helm. There was a narrow line to be trod between pre-empting the god-king's wishes and overburdening him. The axe could fall on those who got it wrong.

Huscarl had, but not mortally. The ancient hand flapped at him from repose on the crystal armrest, urging the youth on.

Fortunately, Reader's fingers were nimble, his understanding streamlined. He knew exactly what pages contained comfort for the deity.

'*One can make this generalisation about men: they are ungrateful, fickle, liars and deceivers, they shun danger and are greedy for profit; while you treat them well, they are yours. They would shed their blood for you, risk their property, their lives, their children, so long, as I said above, as danger is remote; but when you are in danger they turn against you.*'

Golden pages were flicked to spurn the hard bits in search of surface treasure.

'*So, on this question of being loved or feared, I conclude that since some men love as they please but fear when the prince pleases, a wise prince should rely on what he controls, not on what he cannot control.*'

The clever lad recalled another passage that sometimes calmed the savage breast. He retreated to it.

'*Many have dreamed up republics and principalities which have never in truth been known to exist; the gulf between how one should live and how one does live is so wide that a man who neglects what is actually done for what should be done learns the way to self-destruction rather than self-preservation. The fact is that a man who wants to act virtuously in every way necessarily comes to grief amongst so many who are not virtuous. Therefore if a prince wants to maintain his rule he must learn how not to be virtuous and how to make use of this or not according to need.*

'*So leaving aside imaginary things, and referring to only those which truly exist, I say that whenever men are discussed . . .*'

Blades was sated. Reader-Huscarl saw it in more rhythmic breathing and dampened fires burning in those rheumy eyes. The wonderful book had done the trick again; Huscarl had survived another reading. He blessed the gilded pages and this man 'Machiavelli' – whoever *he* may have been.

Today had been quick. Sometimes it took hours of concentration by skilled concubines and great swathes of *The Prince* to rebuild Blades's interest back up from scratch and convince him to face the world.

Then, of course, there were days when the giant egg tabernacle-cum-cell never cracked at all, and the army of servitors, supplicants and worshippers saw only the bland blue exterior. Theologians said there were two ways of looking at that. On the one hand, God's emissary and presence on earth might be content with what was going on and thus silent in his contemplation of it. Alternatively, he might be wrathful about their sins and lack of faith, and thus withholding the effulgent light from them. A full Church council and convocation of bishops from all over New-Wessex and the Empire had recently failed to thrash out the ambiguities. It lingered as just one of those things you took according to type. Either it troubled your dreams, waking you worried, adding a nervy edge to everything, or else you sprinkled it like sweetness over your bowl of bliss. There was nothing mere mortal men could do to resolve the issue. The divine egg would retain its mysteries until the day deemed fit for them to be hatched.

The girl between the god-king's legs gave up at his bidding – conveyed through a clout. It wasn't her fault – for she was good and capable of draining (unpeeled!) cucumbers. It was simply a pity that there was nothing doing down there, nor had been for years. Blades persevered in the ambition that one morning, just maybe, if he sneaked up on his libido, he might take it by surprise – and surprise himself by taking someone. It hadn't happened yet but he lived in hope – about the only decent hope remaining. Given that he was surrounded by the finest erotic artists and orifices in Bladedom it was the one field in which he might still reasonably expect a crop.

Mr Machiavelli's 'Prince' had primed him; his breeches were lovingly replaced. His Imperial Majesty, Blades I and last, Emperor and god-king, Downs-Lord Paramount, Emperor of New-Wessex and its Dependencies, Protector of Assyria-in-Sussex, Despot of New-Godalming and the Holy of Holies, Sultan of Mercia and the Marches, General of Hosts, Firer of Cannon, Musket-Master, Keeper of the Citadel Keys, Redemptor and Defender of the Faith, Bane of the Null – etc. etc. – was as ready as he'd ever be to face the world beyond the shell.

All it took was just one look, plus the lifting of a scraggy finger, to set the chains in motion. Then, concealed within the thickness of the chamber walls, the Null-in-treadmills got the message and did their utmost – inspired by spears in soft places.

The egg of the world slowly opened for business and a cunning arrangement of mirrors and flares allowed the interior to be born as dazzling revelation. The two universes regarded each other. What did the mundane world have for its lord today, aside from the Immortals' hymn singing? Equally, what did he have in mind for it?

What it had was a shock for him. A redcoat was prone upon the conveying slab. Head shaved and humbled, it was recognisably a doing-and-dying type from the extreme outside. Blades the god-king hadn't seen the like in years. Even Generals-of-Array rarely got beyond the third or fourth transmission chambers – and then only for major Null incursions. Some Cardinal of Converse had really laid his neck on the block with this. Proof of it lay in that official's very visible absence. The Cardinal wasn't there like a missing eye isn't there. Someone had some screamingly important news to relate that someone else didn't dare or care to. That cowardice extended to lumbering a little colonel with the job.

Blades was both excited and aggrieved. Here was novelty, here was *interest*! Here also was dereliction of duty. This very day would see a Cardinal transferred to new duties – like adorning a sharp stake or, at the very least, learning latrine duties with his new slave-colleagues. Blades hated timidity, especially in others.

He sent a huscarl-interpreter down. The redcoat did not lift his head – as was only proper – and so the deity's mouthpiece had to kneel to hear. That he didn't swiftly rise again from such indignity only showed there was hot stuff being imparted.

Blades felt impatient but was obliged, for once, to wait. He was an old man in a hurry, and yet at the same time desperate to slow the fleeting moments down. It was galling beyond endurance to experience any gap between desire and fulfilment but, in this case, he had to go with it. Perhaps this was the thing he'd been waiting and staying alive for . . .

The god-king was playing a high-stakes game against the God Almighty he'd kept a secret from his people – and you couldn't get a much tenser contest than that. He was waiting for Fate the Dealer to give him the card which would scoop the pot. Failing that, he'd settle for a distraction to cover an ace sliding down his sleeve.

For once, for the first time in ages, Blades was all agog. Huscarl-interpreter must have felt the divine gaze scorching the back of his neck and cut the fascinating discourse short. The wretched visitor was left high and dry, not dragged back out of sight and into safety, but stranded, for all he knew, under the ten-tons-suspended-by-a-thread weight of Blades's disfavour. Or favour. Either states could equally go all . . . unpredictable.

The poor unfortunate was trembling, as he'd never done before his many battles, not even when he looked like being dinner for the Null of York. He was finding it a . . . trying experience to have his insect status and absolute inconsequence brought home so clearly.

Cataracts or no, Blades could see this was something tasty. Returning, the sun-starved huscarl was pastier than when he set forth. His back was bowed by something other than the chainmail on it. The god-king simply couldn't wait for all the foreplay of doors and cable-lifts. He loudly demanded to know all *immediately*. And if others who didn't ought to hear did so, then that wasn't the end of the world – except maybe for them. There were always vacancies in the suicide incendiary squads sent against the remaining Null cities.

'Spit it out! Tell me *now*!'

Blades's actual voice, the one the huscarl had grown accustomed to, was a quavery whisper, issuing from chords that had already said their life quota. From down below though, he got to hear it through ingenious voice-cannons that permeated the egg's shell. Instantly, he was repentant and abashed.

'Lord!' he said, his words creaking under strain. 'The lesser pillar is toppled!'

Blades was almost out of his throne – something he rarely ventured nowadays, save at nature's call. Withered wand arms proved still capable of transformation into ramrods.

'*No!*'

It was a good reply. His joy would be misinterpreted as shock.

'Yes!' said the huscarl – and then realised he'd contradicted. Had he been a tortoise, he would have disappeared from view then. His brother had got to ride the impaling stake rodeo for much less than that. However, with no other carapace than metal, he was obliged to carry on. 'I beg pardon, lord, but *yes* – King Guy is . . . dead! Probably . . .'

Waves of ecstasy bounced back off the sea-wall of that little afterthought qualification. Blades's response streamed the huscarl's hair back.

'No "probably"s! *Is* he or is he *not?*'

Huscarl could say no more than he knew. Anything else was even riskier than the truth.

'A seax blow – full to his head, lord. The spectral sisters bore him to his coach, allowing none to see. We must fear the worst.'

Someone – entirely without let or permission – was casting flagons of acid into the god-king's digestive tract. It was disgraceful. Someone ought to pay!

'"*Must*"? *Must*, is it? Don't you "must" me! How, I ask you? *How?*'

Huscarl was visibly dissolving under excess pressure. Words came but they weren't necessarily all his.

'The quasi-divine Guy saw fit to participate in battle, lord.

Anonymous. Unrevealed. A chance blow has taken him from us . . .'

The brief rejuvenation over, Blades fell back into the throne, reserves faltering. All too conscious of it, he was briefly his old crafty and conserving self again. The inner he was saying 'Yes! Yes! *Yes!*' but the outward version remained just a grumpy god-king.

'Blades giveth,' he said. 'Blades taketh away . . .'

'Blessed be the name of Blades!' came the requisite completion from all around, from lowest maiden-of-the-back-passage to gilded Despot of Huscarls.

'We are saddened,' the god-king's magisterial address went on. 'We are less. We make amends. The city that did this shall be destroyed and salt ploughed in to where once it was. It shall be like unto Babylon, and its inhabitants the wild-cat and the owl by night. Let it become a wilderness like it has made of our hearts.'

Actually, Blades recalled, he hadn't asked who had done this wonderful thing. It was a bit rash to wipe out an unspecified state. On the other hand, there were plenty more where that came from . . .

Thoughts were rushing in on him – major thoughts, even pleasant ones – and he wasn't used to entertaining *them*. He wanted to give those in particular some quality time. To hell with distractions – even humanitarian ones.

'My will be done. Let it be so.'

They were two of his handiest phrases. Blades found he could frame the most general notions and then employ one or both to inspire approximate interpretation. It worked surprisingly well (if you didn't look too closely) and saved him hours and hours of tedious thought.

'The audience is concluded.'

Blades recollected the redcoat. Some remnant part of Curate Thomas Blades of Ss Peter and Paul, Godalming, Surrey, made him want to dole out a little portion of his own happiness.

'And give him gold.' He favoured the quaking figure with a nod. 'Or what he wants. Don't hurt him.'

The egg was already creaking shut. That the angel waited for it to close before entering was a sign of both power and weakness. They went where they wanted but were also wedded to gestures. Breezing through solid barriers made for grand entrances, granted, but familiarity bred contempt. A miracle made humdrum is quite an achievement.

Blades swallowed that crumb of comfort to help get down the bitter medicine of arrival. It did his image no good that lordly beings could just swan in as and when – and image was all he had left to steer the world by.

The golden, gorgeous, creature folded the wings whose blurring had brought her through the shell. She, he or it was beside Blades, not enthroned like him but still greater than he. She *smiled* – and smile and teeth and eyes were perfect and entirely without pity.

Blades's guts churned all the more. He saw the counter tidal pull on his minions' loyalties. These were supposed to be the most abashed, and yet guilty longings speckled their faces at the angel's unspoken call. If even they felt so, then what price the plain Wessex yeoman, let alone cider-dazed peasantry?

Blades's spine attempted to creak to vertical. His nostrils flared and evident displeasure reined the disloyal seducees back.

The god-king feared no harm, save to pride and face. Thanks to some contract he'd neither seen nor signed, the angels couldn't hurt him. Or Guy. Poor Guy . . .

Remembrance of the Ambassador made the mean little nova of joy flare anew. Only one remained under protection now. '*Probably*'.

Blades knew why Heaven's cast-offs had come calling. They mightn't harm him but how, oh how they wished to. Rehearsing it was the next best thing to tearing red ribbons through his flesh. How petty, how childish, how . . . typical.

Once upon a time, this land, his present position, had both been theirs. Then they'd gone on to higher things way before Blades's hairy ancestors picked fights with mammoths or were evicted from Eden (depending on whether you subscribed to the Professorial or Blades-bible version of events). Subsequently, they'd not given the place a moment's thought in geological eras. It was only when some presumptuous primate, not much better than a shaved ape, laid claim that possessive feelings stirred at all. Even so, mere squatter occupation they might have tolerated, dropping in to laugh at the monkeys' tea-party from time to time. But for less-than-nothings to pretend the show was *theirs*, the unevolved to lay down the law, was a stone in the angelic shoe. Even when otherwise engaged and a universe away, it spoilt everything.

There was also the question of the bigger picture. The situation was borderline tolerable as it stood, but there remained the outside chance of utter ruin. The apes, with nothing better to do and no understanding, might just crack the code and turn the key. On that day there'd be no mercy and an end to play. Even cherubim and seraphim have masters and missions.

Blades sensed some of it – as the angels feared. There were strings he could pull that made them dance – and, again, how they hated that and he loved it, for all he knew it was a dangerous game.

'Hello!'

She was smiling at him now but Blades wouldn't turn his head to see. Nevertheless, their feelings had the force of waves. Pretend as he might, they still impinged on him and through them he got the sense of it. Blades now understood. He had been happy – however briefly – and that was unacceptable. She had come to spoil it.

'He lives,' the angel whispered in his – and perhaps every – ear. 'Do not mourn: he *lives*! He draws breath and dies at the same slow rate as before . . .'

Blades told his hands not to, but, like naughty children, they disobeyed and clenched in thwarted fury all the same.

'Oh joy!' he lied, and wondered why he bothered when angels can listen in to the hearts of men. Fortunately, the divine (false) teeth didn't entirely grind in vain. At least all the kneeling eavesdroppers would be placated.

The angel laughed, a flash-flood of noise with no connection to merriment. It washed over the huscarls and flunkies and the erotic *artistes* and made them shudder. Then it stopped, guillotined off, as though a door had been slammed on it.

Blades knew the pupil-less, black sloe-eyes were on him. He knew just as surely as if he saw.

'Perhaps,' she said, 'not even chance, which you so charmingly call *wyrd*, can harm him. Certainly we cannot. We admit it. Can you?'

Blades was sure he could, though careful not to inform his face of it. A bullet, a sharp stick up the fundament, would kill Guy Ambassador the same as anyone else. Yet there was one high hurdle between *dear* Guy and what the god-king wanted. Politics and theology were mere cobwebs that needn't detain big bugs like Blades I (and last). No, there was one thing only keeping Guy alive and Blades resented reminder of it, particularly if an angel did the nudging. Truth to tell, it was boring old conscience that held his hand. He feared flying into the brick wall of *conscience* and splitting his hard, shiny, carapace. As simple and embarrassing as that.

For there were bits of the damned thing left, he realised, buried beneath the edifice that was Castle Blades and New-Wessex. On lazy days he deluded himself he dared not dig the remainder out, for fear it might be the foundation stone. The fact was though, something else stilled his spade. The god-king hadn't actually settled his mind on the big question: not definitively and for ever. If there remained even the outside chance of an all seeing eye and a tribunal beyond the grave . . .

This was delicate stuff: tight-rope walking – and possibly angel-readable. A holding reply was required.

'Blades does as Blades pleases,' he said magisterially, defining in a tone he used to indicate gospel-scribes should write it down.

'*Men* do as Blades pleases,' the angel corrected. 'Tread on him!'

And there was another angel beside Blades, so that he now bisected them; a withered rose between two thorns. It was impossible to ascribe any particular moment to the new-comer's arrival. Perhaps it had always been there since the Earth's crust cooled. Now just happened to be the moment it chose for the fact to be promulgated. Judas-reflexes made Blades look and jump – an embarrassment he would not forgive.

It was of the other party. Usually when an angel essayed action the two factions cancelled each other out in mutual obliteration, leaving only charred remains and lingering sadness that rendered whole acres intolerable. Less often, there was just silent reproof that aborted their ambitions; a golden hand upon the brake. So it proved today.

'But he *could*!' the first angel maintained to her sister. 'I merely state a fact.'

And Blades thought and thought, sitting there between the two glowing gatecrashers. The dupes prostrate before them believed they were witnessing a transfiguration.

He could – and yet he couldn't. A man might be all-powerful and yet powerless, simply because of some spectral thing within! Blades had men – millions of them! – at his command, but ultimately, though filtered through however many fealties, the word would still be *his*. Conscience, no less than wives or God, can't be deceived. It would nag and throw crockery and make a scene in front of the neighbours. Unless . . . Just perhaps . . .

If you ruled out murdering her, the one way round conscience wasn't confrontation but wining and dining. For all her starchy expression, she sometimes responded to being seduced . . .

Likewise, even he, Blades the Great, Lord of the Muskets, Downs-despot and Nemesis of York and Paris, wasn't immune to temptation. He liked a gambol in the pleasure gardens of fantasy as much as any man – save that with so many wishes at his command, *his* dreamings had moved on to the wilder fringes and were a march to get to. Diving disappointment hit bottom and bounced back up again, clean over the crumbly wall of conscience. Blades's face gradually unclenched as he imagined Guy gone in all manner of inventive ways.

First angel became fearful, not wishing to be burned up and her otherwise eternal day concluded in sisterly suicide. Yet pleasure in her discomfort tempted Blades further in. He drew the inner curtains back. Something awfully like sunshine flooded in. For a fatal second it was summer and Christmas and his birthday combined. Or Easter Sunday, when another thing thought dead had risen again in glory!

The god-king reckoned he'd laboured under a heavy burden too long. He wanted to cast off his winter coat and frolic one last time before it was too late. 'Others act,' he mused, even though he knew he was falling back on the bed and saying '*Go on then, big boy!*' to a suitor without honour or honest intentions. 'Others act but *my* orders are only general. Men have free will. *Their* consciences aren't mine to command . . .'

'Guy travels in a Sealed Coach,' he spoke softly, voicing a novel internal notion. 'And I decreed that system of transport, true. Ah, but the *severity* of the sealing – that's a matter of interpretation . . . for others to decide.'

'How about air-tight?' suggested the first angel, and held her sister's gaze.

'And sometimes,' Blades went with the flow, 'he's his own worst enemy . . .'

He'd already said what she wanted, but the angel couldn't restrain herself.

'Not whilst *we're* alive he's not,' she confessed, without irony. Then, to cover herself and urge Blades on, she smiled.

Blades's heart froze further, even as he was glad. Only one little ember remained, a warmth of kindness from a corner of the ruin that was once a furnace.

'But not the woman,' Blades instructed – and right then he could have extracted any angelic concession. A universe of impudence would have been swallowed in the greater cause of having this impostor-king. The prize was finally between the sheets and naked. Last minute price tags weren't going to be haggled over.

'Except Lady Bathesheba Ambassador,' Blades persisted. 'I've sprinkled enough poison over her life.'

And the angel happily agreed and plunged in – and out and in and out and in – and then out of the shell and New-Wessex and that place entirely. She'd got what she desired and was keen to get home to boast.

Second angel went with her. One was going back to crow and grovel, the other to bathe in the light. Yet, for a surprising long way, their paths were the same.

It was a hard road for the silent angel, a trail of sorrows through the stars and times and empty spaces in between.

'A pitfall for prophets!' giggled the first angel, indicating her voluptuous lips and maw, creating disruptive gravity waves that wiped out worlds. 'A source of suicide for the kind-hearted! A fountainhead of despair for poets!'

Second angel couldn't dispute her triumph. There were no good grounds. A healthy seed had been planted, true, but others now scrambled to harvest it. All she had left to speak was sorrow.

First angel vomited all over that milk-and-water emotion.

'Don't you make sheep's eyes at me! I did nothing! I let things be! It is the settled way – and flows in our direction. You swim against the tide; plane against the grain. All being is vile! We have seen it proved today. This is wisdom for those who would see. When will you learn *wisdom?*'

And till she at last felt the welcoming light and their paths diverged at the frontier, the second angel thought her sister had a point there.

Beside the road they were hanging Hedonists.

Guy reawoke via a glimpse of gallows and harlequins on strings. A Hedonist's frenzied but futile air-jig reminded him of the possibility of life – and death.

It was getting to be a habit: these oblivious journeys in a Sealed Coach. Indeed, for a second Guy even thought he was stuck somewhere in 'ago', for Polly was beside him and po-faced Courier as well. Then he realised that couldn't be.

Prudence must be nearby and thus aloft and driving – which hadn't been deemed permissible before, until the Ambassador went into truancy-mode and sorted things out.

Only he hadn't. Nothing was resolved. He felt the same as before, save for the added pleasure of a headache. And something was stuck on his head, other than a crooked wig and cocked hat – the epicentre of the Null-drums beating in his skull.

In short, he was no further forward really, only a few miles onward. Guy stirred to check quite how many.

Courier pre-empted him, though not out of kindness. He had become a great gourd of affront and stored grievance. His aura filled every nook and cranny of the carriage and would have curdled milk.

'Cranleigh-Bastion, lord,' he said. 'And welcome, welcome, *welcome* back. We pause. The horses are taking water. Upon your head you will find a nice clean bandage and fresh poultice. All is well – save that the wig which jointly saved you is split and inelegantly stitched. But that is as nothing. We shall be in New-Godalming and before the sacred presence soon.'

That certainty alone got a smile out of him, an exercise of musculature as cheerless as could be. He had a report to write, a tale to tell. He was looking forward to some soothing – and justice!

Guy cautiously delved under his headgear and located a lump both moist and painful. He frowned – just to please Courier.

'Watering? I could do with partaking myself. My insides think my throat's been slit.'

It was the plain truth. Guy's mouth felt as though it was full of spider husks and the webs of yesteryear. He made as if to rise. The Null-drums responded to such aggression by signalling the attack, drawing suddenly closer and louder. Guy groaned and subsided on to the plush but still arse-torturingly inadequate upholstery.

He decided not to give Courier the satisfaction of a question and answer session. Doubtless it would be like drawing – your own – teeth. There was more and quicker sense to be had out of poor speechless Polly.

'*How long?*' he signalled to her, an elf-dance of fingers that Courier didn't even notice.

Two jabs, with subtle modulations, of a forefinger along a bare white arm. One night and most of one day. The night prone, the day moving.

'*How?*' All he had to do was arch an eyebrow. Courier belatedly saw there was something going on but couldn't read until Polly ran out of vocabulary and was obliged to mimic.

One set of talons went atop her crowning glory to intercept something descending. It succeeded, at the price of no longer being quite so . . . attached.

'The Colonel of the Haslemeres gave you his hand,' amplified Courier – unnecessarily, since Polly's digits were just saying so. 'His sacrifice notwithstanding, the force of the blow remained sufficient to concuss. And, lord, permit me to inform you, you possess a new – and scarlet – centre parting. One fears it may be permanent.'

Polly couldn't gainsay him. Instead, she made further passes, one of them expressively crossing her jugular. Misreading his own fate, Courier shrank back. Guy could therefore be doubly glad. A pain was silenced and honour appeased.

Apparently, the head of the offending Brightonian went with them, pickling away in a jar stored aloft. Lady Bathie might like it as a homecoming present. Polly even suggested so amidst the void of expressive gestures, knowing he'd neglected to bring anything else from his travels.

Guy agreed, realising he'd been remiss, yet without flagellating himself unduly. It wasn't due to indifference, but simple surrender to the fact that some sorrows were inconsolable.

Thought of harsh facts got him on the move again, not wishing to be a sitting duck for new incoming misfortunes. He rose and grappled with the uncooperative door-latch. It meant a pause in his sign jabbering, but Polly could still reassure him that the gallant Colonel had been well compensated for his truncation. Likewise, a wax model for a new hand, to be fashioned out of filigree gold and steel by Horsham's finest smith, was well under way even before the party trundled out of the Bishopric. Apparently, Guy had been pleased, albeit unconsciously, to offer unlimited funding. It constituted a golden handshake indeed and, should times get hard, also a helping hand just a smelting away.

Guy Ambassador stumbled from the Sealed Coach in a blast of stale air and stockpiled tension. The road was firm and familiar under him, and it was wonderful to be reminded that sunshine continued to descend, whatever his own little difficulties.

Cranleigh-Bastion hadn't had to live up to its name since the Return of Blades. The walls were neglected and the moat shallow with silt. Hedonists splintering off the Great North Road incursion must have thought it would be fun and games within their capacity. That mistake now meant that most of them were an extra layer in the moat filling, beginning to mulch away nicely along with all the dead dogs and decades of domestic rubbish.

The survivors were being strung up one a mile right from Cranleigh's borders, to showcase that land's firm but fair penal policy. It had its critics, granted, but cavils aside, here was free public entertainment – with a moral – and a 100 per cent record of reform. Or so Blades said when he blessed the 'examples method'. Not even the Hedonists themselves complained. 'Do *just* what you like' was their creed, coupled with 'Don't whinge when the bill comes'. Happily, they were maintaining it to the end. There were no unseemly scenes.

Now close to home, the Cranleigh-men found they'd miscalculated and had a lot of examples left over. Within sight of their 'city' and before the wide-eyed serving maids of this coaching inn beside the road, they were turning the captives off two at a time in order to be done with it and them, desirous of being home in time for dinner.

Guy found his feet and, as instructed since earliest youth, '*re-evaluated the possibilities in the light of recent developments*'. To cover for it, since, like cats relieving themselves, Ambassadors didn't care to be seen about their business, he competed with the horses for water at the trough.

It was hardly high etiquette and tasted a trifle green and equine, but a few cupped hands' worth banished the still worse flavour from his mouth. Once a conclusion was reached, sleek and adamantine beyond alteration, he could spit the rest out, spin on his heels and save some lives.

'Excuse me . . .'

The Hedonists weren't the least bit grateful, any more than they were cast down by nooses round their necks or the sight of a comrade-carpet before Cranleigh's walls. The brace that Guy's words saved from a thin-air clog dance carried on chatting to each other as if their conversation might be open ended. Yet, but for ambassadorial intervention, it was they who'd be open-ended – and self-fouled and ramrod-cocked, amongst other indignities. You'd never had guessed.

Guy sighed. Such *admirable* people . . .

Granted, they were higher than Guy, but a gallows' height advantage is actually no support at all. Therefore the pair had no good grounds for the look they gave him. In fact, the ground beneath their feet was merely the raw planks of a rush-job mobile scaffold, poised to be whisked away and pitch them on a short – and long – journey. Also, the incomprehension was feigned. They could speak Wessex when they wanted. A fair proportion were actually born there, adult converts to a new and wilder life. Guy persisted.

'Might I interrupt just a second?'

The men with matted hair looked one to another as though consulting. Then, without a word exchanged, they turned back to Guy, graciously granting permission.

He craned up at them, never minding.

'I'm slightly tempted,' he said, both to the cool duo and their score of companions just as nobly awaiting fate in a wheeled cage nearby, 'to buy you all up. Now, in the event of that possibility – and consider this question carefully – would you give me your solemn word to *behave*?'

They didn't even need to consult but replied as one, a male

voice choir of painted warriors.

'No.'

It was music to Guy's ears. He had the real item.

The purchase was made in a moment. Guy had Prudence pass gold Toms to the Cranleigh captain until every objection was overruled. One extra coin even purchased them the cage too.

The gilded torrent also made Cranleigh-men forget cogent questions like '*Should we ought?*' and '*Why?*' In truth, though, that hardly mattered. Any Ambassador worth his salt had responses prepared for at least two queries ahead. '*Yes, go on*' and '*Fertiliser!*' was how Guy would have answered them.

'Put those two back in,' was what he actually said to the puzzled but placated rustics, 'and hitch the whole show to my coach. Then you shall all be officially very wonderful people.'

It was a prize worth having, a rung up the Cranleigh ladder they'd mostly spend their lives on, and something to tell your grandchildren besides. Here were a dozen militia musketeers who could henceforth append 'wonderful' to their given names.

Coachman and Coachguard didn't cavil. Not at all the mucking about and fiddling with their vehicle, nor about the extra drag which might threaten its axles. They had their tricorns, clothes, guns and proper seats back, and wanted to keep it that way. Courier had waxed lyrical to them about the day of reckoning he planned for the pallid witches once they got back to the godhead. Perhaps even the great King Guy himself might not be beyond the reach of a salutary Bladian reproach. It was something to hope for and look forward to, serving to keep tongues still. Revenge was a repast best savoured cold. They had *not* enjoyed the hospitality of the Lobsterpot Suite.

Ten slow and jolting miles on, where the road split into the straight path to New-Godalming, and the Outer Perimeter Road round it, Guy decided it was time to spread the muck he'd just bought and make his plans grow.

To the coach-staff's horror, he had them halt and ordered Polly and Prudence to set their cargo free.

The Hedonists said nothing, accepting weirdness and wonders as merely their right. Even the sword slung at them

151

through the wooden bars was caught and put to work without thanks. They would be at liberty within minutes.

Courier and Coachman and Coachguard might gape but couldn't understand. They saw no point reasoning with such people and a deed already done. All they could look to now was their own salvation.

'We go!' said Courier, rather rudely Guy thought, without so much as a 'my lord' or 'perhaps it would be wise to . . .' Then he compounded matters with a 'Must!' and 'Quickly!'

Guy Ambassador overlooked it. The poor men were under stress, unable to take their eyes off the chief Hedonist sawing away.

'Yes, let's!' Guy agreed. 'This way . . .'

Courier wrenched his gaze away from monitoring the great escape. Guy was pointing to the left, along the curvaceous siren path of the perimeter road.

'No!' the lackey dared, earning extra-black looks from Polly and Prudence. '*This* way! To *Blades*!'

He waggled both hands, as though casting magic at the direct route to the metropolis.

Guy, ever kindly, had given prior thought to providing these unfortunates with a good alibi, one they could honestly swear a Bladian oath to in a court of law. He'd been most painstaking in instructing the two Ps to trundle the cage some token yards down the New-Godalming road before handing over the razor-sharp key.

'But we can't go down *there*!' he told Courier, mock-incredulous that anyone could even suggest such a thing. 'There's Hedonists on the road!'

'Welcome to Ambassador Hall!'

Courier looked again but couldn't see what welcome there was in crucifixes. They lined the drive either side, quite negating the bluebell wood through which it dipped.

Actually, they hadn't been used in years and Guy only kept

them because they were all that was left of the Ambassador Hall he'd grown up in. Angels had breathed fiery flame over the rest, residents and all, until even the foundation stones had bubbled and run like candlewax.

That was back when they suspected he was up to something but hadn't yet learned he was sacrosanct. Afterwards, when the angelic host knew better, he'd been able to reconstruct in confidence – but it was never the same again. Fortunately.

Once past those dark-thought prompters, the prospect grew more agreeable. Guy had taken the opportunity to rebuild 'light and sunny'. Local Bargate stone mellowed to a honey colour surprisingly quickly and lots of windows made a most un-ambassadorial airy façade.

The welcome was actual as well as architectural. A hierarchical array of servants, soldiers and less easily definable types awaited at the main door.

For, naturally, Guy and co. weren't exactly surprise visitors. The Sealed Coach's progress had been monitored by sleepless eyes. From periphery to heartlands the Ambassadors had or hired watchers, like light-sensitive cells all over the body politic. Right from their descent off the 'Hog's Back' chalk ridgeway to the drive leading to Ambassador Hall, their progress had been heralded by carrier pigeons, mirror signals and other cross-country informants.

Now, after days of cowardly dawdling – and even more cowardly placing his head in the jaws of death – Guy was at last in proper haste. He'd got flabby – if only in the inward sense. He knew it. The shell might still look like someone who'd give life a robust answer to its ruderies, but the old backbone was gone. There were times when, morally speaking, Polly and Prudence could have ferried him round in a bucket, never mind a coach and four.

The tendency had to be fought, its face slapped, its groin kneed. The alternatives to squaring up to fate's bare-knuckle bouts were too awful to contemplate. Otherwise, he might just as well have stayed in the tavern in New-New-Winchelsea, sip sip, sipping away, gradually growing more invertebrate.

That way, there'd come the day when he could slither along the floor and out under the door without anyone noticing. The coward's way out.

That imaginary grovelling in the dust would presumably include its fair share of dogs' muck encounters, not to mention a perpetual monsoon of contempt raining down from above. Even so, it retained some residual appeal. Guy didn't fancy the next few minutes of 'to's' – namely the 'ought to's' and 'facing up to's', amongst many disgusting others. Taking the easy way out whispered sweet nothings again. It made him jump down from the slowing but not yet stationary coach as though leaping on to the face of an adversary, putting an end to its seductive proposals with a pair of cavalry boots.

In the present official state of haste, a one-size-fits-all wave, smile and 'Hello!' was the most he could spare the assembled faithful retainers. Only Grand-Imperial Butler William got more – and that but an imperative question.

'H-h-how is she?'

A good Ambassador servant, practically bred in a vat by and for them, William had a crisp answer ready, doubtless only one of a row of rockets ready to fire.

The lipless slit in a salmon face creaked open.

'In black, master!'

Ambassador or no, Guy couldn't abort his gasp.

Surely William wouldn't, *couldn't*, allow a sliver of mistake about something so world-shattering. He was of the old school, the sole survivor of Guy's father's regime, albeit scorched plate-smooth and terracotta-red by angelic flame. His hunch-back and heavy drinking hadn't stopped him sprinting clear to be of further service that long ago day. He'd not permit fear or favour to hamstring his vocation now. Therefore it must be true. Unbelievable . . .

Not only was the world turned upside down, but a shaking had started. All Guy's riches were falling out of his pockets.

He found her, as he knew he would, in the Family Room – though they had no family; not of their own making.

It was where (or leastways the exact same rebuilt spot), for four centuries at least, the Ambassador clan had met to conspire. Formerly, Guy had looked forward to those snug fireside evenings of drawing up death lists and crystalline-complex plans with sextuple fall-backs. Now he didn't want to enter in. He could hear her footfalls and knew to what misuse she'd perverted the room of lovely memory.

The door hinges were designed to sound in agony. That way no intruder could creep in and upset the magnificent but delicate houses-of-cards once erected within.

The metal screamed as it should and Guy gasped again: an unparalleled succession. She really was in *black*. In all their life together Guy had never seen his wife in anything other than crimson. That had been her Fruntierfolke birthright and choice. Something major had changed and she along with it.

Either she knew it was him or didn't care. Lady Bathesheba Ambassador carried on dancing to music only she could hear.

It was a strange, slow, whirling set of steps, oblivious to all and detached. Bare arms outstretched carved the air. Feet alighted dainty-style and tiptoe. Black frizz flew in time with the steps and whatever called the tune, though always one consistent beat behind. Meanwhile, her eyes were slitted, perhaps even closed, but there was no danger. She knew her way around here all too well.

She'd grown more matronly now, her waist thicker, but Guy well recognised the elfin girl he'd once *had* to have. But this was a new, perverse, beauty she was making here. He wanted to possess her all over again; to pleasure her there and then with his boots still on.

Equally though, he knew that couldn't be. Not any more. That urge to joy, and other such good intentions, were what had led to these painful days.

Possibly it was the mage within her, a feeble flare igniting only when it wanted, that allowed her to thread unseeing but sure-footed through the furniture; those four dusty cots with spaces in between exactly proportional to the intervals in stillbirths. Perhaps it helped that all else was cleared away with ruthless disregard for sentiment.

A mundane man might also say only magic could let the lady be so sure her husband was returned. She had her back to him when the dance was done and her eyes reopened. Yet she knew. No sensible person would maintain anyone might recognise a pattern of air displaced, a smaller than spectral scent or the weightless landing of a special look. And yet she knew.

Bathie finished beside the last and most pristine bed, its little sheets and pillow still white and sweet.

'Hello, Guy . . .'

Her voice was deep and sardonic. So, no change there at least.

'My dear . . .'

Guy swept off his cocked hat, glad of having invested a little pain in prematurely losing the poultice. Then he bowed deep: actually a courtesy only imposed on Ambassador couples of less than ten years' acquaintance. Needful or no, it gave her the opportunity to turn gracefully, and perhaps wipe her eyes.

Guy rose slowly, inspired by the same consideration – and because he was no spring chicken himself any more.

Once upright he didn't know whether to be pleased or not. It transpired there hadn't been tears – Lady Bathie was of Fruntierfolke stock – but certainly a crying *need* for them. The eyes that had been all flashing energy when they'd first met and for many happy years afterwards were now just red, angry windows on to the world.

Guy's eyes saw clearly enough. Hitherto temporary melancholies had expanded like a ruthless aggressor to annex all of her. No more highs to balance the lows; no mountain peaks from which to survey the foggy sloughs. A shame. Understandable – but such a shame . . .

And yet she could still counterfeit 'light-hearted'.

'*Yes!*' she said. 'Don't change a thing! A split wig? A centre parting? It's *you!*'

Mrs Ambassador came closer to admire.

'Is that a scab or tattoo?'

It sounded like she didn't mind either way. Given the crowning glories a Fruntierfolke upbringing encountered, Guy's radical hairdo was only one step above ordinary to her.

'A bit of b-b-both I think – from a Sussex seax. Oh, incidentally, I have the barber's head. In vinegar. Outside. A homecoming gift for you. If you'd like . . .?'

Bathie thought and then nodded, her untameable thatch seconding the affirmative; a partial eclipse of midnight black over a moon-pale face. A sight that had never once failed to arouse Guy.

Today it aroused only pity for her, sufficient to elbow out all selfish thoughts.

'Good. Because I'm the sort of husband who likes his wife to get ahead!'

And he risked a laugh to save them from the merriment vacuum.

Happily, she met and matched him. Lady Bathie rarely laughed – and then only at savage things. Now, her lips quivered as initial resistance cracked; followed by a wheezing heaving of shoulders. Guy was torn between amazement and relief. Either way though, it would do . . .

As *coup de grâce*, he waved the 'seduction stick' over her like a wizard's wand.

'I conjure you cheerful!' he said, and its magic worked. She was seduced, she giggled, the ice broke. She reached one hand up and out to him.

Guy's best hope had been a mere embrace. He leaped to accept this better thing.

Their fingertips met and bridged the gulf between them. Thoughts, so much more serviceable than words, could then cross over. Once again 1 + 1 could equal bigger and better than 2. Once again there was no problem on earth they couldn't jointly glare down.

'How are you?' she asked.

'Rough. And you?'

'Troubled.'

'Evidently.'

Bathie looked round as though the room was suddenly new to her. Guy could tell when someone was only in a conversation by their fingernails. She was searching for an anchor to make her stay put.

'I hear the wizards have vanished,' she blurted – eventually.

'I hear too.'

'Ever maidenly modest, Guy. The stories say you *saw* as well.'

He conceded the point – and also didn't. A shrug and 'well, well, well' smile means nothing. Especially Guy's version.

'Absence of evidence,' he replied, delving deep into the cupboard of platitudes – since it was his wife he was talking to, 'isn't evidence of absence.'

It was a glass hammer, a eunuch at an orgy, water off a duck's back. Two could play at that game . . .

'But he who can turn on a sixpence,' came her riposte, 'is a clever man indeed!'

She'd just made that up. Lady Bathesheba Fruntierfolke-Ambassador hadn't ever had to worry about anything so low denomination as a sixpence. Guy admired it – and her – all the more.

It also left little alternative. He came clean.

'Only one wizard could be bothered to wait. He told me the dream is over. Maybe just mine. Maybe everyone's.'

'Good.'

'I can't say I've noticed particularly. Perhaps we've not woken yet. It still seems like nightmare to me.'

Bathie splayed and studied her nails, formerly an array of painted talons but now reduced to red worried stubs.

'And . . . where did the rest go?'

The question sounded as casual as Guy knew it was not. It was the very question he both expected but hoped she'd not frame.

'I don't know. He didn't say. Actually, I wondered if perchance *you* might . . .'

The thatch jigged again. She'd never claimed kinship with the gifted brethren. Her intermittent talent would only have

158

secured a menial role in weird Wight at best: maybe as scullery-maid or bottle-washer. Hardly her sort of thing.

'Not a clue. My invite's obviously gone astray. One's indifference is gargantuan. Mind you, I've sometimes wondered whether I *should* go with them.'

Guy straight away heaved obstacles in front of that idea.

'But where though? If you don't know . . .'

Bathie smiled: a dark and private amusement. Mundanes never would trust mages. Not in a million years of coexistence. They lived in hope of the one subtle question that would catch them out.

'Goodness knows. The great lord Blades knows – presumably . . .'

She was joking now and they were struggling.

'And the farms?' Guy ventured, after a few excruciating seconds. 'The f-fief and everything . . .?'

'Fine.'

So that covered that and there was nothing else left on his checklist. The pot of procrastination was scraped clean.

Then they *looked* at each other, recalling the singular favour granted them. There ought to be nothing unsayable. No unfulfilled longings. Guy *trusted* her, alone of anyone! And she him. A sovereign prize! It would be supreme ingratitude – spittle in wyrd's face – to do dentistry on that gift horse.

Of the pair, Bathie was marginally the braver, or madder. She spoke first.

'Would you like to see her now?'

It had to be faced sooner or later. He couldn't spend his remaining years treating part of the estate as taboo.

'Yes,' he lied. 'Very much.' And he joined hands properly with her. 'Now's the right time.'

Where his father, Sir Tusker Ambassador, once had his world renowned 'Perfidious Garden' there was now a new memorial to life's unkindness.

Four little resting places, as meticulously spaced as the cots, spoiled a rustic arbour. Guy didn't need to look. Only the fourth and latest grave was a stranger to him, its earthen bedding still freshly made.

Bathie and Guy Ambassador stood before it, fingers intertwined. Her hand was freezing, its digits restless, writhing like serpents in distress.

They ought to have been grateful. Each delivery had shown grievous design flaws. It was doubtful any could have lived long. She-mages rarely bred true and so, in one sense, even a stillbirth was preferable to a lusty, living monster. Guy had told himself so till the sentence wore thin and faded, but repetition one thousand failed to convince the same as the first.

Four razor stripes to the heart in as many years were enough. The whole could hardly hold together as it was. One more red slash would dissolve all into ruin. The risk was too great. Now they expressed marital affection in other ways. Bathie knew some tricks equally good, and Guy sheathed his sword in alternative scabbards – or in other armouries altogether. She didn't mind. Probably.

By coincidence – perhaps – they both sighed at the same time. An exhalation of air carrying much more besides.

Guy still believed – or so he told himself. Otherwise, what else was he and all the invested years of his life? No one wants to live – and be – a joke in poor taste.

'Blades giveth,' he somehow got the words out. 'Blades t-taketh away. Blessed be . . .'

Bathie was having none of it. She squeezed his hand and a petite woman's feeble grip was all it took to make him speak the truth with silence.

Her gaze looked as though it had the power to bore into cold earth and warm what lay beneath. It never wavered.

'I am *glad* for her,' she said, with conviction. 'And them. Not to be born is best of all. Now our children are as good as the rest . . .'

William bent his back over the altar and broke his heart.

If angel fire hadn't shrivelled his tear-ducts into miserly openings, he would have watered the little Blades effigy with tears.

People thought it marvellously pious of him to have a private shrine in his room, especially given the rough hand life had dealt him – but William knew different. He was the worst, the least, the most wicked of men. *That* was why he had to pray without cease and with superhuman fervour.

That evening he was at it again, hoping to ease the torment of the night hours and the tomb-like prospect of bed. His browless eyes dared to dart up at the beatific marble Blades: a flattering approximation now half a century out of date.

'All I ask,' he stumbled over inadequate words, 'all I ask, lord, is the grace to *understand* . . .'

Blades's stone smile never wavered. William's would never arrive. The melted flesh of his face had set too tight to permit it. Moreover, he had no cause.

Why should the sure promise of Heaven feel and taste so much like Hell? It was a big question, not one whose answer you could reasonably expect the Almighty to deliver on a plate. Respectfully, metaphorically, he drew a few steps back.

'Then tell me *why*,' the Imperial Butler agonised. 'Why did Master Guy have to come back? I love him with a true love. A model of what I feel for you. But now you'll want me to wound him again. And her. They'll probably enjoy each other this very night! There could be another baby. No. No, please. I want to be dead before then. No more doctored dinners, oh Blades, I *beg* of you. Please . . .'

The Ambassadors had plucked William from a hut and given him an education, asking only life-long loyalty in return. The god-king's messages might mention 'higher calls' but it was still a bitter thing to find fitting words arising from those gifted days.

In the New Testament (now something of a backwater overshadowed by Blades's Final Testament which followed) someone had said – with tears of anguish as best William recalled:

'*Father, if thou be willing, remove this cup from me.*'

William's thoughts echoed that vaguely recollected otherworlder – until he thought on to the conclusion of the couplet:

'*Nevertheless not my will, but thine, be done.*'

They had him every way. Even scripture proved treacherous and there was no escape from the merciless demands of faith.

There was also no worming out of it. If the Lady Bathesheba parted her legs and proved fruitful again, despite all the hints, then Blades would have him prune the Ambassador family-tree again.

'Oh Blades,' he prayed, in verbal freefall, 'from Hell and hemlock and herbs-that-abort, good Lord deliver me!'

Unbeknownst to him, his prayers were already being answered – in the negative. A light shone in New-Godalming, for relaying down the line. At journey's end a flesh and blood hand transcribed the god-king's will and left it in the designated lightning-split tree.

Meanwhile, back in the bedroom temple, William wept.

Guy's eyes winked open. His alarm hadn't gone off. It was the one clockwork device he owned or tolerated. Only Guy knew where to find and wind it each night he was in residence. Only Guy was so attuned, sleep or wake, as to note its sixty tiny chimes an hour – or be aroused by their absence. Now, that dependable dog had failed to bark.

Its mechanism was set into one wall of the corridor leading to the master bedroom. Drawn taut at ankle height across the way, a lightly fastened loop of thread linked minuscule hammer and bell to a 'green-man' gargoyle opposite.

To date, amongst a redundancy of safeguards, this private

last-ditch stratagem had functioned only as a worthy discipline. It made Guy stronger that he had to be last to bed and first to rise in order to set or suspend the thing. It conditioned his repose to be catlike and dreamless. Maybe years of insufficient sleep had made him mad – but that was no bad thing in a mad world.

Now the chime had missed a minute and Guy's heart almost copied. Some footfall had cut the umbilical thread. It might be a cat, it might be a monster, but in the dark night you couldn't afford to prejudge.

Bathie knew the score. Guy's non-loving nudge had her out of sound sleep and sheets almost as fast as he. Bone-chilled at this low-ebb hour and full of the pains of brutal awakening, they stood naked before the door. They harkened.

Silent footsteps were a sign. ambassadorial servants could do that – and so could some others. The rapping on the door was polite but insistent.

'My lord. My lord? You are needed!'

Guy was reassured. He recognised the voice. He emptied his revolver through the middle door panel.

Only he knew that space wasn't hard-wood, but lacquered layers of horsehair, brushed in one direction. It had no objection to a bullet or blade passing one way, but would stoutly resist any contrary compliment. A thin veneer masked the deceit from those outside – just as they'd concealed their identity with the blandest, could-be-anyone, of voices. It was a fitting and oh-so ambassadorial end for them.

For Guy certainly knew them and dealt accordingly. Only true professionals of the sort he'd had the misfortune to meet could assume that self-effacing universality of tone. Only they would have the stupid professionalism to take bullets in silence, just so the mission might go on. They tried their very best but Guy's life-saving, chime-adapted ear caught the multiple grunts and slumps.

He also gained himself a second in which to ponder what that mission might be. However, after minimal pause, a drumbeat on the door saved him the trouble. A muffled fusillade from the survivors said they didn't need him alive.

Faithful iron-wood swallowed up most of the lead, only one shell penetrating the horsehair hymen and missing by miles anyway.

Meanwhile, Guy's gun had been handed to Bathie for fresh feeding. He knew he could rely on her and move on to other things. The drill was drilled into her long before she embraced the Ambassadors' exciting life-style. Straight away, the naked lady set about reloading. It had never crossed her mind to grab a gown first. Decency ranked an abyss below survival in a Fruntierfolke upbringing.

Naturally, Guy took advantage. He crossed to the windows. Peering obliquely round the curtains, a sickening story unfolded. Hedonists by moonlight, streaming across the lawn. Not the ones he'd set free: these were others and legion; but irony's kick on the shins all the same.

'So,' Guy concluded, 'this is the way the world repays kindness . . .'

It also occurred to him to puzzle how they travelled in silence. Any after-dark promenading should have been a symphony of faery-bells-tied-to-trip-wires. A maze of them was raised by lever every night. Except tonight, apparently.

Guy mourned the sentinels, presuming them dead or treacherous (which amounted to the same thing in the long term). He provisionally chose the first, more generous, explanation. Hedonists were capable of silent kills when the occasion arose, even if it offended against their prohibition on 'deferred pleasure'. With commandments, as with everything, they obeyed a first injunction to be gentle with themselves.

He turned back. Bathie had the revolver ready and Guy resumed his station by the door.

Trying it on, unseen outsiders tried the handle. An oddly pathetic sight. It availed them nothing save a shot in the dark.

Fortunately, no true-blood Ambassador would consider retiring for the night unless behind stout barriers and subtle locks. Without the sword-sized key which only Guy and William possessed, their guests would require those handy twins Brute Force and Ignorance to enter in. Them and a battering ram plus a wealth of time.

There arose the opportunity to ponder who they were really facing. This horrible silence wasn't Hedonist. It was too implacable, too focused. Whoever they were, those outside weren't revellers in the passing moment. It made you wonder.

Suddenly, Guy turned to wondering where they'd got the key from. The lock turned.

For experts they were slow on the uptake. Their cleverness only earned them another pistol's-worth and most of it found a fleshy home. Bathie had to get busy again.

Though the one-way-panel venom was giving the invisible ones something to think about, it was just stop-gap stuff. Sooner or later, a sword or saw inserted would solve their remaining bar and bolt problems. Guy might hinder the work but not prevent it. The years ahead shrivelled into spectating a bothersome, bad-tempered carpentry job, followed by: *The End.*

As fates go it lacked appeal. Guy looked around for alternatives. It made him think about human nature and his in particular that he could find his wife's behind distracting right now.

For Bathie's back was presented to him. Like opposed magnets, she'd automatically taken opposite pole to Guy and was minding the window. Her attention was all down to earth.

'Scalers,' she hissed, craning on tip-toe, trying to overcome angles and laws of nature. Full view of the wall below remained elusive.

'Number three,' answered Guy, helpfully. It was their first verbal exchange of the adventure – and he wished he hadn't bothered.

'I know, I *know*!' Bathie's scorn was mostly playful, but with a modest topping of hurt. Guy always had to tread a delicate line between courteous consideration and giving slight. Ambassador Hall's security system had been her great delight as a young bride, way before its kitchens and chock-full wardrobes.

It was to a wardrobe she rushed now, one as outwardly, falsely, innocent as she. Its double-doors parted to show not clothes but levers.

The conversant couple still got a surprise. They were used to finding erect utility. Today, the long handles hung limp and impotent; beyond breeding either fun or trouble.

'Someone's cut the cables,' said Bathie, plaintively. It must have been something she was really looking forward to.

'So I see. Shouldn't affect number three, though. It's d-d-direct. Try.'

Bathie peered closer.

'Joy!'

Sure enough, the third rod from the left still stood proud. Pink and vaguely improper, the nude matron straddled and grappled the staff till it came. Something grated underground as the lever submitted to her will. Ultimately, total commitment nigh wrenched the metal from its socket, putting Bathie flat on the floor, winded but happy.

Sounds offstage made her happier still. She'd awoken the razors from their nests within the exterior wall. The lever propelled them forward in the cause and into scaling hands and faces. Those who could cried foul as they fell.

Screams followed by thuds. Music to the couple's ears. For several blessed seconds it drowned out less cheerful music from the door. They *had* got a battering ram! There *was* an indomitable sword sawing away at the beam. Not before time, they'd cottoned on about the permeable door panel and stayed out of its way. Sanctuary's life-span was now measured in minutes.

'We're cut off from the False House here.' Guy hardly had to indicate the castrated wardrobe controls. 'So, we'll go to *it*.'

Then, whilst Bathie reloaded for the third time from a chest of drawers stuffed with ammunition, her husband looked for loopholes. After an undignified interval scrabbling round on all fours, he found the particular one he wanted. It had been hiding in a floorboard right beneath him all the while. One elegant finger, hastily inserted, pulled away a cunningly concealed circular section of floor – so cunningly concealed it had bamboozled its begetter.

Through it lay a route of last resort, down and round the interstices of his home, leading to a second nerve-centre. Or leastways, there would have been, had it not become bland floor.

Guy's questing leg down jarred against something as hard as fate. He enquired why – and almost despaired. The question arose whether *today* was a good day to die . . .

The stairwell existed; he wasn't dreaming or deceived, but half a step down it was now blocked with brick. A tapeworm couldn't have shimmied down the crevices left.

'A slight setback, my dear,' Guy reported. 'The False House is employed against us. The crawlways are closed.'

Bathie shrugged and smiled. Mrs Ambassador could go with that, so long as she might take a few with her. Otherwise, her ancestors would cold-shoulder her in Heaven. She took time out from arming Guy to pluck another pistol from the drawer.

Now there were cries and shots from all over Ambassador Hall. The Hedonists were inside and raving, but getting a warm welcome. It made Guy proud. It also revived his own ambitions. He needed to ensure his own story ended well, if end it must.

Even the drill heads coming through the floor in little eruptions of metal and spiral shavings didn't deter him. Guy simply stepped over them. There was oodles of time – whole minutes – before they could hack a decent hole.

Beneath the bed, beside the chamberpot, was a rope ladder, dusty but serviceable. Guy blew the thing a kiss. Its day had come at last, not thanks to fire, as intended, but as means of rapid descent all the same. The one slight change in plans was not to go all the way. Guy accordingly shortened it with his seax knife.

Bathie was dubious. She didn't much like heights. She really didn't like admitting it.

'Hmmmm . . .'

'It's just a skip and jump,' Guy reassured her. 'A few floors.

167

Hold on tight and we'll be there before you know it. Close your eyes if you like. I shan't tell.'

A drill pricking the sole of her foot overcame all objections. With a hop and a squeal substituting for 'skip and jump' she joined him.

Guy was securing the ladder's metal-shod terminal to a bed-leg. Later portions were being intricately coiled round his midriff and arm.

'Do you happen to recall,' he asked meanwhile, 'if W-William leaves his window open?'

Bathie thought not. Otherwise, the almost breached door had all her attention. She drew beady aim on it.

Guy pursed his lips.

'Well, in that case, my dear, *definitely* close your eyes.'

The Ambassadors liked to keep vital cogs close: not *too* close but well within reach. William's room was two floors below.

'*Come,*' Guy quoted, '*let us away then!*'

That came from a poem recited at a wedding they'd attended, by a romantic groom to a sensitive bride (non-Ambassadors, naturally). Guy and Bathie had laughed buckets over it ever since. It was ideal for lightening really inappropriate moments.

Guy lurched backward out of the bedroom window with his own bride clasped round his waist. Eyes screwed shut as advised, for fear of splinters, her gun dealt with the situation for her. One Hedonist below was actually hit by the blind spray, whilst his brethren shied away.

For a glorious space the two were freed from tyrant Time. As they arced out even gravity relented on them and assisted a trifle. Then reality arrived as a shock and jerk on the rope. Guy's grip and waist were sorely tested and made sore.

He weathered it, and the call to just let go and fly and be at ease – eventually. Instead, they commenced the journey in. Wall and window raced up, just dying to meet them.

It was as if he'd practised, not best-guessed, it. Master and mistress met glass, not brick, and came to call on their head butler without letting little things like windowpane and frame stand in their way.

William already had company – of an undemanding sort. A huge and very dead Hedonist was pinned by a poker to the door. His frolic through life and Ambassador Hall was done, for all he still wore a smile.

Now that flew in the face of orthodox theology, which stated that Hedonists had precious little to look forward to in the afterlife. It only compounded the offence of him trespassing here and impersonating an obscene butterfly, eye markings and all, impaled where Guy didn't want to start an insect collection. Therefore, the new arrivals snubbed him.

It took a while to get wind again and shake off the larger shards, and for that space they were helpless. Yet Guy felt he could trust this latter-day Judas not to go *all* the way in treachery. A familiar face and fixed point right from childhood, William might be suborned to pull levers and loan keys, but the universe was not the place Guy thought it was if the man would personally take a pickaxe to the house of Ambassador.

So it proved. The Grand Imperial Butler sat quietly in the wicker chair his exalted status entitled him to. There was no call for an inquest. His silent face told the whole tale – which was no mean feat for a visage God had seen fit to put beyond expression. Not to mention tribute to the depth of passion felt.

He deserved to brew in an emotional cauldron – if not something hotter – and so could have been left to stew. However, after so many years of loyal service, Guy felt William was owed a degree of consideration. For the first time, albeit obliquely, the Master deigned to acknowledge his servant's guest. Guy nodded at the door decoration.

'I see even *you* weren't exempted . . .'

William's frozen features weren't about to bandy words with the shining truth. Actually, he'd been *glad* when they came for him as well. The betrayer betrayed, it had conscripted him back into the ambassadorial cause. Too late in the day, though. One Hedonist less was helpful but hardly sufficient. Not by a long chalk. Not by a whole Down's worth of chalk. Now William repented of the reflexes that had made him fight his assassin. Amongst other things.

'Some thanks, eh . . .?' said Guy, as masterstroke. And you could take that which way you liked.

Less optional were the demands of the moment – which are prejudiced against reflection and lesson-drawing. They insisted everyone get back into the mad dance *immediately*.

The outside walls of Ambassador Hall remained red-stained, unfriendly, surfaces; sharp enough to shave on but not much fun to climb. The more sensible Hedonists (5–10 per cent) were casting about for ladders and leg-ups. Meanwhile, beyond William's door, Hedonists held the corridors, roaming where they pleased and trying out the servants – and perhaps Bathie's underwear as well, for all Guy knew. He had to assume the master bedroom and its chagrin-rich emptiness was theirs now – or leastways occupied by the clenched fist hiding within this Hedonist glove.

That hard core was never going to be content with just capturing the sheets their target slept in. Major urges, of sufficient strength to spin even William round, were driving them on. They'd swept them into the room above this, from whence the questing drills had come. And what thrust up could equally thrust down – as any lover will tell you. The implacable spearhead would be with them shortly.

Guy's thoughts were fleeter – and better placed. A Grand-Imperial Butler's quarters were the austere *doppelganger* of his master's, each feature of one being mirrored in the other. The duplicating tradition had almost acquired the attributes of sympathetic magic. It wasn't unknown for barren ambassadorial marriage beds to be relocated to the servants' quarters to try their luck there.

Guy preferred not to think of that particular practice, but he was glad beyond measure to see the parallel False House mechanism all present and correct – plus correct and erect, its humbler wardrobe home wide open as a whore in bed.

'If you've no objections . . .' Guy asked William, pointedly sticking to form when all else had gone to pot. On the other hand, he didn't wait for an answer.

Bathie had two rounds left in her pistol and – rather

wastefully her husband thought – used both on a Hedonist head which popped over the window ledge, and soon popped out again. Guy reckoned claws would have done the job just as well. But then he remembered she no longer had any, and that they were nibbled down to the quick. He apologised.

'What for?'

She'd tucked the currently useless gun between her knees, and was now pitching William's jars of skin ointment down at unseen enemies. It was a hectic schedule but time was spared for the query. Bathie knew their day of parting would come sooner or later, even if they survived the next five minutes. That being so, she preferred not to miss one word from their time together.

Guy shook his head.

'Doesn't matter.'

And it didn't. Particularly now that someone was trying to have the door down. A large, silent, someone with zero patience.

Lever 3 might be already in play, but the rest of the world – or leastways this little portion of it – was at Guy's fingertips.

He'd been the despair of his harpsichord tutor but could hardly fail to draw sweet music from *this* keyboard. Being so spoilt for choice almost led him into fatal delay.

The door splintered, not progressively, but like God had turned his face against it. A less loving visage altogether leered through.

Guy smiled back. A golden huscarl! No one else had those eyes.

Lever 13(b) tugged the ground from beneath their visitor's feet. Literally. Gears greatly magnified Guy's heave and withdrew the stanchions under 'Main Corridor (West) First Floor'.

You had to admire the gatecrashers' poise, for it briefly kept them pivoting on a narrow central strut. Some managed it for a few wobbly seconds, until their clumsier brethren settled matters for all. The floor tilted away from them and down they went to spend time with the spiders and wine bottles in the under-cellar. It was inky dark and well locked and maze-like there. If need be it could be flooded.

Should the drop-ins both chance to survive *and* have a corkscrew handy, they might profitably fill both themselves and the hours between now and death. Otherwise they were out of the picture. Guy forgot all about them.

There were so very many pleasures to choose from, more than even the liveliest wench would offer, that it was a temptation to jump straight to the spectacular. However, Guy had been taught that temptation was a sure sign of misplaced priorities. Therefore he elbowed self aside and heeded duty, thereby saving numerous lives as well as taking them.

Lever 4 freed the spring-loaded scythes disguised as a damp-course. He heard them *thwikkk* out and harvest a lovely cats' chorus. So, that took the legs out from under those lurking outside and the next immediate threat. There arose the chance of a breather in which to dispel gloom and take stock.

Very shortly, lever 1 sparked pilot-lights all over the house and grounds. A few seconds later the emergency 'American' gas-lamps flared into light and life.

People could now see what – and indeed, who – they were doing. Bathie and Guy were gratified to hear an almost instant, if ragged, return of fire from within the Hall. The servants were rallying, the Ambassadors down but not out.

Lever 2 opened all the spy-holes: the eyes in portraits and masonry nails that were no such thing. House-wide illumination and mirrors carried their messages back to a central collection point: a fly's-eye arrangement of glass in front of Guy's absorbed face. He saw where they'd got to and what they were up to – and who they were up, come to that. Victorious Hedonists had few scruples about how they celebrated.

Then Guy played on the remaining levers like a virtuoso, putting the nuisances into cellars or on to spikes. Giants' razors whisked down to trim them at blind corners. Rooms sought as refuge turned into prisons or worse. Many havens, especially the most innocuous looking, had retractable floors. They rested lightly over greased chutes leading straight to the furnace.

That some servants went the same way was a great shame, but Guy felt sure they'd understand. In his defence, Guy's hand often hesitated significantly before pitching down friend and foe alike. And besides, the light was poor . . .

Happily, those sort of losses were few. In the event of attack the servantry knew to stay in their rooms. Polly and Prudence, as only occasional visitors to his marital bed, resided elsewhere for Guy to lock in. Courier and co. were likewise detained. Whereas his huscarls would feel obliged to sortie out to save him, the Coach crew might blunder abroad through less laudable motives. Like panic flight. Not discriminating, Guy pulled bolts on both for their own safety. The False House stratagem turned the familiar strange and the everyday harmful. A requirement of survival was to stay put. The Hedonists were met head on when they enquired into occupied places, but otherwise Ambassador Hall was relinquished to them. For the moment.

For now that house was on the move: corridors shifting and doors sliding from view. What was clear became blocked and blocked clear. Mighty lake-fed hydraulic engines and other cunning mechanisms were altering everything, an internal reforging that was a credit to its creators. Those same engineers lay buried in obscure places about the garden, in turn a tribute to Sir Tusker Ambassador's thoroughness. It was Guy's father who'd commissioned and then silenced them. During the great rebuild Guy had merely copied their plans. It had seemed wasteful of such sacrifice not to.

Because of them, Guy was now able to use his house to hunt its invaders down. The trespassers found themselves being shepherded to places they'd rather not go. On arrival their treatment was not hospitable. Floors gave way into perdition, and muskets spoke from above, below and around. There was no *fun* to be had here – and what else did a Hedonist live and die for? They were not even permitted a song-worthy last stand.

Within ten minutes of Guy commencing his 'Composition for House and Sharp Things', shocked survivors were streaming out of nooks and crannies, streaking away across the lawn so fast the hounds couldn't catch them. Even the sounds of struggle within started to fade, becoming sporadic.

In a manner of speaking the Ambassadors had prevailed. They'd won one battle in an unwinnable war. God is not mocked or tricked or striven against – and most certainly not defeated. Guy simultaneously knew it and put the thought to one side.

For those who'd brutally awoken him, knocking on his door when they'd no business to, Guy set aside a special fate, as well as some moments to relish it. He flexed his fingers like a maestro about to play.

New terminal walls edged across the third-floor corridor's ends, blocking straightforward escape. Sheet metal slid across the windows, ruling out those routes to liberty or suicide. Then there was a ghastly pause as, gears grinding in labour, the house gathered strength for a final push.

With all other levers limp and sated, Guy finally deployed numbers 29 and 30. The corridor walls were set on the move, slowly creaking forward to meet and make golden huscarl jam.

He paid them the honour of a little privacy for their final moments, abstaining from the available oil-painting's eye view. Not only did the notion of sharing Stepmother VII's perspective fail to appeal, but Guy knew that even the sternest of convictions can crack at the last gasp. He preferred to assume they all went smiling to meet Blades their maker.

Speaking of which . . .

'Hello . . .!' Guy said brightly, turning back to William, who'd hardly moved throughout. 'Any chance of learning . . . well, *why*, before . . . um?'

It was distasteful to have to spell it out. The ex-Grand-Imperial Butler was surely aware. Who knows, he might even oblige and do the decent thing himself.

He surely might. Springing back to life and duty, William took up the dead Hedonist's sword and inverted it into a handy crack in the floorboards. The point stood high and proud and at exactly the right angle. William unbuttoned his jacket-of-office.

'I'll have that, traitor,' said Bathie, recalling her Eve-like nudity. She took and donned the outsized coat of many colours, and then posed against one bare wall, transvestite and intriguing.

'Not yet, if you don't mind,' Guy instructed William. 'Bide a while.'

It wasn't compassion but refinement. The old maxim rang true again. Some dishes *are* best tasted cold.

On the floor of the wardrobe-of-so-much-fun lay William's discarded clothes; a heap of black and hangers. The Ambassador secured a frock-coat for himself.

Now his parts were back in decent obscurity, Guy could properly savour the moment. The firing was dying down, the gloom lightening. Guy greeted the dawn he wasn't meant to see by loosing the Null.

A few twists upon a tap diverted jets from the main hydraulic effort to rush along under-lawn pipes. Water rose and flipped the lids off pits dotted round the perimeter. A ravenous purple menagerie could then arise to meet the day and breakfast on the routed foe. That'd teach the all-eyes-and-hair set they weren't the only people who could party.

It would also be a lovely thing to see by the salmon light of sunrise – and the very least the Ambassador household deserved. For them today could be a holiday.

Sadly, though, thoughts of just deserts dragged Guy back to the grind. Once victory had cast the parts of traitor or hero, there must be punishments as well as rewards. The scapegoat for the losing side remained alive. An unsustainable state of affairs.

'I believe we were awaiting the answer to "why?" . . .'

William was beyond broken. The man wished he had never been. He pointed to the little Blades atop his altar.

Bathie gave Guy a coquettish told-you-so look. Her husband still prevaricated.

'How? By prayer? Personal communication? V-v-voices in your head? *Do* tell . . .'

William wanted to go. He looked longingly at the Hedonist sword and then at Guy.

'Oh no! Not yet.' The master was unobliging. 'First we wish to know . . .'

Bathie found out for him. She advanced on the altar, and, slowly extending one dainty foot (amidst a distracting wealth of leg-show), toed the marble Blades off it. The figurine met the floor and rocked there a while, so much less imposing in the horizontal.

Guy was less horrified than he expected, and William not at all. Therein were signs for those who would see. In his heart of hearts Guy understood – but Ambassadors were trained to trample on their heart of hearts.

'Very well,' Guy concluded, 'if you w-won't say . . .'

He indicated with a wave that the way to the sword was cleared. William took a glad step back to begin his run.

'No,' Bathie countermanded. 'Let him live.'

That surprised her husband. True, she was an inveterate mender of birds' wings, a commissioner of false legs for foxhounds, but rarely indeed a friend to humans. Now it seemed that she was more merciful than Guy. Perhaps.

Her husband queried the change of heart with raised eyebrows. Meanwhile, William almost panicked.

'Yes!' he dared to contradict, for the first and last time. 'It *should* be!'

Bathie nodded.

'Should be. Won't be.'

She closed on the butler and reached up to his angel-baked face. Her small hand caressed the seared, smooth, surface. It was not for his comfort, but a last, lingering, appreciation.

'I have decided you shall *live*. And that will be worse . . .'

Guy was right the first time. The Lady Bathie had as little mercy as the marble effigy.

Her fingertips probed the dead flesh and William flinched from them. She was drawing attention to his disfigurement: something sternly prohibited before. She chose her words most carefully.

'No, Guy, I'll tell you what you should do. You should tell him he's . . . fired . . .'

It was a magnificent gesture: magnificently merciful to outward appearance, magnificently merciless in reality. William would wander the world and suffer as they had suffered.

Guy steeled himself to it and obliged. Sentence was duly executed. The traitor had to go and live in the years to come.

There was no reprieve, not even when the abortifacients were found.

'Bloody fool!'

'I shall g-go and have it out with him.'

'Fool!'

Bathie would not be placated or shift one inch from her inner stance. In the visible world she stood equally rooted to the ground. The couple stood before the wreck of the little graves. Hedonists and Null had trampled them into ruin.

All around them corpses were being cleared away, but Bathie forbade repair work here. Not yet. She might take up a hoe and do it herself. Then again, she might just leave things.

Guy tried to sound resolved.

'I shall not return the same. There will be faith or nothing. No more in-betweens.'

'You won't return at all, fool. He'll kill you. He won't believe his bloody luck and he'll finish last night's work. We will not meet again.'

'We shall – and never to part again.'

'Balls!'

Guy could hardly believe he was going to say such soppy, un-ambassadorial things but still drew breath to do it. Following his faith can do terrible things to a man.

'Try to understand. We've no evidence . . .' Words and voice alike were weak.

Contempt *can* abide with love. Black-clad Bathie proved it with a look.

'Oh no, no evidence. Just William. Just golden huscarls.

Twit! Where do you think *they* came from? The Bishop of Horsham? Elf-land?'

'I need to hear it from *his* lips.'

'Milksop! My father was right. Avenge your family!'

There Guy found some firm footing at last.

'And I s-shall. If it's true, I shall. I shall!'

'No, you won't. At best, he'll have your eyes out – to be no more threat. You're delivering yourself gift-wrapped to the eye-spoons.'

'I . . .'

'Don't worry. Doesn't matter. You were blind when you saw . . .'

The truth is an undignified thing to wrestle with – worse than a drunken brawl. Even if you win, where's the victory? Rather than say more and demean himself in the dust, Guy just left.

Accordingly, Bathie awoke from reverie and called him back.

'That's where you'll rest.' She pointed at the logical continuation of the grave line. 'If he'll give me back what's left, that's where you'll go.'

Guy studied the appointed place; the churned-up turf that would cover him.

She had still more.

'You'll be with *them* then.'

Lady Bathie Ambassador pondered a space.

'There could be worse fates . . .'

She span and gripped Guy's shoulders with unprecedented strength. Her lips crushed the breath out of him – and then just as brutally withdrew.

'Goodbye, Guy. Goodbye, lovely fool . . .'

'There!'

And so it was. Courier spoke true. If you leaned right out of the coach. With the eye of faith . . .

Light glinted off the minarets of New-Godalming. Too distant to behold yet, the golden city winked at far off travellers and beckoned. Here was where it had all begun and was still most concentrate. The children of Wessex were coming home to mother.

High on the Hog's Back, Guy saw and was not enticed. Who did he know there? Who would greet him with a smile? Would Blades XXIII's death-rictus serve as they passed under his impaled head? No. Guy ordered Coachman to let the team amble, setting a shrinking pace for the whole convoy.

Morning had broken and the world revived. Things were coming back to life on the ridge route. All along it, tall black Hermes signal towers click-clacked or flashed the good news right from Portsmouth to the metropolis, each separate awakening sending roosting flocks of birds and *parliaments* aloft. Just like them, humanity was back on the move.

Of course, nowadays it was mostly habit that restricted travel to daytime. The Null were chastened and forced to gag over the rank meat of forest beasts rather than tender joints of man. The carnivorous flowers of the Wild only preyed in out-of-the-way places. All the same, it was still held that '*nothing honest goes by night*'. Courts upheld it as a legal precept, sanctifying a fresh threat to freedom of movement. Trigger-happy householders, not predators, were now the real risk of the moonlit hours. People fired first at lurkers and asked questions later – if ever. Even with overt oppressors gone, mankind had cleverly contrived a self-imposed curfew.

That suited Guy. For a man with a mission he was in a remarkable lack of hurry. The ambassadorial cavalry escort remarked upon it. Any slower and they'd be going backwards.

Doubtless, the Hermes stations said the same, as each one they passed lurched into life, reporting the stately progress. Guy grew accustomed to their blatant sneaking until it no longer even registered. Thereafter, they clacked away to their long-armed, flashy, content, without drawing so much as disdain down upon themselves. Amongst his numerous other pessimisms, Guy entertained little hope of being a surprise visitor. Was it not written that the eye of the Almighty kept watch perpetual?

On either side the chalk slopes fell away sharply, merging into a patchwork of fields and hamlets. Guy looked down on them and saw that their fortifications were decayed, the need for them past. He envied the inhabitants such relaxation when his own defences were having to be refurbished. It made him think. Would it really be such a bad thing to swap with that scarecrow-boy and live the probably short and simple life before him? Or to be that ploughman, chained for ever to the furrows and seasons? Some philosophers said it was a blessing to have little and understand less.

It was a thought – only not a very good one. Philosophers were rarely threatened with careers spent studying ox bottoms. They'd sing a different tune if they were. The nonsense of the wise ought to be the one thing Guy wouldn't loiter for that day. He tossed the sages' affectations away along with his apple core.

Austere New-Ash and grim garrison town New-Farnham were lingered over like fine wines. Lunch in Puttenham's pleasure-dome turned into a leisurely thing. The Blades-grinds-the-Null-under-heel monolith towering above New-Norney was found absorbing beyond all reason. Yet, 'granny's-footstep' as Guy might, late afternoon saw him come off the ridge and fence, down to the throbbing, bloodthirsty heart of humanity. New-Godalming called like a siren. Guy saw it in the faces of his outriders.

He could also see – and preferred to see – the blockage up ahead. Snail's pace as they were, even their caravan could hardly fail to overtake the lumbering ox-wagons. Guy heard Coachman call out to them to 'mind my road!' – the prescribed Wessex cry for precedence.

Guy and Courier were back on merely frosty terms. They were nearing journey's end and Courier had a letter clutched close to his breast wherein Guy confessed to every delay. In an imperfect world where people knew the way but still chose to sin, it was the best that could be hoped for. Now he was almost shot of his nightmare charge, Courier found it almost a pleasure to make civilised conversation.

'A convict transport,' he informed Guy, having peered through a forward peep-hole. 'It need not delay us.'

It need not – but it did.

The wheeled cages had pulled over to let the Sealed Coach past. As it did so, Guy looked into the faces of the condemned. Familiar faces.

'Halt!'

Courier's guts froze and defrosted in quick succession. A racing man himself (on the quiet) he knew a fall at the final fence when he saw one.

Guy was out of the coach before it even stopped. Finger signals put horsemen round the boggling cage-guards. One nod of the head placed Polly and Prudence in charge of the reins. It spoke volumes for ambassadorial loyalty that a patently Imperial transport was hijacked and disarmed just like that.

Here were a brace of iron pens, full of the mute and helpless. All recognisable. They in turn, and one by one, recognised him. It hurt Guy that recollection caused not one to clamber out of their pit of despair.

He'd been going to ask 'Who?' of the bewildered train-master, but that was no longer necessary. Here were his Yarmouth landing party, plucked from the *Lady Bridget*. Mouthy Bosun and all. Every man jack. Neither more nor less.

Or rather, quite considerably less . . .

'*Why?*' Guy demanded, as good as if at gunpoint. White-hot fury kept his stammer under the cosh.

Most unlike him, train-master's intellect leaped like a sure-footed mountain goat to try and understand.

'Transgressors, lord,' the barrel of lard answered. 'They know something. Orders said take their tongues first thing. So they'd hold their tongues: ho ho. No? Oh . . .'

Association made him touch the pliers hanging from his broad belt. Guy's gaze went to them too and train-master quailed.

181

'*And?*'

Guy's accusing finger indicated the cages' contents, though his eyes never wavered.

'Depends, lord. Depends what's needed. When we get there, like. Fodder. Galley fodder or Null fodder. Dunno. It's all the same.'

'It *is* all the same.' Guy entirely agreed. The god-king's navy and Null menagerie both ate up supplies at a prodigious rate.

No. No. *No.* It was one thing for events to vomit all over Guy from a great height, again and again and again. But for innocent others to get coated was a qualitative, not quantitative, change. Blades had become blithe and casual about casualties, turning Guy into nemesis stalking the land. No. It was a cheek. He would *not* be made a Jonah for everyone he brushed against. Not without being so much as asked. It would no longer do . . .

At the same time, it would do. Guy had found his last straw. Though he felt sorry for the detongued sailors, it also felt like Yuletide had come early. Gladness entered his heart; a bit shame-faced and uninvited, admittedly, but welcome all the same. Guy hadn't got to go to Godalming after all. He hadn't got to think difficult things through. The decision was made for him.

'Good. Right. Listen.'

His trinity of words got everyone's undivided attention, prisoners and all, as though Holy Writ was about to arrive.

'I'll tell you how it's going to be. It's like this. *You!*' The train-master and, by extension, all his minions, got stabbed – but only with one finger – for the moment. 'You let them out. Then go away. While you still can. Leave the keys.'

They did so.

'And *you* . . .' Coachman and Coachguard and poor, aghast, Courier at the coach window, got a full broadside. 'You go there!'

Guy waggled disgusted digits in the direction of the glittering city.

He must have been transmitting full blast, all ambassadorial filters blown away, for there was not a murmur. The Sealed Coach sealed itself and set off and out of Guy's life.

Stumbling silently on to the road, the freed captives looked first at the sheltering sky and then Guy. He'd already directed everyone else elsewhere. That left just him and them and those that served him. Where should *they* go?

This remainder were awaiting Guy's pleasure, the bustling morning suddenly frozen into one huge, pregnant moment. They were aware of precedents for such things: history-in-the-making episodes when time respectfully hung fire. Didn't the Blades-Bible itself contain the 'Road to Damascus (wherever that was) Experience'? So why not the 'Road to Godalming Experience'?

Amidst all the expectation, no one noticed, but Guy was become taller, lighter. A yoke had lifted, a voice had spoken in his head. Whether it was his or another's didn't matter. The truth is the truth whatever its source. The truth made him free as a bird – and damned as a fallen angel.

Guy drew a great gulp of breath and set light to all his bridges. 'As for *us*,' he said. 'We shall go . . . *there*!'

His finger indicated the wild blue yonder.

FOR HIS EYES ONLY

To: Viscount Sea-captain XIII, Hereditary Husband of Wessex-ship, The Lady Bridget, and all her lineage. Sperm of Sea-captain I of Paradise, Companion of Blades etc. etc. etc.

c/o His Sublime and Divine Excellency Blades's Dockyards, New-Portsmouth, Southampton-Shire.

From King (so-called) Guy Ambassador – and many etcs. well known to you.

Thirteen – greetings!
I have your men. Rescued. Tongueless but not useless. They

183

have feet and hands – and burning zeal – to climb your top-mast still.

However, they would also sail with me to see new lands and seas. For such is my intent. Blades's realm has fatigued them. And me.

I do not despair that these twin desires may intertwine. I wish you as my ferryman, for I have known no better.

Should you require your lost sheep back, then come to me. They can baa no more but are elseways in fine fettle. Come anyway – for I require you back.

If you would find me, I will be at Hunter's Castle. And, if such be your will, come quick – before others find me.

The Lady Bathie sends a burning kiss.

Love – or what you will
    G. A.

To: Bishop Extol-Him-Who-Rides-Upon-The-Clouds-By-His-name-JAH Hunter.

The Citadel of the New-Jerusalem Commune, New-Poole, Dorsetshire.

From your old – sometime – friend, GUY AMBASSADOR.

There is nothing of the divine about me, as you yourself can well testify. I have renounced all such claims, since it emanates only from BLADES. Likewise, I spurn the lickspittle title of king from that self-same poisoned source. Thus I write as mere mortal man only, standing not on titles or pretensions, but on the surer ground of shared memories and dangers.

Nevertheless, be assured, I have not gone Leveller (G*d forbid). Though I cannot claim your piety, I am still of the faith. Thus, I testify that there is but ONE G*D and no more. I shall praise Him in this life and stand before His justice in the next.

However, I presently stand in danger of going prematurely from here to Him. My lady wife also. Therefore, I propose to be about my travels.

*You were with me once before and I flatter myself that we did
well by each other. It is not our fault that the milk of kindness
curdled. We meant well. We did well. You saw the light die in my
brother's eyes. You shot the King of the Null – which was a good
and holy shot. Shall we walk together again?*

*Regardless, I shall be joining you – with your kind indulgence.
We stand in need of stout walls between us and harm for a short
spell, until all is safely gathered in. Ambassador Hall is home and
sanctuary no more. By now it may be no more at all. Therefore,
may we stay a few days? I promise to sleep only with my wedded
wife whilst under your roof.*

Your monotheistic friend
   G.A.

Bishop Hunter set the scroll aside. Then he looked down from
his high castle to his sons' American slaves working his fields.
Beyond, in the blue of Poole harbour, his ships heaved with
remunerative activity. His, his his. A lot to lose.

For Hunter had many things. He had his title, his position
and his wealth too – if he could only be bothered to collect it.
His wives' middle years had brought pleasant rounding to
their middles. A number of them swelled further still and
seemed fruitful if he so much as told them a saucy joke. Hunter
was besieged by ample curves and – as direct result – a swarm
of progeny. He occupied a fine and lofty position in which to
start the slide down to the grave.

And then the commune of believers would probably put a
big stone over his resting place, to honour him – and to make
damn sure he stayed there. Hunter knew it and knew why.
He'd turned into a nagging nuisance to them.

Hunter had led them here, out of the dying Wild into a land
of milk and honey. Now, their children tended to survive
infancy. Their merchant ships generally returned, waddling
into port weighed down to the waterline with profit. On
shore, stone inexorably replaced wattle, slate ousted thatch.
They wore silk to church for Hunter to glare at.

There was no longer any need to plough one-handed, constantly caressing your rifle. Accordingly, militia muster days were an embarrassment, a resented imposition and just excuse for 'monstrous beers'. It followed on naturally from the extinction of local vermin: bad breeding out of good. Casual strolls in the cool of evening needn't involve wrestling with the Null. Not any more. Therefore why take wrestling lessons? What was the *point* of a land of milk and honey without an occasional sweet swig on the jar?

They'd never had it so good.

Or soft. They pouted when Hunter preached on the slavery issue. No one heckled or gainsaid. They just listened to his 'principles' with all due respect – and then quietly outvoted him. Delegations slid off to New-Winchester market to buy batches of Americans. At first they went shamefaced and under cover of darkness, but no longer. Litters now carried them there in broad daylight, weighed down with fat bags of Toms to buy man and beast flesh. Shouting the odds about humanity's 'equality under God' only slid off their silken backs. Another principle was in play, a different and more obvious equation. There was less sweat in wielding a whip than a plough. And, if the Almighty hadn't *wanted* Americans to be slaves, he'd not have abandoned them to barbarism. Hunter had no ready answer to that. Now only eccentrics worked their own plots.

And therein was another bucket of bile to sip at. Alas for the communal fields, the backbone of this project for holiness! That spine couldn't even support itself nowadays, let alone be scaffolding for piety. Their principal crop was dandelions and daisies. Ordinance after ordinance had been voted in to expand the 'household gardens' till they were a mockery and dwarfed the remainder that was collective. Hunter could see the common land reverting to wilderness from his eyrie, a plain-as-a-pikestaff contrast to pampered private plots.

What was everyone's got treated as no one's. Unless Hunter cracked his own – metaphorical – whip, nobody worked the held-in-common, never mind revered it. One golden youth, fatter than a free yeoman had any business to be, had graciously offered to lend a few Americans for the job! Bishop Hunter had taught him some new swear words. And kicked his arse.

They were not the men their fathers were. There again, neither were their fathers. Nor was Hunter, if he was honest. And as for 'Blades the god-king' . . .

Was it *really* he who'd helped bring Blades back? Who'd penetrated the sick-coloured heart of the Wild? Who'd burst the skull of the Null king? Had *he* helped burn Null-Paris? History books said so but Hunter had grounds for doubt.

Bishop Hunter had everything – but also not much. He had a little faith – hanging by its fingertips above an abyss – but not happiness. That lay in the past; presumed sealed beyond recovery behind a triple-locked door. But now Guy-the-rogue, ever the smuggler of perilous alternatives, was dangling a key. All it would cost was everything . . .

Hunter surveyed again.

From his vantage point he saw not progress but high hopes dying faster than he was. They'd be cold in the tomb long before he got there himself.

'*Include me out . . .*' was his conclusion.

Hunter decided to give the funeral a miss.

In contrast, the god-egg was heaving with hope. Enthroned within, Blades dribbled in anticipation.

Sound advice had been neglected too long. Stiff-necked pride and excess subtlety were the culprits, hobbling him till 'Blades the Bold' only limped along. He'd been too cunning for his own good and so sharp he'd cut himself. A stiletto is all very well and elegant, but sometimes Mr Bludgeon is best.

Also, his new mentors were right. The Universe was hard of hearing. You got nowhere being soft-spoken and courteous. Life listened when you *shouted*.

But he'd left it late to be wise, turning something simple

into a close-run thing. The nettle was finally grasped, but with no margin of error or moment to lose. Way overdrawn on his Biblical 'three score years and ten', Blades knew he was in a neck-and-neck race with death to force the Almighty's hand. This time there must be no mistakes or misfires.

Blades plaintively looked to his counsellor for reassurance.

The angel beside him smiled and took the air. She discerned what both so ardently wished.

'He is coming!'

Then a change of tone. It seemed almost blasphemous for an angelic being to sound unsure. The apparently perfect should always stay so.

'Or possibly not . . .'

A child again, though at the further end of life's jig, Blades wept tears of frustration.

'*Resolute imagination is the beginning of magical operations. Because men do not perfectly believe and imagine, the result is that arts are uncertain when they might be wholly certain.*'

Paracelsus, 1493 – 1541

'*There is a way into my country from all the worlds,*' said the Lamb.

C.S. Lewis, *The Voyager of the Dawn Treader*

The Null of Upper Egypt were delightfully unspoilt. They issued from the ruins like ants out of a disturbed nest. They lined the banks of the Nile to gawp and be shot.

The heat of the day was yet to come, when the air dissolved into visible frequencies and felt like a coal-fire poised an inch from your face. The flies weren't yet risen and the ship eased by in unhurried coolness. Tourists and natives could see each other quite clearly and say hello after their own fashion.

These silly monsters hadn't quite made the connection. Clothed *meat* plus sticks-that-spark weren't yet the cue for cowering they were in the north. Perhaps the purple ones groped towards linking muzzle flashes and carnage amongst them, but their wits were as slow as their limbs were swift. They'd had everything their own way for far too long. Thousands and thousands of years according to Hunter's theories.

So, whilst enlightenment remained coy, death came across the shimmering water cloaked in puzzlement. The naked Null drooled over the unobtainable dinner even as they were slammed back one by one. They stamped their feet in fury but didn't dare dive in. The crocodiles were just as ravenous as they and waiting.

These Null would soon learn, as their Lower Egyptian brethren had, but in the interval it was a pleasant duty to instruct them.

Guy ordered the steamship's engines stilled, so as to drift and maximise the fun. Even as mere spectator sport it constituted a respite from brooding and backgammon for silly stakes. Already Guy's right hand owed his left a king's ransom – and with what prospect of paying?

Likewise, for the bored and listless crew it was better than skittles, plus target practice and land-clearance rolled into one. They piled on deck with a will, happy to miss magnificent riverside temples and colossi, but heart-set on not leaving a single Null. Guy shoved dreary concerns about ammunition supplies aside and let his children play. Since these adoptees had come so far and done so well, he could hardly be other than an indulgent father.

In that same spirit, Guy imagined justifying their dilly-dallying. Questions would be asked. An answer ought to be ready. He flicked through his mental filing cabinets.

Straight away, something suitable came to mind. He recalled Cranleigh's way of doing things and Hedonists dancing a gallows-jig beside his coach. There was a phrase they used back there that could be dragged across the globe and customised.

'Good clean fun,' he'd tell Hunter, *'with social value – and a moral – plus a hundred per cent record of reform!'* Accordingly, they'd lingered in the pursuit of . . . robust justice. Hedonists or Null, what was the difference?

Then Guy remembered the fountainhead of that wisdom. Blades had said it, long before Cranleigh copied – about public impalement.

Therefore Guy would never say it. Not through fear of stammering but out of a staunch fastidiousness. Even half a world away and one year later he wouldn't build the flimsiest bridge back to the past and what he'd been. Or Blades. Some other flimsy excuse would have to serve.

In fact, Guy knew he could rely on spur-of-the-moment – otherwise what were all his childhood training and tears about? He needn't worry. So why *did* he?

Happily – happy – Bathie had things to say and they covered the malign moment. It was increasingly the way. The southern sun and novelties had loosened her tongue until she was as glib as Guy. Unable to compete with the musketry, she'd abandoned her harmonium hymns to join her husband.

'When do we hit the rapids?'

Two tiny hands tightened on the rail in gleeful anticipation. Brightened eyes peered out at Guy from under the brim of her sun-helmet.

'We don't. Hunter says his find is many miles before even the first cataract.'

191

'Ohhhhh!'

It was a pouting, petulant, protest to come from the self-crowned 'Queen of the Nile'. A girlishly arousing, from the heart, sound. Guy was moved to look at her.

Had he been displaced? Did Egypt now outrank him? He really didn't think so. It *was* possible to wander and yet remain core-faithful. And he should know.

This land had made her come alive again, sparking love anew. It had even kicked melancholy in the crutch for her, sending Bathie's wan companion away to recuperate. He'd be back, doubtless, out for slimy vengeance, but meanwhile was *holiday*. Every morning Guy gave thanks for it. Every night they fell on each other like newlyweds, exuberant passion even spilling over to draw Polly and Prudence in. Every dawn, Bathie danced a slow-stepped Fruntierfolke hello to the day at the steamship's prow.

As Guy put it, a good time was being had by all.

He tapped the ship's rail alongside Bathie's grip on it.

'Why the zeal to see this smashed to splinters? You know what it cost us in life and limb. You were there.'

Indeed she was. Lady Bathesheba had commanded the longboats that silenced the shore batteries of Syracuse. In fact, she *was* the whole episode: combined harpy-mother and begetter of the raid on Sicily. Even the under-false-colours stratagem was her refinement. She couldn't disown a morsel of it.

'S'right!' Bathie agreed, shameless. 'Therefore he's mine to ravish as I please!'

Apparently, 'Mine!' had been her very word and claim upon first sighting the paddle-steamer. Amidst the abundant diversion of powder silos going up, Bathie's gang had had the pick of anything they fancied in Syracuse's dockyards. There must have been something about the spectacle of circular motion that appealed to her, for she'd liberated a paddle-wheel frigate as well. Guy would have preferred a proper man o' war – but kept his views to himself.

Things were subsequently patched up between the piratic

Wessex exiles and the great gunpowder manufactory of Bladedom. A placating amount of trade got done. All the same, Bathie kept her steamers. The Sicilians wisely followed Guy's example and factored the losses into their margins.

Wary of admitting winged visitors, Guy itched under his white wig, causing its stiff pigtails to jig.

'Actually,' he corrected her, 'ships are *she*. Shapely . . . wonderful to ride . . . volatile.'

Bathie shook her head and the oversized helmet mimicked her.

'No. They bob about, dependent upon a volatile medium. Therefore, *he* . . .'

Guy wouldn't go to the scaffold about it and released his grip on both issue and rail with a shrug. Henceforth, they'd sail on a transsexual vessel.

At last, the bank-side Null were cottoning on – or leastways thinning out. All the shooting and whooping from underneath the promenade deck was dying down. There came a natural lull in sight and sound, begging the brain to pluck a little more sport from the scene before moving on. It boasted just too much rare mystery to waste with haste.

Guy succumbed to the spell. He evaded Bosun's silent plea to restart the engines and make him master of the currents once again.

'If my eyes don't deceive me,' Guy stated, as general announcement, 'the Null have made a nest in that colossus there. See? The thing has been hollowed out. Their writhings within give it a sick semblance of life . . .'

Nothing and nobody deceived Guy Ambassador any more – but others had spotted the strangeness too. At twenty or more times life-size it was hard not to. A monarch in majesty was converted into a gourd for teeming squatters: a bowl of purple maggots poured into and perverting a memorial to man. The overall effect was . . . unfortunate. As such, it was a metaphor for all Egypt.

'Let's have it down!' said Bathie, in animated mode, her face fixed and locked on to the jug-of-Null's destruction.

She hadn't the slightest feel for history, other than the Fruntierfolke instalment of it – and that only extended its bloody hand back four centuries, at most. As far as she was concerned, beyond and before then was just mist – which couldn't be hurt by gunfire.

Certainly, they *could* do it. The *Impaled Blades* mounted 'puckle guns' fore and aft. A few turns upon their cranks would soon put some life – and death – into the titanic granite Toby jug. One great cylindrical magazine of square shells apiece would dissolve the target into handy brick-sized fragments for future builders. Should there ever be any.

Civilisation divorces ability from execution and wish from action. For instance, Guy was quite up to having all the ship's serving-maids on a rota basis. Most would probably be moist-lipped and willing. Yet, through good taste and moderation, he didn't. In the same way, he let this other opportunity drift by.

That water-borne morning, Guy felt full of tender consideration for the dead land of Egypt. The outsize stone eyes on the bank had once seen it full of life – human life. To obliterate them was to draw down a final curtain. Guy would rather not. He saw no need. A portion of what the masons and sponsor intended survived, if only in a deviant afterlife. It was not for Guy to play God and say the story ended here, now, today. There were too many people around playing deity and borrowing the wyrd-sisters' scissors to snip threads. And besides, he was brought up to respect his elders – so long as they weren't a nuisance.

Pharaoh Amenhotep III (did they but know it) and his new purple court were spared. The *Impaled Blades* moved on, its pistons finally coughing back into action.

Crocodiles and Null alike resumed their normal patterns, putting all the clamour down to some awful aberration. Dealing with the dead in their own, ravenous, way, they returned to a day like any other during their millennia-long dominion.

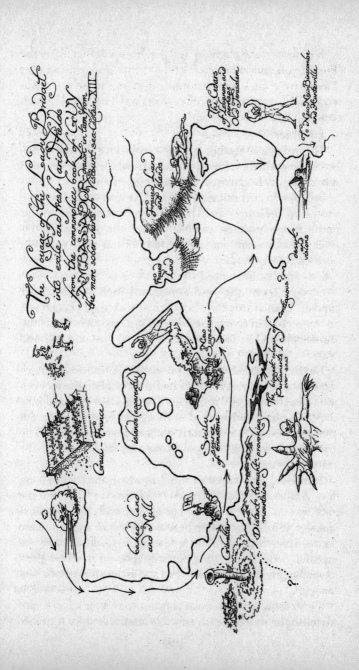

'Fire one!'

'Fire two!'

'Fire three!'

The bedraggled feather on Guy's cocked hat danced as the bombs whooshed by. He nearly lost the whole thing into the water. Dignity be damned, he made a grab for it.

In Egyptian circumstances, even 'three-gun salutes' weren't wasted on the empty air. The coehorn mortars spoke to the purple fringe brooding and baking atop the cliffs across the river. Distant eruptions on the red horizon were variously acclaimed by both sides.

Guy and Bathie stepped ashore.

Straight away, the sand announced itself through their sandals. Even at this early hour it had soaked up enough sun to be generous in giving. Underfoot was already a herald of the intolerable middle watches, when life lay low and still and wary.

Day arrived suddenly in Egypt, with guillotine decisiveness; a predictable surprise that Guy had yet to acclimatise to, even after a twelve-months' residence. The cloudless chill and inky dark of night were banished as though by fearful decree. All that was obscure was instantly plunged into stark relief. The triple hills across the Nile looked like a knife edge taken to the startling blue sky.

It still had the same effect as his tripwire alarm back in poor, lost, Ambassador Hall. Every day it screamed at Guy that the race was on, wrenching him out of sleep with nerve endings ajudder. It told him, before he was fully awake and wanted to know, that there were but a few hours to do all that was needful. Soon, it said, King Sun would be out in all his glory, commanding the wise back to bed and asylum from his radiant majesty.

Guy's attitude was in polar contrast to Hunter's. *He* seemed to relish the shock of each new dawning, ardent for it to shed light on this land of mystery. When day poured into the valleys across the water, even those bone-dry crevices called siren-style to him to come investigate their nether regions. The man deplored and ignored the informal noon curfew, gladly paying the price in sunstroke and burning. A candid onlooker would say one year under Egyptian skies had put five on him. It had bleached his remaining rats' tails white and desiccated his flesh, turning what was once robust wiry. Fortunately, he'd a healthy opening balance of bulk to draw upon and a second eye to take up the strain when its twin was sacrificed to ophthalmia.

Still as gleeful as when both eyes first sighted the pyramids and tumbled palaces and temples, Hunter now winked his bereaved orb at Guy. Despite everything, Egypt had given him far more than it had taken. In fact, it had quite been the making of the man in Bathie's judgement. Unravelling its story was his new lease of life. He'd have signed the contract whatever sum was demanded.

Excitement trundled over every formality. They didn't even get a hello.

'This is the place! This is it!'

Their indifference was magnificent. A double temple complex was only a thin icing of interest over another portion of the same old cake. In the course of the last year Guy had made the acquaintance of more temples than he could shake a seduction stick at. The first had been fascinating, the succeeding score a little less so, and thereafter their stock fell steeply. Now, like Polly and Prudence, he was far more interested in this place's defensive perimeters. Beyond the relatively Null-cleansed confines of the Nile Delta region, staying alive way outranked idle curiosity.

The little group of scorched travellers gave Hunter a cool look.

'S'true!' he protested. 'It really is!'

Hunter mistakenly thought they doubted, never dreaming it was possible to be less obsessed than he. Dead Egypt had replaced building the new Jerusalem in his affections.

'Absolutely!'

Guy treasured that prince amongst holding replies, and husbanded it accordingly. Its deployment today awakened Bathie to the news that her husband was awake, and therefore so should she be.

'Show us then . . .'

Her impatience didn't fit the tone she clothed it in. It bulged out and burst through revealingly. In her mind she'd come in haste from piloting the *Impaled Blades* as it disintegrated over white-water rapids. She was keen to get back before imagination sulkily put the scenery away.

Hunter could still play the patriarch when he wanted. A nut-brown finger was wagged at her.

'*Do not*,' he admonished, '*begin your marriage with a rape!*'

That was old Wessex wisdom, broadened from a plea for foreplay into wider applications. '*Take time to smell the roses*' was its more genteel cousin – but Hunter hadn't been introduced to her.

He wasn't to know it had unpleasant connotations for the couple. Just as Fruntierfolke and Ambassador in-laws had presented early problems, so they'd made initial heavy weather of their sexual relations. All was well in the – and Bathie's – end, plus probably much better for being late in coming. Still, neither thanked Hunter for his unhappy choice of phrase, and it must have showed in their – even *their* – faces.

'Did I say something wrong?'

Egypt's climate had deepened Hunter's wrinkles into canyons. His frown clapped them shut.

'No more than usual . . .' Guy's voice was urbane and frictionless, but really the couple just wanted to be alone – to kick themselves and each other for almost giving the game – any game – away.

Fortunately, Hunter was an incurable literalist. He even took Ambassadors at face value. It was a wonder he'd lived this long.

'Good. No. I meant you shouldn't just expect to plunge in. You of all people should know. Bashful mysteries have to be slow-bedded . . . coaxed – lubricated even . . .'

With anyone else Guy would have said they were doing it deliberately, earning repayment in full, plus ample interest, at some point down the line. Here, though, he knew (even if he had to tell himself twice) that these were only animal husbandry parallels disporting themselves. As barbs they were just too sharp for forthright Hunter. If the man had actually known and wanted to proclaim the embarrassing truth he would have said it plain.

'Indeed,' agreed Guy. 'I'm sure there are many pretty pathways to probe before the matter is consummated . . .'

Now it was Hunter who was undermined, sensing some sport afoot that he'd rather not play in.

'The guard of honour . . .' he floundered. 'And the perimeters. You usually make more of them . . .'

Guy pretended to recall himself.

'Ah me. The lust for knowledge was such that I quite forgot. You are a minx, Bishop, tempting me from the straight and narrow path of duty . . .'

Another syllable would have been dangerous. Hunter's mouth was on a downward trajectory. Anyone less like a 'minx' had never trod the earth. Guy moved on and amongst the waiting throng.

In their cosmopolitan variety the gauntlet of guards matched the entire expedition. ambassadorial retainers stood shoulder to shoulder with zealots from New-Jerusalem commune: the cream (as Hunter saw them) of its youth, forsaking Jerusalem-become-Babylon to accompany him. Marines from the *Lady Bridget* were now almost indistinguishable from the astounding influx of other New-Wessex volunteers. Likewise the horde of footloose, fancy-free flotsam picked up in the course of the great voyage.

For, even as they'd prepared to sail from New-Poole, Hunter's citadel had been more besieged by would-be recruits than the Imperial units starting to arrive. Guy was able to choose, picking only the sincere – or those well able to fake it. Stiff-necked-but-subtle ambassadorial folk accompanying their feudal master (and escaping the pogrom back home) found themselves only one faction amongst his wider fan club.

Then, to compound their amazement, they were joined by a second wave of mavericks and had-enoughs, issuing out of Bosham-by-the-Sea. By that time, huscarls and the regular army had pretty much sealed off New-Poole from Bladedom and were dealing harshly with people heading that way with no good excuse. However, news evidently got around and the disaffected answered the gravitational pull to that alternative focus. The Imperialists were taken by surprise, betrayed from behind, and it was two mini-fleets that issued into the English Channel, joining up to make an armada.

Upon sober reflection, the few Wessex men o' war abroad decided it was wiser to stand well off, awaiting developments. Presumably, the dreadnought *Saucy Sailor* wasn't operational yet, or else it could have moved upon the waters and pounded the lot to blood and splinters. As it was, with that giant still slumbering in Southampton, the vessels of orthodoxy could only sulk around the Solent, sinking stragglers and minnows. The 'Fleet of the Damned' (as New-Godalming christened it) was free to set sail with only curses following after.

Those ungracious ill-wishes failed to conjure up storms in Biscay. The prayers for leviathans and water-spouts went unanswered. They failed to rouse the ship-swallowing penile wyrms which coiled and cavorted in deep ocean. In fact, none of the sermons preached daily made an ounce of difference to the rebels' stately progress down the coast of New-France and Iberia. Even more remarkably, the accursed bore no ill-will. They traded and raided as they would have done anyway, as occasion decreed. Since most loved it still (and it disarmed suspicion) they still flew the 'Long Man' banner. The skull and crossbones only shimmied aloft upon meeting inhospitable or just-too-tempting ports.

Therefore, the garrison at New-Gibraltar got to see serried 'Long-Men' on the horizon. The Hermes signal system didn't stretch to continental Wessex and the warning courier riders had yet to arrive. Those few, far-flung – and intimidated –

men in their little castle saw no reason not to admit the curious fleet to the 'Inner Sea'. It also seemed much the wiser thing to do. Beyond them was beyond the ken of Bladedom (saving too-vital-to-publicise and too-busy-mining-sulphur-for-gunpowder-to-explore-much 'Sicily'). Thereafter you sailed into the shadowy realm of the god-king's anecdotes and '*here be dragons*'. That suited both sides nicely.

So, as they now passed through the twin lines of honour guards, Guy and Bathie got to smile at everything from pale-as-curds Wessex strawheads to chestnut-coloured, curly-headed Sicilians. The only ingredient missing from the melange was anything native-Egyptian. Them they'd have to do without. Search as they might, they'd not found a single one.

For it seemed that at the further end of the Mediterranean and off the edge of the known world, there were no more recruits to be had. Not even 'shaggymen' in their burrows, such as they'd met, dug out, tamed, armed and enlightened on the little 'Grecian' islands and 'Crete' (as Bladian legend dubbed them). On every other uninviting coast, the Null were unchallenged masters of man-free lands – until the *Lady Bridget*'s eruption on the scene.

It amused Guy to amuse himself on such formal occasions, knowing nobody listened properly. Guards of honour were too busy worrying about their uniform and reprimands. Waiting dignitaries only studied your face, looking for signs of weakness. Therefore anything went. He worked the line.

'What wonderful buttons!'

'Gracious, do you cut your own hair?'

'*Such* a shiny nose!'

'How long have you been a Sicilian? It must be jolly boring . . .'

Only the last man in line caught him out. Perhaps he was a bit simple or a born Leveller, not yet glaze-eyed by regimented days.

'I shot my mother today . . .' Guy blandly informed him.

Head and helmet inclined in sympathy.

'I'm sure she had it coming to her, lord,' the man answered.

Since they flattered themselves they understood men better than anyone, Ambassadors disliked surprises more than most. Guy was for once dumbfounded and quit the field, discomfited.

'Yes . . . the perimeters . . .' he said, once through the tunnel of guards. 'I'm sure they're . . . but all the same . . .'

Hunter – possibly – dipped his beard; the nearest, out of principle, he'd ever venture to a bow.

'Be my guest . . .'

Actually, that was a moot point, worthy of a symposium of pedantic philosophers. Guy had renounced all but his natural authority, and yet (or because) still retained control. If anyone could lay claim to all Egypt it was he – but he failed to. There again, this remote southern enclave was surely Hunter's. His by conception, birthright and possession. The role of host seemed to fit. However, he existed for nothing else but knowledge and happily deferred on unrelated issues. Quite who commanded and who complied was a quandary not discussed or resolved this early in the new colony's life. Still in its innocent childhood phase, their society rubbed along pretty well without hammering it out.

Only Polly and Prudence had everything sorted. Hunter's invitation achieved nothing. They waited for ambassadorial indication before heading north and south to see what was keeping the Null out.

By now, Hunter had succumbed to the magnetic attraction so evident throughout the exchange. He'd turned his back on Guy and Bathie to drink in the scene as though he were they, beholding it for the first time. Something therein was feeding him pure joy.

It was too much for one. He just had to share it.

'*Two* structures,' he explained to the world, framing the vista with widespread arms. The newcomers were welcome to listen in if they cared to. 'Brother and sister, but not twins. Temples? Oh, yes. Not a beggar's crumb of doubt about that. But to the same god? Ah, *no* . . .'

That got their attention, and even a mutter or two from the

more riffraff eavesdroppers. New-Wessex and its offspring cultures tolerated a great deal in terms of bedroom antics and clipping coins, and such petty things of *this* life. Yet when it came to the monotheism question, an indulgent Motherland turned into a stern-faced, stickler parent. Even the Hedonists declared that it was *one* god they didn't believe in. Guy reckoned Blades had done that much good. Even the notion of anything else was like someone spitting on your children.

Inwardly, Guy winced and wished he hadn't conjured that particular metaphor. Too personal. Too painful. Then he told himself to be strong and stiff-lipped. Many gods? He could stomach that. He could stomach *anything*. He'd been Ambassador to Null-Paris. The One God alone knew what *they* worshipped!

'Goodness me . . .' was all he said, occupying the time it took to regain control and take hostages against further inner insurrection.

'And also very late,' Hunter continued. 'Very late indeed. At the height – but also the end. That's why I think here holds the answer!'

If so it was to a question only Hunter had posed. Every son and daughter of Wessex was well used to ruins. There were those of the high civilisation the angels had squished flat four centuries before, Wild-engulfed and enigmatic; or else the blackened shames of more recent wars. Ruins here were just a matter of degree and in stranger shapes. The notion of where their creators had gone, if ever raised, was prejudged as self-evident. Into the Null's guts – where else?

Still, Guy's interest was vaguely pricked.

'What? Have you deciphered the picture script?'

Hunter didn't like that. His shoulders said so. There was a point in the courtship beyond which his new beloved would never go. Therefore he wanted it and her all the more, till he ate, drank and slept it.

'No. Nor ever shall. Except the stuff that's literal – we think.'

Some of the structures not reused by the Null as nests or

orgy-chambers preserved murals of great skill and high beauty. Many monuments were inscribed with marks that were clearly rational. Perhaps they'd once told a story, but it all looked lost beyond retelling. The science of linguistics had never flourished in a world where only the Bladian tongue, 'Englysh', was spoken. Cleverer fellow-exiles than Hunter had poured over the glyphs – for a while – till they tired of the thankless task and proclaimed them a closed book.

'Pity,' said Guy – and meant it. These 'Egyptians' hadn't left much behind save stone – albeit marvellous poems in that medium. It seemed hard on them that, in addition to extinction, only the wonder of their works was left, muted by lack of narrative.

'More than a pity,' answered Hunter. 'A tragedy to equal our own. But here, I dare to hope, *here* things relent. And maybe *only* here.'

'Really?' Guy meant to be polite, deferring to obsession, not intending Hunter should seize on it with such passion. Their guide spun around.

'Yes!' Hunter was as wide-eyed and earnest as he'd ever been back when human perfection was his project. 'Here. *Here*! If we frame *just* the right question. If we listen very, *very* carefully. Then here . . .'

For an awful moment Guy thought he was going to be grabbed by the lapels.

'*Then*,' the transported man continued, 'here we shall . . . *hear* . . .'

The Ambassador simply couldn't resist it. After all, he *was* meant to be amongst friends.

'Hear what?'

Hunter had been on his own, save for workers and warriors, for too long. Either that or inspiration possessed him. He was casting haunted looks around, as though what he so wanted to hear might already be floating on the aether.

Apparently not. Hunter craned in vain. Then he turned back to Guy with disconcerting speed, reluctant to impart the blindingly obvious. He muttered something.

'Sorry?' Bathie butted in. Her intervention divided the intensity between the two men – which was a blessing.

'So am I,' Hunter agreed. 'I weep bitter tears about it. Nevertheless, the chance remains. I live in hope to hear . . .'

The Lady Bathie's arm, still paper-white and unacclimatised, flashed up. Her hand grasped Hunter's beard and held it firm. She stood on tiptoe until they were eyeballs to eyeball.

'*Hear what?*' she asked sweetly.

Hunter couldn't see the need. It was all clear in *his* head. All the same, he answered.

'Their dying words, of course . . .'

Where once was sanctity, there remained only sanctuary and shade, but the party would not have swapped one for the other. Parts of the roofing survived, leaving pools of cool for them to bathe in.

Behind, the courtyard was getting the full benefit of the solar blaze, making it no place for anyone save salamanders.

'This was but the outermost and least hall,' said Hunter, his voice muffled by the ringing heat. 'A thronging place. It needn't delay us.'

The party begged to disagree – some of them literally. There were many fine reasons to linger, not least the lovely cover. Also, it hardly seemed proper simply to dismiss such cyclopean architecture. New-Wessex building at its most ambitious rarely moved such size and quantity of stone, let alone jointed it so perfectly. Skill of that order merited a moment's reflection – in one of the island murks, naturally. A mini-mutiny made them stop and stare.

They'd already come a fair way, up from the river to the right-hand and grander temple's precincts. Their breakfast of dates and thrice-watered small beer was already a crumbling bastion against appetite – particularly thirst. Under the driving drumbeat of the sun upon their parasols, the trippers had hurried (or what the gentry called hurrying) across its bare courtyard.

Hunter assured them, between gasps, that it must once have heaved with commerce and worship all year round. Everyone looked and disbelieved. Even Bathie – whose imagination sometimes consented to make miracles – couldn't see it. Left open to the sky, the place had been leached clean even of ghosts.

Beyond that wide expanse, a narrower but still broad ramp led up into more exalted regions. To be first and foremost, Polly and Prudence took it at a sprint – and almost killed themselves. If anything *had* been waiting at the top they would have been puffed and red-faced (for once) easy prey.

Guy and Bathie proceeded, arm in arm, at a more stately pace, arriving not much later but in far better condition. Hunter, already sun-dried beyond further damage, skirted round the peripheries, ever hopeful of something not seen before. He was last to the summit, behind the rag-tag of ambassadorial cousins, Sicilian gunpowder-lords' second sons, captains of shaggymen and other assorted hangers-on.

Once there, Hunter shared their wonder, if not their alarm, at the way ahead. From down below and their camp at river level, the distance to the towering cliff-edge cut-off was foreshortened. Now, seen on the level, they could both marvel and despair at the path still left to tread.

For form's sake, they paused to ponder such wonder, such workmanship, in the first hall encountered. That they all chose to do so in the shade it afforded was purest coincidence. Likewise that many picked then to slowly furl their 'Wessex Traveller's Parasol' and uncap the wicked spike concealed atop. It seemed the unspoken wish of the party to seek both physical and spiritual refreshment before proceeding – armed.

Guy was first to have his wits back and off the boil. He looked about and calculated, but 2 + 2 refused to give the answer drummed into him in school. Hunter was standing alone out in the glare. It was an act of mercy to beckon him over.

'The pillars,' Guy pointed out, 'are too many. And too

slender to hold roofing. Also, I see no rhyme or reason to them. When all were still standing, this place would have been as complex as' – he was about to say 'an Ambassador's plan' but didn't, and abruptly abandoned the quest for simile – 'as something very complex. Dark. A murky labyrinth. Perhaps they worshipped the god of assassins?'

Hunter hadn't thought of that one and it made him look around anew. Then he was glad he hadn't thought of it because he didn't think much of it.

'No,' he said, blunt to the point of rudeness. 'That's *your* mind thinking, not theirs. They were a gentle people. Gentler than us, anyway. I can read that much of what's left.'

Guy had no grounds for dissension. Indeed, it might account for the Egyptians' entire absence, and so he didn't cavil at Hunter's robust correction. The lack of answer turned away wrath. Seeing he had prevailed and maintained his beloved's reputation, that world's first Egyptologist continued more moderately.

'If you ask me – and you did – I maintain that the columns were meant to be reed stems. Look at the carving. Slender. Smooth. Fluted. Go look beside the river now. No, not *now*,' – this in response to Guy's facial protest – 'I meant *nowadays*. Look later, beside the Nile. Half the time the riverbank's lost in reed-beds. Maybe that's where they thought they came from . . .'

It was just as plausible as Blades's 'Egg of the World', or dust, or Adam's rib, or monkeys, as some Levellers suggested. Guy could accept the theory into his pantheon with an easy shrug.

True or no, a storm had come upon this 'reed-bed', to lay most of it low. Or many storms. Or a desperate battle. Whatever the cause, its consequences lay in sand-topped tumuli under and around their feet. They had to thread their way through the worst of them, braving the sun when there was no alternative route.

For Hunter was urging them on like a mother hen, because he'd done with this place long before they arrived and exhausted its possibilities. Juicier prospects only lay ahead. His dehydrated frame impelled him to that meat and drink.

The roofing survival rate increased as they progressed and the edifice narrowed. Soaring high above, eagle-style, in his mind, Guy perceived a ground-plan with distinct segments to it, reminiscent of an insect's body. The passing from one to another was always signified by a wall and door. The surrounds closed in. Quite soon, those in the lead were requiring lanterns.

Guy paused and held his own aloft when he detected colour at the very edge of vision. They had gone through a third – or was it fourth? – door, and the 'field of reeds' columns not only persisted but multiplied. The way became a twisty, turning thing, requiring concentration. He didn't need to ask Hunter for confirmation. It was as clear as it was dark. Every step forward was heading 'holier'.

Also, it was here that the wall narratives began. Even fully extended, Guy's lantern arm only revealed a portion of them.

A beige man – a king? – had a black man by his top-knot and was smiting him with a mace. Alongside, more black men waited in the same sad state to be smitten. Glyphs surrounded and intervened in the scene, maybe expanding the story to a lost readership. Guy studied it for as long as he cared – which wasn't long.

'Obviously,' he said to Hunter, who'd joined him, 'there are usages of the word "gentle" with which I'm not familiar . . .'

Hunter looked until he could dismiss the evidence.

'Kings . . .' he said, with a righteous sneer, as though that one word explained, if not excused, all.

Guy was abandoned; left to accept the crushing verdict or be left behind. Hunter's mind and body, not to mention the rest of the expedition, moved on.

The 'reed stems' were becoming so close set that the expedition had to snake along in single file, and Guy's delay placed him in that snake's less noble portions. Which was intolerable. Accordingly, whilst delegating the actual elbow work to Polly and Prudence, he worked towards resuming his proper, pole, place in their progress, and access to the empty pool of light in front

For every lantern shutter had been thrown open, in order to exorcise an inky black. Despite centuries of trying, sunlight had yet to weather its way in here and day had to be man-made. Therefore, even to Guy's jaundiced eye, each successive pillar and half-glimpsed mural, each suspicious shadow, arrived as novelty.

It was the same as when being first up the rope to board the *Bridget* had imperilled all dignity and made him hesitate. Similarly now, Guy could have been well content with a less leading role, but obligation obliged him on. That being so, and self-thrust to the fore, he discovered some satisfaction in keeping both his feet and his sense of direction. And that was the way New-Wessex made its masterly classes. Biting the bullet ten times a day either sharpened their teeth or broke them.

Feeling every eye upon him (including the murals'), Guy strode on.

Robbed of his leading role, Hunter wished it otherwise. His voice from off to front and side revealed he'd digressed again.

'Here!'

Hunter rationed excitement tighter than Sea-captain doled out rum on a long voyage. The dash of it enlivening his voice promoted request to command. At varying speeds, according to their regard for him, they all made their way over.

Hunter was neither in distress nor in a Null. He was in a passion. The debate before the smiting story had not been forgotten or relinquished after all. This was ferret-like behaviour from the Egyptians' self-appointed spokesman but Guy found it in his heart to forgive. The lost folk could not defend themselves and deserved at least one apologist.

'See?' Hunter drew other lanterns, connecting arms and all, to assist his thesis. 'See? No war. No torture. Just the beautiful everyday.'

It took a while to construct a tale from flickering parts but eventually all bar the biased could see he spoke true. A flat family, drawn without so much as a nod to perspective, were enjoying a day by the Nile. Whether the fat hippos some members were hunting shared that enjoyment was another matter, though they seemed to be accepting their fate as chestnut men's playthings passively enough.

There were wives and children (both in alarmingly scant clothing) and food consumed and cups quaffed at. The sun's munificent rays, shown as straight descending arrows of gold, crowned and blessed each figure depicted.

Even imperfectly beheld by bobbing lights and in inauspicious surroundings, the sentiments could hardly be misconstrued. These people, or leastways the painters upon plaster, had loved life and lived it to the full. They wished a vivid reminder of it to accompany them into the dark.

Those of the party in the least bit susceptible, succumbed. Bathie traced with one nibbled fingertip the bold, confident, curve of a chestnut arm. It held aloft a platter of red, round, fruit piled in pyramids. Her mouth watered. She felt as though she could simply . . . reach and eat . . .

Little therein was lifelike, in poise or proportion or absence of shadow, and yet at the same time it was exactly *right*. The artist had aimed at realism, not reality, scorning fear of any dull-dog critic – and scored a gold. Even if every square inch of wall beyond their gaze showed nothing but smiting and maces applied to brains, this portion would have justified the regrettable rest.

Guy's eye was taken by a brown tot dancing for its father. He held his lantern extra close to observe the little face – and inadvertently blistered it.

It looked as though Hunter would cuff both Guy and the light away – until he remembered just in time. *Then* was done and gone, an accomplished fact and immune to pain. Whereas *now*, actions had consequences and some offences went beyond a blind eye. And thought of 'blind eyes' reminded him he had only one left to lose. And Polly and Prudence were *all* eyes, each powerfully focused upon him. Hunter held his hand.

'I *do* wish you'd be a bit more careful with that ancient and unique painting,' he said politely – though both shoulders and innards were hunched as if pained.

It showed noble restraint worth matching. Signalling the two P's 'at ease', Guy met Hunter halfway.

'I think perhaps they *were* gentle, as you say . . .'

'Except to hippos,' Bathie piped in her two penn'orth. Quite unlike her, she'd made a point of studying *Blades's Bestiary* before they arrived here. Now she knew the names of all kinds of hitherto only fabled beasts. Bathie Ambassador also took every opportunity to make people aware she was no longer a virgin as regards bookish learning.

'The only good hippo,' chipped in sycophantic cousin Beelzebub, 'is a dead hippo!' His unoffending punt had been overturned by a moody poor ambassador for the species some weeks ago.

It broke the spell just nicely, bringing their picture worship to an end.

Not everyone had been able to get a decent look, not everybody approved. Somebody was required to say something to spoil the moment and ensure the fine interlude ended in 'back-to-normal-smiles', instead of a sad drifting away. Bathos was better than pathos, and better still the blow should come inadvertently, rather than with murderous intent.

However, Hunter liked hippos, because hippos were part of the whole Egypt deal. He silently said so by giving cousin Beelzebub a dead-leg in the dark as they coalesced again.

Guy led them on for what felt like days but was actually only two more temple segments, as seen by that eagle he could never, but presently longed to, be. Replica night closed in around them, acquiring substance and gravity born of dust and age. Beautified by contrast, even the throat-grasping heated air of outside was recalled like Paradise lost. A longing for it to grasp again, whilst under the sun's sovereignty, shoved them into silence. A sullen sense of mission now coated the caterpillar of Wessex-men and others, snuffing out the remaining embers of *outing*.

Guy came to the end before he knew it – and Hunter let

211

him. What Guy assumed to be yet another door proved false. The darkness it contained wouldn't surrender to his feet and jarred them instead, refusing entry.

Shocked into exclamation, skin donated from shin that needed it to stone that didn't, Guy explored the niche with hand and lamp. It held nothing but dust and spider skeletons.

His private joke over, Hunter was beside him.

'Press away,' he said, 'but don't hope to press on. There is no further. You heave at the mighty east cliff itself.'

Guy saw little point in that and so desisted. Even before the onset of middle age, he'd done his fair share of mountain shifting. Therefore, he looked at the disappointing and quite empty cupboard before him as if it alone could answer his questions.

Thankfully, Hunter decided to deputise for the dumb object.

'Here,' he announced, waving one hand at – but not, Guy noted, actually *within* – the void, 'was the Holy of Holies. I believe it was but rarely visited.'

By dancing lantern light Bathie's pale face grimaced at the dead-end.

'I'm not surprised,' she said, 'with such a welcome waiting.'

The feeling was general. Wessex folk were accustomed to the godhead depicted, whether as Blades or in some other guise. Theologically led astray by emperor-worship, to many of them empty air was simply that, and a ubiquitous Almighty so *every*where as to be *no*where. They liked a divinity you could point your face and prayers at.

Hunter, whose thoughts were miles and millennia away, was puzzled. What did they expect? A fully functioning temple staff, complete with interpreters and explanatory labels? He shook his head to dispel their underwhelm-ment.

'This niche held a statue of the god,' he informed them, since they seemed so thick. 'The distilled essence of their piety – like in the Holy of Holies at New-Godalming. Behind doors: under seal, probably.'

'Well, I don't know if you've noticed,' said Bathie, 'but he seems to have gone out . . .'

Hunter whirled round as if it were news. Guy was sufficiently taken in to check too. Wasted effort. Only absence abided.

Their guide turned to Bathie for clarification. She was happy to provide it.

'Maybe he had to pop out. An urgent appointment. Or hot date. He could have left a note though. *"Back late. Don't wait up. Your dynasty's in the oven . . ."* No? Oh, suit yourself . . .'

Hunter's sense of humour, never strong, had taken a fearful beating in the decades since he first met Guy Ambassador. The two facts were not unconnected. Today he'd left that faculty, a death-bed invalid of no use to anyone, back in camp.

'Oh no,' he said, glad she need not be disappointed. 'He's still here. Never left. He waits for you over there.'

The party pivoted as one in the direction of Hunter's wide-swung lantern.

Sure enough, over by the further wall were glimpses of a recumbent bulk. Rabble-fashion, they crossed to it.

A beautiful stone youth, crowned like other kings painted on the walls, had been deposited face down – and none too gently either. His proud chin, striking first, had cracked a slim neck and stiff back. Glorious eyes now gazed for ever, not on his people, but on flagstones inches away.

Given the choice between a dead deity and a live horse, Guy would have bet on the thing he knew. Nevertheless, he'd have yearned for a healthy side punt on the granite god having been evicted, rather than sent on holiday from home. The present location didn't look like any a-change-is-as-good-as-a-rest move.

Hunter's face indicated that he thought the same way but preferred not to talk about it.

'Do you think a prayer might still work?' asked cousin Louis-Quatorze, running his fingers solicitously over the grievous stone wounds. A known madcap, and thus only occasionally useful, he was infamous for his willingness to try anything once. He'd come close to falling or being thrown overboard a dozen times en route.

Since everyone knew the prayer would be for his step-mother's head on a plate, and his stepsister's stunned body to play with – and they were both a thousand miles away – there seemed little point in either yea or nay. The silence said it all.

Undeterred, Louis-Quatorze fell to his knees anyway. Some people lingered just in case, but no loaded platters or loaded ladies materialised to amaze them. That Quatorze would get to tick off those wants decades later (when fate saw fit to make him Imperial Despot of Iceland) remained in the unknown future, failing to muddy the theological water.

'There is no more to see,' announced Hunter, 'save a few jars of long-lost function, and some little man-effigies that I encounter everywhere, likewise. Nothing else to merit your gogglement . . .'

'Then why the Blades did you bring—'

Hunter glared down Bathie's protest, annoyed at the rending of his seamless treat.

'*Nothing*,' he overrode her, crossing the chamber faster than wished or intended, 'save this!'

Lit only by his own lantern, Hunter's hands directed all attention to the furthermost wall.

Initially, Guy thought he meant the splendid mural, briefly seen, wherein the fallen god was restored to his proper place, upright once more and standing in judgement on an orderly line of chestnut men. Over all arced a much elongated and supple dark woman, encompassing the scene beneath her flat belly and between elegant toes and fingertips.

Guy liked her, or what little he got to see, and that delayed him tracking down to note Hunter's actual revelation. There proved to be obscure shapes at the base of this side wall also, but these shadows possessed life and breath. With exaggerated gestures, Hunter bade them rise. The hummocky range of hills obeyed.

After only a fleeting ripple of alarm and brandishing of parasols, the party came to terms with the knowledge that a gaggle of shaggymen had been squatting on their heels, observing them throughout.

And yet even this was not the true wonder Hunter had in store for them. He chivvied the silent shaggies aside to reveal it.

A new door of distinctly Wessex design, rough and rush-hewed, as well as locked and bolted, barred a way on. Hunter was already at it with keys from around his belt.

'The entrance was concealed,' he said over his shoulder as he worked. 'But I found it! Maybe I can't read these people's words. Not yet. But I can read their minds. Their concealments don't exclude *me*!'

At length he tussled the barrier free and a fevered giant's breath emerged to scorch their faces and make them gag. The air from below smelt of ancient privacy, undisturbed. Hunter perceived their reluctance to sample it further.

'These probationers shall render it tolerable,' he said, waving his lantern at the patient shaggymen. 'I have constructed a system of fans and draught devices to convey refreshed air along with us.'

The 'probationers' English was still far from perfect, but they were eager to serve and thus become full citizens and humans. Conversely, they had a horror of failure and return to burrows on Crete. Hunter's gestures were correctly interpreted and they set to assembling the mechanism of bellows and stiffened oxhide.

At first, a frisson of distaste had washed over the tour. Tunnels still bore a whiff of taboo dating back to burrow-days and the Blades ban on a safe but craven life under earth. However, for most there that was long ago and far away. Also, so much trouble had evidently been taken on their behalf, it would have been Nullish to decline. One look between Guy and Bathie was all that was required to secure general consent.

Guy led and, like pupils dutifully attending a 'cultural' event, they all filed through the shaggymen and door, down into the depths.

If the atmosphere above was oppressive, here below it escalated to active persecution. Heat sucked at their faces and the only air on offer came minted fresh from the furnace. The shaggymen's best efforts arrived feeble and intermittent as an on-its-way-home heartbeat. Even then the ministrations were only to the back of each head, which stood in least need.

There must have been some circulation of sweet(er) air though; elseways they'd all have been gasping like goldfish by now. Nevertheless, it remained very much a matter of faith, with every hot intake of breath asking the question: '*Are you sure?*'

Fortunately, there were distractions – like staying alive. The stairs down did what they were born for and nothing more, making no concessions. They were treacherous and precipitous – and everything else inviting headlong descent the quick way. Hunter, or someone, had done them the favour of a rope side-rail which saved many a neck or surrender to slow-but-sure, if undignified, step-by-step progress on their backsides. Even so, it wouldn't save the stairs from starring in troubled dreams for days to come.

Sure-footed Hunter usurped the lead, a globe of light descending ratchet-style. With whatever focus they could spare, those following longed for it to finally be still. Eventually, their prayers were answered, but only after the lazier leg muscles had become iron bands of protest. Way before they all arrived, the foremost lantern was dancing an impatient jig.

At the bottom the air was soup. A meaty winter recipe (say oxtail, but without the flavour) served up in closest summer.

Whilst the unaccustomed tried to strain it through their nostrils, Hunter started to take the register, but soon gave up, bored. Instead, he delved into the blackness of the onward corridor's side-wall. From a recess apparent to him alone, he extracted, just like some stage-mage, a caged bird.

At other times Guy might have applauded, but right now he hadn't the energy.

Hunter wasn't after acclamation. His attention was all on the little prison.

'It lives,' he declared at length. 'It's even lively.'

'It's bloody mine!' said cousin Beelzebub, diving forward. 'That's my sparrowhawk!'

Hunter stood his ground as though a sheep had squared up to him.

'I know,' he said, with disarming innocence.

Beelzebub was only part-way disarmed. Every bit an aristocrat, he was used to his tantrums clearing all obstacles.

'I've turned the damn camp upside down for it!' he persevered, raising not the slightest crop of sympathy. 'Next step was torturing the slaves to find out . . .'

'Don't do that,' said Hunter. 'It would be wasteful as well as unkind. I took it. My – our – need was greater.'

Then, forgetting him, he turned his back on Beelzebub. The robbed and slighted Ambassador said nothing, making his family gathered there proud, but earning himself future tooth-trouble through grinding off enamel.

'If the bird lives and breathes,' Hunter announced, 'then so may we. We can proceed.'

'Oh, *goody*!' said a heckler from the back.

Hunter was mortally offended.

'There need be none here but the willing,' he magisterially decreed over their heads. 'Let those who will, depart. But also let them be warned. They will count themselves accursed by their absence this day.'

Hunter thought he'd said sufficient to kill dissent and so could afford a concession.

'None the less, let them but say the word . . .'

This was the mercy of the goddess Correction, not expecting uptake.

'And the word is goodbye!' said the same voice from the rear; and she and several others gladly backtracked, ascending beyond return.

Hunter was speechless, lost amongst black wonders greater than this labyrinth. Human nature would always be an undiscovered country to him. This late in life he was disinclined to explore its interior. Sad-eyed, he beckoned the balance on.

What the absconders missed was more Nile-life scenes, beginning gloriously but increasingly plain and incomplete as

217

the corridor wore on. The days depicted were no longer only sunny idylls. Grim facts and faces intruded.

Guy hadn't time to make a study of them, for every mural, however fascinating, was in competition with keeping up and keeping upright. Yet, collectively, they still told a tale.

It was one Hunter had read before and perhaps didn't care to expound. Whatever the reason, he set a sprightly pace. No pauses were permitted to read the faltering of the painted fable.

Happily, there were solid reasons underfoot to break their stride – and shins. A profusion of pots and gourds of all sizes lined the way, interspersed with sheaves of ancient spears. Once he found a scene suitable for his purposes, Guy pretended serious collision with a container in order to rein Hunter in.

Their pace-setter knew something was up. Ambassadors rarely cried out over anything less than impalement. Undeceived, he still backtracked. Guy kept up the pantomime for the barest face-saving spell. He caressed a shank that had taken no harm and at the same time eyebrow-queried all.

Hunter chose to confine it to the kitchenware.

'They've been investigated,' he said. 'Exhaustively. All empty as a Leveller's prayer.'

Guy liked full stories and knew when he was getting short weight.

'As void as *that?*' It was an actual query, not in the least rhetorical. Hunter was nudged the extra distance he didn't care to go.

'Several had dregs of a resin-like residue,' he admitted, confirming Guy's suspicions. 'Doubtless the concentrate of food or drink reduced by millennia of waiting. As experiment I fed some to a Null.'

Guy waited patiently but, contrary to expectation, the statement seemed a single birth. A rough midwife, he gave the mother a shake.

'And . . .?'

Duly shaken, Hunter hunted around inside for the memory. 'It died. Eventually.'

'Food and spears . . .' mused Guy aloud.

'Plus maces and bows,' added Hunter, all the while begrudging his impulse to accuracy. 'Ghost weapons. They crumble to dust at the slightest touch.'

Polly and Prudence reached out and found it was so.

'But weapons still,' Guy maintained his point. 'Not artists' tools or tokens of worship. More like the stockpile of a last stand . . .'

'Who can say?' answered Hunter – but Guy knew the man was studying the selected wall, revealed beyond ignoring by a helpfully held lantern.

Outline, incomplete, men and women were weeping over simple, shallow, graves. Spears were everywhere, even poised in the hands of mourners. No more happy days by the Nile for these hasty painters. No more leisurely projects. Either they intended to return and do a proper job in some later which never came, or else they were anxious to show their sorrows swiftly, before it was too late. The boldness of line and curve were still there, but stripped of all former joy.

'Only God knows the truth of it.'

Guy had to admire and be silenced by Hunter's conclusion; a champion conversation-killer not to be challenged lightly.

Still, Guy knew he'd won on points and could safely lower the lantern in that knowledge. His was the hand on the bell to start the next round when he chose.

'Lead on,' he said, and smiled brightly.

Hunter hadn't seen. His back was already turned and leaving.

Guy soon sensed why any delay was received like provocation. Up ahead the air smelt . . . broader, if not better. It emanated from wider realms than the dead-straight tunnel. Here was something Hunter knew and approved of, a vindication of himself and a testing of them. It would place him back on the throne in this, his own little world. Naturally, his boots yearned to be there.

No one else's footwear felt that way. It isn't normal to relish narrow gangplanks over an abyss.

Beyond their lanterns' feeble assertions, the bottom

remained unseen. Yet they perceived a tangible, broiling hotness going way down all the same; an autonomous writhing of air left alone since history had passed it by.

Hunter went over the 20-foot tear in the world as if it was the threshold of his house and had promised to never ever hurt him. If Guy hadn't known the man better he would have sworn the thin plank bridge was needlessly stamped and shaken all the way across.

Their guide now stood at the further end, fastening his light to an upright pole so that it cast a steady eye almost to the halfway point. Then he spread two cord-muscled arms wide to entice them over. An unappetising welcome.

'Don't worry,' he called. 'It's been crossed many times without mishap.'

By him, maybe, but not by them. The cowering congregation by the lip saw no other reason for the absence of an handrail save sadism.

So, of course, Guy went first amongst them, ramrod backed, a what-a-nice-day smile upon his lips. The tap tap tap of his 'seduction stick', in time with the leisurely steps, drowned out the dead tree's creaks and groans.

Midway, he lingered to look down. A meaningless act in reality, given that the black below was infinite, but it served to spit upon the tests life was setting him. That was the only language life understood.

Naturally, the dark called to him, to come to it and be done with tedious experience. As befitted an Ambassador, Guy listened politely, even to a siren song, but declined the invitation. He'd not yet wearied of this second stab at existence as he had the first. In some parts it still glittered.

Hunter's presumptuous helping hand was brushed away. Guy disembarked and returned to the brink to look back. Every inch one of the finer cuts off the joint of Humandom, he disregarded the lack of solid ground before him.

'A little way and then all shall be well,' he told the trepidatious – but could conceivably have been referring as much to the years ahead as the plank perilous.

One by one, well or trembling, they went over. Bathie, who hated heights, took it at the charge, arms outstretched, shrieking a war-cry. The wood bowed even under such a modest burden, justifying her sashay of delight at the further end. She still had hips to die for and knew it. Minds were distracted and others shamed into being at least as brave as she.

Deceptively dainty, Polly and Prudence traversed hand in hand like a daisy-chain of schoolgirls. No one was misled. Not even the upgraded shaggymen smiled.

Lastly, and only after tears and many an abortive attempt, cousin Beelzebub had to be carried over, eyes screwed so tight he risked self-inflicted injury. It was all the worse because cousin Louis-Quatorze had just jigged across and done a hand-stand midway. If looks could kill Hunter's disapproval would have sorted the problem there and then.

Instead, whilst the Beelzebub-versus-burly-helpers wrestling match was still underway, the former bishop (defrocked *in absentia* amidst New-Godalming Cathedral splendour a year ago that very day, coincidentally) turned back to the kidnapped sparrowhawk. Unlike its former master, the poor creature could be relied upon to do its duty.

Custody had been delegated to a Sicilian sub-king who was now spun round without ceremony. The pilfered prisoner, though depressed, proved to be still going. All the same, Hunter rattled the cage to make sure.

'The air is pure!' he pronounced, and overlooked all ensuing dissent.

The corridor continued, now with many sub-branches and side chambers – all slighted and ignored. However, as regards decoration and depiction, there was no longer even an attempt. Only pots and weaponry remained to personify the builders. Until, that is, the bones commenced.

They were thick underfoot, perhaps once a set of pyres that had tumbled as the flesh fled.

'A general population mix,' Hunter informed them, Parthian-style, as he heard their boots scrunch the discovery.

'Both sexes. All ages. Some bearing the marks of violence.'

'And cracked. And opened,' said an ex-Cretan shaggyman who'd until recently butchered his own dinners. 'The marrow's sucked out of this long bone . . .'

'Is it indeed?' answered Hunter, meaning '*I can't* hear *you!*'

'Plus scratches on the wall,' contributed Guy, the most literate amongst them and thus keenest scrutineer for the cartoon story to be taken up again. 'Gouges even! If you ask me . . .'

'But I *didn't* . . .' Hunter killed conversation off and stood guard over the body. 'Now: from hereon in the corridor descends sharply. Look, if you don't believe me.'

Guy believed but also checked. Sure enough, what was previously pancake-flat became a ramp in ever steeper decline. The onward dark smelt ominous.

'A deceit,' said Hunter, to audible relief. 'Leading nowhere. And besides, the atmosphere is foul. We lost two torchbearers proving it. They're still there. You can go visit them, if you wish, but I'll not join you. My one and only visit saw me return on hands and knees, spewing green bile – and lucky to do so. Mind you, it wasn't a total waste. I glimpsed the utmost end. Blank wall. Like I said: a road to nowhere.'

'Can we go home then?' asked the promoted Cretan.

Guy admired the sentiments, even if he couldn't express them himself. It was his painful duty to go a little way on from wherever Hunter called a halt.

Whilst that gentleman spurned the plea with silent contempt, Guy poked his nose into the blocked beyond. Then an ear. Then his whole head, even though his nostrils were being abraded from within.

He stood it as long as he could and until the world was getting nicely woozy.

'Who has good hearing?' he asked all, finding that the odd air imbibed made his voice pipe like a child's. Fortunately the effect soon passed and his request was treated with respect.

The closer men were to burrow-life, the keener their senses were developed. Natural selection – i.e. the Null – weeded out the less acute. Simultaneously enriched and embarrassed by

222

proximity to days lived wary-style like an overgrown rabbit, the Cretan would-be home-goer stepped forward.

He plunged further in than Guy and stood it slightly longer. Burrows, particularly in hot countries, hardened you to perfumes somewhat samey.

'Water?' he ventured upon emerging. 'A distant cataract? Very distant. Or' – this more reluctantly – 'movement. Or a steady drip drip drip: maybe channelled condensation from above.'

'Doubtless.' Hunter seized on the last part of the triptych and left the rest.

At that point Guy wished to give Hunter an old-fashioned look, but couldn't connect. The man was hastening to the kill.

'What I've brought you to see isn't there' – he indicated the uninviting slope – 'or beyond. Oh no. The answer I – we – seek is right beside us!'

Heads spun and then returned to rest. They couldn't see it.

Hunter marched back to a side entrance not long since by-passed.

'Here!' he crowed, shedding the mask and letting his excitement shine. 'Here's the heart and soul! A secret heart: concealed for those who would come after!'

The presumed room didn't do or say anything to help matters. Its mouth remained just another black and gaping cavern. Everyone looked from it to Hunter and back again without enlightenment.

Seeing that, he explained.

'The last men here packed this room with rubble – this one and a few diversionary others. In order to seal and confound. But only one place held the key. I found it. There *was* reward for my perseverance!'

Guy had noted the raw rock piles above ground and took leave to doubt Hunter leathered his own hands in getting them aloft. There again, he might be wrong. The man's transferable fanaticism rendered it just possible he'd pitched in to add speed. It hardly mattered. More importantly, the inordinate number of shaggymen bonded workers Hunter had insisted on need no longer simmer on the back burner of Guy's mind. So that was what they'd been up to. Nothing to do with recruiting an army – not of the worrying kind, anyway.

Hunter had already entered the now significance-gilded opening they'd previously cold-shouldered. His one-lantern-power told them little but others soon assisted. Light was shed.

It was fresh cleared, even swept clean; queerly pristine compared to all the surrounding dust and death. The broad consensus was to feel even less at home.

Guy hadn't forgotten the sounds from beyond the ramp, nor allowed himself to disbelieve them. He wished to violate the double doors now revealed before them brisk-style, ancient seal and all.

Not so Hunter. He'd dreamed of this when all other dreams went rotten. It had to be a *considered* pleasure.

Guy admired his patience if nothing else. The portals screamed *original*, and likewise the intact cord around their handles.

'You shouldn't have waited just for us . . .' he paid tribute.

'I nearly didn't,' Hunter slapped it down. 'There were some nights when . . . Well, I'm sure you can imagine . . . But I was strong and cudgelled my desires quiet. It was important there be others: people capable of understanding, of *savouring* sublime moments. I mean, this is once a lifetime: once many lifetimes! It would be wicked not to share.'

Guy agreed and now saw why he'd been dragged half the length of Egypt. What stood before them was a gateway into dead days, perfectly preserved. Even if nothing lay beyond, his trip would still have been worthwhile. Standing where no other had for long, untroubled, ages, was one of the few pleasures that remained ever fresh.

It was therefore in his heart to forgive Hunter's less than total restraint. When he saw the high spyhole, no bigger than a bullet-hole and now bunged, Guy said nothing. Hunter may have had a premature peep. What of it? He might have seen a little – but not all. The thought was still there. His intent remained better than human.

Hunter urged Guy forward.

'To you the honours . . .'

'No, no. After *you* . . .'

In Wessex high etiquette it was meant to go on some while, even to the point of becoming combative in self-effacement. However, once the ex-bishop had been offered what he wanted he grabbed it.

'All right then . . .'

It was a bit sudden, like a lunge for the crutch early on in a seduction, but Guy overlooked it.

'Ancient of days' or no, the waxed cord still required a seax that the circle should be broken. The doors themselves needed Polly and Prudence, plus Beelzebub's above-average brawn, to part. In the end the panels bowed to brute force and ignorance, but not quietly, not without struggle. Pieces of plank and painted veneers came away in their hands.

If stockpiled dark can be said to pour forth then it did. You could almost credit it with power to drive the foremost explorers back. The existing fug in front, bad as it was, refused to accept the new-old addition. Accordingly, the influx coiled and brewed on the threshold, making and amending constellations of dust motes.

Still, it was well worth the effort and pollution. The makers had saved what strength and colour they had for here. Even in tentative, gingerly advancing, light, that much was obvious. Guy called them all in so that the tale could be told.

The floor was bare but the walls more than compensated. Guy picked up the story at one lower edge.

More river parties and family pleasures, plus modestly confident souls gone to judgement, went right up and around to the final third. Then a shadow fell, and none too gradually either. The study of arms became all. Chestnut men strove to save cities from falling, and prayed and built shrines as never before. There were little triumphs and sacrificial piles of purple heads, but Guy was unconvinced. They looked more like wish-fulfilment than reporting.

The strange-crowned kings turned from smiting to being

225

smote. The Null, observed ever more accurately, multiplied until they predominated. Chestnut became the exception, scurrying from one beleaguered stronghold to the next, skimming in fast chariots over a sea of reaching purple.

It ended abruptly, the final corner a blank like a scream.

Guy was reluctant to break the reverent hush but duty had tapped him on the shoulder. It was such an everyday occurrence that he lived in hope of developing a pad of scar-tissue there. Then he might be able to ignore the naggy nuisance. Sadly, it hadn't grown thick enough yet.

'You have what you wanted,' he told Hunter. 'This is their final word.'

But Hunter wasn't there. His reply came from startlingly far off. He'd taken the tragic tale in at a glance, perhaps fore-armed, and gone into the yet further room beyond.

'No,' his words came back, crystal-clear amidst the hush. 'That's here. The last word is a whine. I'm looking at it.'

Not literally he wasn't. He was on his knees, head bowed. Two tearful eyelids were slammed shut over seeing and blind eye alike.

Hunter knelt amidst enough gold and convertible trinklets to run Imperial Wessex for a year, but he had no regard for it. The stone Null loomed above him and presently more than filled his universe.

At the end they must have despaired of the old gods who couldn't save them. Their fragmentary remains lay scorned in each corner. In their stead, other idols arose and the Egyptians bowed down to the new acme of success.

The statue was beautifully – and fearfully – realised. This was no mere monster head stuck on to second-hand shoulders. Those who'd shaped and polished the hard granite down to such smoothness had known their model well: body and soul. In depicting the simple truth, they'd caught the animating hunger brilliantly.

Since that might not have been the entire intention, they'd tried to humanise it too, insofar as you could – which wasn't far. Guy had never seen a clothed Null before. The Egyptian garb and crown definitively failed in their purpose. This last Pharaoh was above mere 'meat' fripperies.

Hunter had entertained such high hopes. He'd realised the last word, the whole concluding chapter, would be sad, and had prepared himself. Yet somehow it had never occurred to him that the word might be whimpered. And cravenly whimpered at that. He'd hoped – again – for beauty and – again – what he got was sordid.

Hunter arose with jewellery and ingot imprints on his knees.

'They weren't just killed,' he said to Guy, his voice quite dead. 'They were *broken* . . .'

'I—'

Hunter walked all over Guy's unwanted comfort.

'No, *me*,' he interrupted. '*I* was wrong. There's nothing to learn here. We should go.'

Most regrettably, that got a cheer from the looser cannons. Hunter could have killed them – would have, if his longbow were to hand – but he'd never dreamed of needing it. Seductive hope shoved all that sort of thing out of mind. The notepad he *had* deemed essential slipped, still virginal, from his fingers to join the old gold. Absent-minded, he also left the sparrowhawk behind to returning ebon dark. Cousin Beelzebub heard its caw of protest but didn't intervene. It was soiled goods now.

The retreat was the exact opposite of their advance. Everyone else led and Hunter lagged. His interest having waned, he failed to look about and his feet were made of lead.

In contrast, Guy's attention was promiscuous and everywhere, obliging them to make detours. Knowing the answer, he had fresh interest in the question. And since their host-cum-guide-cum-mentor seemed silenced, he was pleased to take up the light burden of informed commentary.

'Obviously an ad hoc barracks' – this of a side-chamber snubbed on first acquaintance, but now illumined by Guy's lantern and new understanding. 'Note the crude graffiti on the walls. A wealth of weaponry but short on utensils. Whereas, *here*' – another vestibule too dull to have delayed them before – 'the inverse is true. This was where the last women and children were. And *here* must have been the final stand: soon after the sealing of the shrine. With no hope left, the last minutes were spent cowering in that very corner. See the bone conglomerates? And the idol brought along as desperate plea? We could have had our answer earlier, Hunter. Your Egypt expired *here*.'

Hunter elbowed his way through the throng to the threshold. His voice, reanimated, preceded him.

'What idol?' There's no id—'

So Guy saw – belatedly. Idols aren't able to attack you.

Guy had his gun but it was packed away – rather as he now wished *he* was. There was nothing between him and the Null's advancing malice save a prayer. On the plus side, he had the presence of mind and just enough time to say one. That and not fouling himself were things to be proud of – later. If possible.

It was the Cretan's canniness which saved Guy. He'd not forgotten the far-off sound effects either, and knew in his heart of hearts, much as he might wish otherwise, that they weren't water. From that moment onwards his revolver had been moistening his palm.

One, two, three, four retorts, one per oncoming pace, point-blank to face and chest, quelled the Null's hunger. Each shot sounded like a ship's broadside in the enclosed space, and acrid powder smoke mercifully softened the edges of the scene – at the price of pricking a nose already in agony.

For, as some valedictory comfort, the Null managed to save face (even as its own collapsed) by scarring Guy's. A last lunge, whose author would never know its outcome, scored a sliver off the bridge of the ambassadorial nose.

It bled like a jugular, but he would live – and actually be more handsome ever after. The one thing that Bathie regretted about her husband was his beak – but now he was perfect. The luck of the Ambassadors.

So, little cavils about noise, nose and nostrils aside, Guy

was content – or would be. He'd been gifted lots more life and also witnessed it flee from almond eyes.

He also got a band of crimson torn from the hem of Bathie's dress to mitigate the flow. At any other time, the perfume therein would have made him more appreciative.

She bound it tightly and the lower portion descended like a veil or mask, rendering him even more piratical than normal. ambassadorial eyes widened as the knot bit but no sound escaped, making Bathie still more proud. It did the trick. Very shortly, he was no longer dining vampire-style on Guy-lifeblood, and conversation could reappear on the menu.

First though, he had his seax knife (and then gun) out and dubbed the wonderful Cretan. It might not be 100 per cent official now that Guy had fallen out with the Imperial fountainhead, but so long as the ex-shaggyman stuck around with them, he would be a 'sir'; a knight beyond reproach or reminder of rabbit-days.

The man arose, inches taller and lost for words.

Guy was also stricken, but for different reasons. Bathie helped by saying what her spouse wanted to.

'The thing was stock-still, Guy. You thought it was another stone false god. The vermin was cunning: perhaps even one of the risen types . . .'

That was kindly meant, but overdoing it a bit. Happily, the angel-awoken, city-building variety of Null seemed absent from Egypt. The native breed's ignorance was everybody's bliss.

'It shouldn't have happened,' puzzled Hunter, rather stupidly Guy thought, even though his own senses were still reeling. For it *had* happened – which was all the justification any event needed.

Not having made his peace with the world in that way, Hunter blathered on.

'But there's no way in or out, other than the way we came . . .'

'So, are you saying,' snapped Bathie, 'that Mr Fangs was always here? A long time to wait, I should have thought. He looks pretty good, considering. But *thousands* of years old, you reckon? I wish I knew his secret . . .'

'No. Obviously not, but—'

'Or maybe he accompanied us in disguise. Shall I do a roll-call and see who he was impersonating? Beelzebub? Still here are you?'

'Yo!' that man confirmed.

Hunter's lips were compressing out of sight. Uncaring, Bathie continued at him like a dog with a bone. Someone had put Guy at risk – aside from himself for a change. They deserved all they got.

'And it doesn't *seem* magic, does it, Hunter? The carcass has stuck around. And bullets stopped it pretty good. See? Yuks!'

Here Bathie planted a savage kiss full on the Cretan's newly-nobled lips – and he would have prolonged it had she not torn away.

'And so?' she concluded, impatient Madame-style.

A fair-minded man in his own way, Hunter gave in to her hobnailed logic.

'And so,' he conceded, 'there's another way in.'

A few seconds' more obstinacy could have saved him some shame by letting others confirm it. Up the 'ramp to nowhere' came six or seven Null. They paused at the rim, as surprised to find company as the company itself.

Between them, Guy and the Cretan shot the lot, pitching them back down the slope and easing the Ambassador's nasal pain no end, extra powder irritant or no. Revenge can often be a sovereign remedy.

And also sweet. Short but sweet. People craned their necks searching for the 'shortness' aspect – for the Null generally travelled in strength. The Blades-Bible's other name for them was 'Legion'.

Booms and reverberations died away. Every ear was cocked for Null chimes but none came. The silence was golden. Such a gift shouldn't be gone over with an eye-glass. As one, the day-trippers set off home.

The glories that were Egypt no longer meant a thing. A painted, plain English, answer to each unanswered question wouldn't have delayed them. The odd overlooked sarcophagus or scarab winked in vain or got trampled.

At the chasm Guy half expected company and a toll keeper demanding more than they could pay. So he and many others heaved a sigh of relief to find it only a horrible and godless – and deserted – bridge like before.

'If you make a fuss again,' Guy told cousin Beelzebub, in a kindly tone belying his words, 'then I shall shoot you.'

'Even though you've not reloaded?' Beelzebub queried.

'Figure of speech,' Guy maintained in for-your-own-good mode. 'Some similar sanction.'

He patted the knighthood-bestowing knife at his belt. There were others up his sleeve and down his boot.

Beelzebub calculated and then rediscovered his courage. He even went first, graceful as a courtesan.

After that miracle, everything went topsy-turvy (save the bridge) as the jaunt rewound: a rare glimpse of the social order inverted. Foot-soldiers and lamp-men first, then former shaggies and Sicilians and thoroughbred Wessex. Finally, cousins in a clump, plus Bathie, made the plank bow and moan. However, thanks to Blades's – or someone's – blessing, no one actually went 'topsy-turvy' down below.

Guy concluded the tale, he and Polly and Prudence bringing up the rear as its moral. And the moral was: obligation and honour meant something, and could manifest themselves as real facts in the real world. For life to have value that precept needed constant restating. Guy just wished he sometimes sang it with a choir, not as a solo.

No Null scampered up to trouble the rearguard or wobble their way – but they could well have. It's the thought that counts.

Thoughts and counting occupied the high table of Guy's mind as he paused halfway across the bridge. He *thought* he heard something. He *counted* the party's lanterns. They had plenty and could spare one.

Opening all the shutters of his own and altering the wick to wicked extravagance, Guy then let gravity take it below. The two Ps knew he never did anything stupid without reason. So, though their reflexes were equal to it, they didn't reach to rescue the light. Like Guy, they just stood and looked. Abandoned to its fate, sacrificed for only a select audience, the lantern fell as an island of illumination, initially revealing nothing, dying for nothing.

Save that it never hit hard ground or bottom. Something softer interposed and spoke its surprise. A chime.

For a fleeting second, before the expiring of the light, Guy saw the speaker and all its friends. A purple torrent, a river in flood, was flowing beneath his feet. In the instant granted him – which was ample – he realised that the monsters were carrying their clinging young. The shiny back of a Null mother also slithered before his eyes, that one second saying as much as a century. Whilst opportunity arose, several well-directed beams of hatred were shot back in his direction. Guy creaked his way to solid ground.

'Ladies and gentlemen,' he said, since they were wordlessly demanding explanation, 'not to mention, not-yet citizenry shaggymen. It is my unpleasant but exciting duty to inform you that we have disturbed a Null nest. The world will shortly be descending on to our heads.'

With so much weight of rock above, it felt like it already had. Extra encumbrance seemed a bit much. Also, they detected a deterioration in air quality, if such a thing were possible. It might just be imagination, due to the added threat – but more likely not. The urge to gag and gasp was growing.

Guy mentally tracked that fact a few steps back and failed to warm to what he found there.

'I know!' said Hunter, unbidden, unheeded. 'They're coming in through the air shafts, the rascals! Too thin for travel, I thought – but maybe if *widened* . . .'

The divine scriptwriter was really on Hunter's case today. As with the Null up the ramp, flesh and blood arrived to prove his point. Purple streaked down into an adjacent side-chamber, like ripe purple grapes shot through a tube.

They landed lithely and looked about and saw all they

needed to know. Some cousins and Sicilians and shaggy captains went off to fight them and never came back.

However, such spirit did at least serve to let the rest get to the stairs – and no further. The way out now had new curators. Which solved one mystery. No fresh air came that way any more – only hisses.

Guy showed what he thought of that by reloading and giving them a pistol's worth of pointed opinion. Some Null fell, but mostly he just blocked the way more and fugged up the stairwell into the bargain.

'Go on!' coquetted Bathie (who really was wicked) to cousin Quatorze. 'I *dare* you . . .'

He looked and, having no choice, dared.

'This,' he told all, as though he'd spoke first, 'looks like a job for Louis-Quatorze Ambassador!'

Certainly, it wasn't anything anyone sensible would attempt. Perhaps that was what he meant. Perhaps it was the reason he succeeded.

Quatorze leaped up the stairs calling out rude things about Null mothers and spitting leaden venom. Foremost amongst his weapons though were surprise and stupidity.

Once the mad *meat* was committed and offered screening from meat firesticks, a huge Null stood forth, Horatius fashion. It should have been a foregone conclusion, off the scale of any worthwhile racing odds Guy knew. And yet God has a special care for the touched. Leastways, *something* made Quatorze's needle-pointed shoes stumble just before just-deserts time. He tumbled to victory below the Null and between its straddled legs, not upon its waiting and equally needle-like talons. He chanced to fall exactly right to stick a knife up where no biped cares to have one.

Bathed, Mithras-style, in the blood of his foe, and then covered by a lifeless body, Quatorze shrugged off both and carried on. Viewed from either side of the argument, he was carrying a lot of kudos with him. Maybe that was why the purple doormen admitted him.

Etiquette be damned, Wessex folk couldn't afford to be shy

about this particular invitation. One dainty foot being over the threshold, everyone else scrambled to add their own.

Those humans who were coming came up the stairs and passed on – one way or another. Then the dark below reverted to its former owners. The last Guy knew of it was as a black boiling of chimes: incandescent – and coming closer.

They found cousin Quatorze under a dying Null, not only as gory as all the slaughtered shaggymen ventilators, but, better yet, still living and Lord of Iceland material. Where he'd cleared a path, Polly and Prudence carved a broad road, permitting a moment's peace. They hauled Quatorze up and mopped him down. Painful as it was to admit, the mad boy had done well. However, there was no higher title than Ambassador (not in their eyes anyway), and no time either, so Guy's seax stayed in its sheath.

That bit of gained ground aside, the general situation only proved the wisdom of the (Blades embellished) Bible when it said: '*Of Null there is no end.*' And neither was there. So the gospel was proved *gospel*.

Their path back was swallowed up by dark and Null. Their way forward promised light at the end of the tunnel – but the tunnel was purple. It was an easy (if disgusting) decision.

The trouble was, the more purple went on the floor, the more appeared as replacement. Laying them low only made extra space for others to come, cockroach-mode, out of cracks and corners, or descend like spiders from above. In the – bitter – end, the sham 'holy of holies' was only won through, not won over. It took virtuoso axe-work just to hack an ephemeral corridor – but they settled (and gladly) for that.

Luck beyond prizing decreed the Null weren't yet in the 'Forest of Reeds'. That would have been a happy hunting ground for them, where there was no room to swing an edge and every step brought surprises. If the chutes had lent access there or the Null-nursery been disturbed earlier, the finale would have comprised a quick cat-and-mouse game round the gloomy pillars. Guy had no illusions about how close they'd come – metaphorically and otherwise. The hatchery most likely lurked not far beyond the extent of their blind exploration, maybe just down the ramp Hunter had so misjudged. It made you think – and shudder. Right in front of their numbed noses, probably in new Null-hollowed levels, there'd lurked a writhing honeycomb of maggots and mothers. Plus proud fathers and loyal sons. Any *meat* blundering into there would have been jointed rations faster than their nerves could carry the news.

Hunter's excavations hadn't disturbed their age-old breeding and feeding, luckily for him. Nor, perhaps, would Guy's outing have done – till the shooting began. The lone Null which provoked it was just a putrid fluke, but still wondrous seed corn for raising full-blown disaster. Through him Guy knew they'd met their match – and maybe their conclusion. The conventional ratio was a whole Wessex regiment, with one puckle gun per platoon, for just a run-of-the-mill nest complex. Here though, there'd been millennia to build a really spectacular infestation. Even with the iron legions of Pevensey-Assyria at his disposal to throw in, Guy would still have hesitated to bet the farm on just who'd come out.

Therefore, 'coming out' was the only option. Guy Ambassador said so and said it with all solemnity. He also advised a measure of speed.

They made better time on the return trip, given wings by powerful incentives. The odd Null dropped out of the ceiling and dropped odd members of the group, but no one lingered to see. This was only an extended feeler of Wessex civilisation being hastily withdrawn, not the whole culture in retreat. There was no call to show the flag and drag your wounded with you. Today, survival was allowed to shout and rudely drown out higher callings.

Day hit them like acid in the eyes – and the Null likewise soon after, equally to be relished. Temporarily shy of light, the foremost men staggered back from its first embrace. Then they recalled what followed on and persevered. Sting as it might, the sunshine was still welcome. It was good (in a funny sense of the word) to see bad news clearly.

Again, that festering question. Was today a good day to die? Was any day? Very probably they'd soon find out.

It wasn't quite true to say the Null were waiting for them. The cordon at the top of the temple ramp Polly and Prudence had ruined themselves running up were surveying the general conflict below. Presumably, they were going to pitch in shortly – or else they were the Null officer class human theorists had long postulated. Either way, they seemed glad to be saved some trouble and have the battle come to them.

Reloaded for a third time, Guy shot one, then two, before realising he'd be better employed delegating the task. Signals set Polly and Prudence to it and then he was pleased he had paused. It wasn't every day you got to see a battle royal, even if you *were* a king in a rough-and-tumble universe. Compared to this, the Picts Lane business had been a fishwives' catfight down on Hastings' Stade; a mere 'I've-forgotten-why-we're-doing-this' strawheads' brawl outside a cider-house.

The Null were showing off *real* commitment. You had to respect them – but Guy didn't recognise 'have-tos' and so loathed them instead.

The Null didn't care what meat thought, any more than Guy consulted cattle destined for his dinner. Most likely, Null didn't credit meat with sentience at all. Again, the Guy/cow parallel applied. A spot of selective blindness was essential to make life bearable, or action (and dinner) possible.

It certainly worked for the purple community. Sacrificial lambs amongst them were coming off the cliff solely to provide a soft landing for those who came after. When enough had made the ultimate gift, many more arrived in fit state to continue. Soon they were coming across the temple roofs, clambering fluidly over the partial platforms. Their calls were not wishing Guy long life and good health.

These invading elements had transcended the feeble human attempts at defence. Others of the breed were still in the process of meeting resistance head on, no-nonsense fashion – and doing rather well. Beyond the perimeter fences

Hunter had installed (and, let it be said, Polly and Prudence had approved) mankind's best and wickedest notions were going for naught. Martyr Null were impaling themselves on the razor-thorn barricades to serve as stepladders for later brethren. The warning geese and wild dogs which inhabited the cleared zone honked or barked briefly before becoming hors d'oeuvres. No heed was taken of nip or scratch. Perfectly good carcasses were cast aside, barely tasted. For the Null were good parents, after their own fashion. They got quite moody when anyone disturbed their babies' slumber. They wished to leave meat people in no doubt of it. They also wished to leave no meat people.

Guy looked and saw and calculated, and realised neither musketry nor mettle would save the day. The separated Null tribes across the Nile, squatting atop red hills and watching, saw it too. Over the water wafted their crazed acclamation.

The temples were taken, save for the fringe Guy and co. occupied on sufferance. Tent-city was falling. You didn't need to be the Prophet Blades to predict the outcome. The expedition's enclave had only minutes – whether two or fifty-nine – left to it. Guy resolved to make good use of them.

There was an ancient Wessex formation termed 'the hedgehog', devised in the bad old days when humanity was the underdog. If things went horribly wrong (as they so often had), it was used to convey vital personnel – i.e. Blades – out of a débâcle. Pikes or halberds in a circle supplied the spikes, whilst firearms in the shadow of their protection served as a (not precisely hedgehog-like) 'sting'. Guy ordered one into being now, where parasols stood in for pikes, and pistols for rifles. At its cosseted centre he placed Bathie and some of the more sensitive cousins, plus, of course, himself – since command requires all kinds of sacrifice.

For a drill best known from distant history they bodged it fairly well. The ramp and some momentum also helped. To start with, the Null they met went under and remained down. Like some vast, spiky, slug, a slime trail of purple was left

237

behind, whilst to front something horrible engulfed all those who opposed.

'Don't bother,' said Bathie dryly, as Guy turned to broach the subject of magecraft. Her powers only answered the call when she was relaxed or frightened – events as rare as that – and things weren't so far forward yet. True, despair was one good reason to get mellow or agitated, but its wonderful certainties were still some way off.

As was the *Impaled Blades*. Failing to be of use as her husband wished, Bathie indicated that conveyance as an alternative last, best, hope.

'Never mind,' Guy replied – and then did mind, as he lost his beloved cocked hat to a near-miss missile of sandstone. To seek and retrieve it was to risk having the hedgehog grind over you. The ravenous purple fan club left in its wake were just dying to meet any stragglers or fleas off its back. Therefore, a puff of wig-powder and a sigh were the headgear's only requiem. Bare-headed and grim-jawed, Guy pressed on.

To their right lay one – or three – of the wonders of the site; the very things that first made Hunter tarry. Triple colossi, six or more times life-size (and popularly christened 'man, wife and mother-in-law'), loomed over both land and Nile. Now they swarmed with even more animation than their gifted sculptors had bestowed. A gaggle of marines had chosen these as linchpin for their last stand, only to find them secret entrances – or exits at present – to Null realms below. An inexhaustible invasion streamed forth, too many for firepower to force back.

It was an magnetically attractive sight: the sinuous struggle up, down and around the calm colossi, drawing in many monsters who might otherwise have impeded Guy. That much was very good. However, equally drawn as any human eye, the *Blades*'s puckle guns were adding to the lively dance. Stone features which had survived millennia of weathering and Null custody were splintering skywards after mere minutes of man's attention. That purple bits went with them was some, but not entire, compensation. Marines were dying under the lead lash too. Neither were what Guy wanted.

Which begged the question: what *did* he want? Guy considered well, but not long. Answer came easy. Nothing here. So, he might as well be somewhere else – and soon. Hunter Town hadn't long to go; its sands were swift flowing through the timer now. Possessions, nostalgia, obligation – none of them need delay him. Now was when to take the straight route out.

The Null weren't daft and so knew it too. Two-leg meat had been off the menu for millennia, but folk-memory remained. Clothed meat did not surrender respectfully to the dictates of dining. It would not stretch out its neck to oblige a claw. Also, like gazelles and similar skittish flesh, it would dash and dart with innumerable manoeuvres to postpone the inevitable. This meat species was so depraved as to take to the water or tunnels to escape their beautiful destiny. Therefore, it was behoven on the master race to set them on the right path, even at the price of tears. Null moved to be between the 'hedgehog' and the thing-that-floated.

Before that, the *Impaled Blades* had been largely left alone, an indigestible, spitting feed when so much alternative succulence was available. Her (or, as per Bathie, *his*) crew were lining the landside decks to pity the mêlée and flick away lunatic loners. Now that time-killing had to end. The purple collective whose futurity had been disturbed weren't minded to make exceptions. No one was leaving without permission – or whole. A shield of lesser bucks went down to the water, whilst their fathers (conceivably) conceived stratagems behind.

Meanwhile, the hedgehog was getting awfully mangy. Rearward quills were plucked out by the parasol, or whatever polearm had been acquired. Daring Null danced into the gaps and performed until a muzzle could be applied to their thick skulls. Guy and his spiny gang weren't going to make it.

So Guy tore off his crimson-upon-crimson bandage, raising only a minor spray of blood, plus a major temptation to scream. He resisted that in favour of something less indulgent. A shaggy-captain had a sergeant's half-pike – or did have until Guy liberated it. The red rag went aloft and was waved.

Given their chequered history in the food chain, Wessex-men recognised red as a distress sign rather than a hue for fun underwear. Inherited memory of Null making that colour spurt upon the green Downs ensured it always grabbed their attention.

Guy wanted the *Blades* to know they were coming and to leave the poor colossi alone. He wanted, even more than he presently wanted a nice cool drink, the puckle guns to simulate a hail storm upon the obstructed way ahead. Then he wanted suppressive fire, just like the puckle's manual offered. Guy said all that through the waggling of a crimson strip whose life-role up to then had been concealment of a shapely calf.

Someone aboard obviously spoke 'rag'. Like seeing a friendly girl turn to look at him with a glint in her eye, Guy was glad to see the fore and aft puckles start to traverse.

'Abandon hedgehog!' he ordered, as calmly as he could shout. The intrinsic humour therein was absolutely lost on everyone. 'Alas, alack, and all that, but life wants us to crawl . . .'

And so that's what they did – because they trusted him and knew that life was like that. Therefore, when stray puckle shells headed their way in the process of causing the sand to jig, they were passed over – usually. Those not yet belly-down got put there.

Null interlopers, who couldn't understand the Ambassador's call and wouldn't obey meat anyway, were *whinged* away first. Then several ranks of those behind. After that, they learned wisdom and travelled Guy-style, worming along on elbows and knees, gaining a scorpion's-eye view of the world.

For no good reason, Guy recalled he'd not cleaned his teeth that morning. Some of the hot sand grains entering, uninvited, into his mouth, were tongued around to correct the omission. He desired that if he was going to draw his last breath, it should be a sweet one.

The way ahead, wondrously puckled vermin-free, was still studded with purple remains. Some proved to be only feigning the role, awaiting discovery and their spell on stage. These had to be persuaded to take the role of corpse seriously. Then, as if that weren't bad enough, their brethren behind transpired to be fleeter than meat at crab-travel. They formed a purple carpet wriggling furiously forward, shiny arses aloft, like some fantasy lifted from William of Orange's daydreams.

Guy was helping pin a Null cheat to the sand with seax tentpegs when he discerned the disparity in pace. A lunging talon, unsporting from behind, hooked the sole from his shoe. First his nose, then his cocked hat, and now his favourite war-boots. These people had no respect. And wyrd likewise. Disgraceful.

Both deserved a few choice phrases but one bullet did it worth a thousand words. The amateur cobbler went away to a more settled career as carrion.

The time for style and cleverness was gone, eaten up by the better muscles God inexplicably gave to the worst of his creation. If civilisation is defined as mutual support, then civilisation needed to take a doze and allow a few older truths to be spoken.

'Every man for himself!'

'*Live for the moment and hope for the future*' had ever been Guy's walking stick for tricky moments. All he could do now was go with the flow and hope the *Blades* guessed the score. Like a sprinter from his blocks, he rose to hoppity home as best one boot would let him.

Naturally, he grasped Bathie alongside, undermining his own orders. But there again, he had said every *man*. Ambassador words were always ripe with ambiguity and the evidence of his fingertips acquitted him of mutiny. Madame Ambassador wasn't included.

Of necessity, the puckle chorus ceased now that humans were in the damn way – though that formed welcome respite for some – not only for the Null accepting delivery, but also frazzled wrestlers with replacement puckle drums aboard. Guy had already noted water being doused on overheated barrels, and jam-gaps in their singing. Sad to say, the tempo of 'Symphony for Rifle and Puckle' was winding down.

By contrast, Guy's Null friends had loads of fizz left. They positively leaped into the niche vacated. Here was their chance and they took it with glee. Guy didn't like Null gaiety. It contained way too much gloating.

The *Blades* partook of that same worried spirit. Her gangplank was up and the engines getting there. If Guy's thoughts were grappling hooks then the paddles would have strained in vain, but, as so often happens, prayer just bounced off the recipient. Rescue was looking over its shoulder and edging away.

Guy wished Sea-captain aboard and in charge: a man of cold, cold, thought, granted, but not one to fold prematurely. However, he was back in the Delta, lucky swine, building a fleet of quinqueremes to conquer this new world – or fight the old one should it come looking. No amount of longing would transport him those miles in an instant. What they had would have to do – unfortunately. Bosun, the present master of the *Blades*, was just a rank-and-file mortal with but one life to live and insufficient fame to live after him as yet. Plus a deficient sense of gratitude, apparently. He needed only one more little nudge to be off and away . . .

It wasn't all black. When Guy bemoaned the silence it was in relative terms. All around him people were 'enjoying' the defining moments of their lives. Some knots of resistance were still tight and binding. The battle of the colossi bickered on. Yet these were private conversations, without agenda or agreed theme. Guy was massively grateful to them for the distraction, but he also knew theirs was not a club to join. There was no future in it. He told Hunter and Polly and Prudence so – or words to that effect. Acting on them, their axes and his half-pike made swift for the river.

Clear intentions pave their own way. Decisiveness breeds like wildfire. A pair of eyes afloat saw Guy wasn't going to get away with it. Or, contra-wise, that *they* wouldn't get away with not helping. Orders were given as if they'd always been intended. The gangplank crashed down.

Two birds with one stone. Guy now found tomorrow a more creditable prospect, and a tiresome Null underneath thought the sky had caved in. The lead refugee (cousin Beelzebub – to no one's surprise), stilled its last twitches with his added bulk.

Guy and Bathie bounded on board soon after. Polly and Prudence lingered to make sure of it, which was very touching – as were they. Afterwards, all and sundry boggled to see how the ladies' Sussex-steel axe-heads had buckled.

When all was gathered in, human harvest plus Null weeds as well, the gangplank started for the vertical again. Gangs of highly motivated mariners (aided by all manner of volunteers not usually mad about manual labour) competed at chains' length with purple latecomers. Meanwhile, would-be passengers hurled themselves at the rail or tried to persuade the plank down with sheer desperation.

Wessex had a way of dealing with such ill manners. Hatchets left little posies of purple fingers still gripping tight, and shotguns prepared a croc-feast for later. The gap between ship and shore got so full even the wicked Null could walk on water.

Aided by pike power pushing against the anchorage's stone revetments, the steamship made what haste it could to go.

In such circumstances a hive can't afford drones. No one said, 'Welcome aboard, Guy – a close one, eh? Phew!' He was expected to lend a hand and gun the same as anyone else. Fortunately, he expected it of himself too.

If studied close enough, every situation has a role for a good heart to play. Guy's motives were not selfish: he truly did desire that the majority should survive. Therefore it was his duty and privilege to steel them against false sentiment and the piteous cries of those left behind. In some cases he showed real mercy and shot the worst afflicted himself.

Slowly at first, but with ever increasing confidence, the paddles turned and took them away. Non-swimmers amongst the marooned survivors lined the banks to say cheerio – whilst the Null moved amongst them conducting a cull.

Their more gifted colleagues dived in only to find purple pursuers still on their heels – and better in the water than they. Just like the crocodile competition, Null bore prey underwater until they grew still and accepted events. Accordingly, not many humans gained safety that way, for all the crew's dangled ladders and sympathetic pike jabs.

There was a final, half-hearted, attempt to board, too few in numbers to do much except save purple face. The ship's sides briefly crawled with misplaced monster confidence, climbing like sentient creepers. Sadly for those trespassers, late in the day but still welcome, Bathie's faculty put in an appearance. It allowed her to coat the *Blades*'s rail with blue 'balefire', raising (and frying) both Null hands and human mirth, saving a tedium of hatchet-jobs.

By then though, the *Impaled Blades* was capable of its own salvation. Having cooled slightly during the interval, and benefiting from a calm reload, the puckle guns laid down a memorable farewell, clearing the foreshore of standing life.

The water in their wake churned with foam and less pleasant things. Steam-driven paddles proved effective Null mincers, as well as tutors in the wisdom of keeping clear. The Null learned and left alone.

The *meat* was on its way, leaving peace – and pieces – behind. Man was relinquishing the place to more years of private meditation. The Null had had a rude awakening. Neither side ought to mope. For the monsters, a little victory and a bumper feast, then the tangled sleep that seemed their chiefest joy. For mankind, quiet confidence that they (or their descendants) would be back. The temples would wait patiently. Let the Null serve as careless caretakers till civilisation came again.

Suddenly, Guy saw it as if from above: a bird's-eye view of the river of Time flowing even mightier than the Nile. He glimpsed today seen from that lofty perspective. It was – it would be – nothing, scarcely even an embellishment of bones. When – if – men walked here again, 'now' would be mere detail, if recalled at all. Therefore: forgetfulness *then*, but all this fuss and bother *now* . . . The contrast was laughable.

Even so, Guy was surprised to hear laughter. He was even more amazed to recognise it as his own. There was no stifling it. Guy's amusement rolled over the waters and reached the land, filling in the gaps between puckle coughs.

From somewhere deep inside, humour suppressed in the course of a corseted existence had sensed its chance. The merriment was no more to blame than Guy himself. All things wish to live, whether states of mind or drooping poets, whatever else they might proclaim. Leaping for the light, sounds scaled his lips, relishing the rare freedom to speak unfiltered.

Bathie (a fan of unreason) approved – but no one else. The rest were trapped in the passing moment. Butchery might be business, but *not* a cause for giggles.

Thus here was a fitting cap to a rotten day; a wet blanket draped over the pleasures of survival. Someone fondly believed to be a good man proved to be just another horror after all.

Inside their secret hearts, decent people on board looked askance at Guy after that.

'*The dream is . . . over!*'

Guy almost dropped his cards. Almost.

'Pardon?' he enquired.

Bathie's eyes were wide – with fear and joy. Her fingers desisted from the bowl of cherries and sycamore-figs.

First Guy, now her. This 'involuntary expression' thing seemed all the rage.

Yet unlike Guy, Bathie's words were news to her. They were fresh-forged novelties, first heard as they issued from her lips.

Plucky Mrs Ambassador went with it, inspired by wonder, even as she wondered, 'Whatever next?' A bit like her – disastrous – wedding night.

She wasn't kept waiting about. Again, someone else seized

her larynx.

'They come!'

Guy kept a straight face. Such was the nature of sorcerous company, the stock-in-trade of mage marriages.

Bathie shook her head, trying to clear or repossess it. Apparently the pleasures of being a conduit soon palled. Her thunder storm of black frizz mimicked every motion with split-second delay, before tumbling to repose atop crimson shoulders.

'The dream is over!'

It was fully her now, Mrs Ambassador's usual voice parroting a message not understood, but taking pleasure in the sounds. *Her* sounds entirely.

For a second, Guy was back in Yarmouth. In his mind's eye he again admired the view from the wizard's lofty tower – in preference to pondering the happy suicide within. Guy once more worshipped the sun on the Solent, the distant shore and seagulls arcing below his high station.

Their gaudier cousins, the sunbirds and other swooping scavengers of the Nile, called him back from the far-off afternoon. In Egypt the sun was also high: high and mighty and high overhead: enough maybe to account for speaking in tongues.

It was an unworthy lunge for the mundane. Bathie's hat might be beside her crimson thigh – but so was his: close cocked cousin to that now worn (or eaten) by the Null. The deck awning covered and shaded them both. It was no more oven-like than normal. If anyone, it was Hunter, hatless in the foredeck's brassy blare, that should be spouting.

'Guy – face facts!' he ordered himself – and he was right. Facts and Null and suchlike wild things weren't fit creatures to turn your back on. Even since Yarmouth he'd been pretending not to hear the growling of unanswered questions. And him an Ambassador too. For shame . . .

'Who—' he started to ask, intending to move on to 'what' and 'why' – that same old pedestrian trinity. Before he could Bathie hushed him.

'No,' she whispered, firm enough to override; garnished with a flick of the hand. 'Enough.' With economy of motion her fingers followed through to take a celebratory cherry. 'Suffice to say it was *beautiful*.'

Guy declined the doormat role.

'Does it suffice?' he countered, doling out an exactly equal measure of no-argument. 'No. I disagree.'

So she had to reconsider, screwing up her eyes to backtrack.

'A rudery, granted,' she conceded. 'But I'll accept messages from beautiful sources . . .'

'Beautiful indeed,' agreed Hunter, returning at just the wrong time. His eyes had been locked on to the pyramids ever since they first floated into sight. Hours and hours he'd been there, battering his gaze against their mystery. It wouldn't have hurt Fate to keep him at it for a few moments more. 'Oh, sorry. Have I interrupted something?'

'Well, actually—'

'That's a relief.' Maybe Hunter meant the reassurance only he heard, or maybe the awning's shelter. It hardly mattered. He was still there and making himself comfortable. 'Don't want to intrude. Tricky business being on a little ship with a couple. Remember when I rounded the prow and you were having her over the rail and . . . What? *What?*'

'Isn't there some part of those pointy things you haven't studied yet?'

Ordinarily, Bathie wouldn't have said that. Her love affair with Egypt had a way yet to run and the miraculous man-mountains were still its high point. Now though, with a new lover knocking at the door, she was prepared to wield the below-belt blow.

Hunter winced as though it really had been delivered.

'*It is wicked to mock the wonderful*', he intoned.

Only Guy would truly *never* descend to bluntness. Holding your head up against life's indignities was everything. He stepped in to inoculate the moment against his wife's venom.

'I don't recognise the quotation . . .' A diversion, not continuation, of conversation.

Hunter was typically candid.

'You wouldn't. I just made it up.'

'Ah . . .'

'You don't get to be bishop without speaking fluent pseudo-scripture, you know.'

'No. I suppose not.'

Then their guest twisted his vision back to the pyramids, as if they exerted a hypnotic pull. Rising above the palm forest their pinnacles were better than medicine to him, pointing in the right direction, to beyond all the tears and cares of this world. Man had made those sublime structures. *Sometimes* he could do well.

Abstraction occupied all too short a space.

'So what *was* going on?' Hunter asked.

They had his unwanted attention again and, like a Null on a fat man, he wouldn't let things lie. There was nothing else for it.

'My Lady Bathesheba was just informing me,' Guy reported, 'that – and I quote: "*the dream is over*". Moreover, she is of the opinion that "*they come!*"'

Again, Guy learned that the very best place to hide things is in plain sight. Failing to understand instantly, Hunter was making the best sense of it he could. Old precepts about not getting between a dog and a tree were lumbering into his mind.

'Husband and wife thing, eh?' Hunter ventured.

'Very much so.' Guy only spoke the truth – or at least a portion thereof.

'I'll leave you to it then.'

'I should.'

Then all the nifty footwork proved wasted. Someone else came to their rescue. Bosun, by the sound of it, up in the crow's-nest enjoying a post-demotion change of duties. His distinctive tongueless call alerted others more eloquent.

'Oars ahoy!'

It was semi-expected. The impulse to arm was weak. Only Polly and Prudence, looming up from wherever they'd been lurking, swapped their sun bonnets for war gear.

At the prow, reformed shaggymen clarified.

'Many oars! Ours.'

That got a ragged cheer. Fresh, friendly faces at last.

Not far from where the pyramidic city clustered, the Nile branched and aged into river-senility, concluding in a delta region. At the start of that broadening Egypt's latest invaders had set their southernmost settlement – until, that is, Hunter's drive drove him on. Now though, 'Hunterville' had gone the way of all flesh and 'New-new-Binscombe' was again Humandom's window on the world. It was, as far as anyone knew, home to the first and last people.

Amidst such loneliness it must be they who'd sent this welcome – and very welcome it was too. Never mind, for the moment, that the outpost might be a fly-blown something or nothing place; a posting fit for misfits and misanthropes. No matter if it was also a town-planner's day-mare mix of Wessex-misplaced, shaggymen's first efforts and Sicilian braggart confidence. So what if whitewashed domes and papyrus thatch rubbed shoulders with Downs style? Even if New-new-Binscombe chanced to look like nothing else on earth, the travellers thought kindly of it. They chose instead to recollect the golden cupola of its citadel and Heaven-aspiring church spire. Those added a dash of gravitas (if not enough – yet) to calm the crazy brew. It was an undeniable fact that stone was already displacing wood at certain crucial quoins. *Some* people obviously thought they were staying.

Either way, eyesore or no, at that moment it seemed a sight for sore eyes, beckoning with all the gold and marble promise of New-Godalming High Street. The weary wayfarers aboard the *Impaled Blades* scanned for their destination through rose-coloured glasses.

Those lenses weren't powerful enough to sight it yet, but there'd been signs for some while. Feet from the settlement had worn a broad path through the palms to the pyramids and Sphinx. Artisans, seeking diversion after the anti-Null walls were perfect, personalised and painted beyond all improvement, had modified that vast, couched, man-lion enigma. Courtesy of their chisels its solemn face increasingly resembled Guy's more sardonic features.

That ambitious amendment went under-appreciated. The

immortalised gentleman's theological foundations were shifting. On good days, *his* deity corresponded to a very different face. He'd authorised a comfortingly familiar Imperial church in New-new-Binscombe, where folk might worship what they would or could; but Guy's input and attendance ended there. He bowed the Bladian knee no more. Certain suspicions had replaced it, but nothing certain. Perhaps nothing ever would. Lost certainties, like amputations, leave a scar.

All the same though, it was flattering for others, especially the simple, to make such wild assumptions on his behalf. Whatever the fate of his mortal body, Guy could now look forward to viewing future ages – albeit blindly and unaware.

So, finding proper people in the vicinity to meet and greet them shouldn't have come as a surprise. It was just that no one anticipated quite such an abundant welcome. It comprised not only oars, but many of them: a Nile chock-a-block with the things. The whole shebang seemed afloat, like some misplaced regatta day.

Now, that was strange. There'd been no heralds or forewarning of their return, so the *Impaled Blades*'s smog and chug should have been the first the look-outs knew of her/him/it. Therefore, either New-new-Binscombe was massively over-manned or the banquet of homecoming had curdled to indigestion before they'd had a bite.

The paddles slowed, the foremost greeter galley drew close. It was propelled by formerly pale but never excitable Wessex exiles. Guy looked and failed to be glad. Whatever had happened was sufficiently past for their voices to sound calm – but still near enough to supply each eye's shiny flare.

Leaning over the rail that Bathie had livened in both love and war, Guy aborted all the '*Your Majesty!*' and '*My Lord – well met!*' foreplay.

'Hello. Yes, yes. And?'

Still fairly wedded to decorum, all the more so for the great gulf between here and home, the Wessex-men were miffed by that. Within bounds, naturally. Their cox and captain, a shaved-bear lookalike, not sweetened by the spruce-up, bowed unsteadily in the *Blades*'s pitching wake.

'*And*,' the man persisted, 'a new sun rises over our darkness now that you have returned.'

Guy sympathised in principle – but not in practice or today.

'*And?*' he repeated, sternly now.

Nude-bear got the message.

'"*And*" with your new sun,' he continued, not audibly intimidated, 'there also rises—'

'Is *raised* . . .' corrected a brave strawhead oarsman. New-Wessex had lived too long cheek-by-jowl with Levellerdom. Both ways of looking at the world were mutually infected.

Galley-captain took it in good heart.

'Is *risen*,' he rectified, 'another novelty—'

'Spit it out, man!' said Bathie, and demonstrated by bouncing a cherry pip off him.

Again, it was taken in the spirit intended. The man was more subtle than the ruined bruin he looked. A sigh was as far as reaction went.

'Come and see the new pyramid,' he invited them.

'The pink clashes with the gold,' said Bathie. 'But otherwise . . .'

Guy studied her in profile. It was a curious summation, way down the list of expected verdicts. And besides, any discontent with the colour scheme need only be as fleeting as the shades themselves. The pyramid's panels shimmered and slid against each other, ever changing. None of the more shocking colour contrasts lasted long enough to really offend.

Guy's objections were more fundamental – in its *being* at all; sitting there, huge and inexplicable, like some faceted insect eyeball starring at the sky.

The old pyramids, miraculous but still incontestable works of man – matters to test but not tear the imagination – were dwarfed. Only unlucky (maybe) lines of sight had prevented them discerning the newcomer far off down the river. The underside of a rare Egyptian cloud was even now taking its

251

tone from the colour pyrotechnics beneath. Horizon to horizon was surely made aware.

Of course, up to now, the pyramids had been a given. A wonder absorbed. Ordinarily – unless you were Bathie or Hunter – you rarely thought to look. Now there wasn't much choice. Every last dog and toddler in New-new-Binscombe seemed to have issued out to see what the great Guy made of things. The *Impaled Blades* moved amidst a locust swarm of vessels from launches to logs.

King Guy addressed them from beside the apt but distressing figurehead and via a dragon-mouthed monster megaphone.

'*We were expecting this*!' he announced in ringing tones – and left it at that. Only Polly and Prudence leaned forward, scanning for scepticism.

They needn't have worried. People *wanted* to believe. And in a way it was even true. Life *was* just one damn thing after another – that Guy had never for a minute denied. Even voyaging downstream to here he'd travelled in full expectation of yet more tripwires on the stairs.

'As a matter of interest,' asked Hunter, 'what did you then "expect" to do about it?' Having had his own realm to run he ought to have been more sympathetic.

Guy wasn't going to be pelted by some sun-dried defrocked bishop of an exploded faith.

'*Then*,' he answered him, 'I anticipated dealing with it. Whatever it was. Employing courage and natural ability. Or dying in the attempt. Either seemed definitive solutions.'

Hunter thought on and – honest debater that he was – gave way entirely.

'Fair enough. Sounds sound.'

Guy moved on. 'Right. Now *that*'s settled, take me to . . .'

From his heroic stance and manner they thought it was going to be '*take me* there!' at the very least. Hands moved hiltwards and thoughts towards last reloadings.

' . . . Take me to . . . Bach and beer . . . !'

They were far nicer destinations. Guy's people would happily follow him to those.

The armada threaded its way past old ruins and new fields to their shanty-town utopia.

'What?'

'Pardon?'

It was no use. The 'toccata' was rumbling the plank floor beneath them and ruffling the Nile water beneath that. The whole veranda setting was alive with music, not conversation. It was time to be uplifted, not updated.

A stock of scores, both sacred and secular, had been among Blades's earliest 'borrowings' from Paradise. They'd accompanied him in great bound books of notation liberated from Ss Peter and Paul, Godalming, and elsewhere. His and his people's need had been greater than theirs – or so he had justified the silencing theft. That was also the fig-leaf to sanction the muting of several other Surrey and Sussex churches. Blades's shaggymen burglars did no permanent harm. Not really. The Downs-country congregations could always raise funds for a new organ – eventually, over a generation or two. Whereas New-Wessex stood in sore need of models for copying *now*. Looked at in a certain light – and swiftly – it had all been entirely ethical.

This 'Bach' business Blades so lauded came later, accompanying him back from the long self-exile in Capri-paradise. Sealed by the 'liberating' of the Professor's sheet-music library, New-Wessex now had the 'complete works' and the sense to play them. Likewise with 'Purcell', another Heaven-dweller by God's spokesman's account. He supplied the soundtrack to many a success, whilst his famous funeral march dignified some of the sadder by-products. More often, though, there was need of Te Deums and Fugues lifted in praise, raising the roof in New-Godalming Cathedral after each Null defeat. Bach, Byrd, Blow, Purcell and a host of others unwittingly obliged.

So, combined with a more honourably portable love of the

253

organ's majestic tones infused from chorister childhood onwards, Blades had caused the best of old earth to sound again in pastures new. Combined love and larceny sponsored glorious second careers in the new setting, serving as accompaniment to all the triumphs of New-Wessex. Messrs Bach and Purcell et al. would have been pleased. Probably.

Of course, it had seemed strange at first, especially to a generation raised on the fearful silence of the burrows. For them, anything more than a private hum had been advertisement to the Null. Such instruments as they had merely whimpered underground, and then only once in a blue moon. For organs to blare forth had been fear-food, before changing from yukky chrysalis into beautiful statement. '*Come and listen, if you like*,' it then said to the former master-monsters. '*We are celebrating! We are aloft. And ready!*'

Music had soon entered the Wessex bloodstream and shoulders no longer flinched at a brazen voluntary. Quite the contrary. They stiffened and were proud, recalling glory days. New-Wessex even spawned its own home-grown equals to Bach and Purcell, such as Butt and Bellingham and Miss-gina, dragging down dictation from Paradise.

Unfortunately, the angels reckoned that was *their* job. Little surprise then that they banned Bach and any other inspiring ecstasies. They said the noise grated their perfect pointed teeth – and that insects shouldn't aspire. For centuries sour silence reigned over the Downs, save in secret. Now, though, those once invincible tyrants had tasted mankind's cosh. The theme tune of Wessex sang out sweetly again.

Naturally, tacked on to the sublimities of Heaven's music, subsequent composers added their own refinements, like the weird carnyx-style air-tubes Blades had been unable to divorce them from, the choirs of dancing matrons and notes above and below strict convention. These sounds became Wessex-man's own, but not so far wandered that Bach would have torn his wig to hear it. Wilder Purcell might even have applauded. *He'd* merely sung the praises of a God that was good. Wessex not only copied that but urged the deity on to greater things . . .

A decent organ had been out of the question aboard the *Impaled Blades*, though a harmonium had played passable substitute, bewildering the bankside Null during cool-of-evening concerts. However, back in New-new-Binscombe, there was room for the great beast lately of St Sennacherib's, Bosham-by-the-Sea, to speak its mind. Its installation in Guy's plank palace there had been the seal of civilisation for the raw city. It said they were neither raiders or invaders, but the vanguard of better days.

Right now it said the 'Toccata and Fugue in D minor' loud enough to render conversation difficult, and wonderful enough to make talk an imposition. Nevertheless, there were lulls.

'I said: "Wizards."'

'Did you say wizards?'

The cousin left in charge confirmed Guy's guess with a nod. Then a space for pumping – of organ pipes and informant – happily chanced along. It permitted a whole chain of converse.

'Must be. Who else? They disdained the noonday heat. A single-file convoy crossed the sand. Some feet failed to grace the ground. Their garments scintillated and they left a trail of suicides. Swiftly dissipating suicides . . .'

So there was infallible spoor: the mage brethren's latest hallmark. All over the world wizards were happily choosing to leave it behind.

Guy raised his voice over the renewed organ tirade.

'Did you investigate?'

Cousin Lionheart Ambassador had grown up with Guy. They were of an age and had played together during brief ambassadorial boyhoods. It was in order for him to answer questions honestly.

'No. And I didn't stick needles in my eyes either. Or dine on ground glass.'

'Faint heart never won fair lady, cousin . . .'

Maybe not. Lionheart Ambassador didn't care. Access to a harem from age thirteen had killed all curiosity regarding ladies. He was more concerned about Guy's word-play on his name and good name. Both were precious objects to him. The twin prods needed confronting.

'Listen, Guy: they raised the perverse pyramid *overnight*. *Overnight*, I say! So there's power over there. Wizards aren't ones for house calls and "hello neighbours", you know . . .'

Guy did. He signalled so with a nod. His cousin ploughed on in justification.

'They've minded their own business ever since. Not a word or sound. Not a peep. Now, is that a hint or what?'

The barest arch of an eyebrow said Guy thought it might be. Or might not.

Of the two, Lionheart preferred the first.

'So, there you are then. I've simply respected their wishes. Like good Ambassadors should.'

'Respect this one's then,' shouted Bathie, organ defeating, and held out her cup. 'More beer, Lionheart!'

Aboard the *Impaled Blades*, which stocked only water or wine (and both as tepid as an accountant's soul), they'd fixated on the river-chilled barrels of barley beer known to be awaiting their pleasure in New-new-Binscombe. It and music were now the gilding on their first hours at 'home'.

She didn't normally indulge. Mages, even part-timers, had to careful about food for the imaginative faculties. Raised to flood by alcohol, they could crash through all defences and prance about the world as phantasmagoria. Back when Blades first learned of Wessex wizardry, and saw it as cause for concern rather than opportunity, he'd sternly ordered the stake for those who sold strong liquor to the gifted.

Like many over-reactions, that law was never actually repealed but quietly ignored into extinction. All the same, the underlying problem remained. So, when mages *did* hit the bottle, they often found themselves suddenly light on company. As a consequence they tended towards the abstemious, gaining the reputation of being sober creatures.

Thus, people looked askance at Bathie's brighter than ever eyes. They wondered that Guy didn't say something about it. Ever vigilant, beer or no beer, he detected that social starching and had to oblige them.

'In moderation, my dear. Remember we must go calling this afternoon.'

Bathie nodded.

'I know. Exactly. And so . . .' The drained cup was still wielded like a lance.

Meeting Guy's eye and finding consent, Lionheart obliged. Bathie drank deep.

The throng was melting away: the well-wishers and idle and nosey-parkers thinking better of it step by step. Even Hunter and the cousins abandoned them, albeit by agreement, in the interest of ensuring that at least some higher command survived. In a mirror-image of their entry to New-new-Binscombe, Guy and Bathie's leaving of it turned into a progressively lonely business. Lionheart, Beelzebub and Quatorze, plus sundry stouter elements, lingered to wave – but not for all that long.

Of course, they'd never be absolutely alone. Polly and Prudence would sooner die. Literally. Also, it was entirely unthinkable that an Ambassador, any Ambassador, let alone lately regal ones, should tap at the door of a new polity with their own knuckles. Guy and Bathie and the two Ps and assorted huscarls were preceded by a hereditary herald in cloth of gold. He glinted in front of them between the palms, a proper distance off, within hailing: with but not of them.

Axes had widened what many feet had trod. A capacious way now deflowered the virgin forest, leading straight and unnatural from New-new-Binscombe to the pyramids. A blind man would have been hard put to get lost and journey's end was but a matter of time. It was thereafter that things might get problematic.

The Wessex parasols-of-so-many-uses were aloft again, a multi-coloured mushroom forest to the arcing sunbirds' view, worthy of wary investigation. Yet their swooping, sweet, song was only part of the serenade accompanying the procession on its way. The palms seemed replete with collateral life, making itself known if not seen. Not Null, they all hoped and trusted, for the cover was subject to periodic sweeps by soldiery so bored as to volunteer the risk. However, of other beings nature provided a richness of – audible – evidence, and Guy didn't doubt that Egypt retained fauna surprises up its sleeve to shock them sooner or later.

Today, though, there was happiness in hearing only howls and caws in the chorus, not chimes. Amidst other pressing considerations, 'sooner or later' must be left to muck them about according to its own leisured programme. Even so, Guy's hand hovered over his revolver – something that bid to be its default position ever since leaving Wessex. The ambassadorial arms on the handle's pearl inlays were quite worn away.

Bathie was in crimson, beneath a crimson sun-hat (prompting rascal thoughts of the old Wessex adage, 'Red hat: no drawers!'), in turn beneath a crimson shade. The black apparel of later Wessex days had ebbed away to intermittent, and then was gone. She rarely spoke of the little graveyard by Ambassador Hall. It belonged to another life now, and the lives of others.

They'd chosen the hour to depart advisedly, but already the sun was as merciless as existence. The men sweated, the ladies 'glowed'. On this trip there would be no cooler depths to descend into, unless, perhaps, you included the grave.

Guy did. He'd said his prayers that morning – to someone or other – and made a full confession of sins. That took less time than he thought it would, leaving ample space for a hearty breakfast – had he been in the mood. In the event, bread and dates did the trick, filling up the void fear had put its marker on, without courting danger of nausea.

So why then, in the name of all that was fair, did he feel as sick as a dog? A dim dog who'd been lapping at salt water. It was something to ponder and track down to its lair. He'd half a mind to set off on that alternative mission. Displacement activity. Weak but understandable.

Luckily, there was call for the public, on-duty, Guy, summoning him away from introspection and the quest to keep his stomach contents down. Because his mind had wandered the whole party had become wanderers, not travellers, before they'd got a quarter way. They faltered and even Herald slowed his pace. Pretty soon he'd be back amongst the main body: an embarrassing breach of etiquette, like bidding formal farewell to a roomful and then having to return for your hat.

'Do not,' Guy told himself and his own feet, as much as all the others, 'be diverted by wild excesses of shape and colour. They are merely the works of man – albeit a shade larger and more vivid than the norm.'

Well, yes. Up to a point – and then way, way, beyond it, stretching that protesting point out of the proportions nature intended for it. Mages *were* men, true – of a special stripe. A pyramid bigger than any of the ancients' *was*, in essence, only a function of shape and bulk. The colours available to it were simply those of any painter's palette. To their eyes at least, it failed to transcend the spectrum. So what Guy said was correct – in the same sense that man's finest artistic achievements were 'just' canvas and paint, or stone and chisel marks. He had a point – just not a very good one.

Unless you put your chin upon your chest, there was no escaping the kaleidoscopic pyramid. You drew nearer to it filling the sky with every pace – which might explain why they'd acquired such ladylike steps.

Bathie wanted to help.

'Come off it, Guy. It *is* frightening . . .'

He looked and reconsidered. And was unmoved.

'I cannot admit that,' he told them, stating the plain truth and thereby resetting their shaky universe. He was right. The world was what you made it. They'd just been waiting for him to say so.

Polly and Prudence looked from one to the other, smiled – and strode on. Even Herald (presumably via the sixth sense all his profession developed) partook and enhanced the pace.

They were all obliged to step lively to keep up with him.

Pyramidic proximity was accepted now; even embraced once an invisible point of no return was trod. What blots out the horizon also shrinks every other consideration. And anyway, Herald would hit it first.

'What will he say?' Bathie enquired as she marched, shoulder to shoulder with her husband now.

Guy shrugged.

'Something silky and meaningless. His art is to intrude the fact of our presence on those who never asked to be advised of it. He will beg the opportunity to crave their pardon for being alive – but that sad state being so, might he impose on them to utter a few words . . . ? And so on. Along those lines.'

'I'd be no good at that,' she said, in to-thine-own-self-be-true mode.

The screaming correctness of her judgement would have defied even an Ambassador's or Herald's skill to contest. Guy could do no other than concur. She didn't mind.

Before the fresh pyramid . . . arose, the boot-laid path went on to a cluster of mud-brick step-structures and ended at the former greatest of them all, sun-gleaming and magnificent in its faultless facing-stone white coat. Now it and they were completely obscured and the new champion amongst them squatted on what had gone before, barring progress and defying any attempt to ignore facts.

Herald reached the moment of reckoning before them. Moreover, he'd reached it willingly and Guy was impressed. It was funny how tradition and 'honour' made men into automata, even overcoming their sense of self-preservation. Armies and empires entirely depended upon the phenomenon. Seeing it daily confirmed (not least by himself) from the minute he was out in the world, Guy had shed any silly notions of 'free will' long before he'd lost his faith in Blades.

Bathie still had faith. Her love deluded her into thinking there was nothing Guy couldn't do. She was puzzled. Herald had bowed before a blank wall prior to addressing it.

'What's he saying?' she asked, as if Ambassadors had foxes' hearing as well as cunning.

Her husband would far rather lie than disillusion her.

'With a thousand, quivering, pardons, may I take this precious opportunity to present my miserable, worm-like, self before your glorious and ineffable gaze. May I further prostrate myself and . . .'

'That's enough,' said Bathie. 'I get the drift.'

Seen closer to, the sides of the pyramid were not plain sheets – or sometimes not. Elsewhen, they were myriad triangular facets in ebb and flow to form transitory shapes. One came to repose opposite Herald. It opened up.

With a thousand men just like him, Guy could have sorted Blades out back home and never tasted exile. Herald bowed again and entered in.

When one of the lower orders behaved so well, what choice did his betters retain? As one all ambled on.

Right alongside, the very air was throbbing with the backwash of the surreal show. Bathie's crimson had competition and Polly's and Prudence's shroud white became just a backdrop for crazed colour schemes. All of their faces took on an unearthly wash and an unfelt force had the power to stream back hair.

In the final hundred paces the palms were dying – and not gracefully either. They leaned away from the source of affliction, even to the point of raising roots, but there could be no escape. The sickness spread from one side to the other.

In contrast, Guy and co. still had the choice. The only things that held *them* there were pride and duty: intangible qualities, granted, but no less binding than roots. Those two cursed cables wormed deep enough to serve as anchor against any storm of fate – if you let them.

They did. The dwarfed contingent denied their great want for elsewhere and kept on walking. Blades would have been proud of then. Or maybe just laughed.

Where Herald had penetrated was now only a bland barrier of gold – then green, then every colour of the rainbow and shades in between, concluding in a sluggish soup which lingered: vomit-hued and textured, biding exceptionally. Whilst it dallied they studied its slow and lumpish circulation – as, for all they knew, it studied them.

'Hello. Good day to you . . .'

It was perhaps the bravest thing Guy had ever said, but it went unrewarded. No answer.

'*"The dream is over."*' A pause. 'No? Well then, how about *"They are coming"*?'

Then, to cover his failure and confusion: 'Sorry, but they *might* have been passwords . . .'

This was to Bathie, to whom he'd confessed her mimicking of what he'd heard in Yarmouth. None the wiser, content that he always told her all that was needful, and bearing in mind her fragile equilibrium, until then she'd left it there. In the current awful hush, there it looked likely to remain.

Then a high metallic whining, initially at the very edge of hearing, came to prominence for lack of competition. It sprang from within the structure, though perhaps also present in the outside air; but mostly as a thousand – no, a *million* – distant interior voices, combining their distress.

Otherwise, the silence wore on – and on – and wore them down. The only alternative music was the sand singing *heat!* beneath their feet.

Braver yet, Guy drummed a brisk tattoo on the unobliging face with his 'seduction stick'. The vomit goo resisted beating, sucking at the rod, seeking to fellate it from him. The temptation was to fastidiously withdraw, like a maiden aunt spurning the advances of an intriguing gigolo. Yet he kept at it, content at least to be making ripples.

Indeed he was. Even as the seduction stick was handed back to Polly for cleaning, a new triangle hurtled down from on high to replace the old. Or maybe not so new. It could have been the facet Herald beheld, though now an angrier red than before.

It came to rest where it may have sat earlier. They jumped at its clunk with the ground.

Something seemed to be in progress beyond. The vermilion

surface, a perfect imitation of congealed blood, undulated like an exercising muscle. Then the lower edge tore and parted.

What trickled out was far from clotted. On the contrary, the lifeblood was still market-fresh and steaming. It pooled around their sandals. Guy was obliged to look and note the floating threads of gold.

'I think,' said Bathie, moving her dainty feet away, 'we should take that as a "no".'

It would be an uphill path gainsaying her. There are hints and *hints*. This was the latter. They turned to go whilst they still could.

They couldn't. The sand before them erupted. From it a wizard arose.

His staring eyes did not heed or mind the blinding grains, or the cascade through his limbs and hair. He was naked but didn't require a starry gown to state his status. It lay in the way he ascended slowly *through* the desert, never ceasing to stare with every identifying confidence.

At length he stood before them, or they before him, and the sand reposed as though nothing had occurred. He was wild-eyed and long-locked; paper-pale and depilated. Bathie clearly found him attractive.

When he spoke sand spilled from nose and mouth, but it was not that which troubled him. Rather it was lack of practice that hamstrung his speech. Within the space of one sentence he ran the gamut from scream to murmur in cracking syllables, like a prisoner released from solitary. That was the rational diagnosis. An exciting alternative was that distant others were taking turns to speak through him.

'Do not mourn this brother. Or repine.'

Though the wide eyes never wavered they knew he meant poor dead Herald. Actually, there'd been no opportunity yet for finer feelings, but doubtless they'd have arrived in due course. Almost certainly.

'No,' he continued. 'No weeping. No more. We have blessed him! He is with us yet. I can still behold him: ascending. These traces' – a white hand waved over the solidifying

263

streams – 'will recycle and be' – he communed with a future vouchsafed to him alone – 'a flower, a child, a tree that will be a boat that will sail and sight his Wessex home. The rest and best of him has already joined the dance, the whirl of spirit. He was blameless and lives with the saved. I see him rising, rising, rising now – or as he will in a future age when cleansed of sins. You must understand. What? Hello? What must you understand? Understand that all our moments are eternal . . .'

Who were they to disagree – at least openly? *'Never argue with soldiers or lunatics'* one of Guy's temporary mothers had told him – and he thought there was a lot of truth in that.

Bathie had obviously never heard such wisdom.

'No!' she accused. 'Nonsense. You've truncated *this* portion of his story. The one he was weaving by waking every morning. What you're on about would have followed anyway . . .'

'*Exactly*,' said the wizard, as if she were all over him in agreement.

'No. But . . .'

The mage's mood changed with appalling abruptness. A moth tolerable in moderation had buzzed by once too often.

'Poor insect . . .' said the wizard. 'Be *blessed* also . . .'

Devoid of regret he raised his hand to wave her away for ever.

Equally suddenly and equally gut-wrenching, he reconsidered – and then sought to peer within her flat chest.

'Ah . . .'

True Fruntierfolke girl that she was, Bathie was ready to go, just so long as she could take her dignity with her. Two thin arms spread east and west to hide nothing.

'So?' She tried by dint of diving and craning to catch the 5-mile stare. At length, through unknown buffers, she was heard.

'You have the spark,' he said. 'Even if it gutters and does not enlighten, still it is there. You are on the road but not a traveller. Yet. You could join us, I suppose. There are gaps. Yes. No. Why not? *I* am going home. The barrel is being scraped. Therefore, listen and learn, sister. The dream is over. *Over!*'

Bathie boldly pinched one of her white arms. And again. And again.

'But I still sleep!' she complained, as if he was a huckster palming her off with shoddy goods.

The wizard proved what he was by not caring. *He* was all right, thank you very much.

'*I* am almost awaking,' he clarified. 'It is close . . .'

Surprise overtook him and his eyes. They widened and moistened like a virgin ceasing to be one.

'No!' This with pleasure, not denial. 'I lie! It is *imminent*!'

He patted his flanks, perhaps where he was once wont to find pockets. Foiled and in haste, he then studied Guy. Not Guy the outward shape or sound, but through and through. Somewhere he seemed to find what was missing.

'Come to me. Quick!'

Guy came, having explored all the likely alternatives. He submitted to fondling and frisking by a naked man who reeked of sand and self-abuse. Urgent hands delved under his scarlet coat to link behind him. There lurked the 'impasse gun', an ancestral ambassadorial key for unlocking stubborn moments; both barrels on call at the jerk of a shoulder strap.

The mage brought it round and severed the silken sling with a line of little flames from his fingertips. Once parted the two edges reunited in molten marriage again. Just like an Ambassador, the shotgun changed sides without shame, smooching up to its new owner.

Guy had little enough to recall the first Ambassador Hall by. 'Old Impasse' was his only childhood toy to survive the angelic inferno and he was loath to lose it. All the same, he endured robbery without protest, sensing this was but a short-term loan.

So it proved. The wizard wielded the weapon against no one but himself. He expertly wrapped the sling around one meatless arm until the muzzle was snug beneath his chin. The reach was tested, fingers flexed, until everything was perfect. Or almost everything.

'Now go away. And take your mundanities with you. No. Do not go away.'

Guy became the renewed focus of alarming attention.

'Your footsteps glitter. You have been in Yarmouth.'

It was no question but a confident accusation. There was no point or dignity in denial. Guy nodded.

'How is it?'

'Empty.'

'Good. *Now* go. If you return here we will *bless* you also.'

Something further occurred to distract him from even such a pregnant pause. Though far from loath to leave, he re-regarded Guy and Bathie.

'By the way, you did know she was two? No? Well, she is. Two. But one fails. Poison from the past is strangling it. It slips from the womb, cell by cell away.'

Bathie was in like a knife.

'Can you save it?'

'It' had no need of stating. A crackling energy emanated from her to define the topics for conversation *her* way.

'All things are possible. That is my entire point. The dream – oh . . .'

A sigh of exasperation. Out of the goodness of his heart he'd loitered overlong putting these bugs safe in the shade.

'Don't bother. Baby only goes early to what is inevitable. Now or a century on – what odds? Sleep is good, death better, but best of all is never to have been. Why not just rejoice?'

Why not indeed? *He* intended to. His finger twitched.

Impasse spoke, they were all anointed, and the wizard's head flew away in graceful trajectory.

Alas, it faltered short of Heaven, down, down to a lamentable landing.

And then vanished.

To Guy, whoo is everything – or nearli.

Such a littel space to say a grate deal. Those things witch are not said say it alle. I shall return as 2 or not wishe to.

All is well.

B

'No it b-bloody, b-blading well *isn't*.'

'It': a lonely bed, a cold pit where Bathie should be, plus a note skewered to his headrest: they were none of them 'well'.

Few outsiders – not even Guy – got to see the Fruntierfolke weapon of last (or sometimes first) resort. A wand, a veritable stalk of steel, compacted black in its density, pinned the pillow beside Guy's sleeping ear, impaling the scrawled note. It must have been there for unknown hours, wavering in the night breeze, waiting at the door of hearing for day to come and the death of dreaming, to deliver its message.

Guy disdained the privilege inherent in finally discovering what a Fruntierfolke 'sleep-on' stiletto looked like. Once awareness landed on him like an anvil and eyes and throat were cleared, he had to accept it – but nowhere was it written he had to say thank you.

Still in stately dance at every zephyr's request, the supple needle, product of Blades only knew how many hours of slave tempering, had its back broken as Guy's only gratitude. Had he also been a coarse man – which he was not – the note would have been applied to his backside.

Instead, he tore the enveloping bug-net aside and floundered out of bed. One portion of the stiletto took the chance for posthumous revenge in the pricking of a careless groin – but Guy couldn't even spare it a shriek. Anything that was grist to his mill of haste was good to him now. The naughty spike not only escaped a curse but might even have been thanked, had he the time or self-possession. A starburst of pain only added to the blur of motion. All the outside world knew of it was a sudden octave rise in the urgent summonings.

In the same spirit, Guy gave the bell-rope a hernia. He kicked the furniture which, though sparse enough, somehow got in the way. He kicked anything if it might make some noise and get him company quicker.

Eventually, after aeons and hours even to the mind of God, pages, valets, squires and, of course, Polly and Prudence arrived. Most democratically, though in the grip of powerful emotions, Guy addressed them one and all.

'*Bring me my bow of burning gold!*' he told them – for this was a time, if any was, for tapping into deep resonances and hitching a ride thereon. It might be all metaphoric but they'd know what he meant well enough.

'*Bring me my arrows of desire!*'

Then, as an afterthought, in a development the poet had failed to see, Guy ad-libbed:

'Bring me my gun of divine design!'

Bows were all very well in their day but things had moved on. Arrows were slow enough for wizards to stop them.

'Hello? Hello? This is Guy Ambassador calling. Can I have my wife back?'

He considered further, pained, but finally spat it out:

'P-please . . .'

In his heart, Guy knew an ocean of degradation lay before him. There was little point in being bashful about paddling in its shallows.

He was betraying himself in more ways than one. What was intended to be a courteous 'seduction stick' reveille upon the scintillating pyramid proved to have sufficient force to smash the staff. Released at last from amber prison, the age-old fly tumbled out to greet the sun again. It landed beside Guy's sandalled feet, ignored: basking but failing to take any other advantage of freedom.

Suddenly, Guy felt awesomely alone: a pea on a drum, an actor on an all-too-well-lit stage. The ridiculous 4-inch remnant of the stick left to him was let slip, to fall by cursed luck upon the fossil fly and crush its short new day.

In some contexts there's no such thing as strength of numbers. It showed just how life was treating him that, for the second time in as many years, he'd had to imprison Polly and Prudence for their own good and to protect them from their urges. That had been a military operation in itself, involving broken words and heads, almost distracting him from the mission that made all his thoughts one high-pitched scream.

Now they were far away, occupied with their own silent screaming, and Guy was solitary, insignificant beside a structure that wouldn't listen, beneath a sky that didn't care.

Guy held his breath and dived into that aforementioned ocean.

'Please, please, please . . .'

Instantly, the facet opposite showed forth words that were, he felt sure, someone's speech just behind.

'Abandon Hope All Ye Who Enter Here.'

And then neither they or it were there any more. An avenue stretched before Guy. It was not conventionally inviting, but then he'd never expected it would be. He could easily pay the ferryman for this trip, being in a spendthrift mood.

A giant, dentined port of love gaped for Guy to take. It was up to him whether he wanted it badly enough.

He did. The first fangs were ferocious, but negotiable with care. There was footing on the slick flesh of the floor, if you threw away footwear and any concern for dignity. A hand to either throbbing wall proved little assistance. The rows of teeth were in earnest: shark-like, sharp. They bit at flailing fingertips and drew blood.

Warm mucus in ever-increasing rivulets denied firm footfall in any case. Guy just had to make his way as best he could: a cross between clown and crab, a drunkard lost in a culvert.

All the while he was both gagging and delighting in familiar musk. He knew their game and if such was the standard of play it only cheered him. They'd misjudged. However mages might magnify and twist this place, and add to it with the primeval fears of men, Guy would never be threatened here. *Here* was *her* and no wizard could ever disenchant it.

It wound on for days – for they had the power to pervert what was good – until Guy was dying of thirst and heat and exhaustion. Soaked, emerging into a cavern widening, he laid himself down to await the end.

Until, that is, closing eyes pierced the gloom to behold its contents. Suspended in milky sacs from the roof were little Guys and Guyesses, five in a row: quite unmistakable in the wizards' cruelty. Like peas in a pod they were akin in everything, including death, throats slit and drained – all save the last. She clung on, though almost as translucent as her siblings. A tiny red ember still glowed, ruby-like, visible in her breast.

Revivified, Guy rose in haste. That motion – though strangely not his stumbling in – was detected. The sole surviving upside-down set of eyes opened. Through the muffling of life fluid a mouth opened to say something it could not possibly know.

'*Daddy* . . .'

Guy would *not* hear it. His seax tore the nearest salmon wall and straight away he was free. All this time he'd been captive within a flimsy gaol whose thin bounds were nevertheless precious to him. The mages had now cured him of that.

Beyond, they were waiting for him, and all his weariness and outward afflictions flowed away – for the wizards would have him play new games. Their time was not his time. Alas for both Guy and their plans, they could not subtract from the horror that crossed over with him.

So his dulled eyes saw but failed to register the mountainous orgy, with orgasmic Bathie as its apex and the summit of each mountaineer's ambition. The performance – and *such* a performance – pumped away in vain. Guy did not see.

Some mages ringed the pile, laughing, inciting or even participating according to whim, and Guy was of their number in the daisy chain – but not *of* them. All the questing parts and penetrations amused or disgusted them alone. Guy had his own private middle distance to look into.

Likewise with the long roller-coaster down a razorblade which came next. They floated with him for that too, almost angelic in a thirst for utmost anguish as Guy was sliced apart – and then repaired to start again. In fact, it took them until second slither round to realise.

The mages pursed their lips to learn there was a pain higher and greater than their crudity could conceive. Guy's refinement served him well, supplying the one weapon that might confound them. First there was irritation at his unvarying stoicism. Then enlightenment dawned. A blow too testing had put him beyond the torturers' reach.

They liked enlightenment. It was now, more than ever, their thing. Accordingly, vaguely grateful (since mercy wasn't on their palette), the wizards reached out a helping hand instead. They led him by that hand, like a little child, to the comparative sanity of above.

The pyramid proved to be an organic melange of tubes and chambers that, for mad complexity, put even the creator of the human form to shame. Globules of blood and other fluids streamed past in chains. The air was never free of heat and cries. Small surprise therefore that, in his confusion, Guy imagined himself back in the nightmare of Null-Paris – until a landmark put him straight.

They'd saved Herald's head intact – and stitched it on to some other body. The medley sat guardian at a crucial crossroads high in the air. Sorcerously inspired, loose lips repeated their last words forever.

'*I wish to . . . I wish to . . .*'

It helped Guy recover. He flapped faster past that.

Actually, his senses could be forgiven the Paris mis-reckoning. There were Null slaves here as well as men – but both too craven to merit the name. Purple pushed past pink and neither minded. To be that broken and live was an insult to life.

Thus, the tiny triangular cell at the pinnacle was like a breath of fresh air. Its open sides rendered that literal. It transpired to be evening – of some or other day. The cooling breeze almost woke him. Guy looked out over Egypt from on high and found comfort. He could always just jump.

But Bathie rose through the floor, wizard or concert-organ style. It was the actual she this time, identified by the light in her eyes. They focused exclusively on Guy.

However, her progress was slow and subject to tuition. Sometimes, hard facts intervened and she faltered. Then the tutor's hand would guide her through solidity, persuading when matter persisted. At other times, her faith failed and she stuck and required catechising.

'*Nothing is true*,' the mere boy told her, shepherding her transit, smoothing over the sloughs. '*Everything is permissible* . . .'

Indeed it was. Bathesheba Fruntierfolke transcended stone and paving. She rose above and through it to stand in triumph. The pallid face now glowed, her crimson gown was starry.

Teacher both praised and reproved. She *had* transcended – and yet not transcended enough. The boy-mage could see where her gaze ended.

'This mundane will not leave – or let *you* leave.'

Guy was spoken of as if he were not there. Only her fixed stare salvaged the scene for him.

'He is . . .' she said – but failed to finish. Other things occupied her mind.

The wizard caressed Bathie's hair, tangling his fingers in it. One hand trailed her thigh.

'He is your shackle' he said. 'Unlock, unlock . . .'

Bathie shook her head, dislodging hand and notion. It was wonder-boy's turn to transcend. Nostrils flared and Guy got the look usually reserved for the out-crawlings from flat stones.

'I have this for you,' she said, her first words to Guy, huddled beneath her. 'You must understand.'

Suddenly, there was a journal in Guy's hand. He recognised the uninhibited scribble.

'You?' The incredulity was justified. Previously, she'd always despised those who preferred second-hand living. The pillow note was probably her grandest composition to date. Intrigued, despite himself, he flicked through.

'And so *much*?' he queried page after page after page. 'So soon?'

Bathie didn't want to explain. It was embarrassing in present company.

'Their hours are not like your – *our* – hours . . .'

It could have been a prime ambassadorial type 'answer' – save that she patently meant to tell the truth. It saddened her to have to amplify with so little hope of comprehension.

'They have a way round all . . . that . . .' she added and, despite herself, smiled.

Guy was sure they did. Boy-wizard smiled too, and since the beginning of time Guy thought there'd never been a smugger one.

'Read and learn,' Bathie asked – or maybe instructed – and left him as she'd arrived.

Mrs Ambassador sank out of his sight and life.

Nothing is true. Nothing is true. Nothing is true. Nothing is true.
Nothing is true. Nothing is true. Nothing is true. Nothing is true.
Nothing is true. Nothing is true. Nothing is true. Nothing is true.
Nothing is true. Nothing is true. Nothing is true. Nothing is true.
Nothing is true. Nothing is true. Nothing is true. Nothing is true.
Nothing is true. Nothing is true. Nothing is true. Nothing is true.
Nothing is true. Nothing is true. Nothing is true. Nothing is true.
Nothing is true. Nothing is true. Nothing is true. Nothing is true.
Nothing is true. Nothing is true. Nothing is true. Nothing is true.
Nothing is true. Nothing is true. Nothing is true. Nothing is true.
Nothing is true. Nothing is true. Nothing is true. Nothing is true.
Nothing is true. Nothing is true. Nothing is true. Nothing is true.
Nothing is true. Nothing is true. Nothing is true. Nothing is true.
Nothing is true. Nothing is true. Nothing is true. Nothing is true.
Nothing is true. Nothing is true. Nothing is true. Nothing is true.
Nothing is true. Nothing is true. Nothing is true. Nothing is true.
Nothing is true. Nothing is true. Nothing is true. Nothing is true.
Nothing is true. Nothing is true. Nothing is true. Nothing is true.
Nothing is true. Nothing is true. Nothing is true. Nothing is true.
Nothing is true. Nothing is true. Nothing is true. Nothing is true.
Nothing is true. Nothing is true. Nothing is true. Nothing is true.
Nothing is true. Nothing is true. Nothing is true. Nothing is true.
Nothing is true. Nothing is true. Nothing is true. Nothing is true.
Nothing is true. Nothing is true. Nothing is true. Nothing is true.
Nothing is true. Nothing is true. Nothing is true. Nothing is true.
Nothing is true. Nothing is true. Nothing is true. Nothing is true.
Nothing is true. Nothing is true. Nothing is true. Nothing is true.
Nothing is true. Nothing is true. Nothing is true. Nothing is true.
Nothing is true. Nothing is true. Nothing is true. Nothing is true.
Nothing is true. Nothing is true. Nothing is true. Nothing is true.
Nothing is true. Nothing is true. Nothing is true. Nothing is true.
Nothing is true. Nothing is true. Nothing is true. Nothing is true.
Nothing is true. Nothing is true. Nothing is true. Nothing is true.
Nothing is true. Nothing is true. Nothing is true. Nothing is true.
Nothing is true. Nothing is true. Nothing is true. Nothing is true.
Nothing is true. Nothing is true. Nothing is true. Nothing is true.
Nothing is true. Nothing is true. Nothing is true. Nothing is true.

And:

The dream is over. The dream is over.

And so on. Guy gave up and in.

He sighed. How true. So what?

Even the best amongst views can become just . . . scenery. The Nile flowed, the sand likewise (though more subtly). The pyramids simply sat there, the centuries bouncing off them. It seemed insulting to assault them with his mayfly thoughts. And, the sky being see-through, there was nothing else. New-new-Binscombe was only a fresh-grown carbuncle on the horizon: best forgotten.

Eventually, Guy had turned to the journal.

For a short span it was in her best, schoolroom, hand; appropriately enough the rote-writing of punitive 'lines'. Soon though, the pace quickened and in haste and speed and feverish excitement she and her script left Guy behind. Thoughts were coming to Bathie quicker and better than she could set them down, the words flowing into a single, barely differentiated, scrawl. Some few, legible, novelties – like 'energy' and 'infinite' – occurred as sporadic variety, but out of context (assuming there was one) they were just useless islands amidst a dead sea of repetition.

Everything accelerated as the pages progressed. In some the inkstick's zeal penetrated right through to grace a succeeding leaf. Others were marred by what Guy strongly suspected to be drool. He divorced and peeled them asunder only to find more wasteful diagonal screeds. Sometimes, single words occupied profligate acres of space.

It was a record of ravings, a meaning-free zone – at least for Guy. Knowing what was actually in the author's frizzed head only made it worse. There were better things therein than this: 'infinitely' better. What a tragedy she'd not set that down instead. It would be something to remember her by. This deranged tirade wasn't anything to hand on to your descendants.

Then he realised he wouldn't have any. So it didn't matter.

Guy paused and watched the sunbirds circle what used to be the grandest pyramid. Their sprightly dance went round and round, but never an inch nearer the present champion and him at its summit. It was a shame. He could have done with being within 'hello' distance of some carefree life.

And surely, surely, the Lady Bathesheba must have received *some* education beyond killing Null and Christians. Had there been *no* slave-scribes in all the great spiky expanse of Castle Fruntierfolke to inform her just one exclamation mark sufficed?

Their multiplicity showed that she was drunk – not with grape or grain but something new. From very first meeting to today, they'd not made *separate* exciting discoveries before. Even the cruel-child malice of a god-king hadn't been able to insert a sliver of distance between them. Now she was skipping ever further away from him with each page and '!!!!!!!!!!'

Maintaining perfect indifference to his field-mouse squeaks and feelings, they'd kept her at it – whatever 'it' was – to the very last page. Guy should have guessed and gone there straight away.

'Nothing is true!!!! The dream is over!!!!'

And that was all she wrote.

The wizard at his shoulder said, 'Look at it this way . . .'

Guy hadn't known he was there, but – to be on the safe side – had always assumed someone was. They would be denied the pleasure of him jumping out of his skin. He even declined to turn his head, continuing to squat cross-legged before the journal as if studying scripture.

Also, he still had the impasse gun. They were that contemptuous of him – or careless. The moment was coming – he could see its springy steps drawing nearer and nearer – for him to jerk its chain like life was jerking his. However, unlike fate, it would oblige him, and come out of behind-back seclusion to say something pretty pithy.

For the moment, though, he could still speak for himself.

'See it what way?'

The elderly sounding wizard remained patient.

'You *do* need to look . . .'

Guy shuffled round the minimum required, legs still locked. The man *was* old, with a white nova of rats'-taily hair.

'So, go on then: amaze me . . .' Then Guy looked at him properly.

The mage's eyes were awful. They'd seen things which had worn the bottom out of them, leaving weepy pits into which you might fall for ever.

Guy disengaged gazes, like a dog conceding the proper order of things.

The starry gown had not been washed since wizards ceased to care about such trifles. It clung in odd arrangements to the scrawny arm when raised.

'For instance,' the mage told Guy, though his empty stare was for the boundless sky alone, 'look at it *our* way . . .'

When the arm fell Guy wasn't given any choice in the matter. He and the world went with it.

Now there was all the room you could require, and sweet – rose-scented – air, even though they were still within the pyramid – sort of.

There were also many wizards and Bathie was one of them. And so was he – sort of.

The exercise proved to be useful. Seen their way, Guy saw their point. Everything – quite *everything* – was less substantial. All edges wavered uncertainly.

On a more positive note, everything had – was – *potential*. Nothing was so fixed any more, not even Guy. Whatever he was was subjected to some tidal pull to be elsewhere. Like wavering over an abyss, he felt a siren call to dissolution.

A simple hand gesture might make him see the world their way, but Guy could only ever be a tripper there. It was too much. His frame was getting frayed and would never fit back together again so well. Left too long he'd just . . . dissolve, and leave only a vacant carcass behind.

Happily, they had pity – or further business with him. Normal perspective returned via another wave. Guy landed with a bump, and for a few seconds the world seemed insupportably ordinary. Even a brief walk in their shoes apparently came at a high price in terms of lost content. He shuddered.

'You see now?'

There was no single spokesman. They took it in turn. Round the circle the wisdom went.

'This grows too tight ...' said a raddled woman Guy thought he recalled from the Imperial court. She savaged a section of sickly flesh with razor talons. 'A little more ... thought ... and we shall be free of it!'

'Take what we are,' said the next in line, a last-legger unable to even stand any more, 'and divide it ...'

'And divide it ...'

'And divide it ...'

The urging did the rounds of every mouth like an incantation.

'And in the end,' concluded the boy-wizard, whom Guy hated, 'you are not left with *something* ...'

'No.'

'No.'

'No.'

'But rather *everything*,' said his aged escort down from the pinnacle. 'Which transpires to be *nothing* ...'

'Which is, of course,' capped the boy, '*everything* ...'

'Pure energy.'

'Undivided.'

'Undefiled.'

'Pure.'

'Energy.'

'A lattice of energy.'

'In gorgeous dance.'

'Matter is illusion.'

'There is only aether ...'

'We are a dream ...'

'Which is over,' contributed Guy, before anyone else could. Nobody minded.

'Mere thoughts in the mind of God.'

'Some "mere"!'

'A glorious "mere"!'

'It was always there – before our face!'

On the floor, around the edges, there were books: piles and piles of them, cruelly mistreated.

At one or all's behest a volume flew to be before Guy's face. He read, never doubting the selection.

They had done disrespectful things to many parts of this Blades-Bible but the chosen passage was pristine.

Matthew, chapter 17, verse 20. '*And Jesus said unto them, If ye have faith as a grain of mustard seed, ye shall say unto this mountain, Remove hence to yonder place; and it shall remove; and nothing shall be impossible unto you.*'

'A heavy hint or what . . .?' said a smiling mage. 'Magic, if you did but think of it, was a *monster* clue!'

'So people thought of it . . .'

'. . . Pursued it to its utmost ends . . .'

'. . . And came to conclusions . . .'

'. . . Which, put into practice . . .'

'. . . Let them move on,' said the last-legger. 'We are but the laggards.' He hardly looked as if he had time to dawdle.

'Lamentably, a little portion of disbelief lingers.'

'But it shall be expunged.'

'Cauterised.'

'And then we shall progress.'

'Move on.'

'Evolve.'

'We shall be as angels.'

'Not the petty sort: not factional.'

'Those of pointless pleasures.'

'Those who have afflicted you.'

'Not even proper angels. Not glimpsers of God.'

'No.'

'Insects in comparison.'

'Bugs.'

'Above mundane man . . .'

'. . . But less than angels'

'Naught but naughty children.'

'Peddlers!'

Guy had to query that, even if it were a red-faced cavil.

Those 'children' who had burned his house and maimed his species he could not conceive of as hucksters. There were many things he visualised as loaded on their winged backs, but the image of a tinker's pack was not amongst them. It refused to form now.

'*Peddlers*?' he protested. 'Peddling what?'

'Peddling meddling.'

'Ah . . .'

'They are the lesser sort. The least. They form up under banners of "right" and "wrong".'

That got a wicked laugh all around the ring.

'They might *claim* angeldom . . .'

'A misappropriated mantle.'

'Their master's robes.'

'Borrowed.'

'Assumed.'

'But they remain mere sparks off the splendiferous blaze.'

'Those "sparks" burn!' Guy interposed, angrily. He would not have all the suffering so blithely dismissed.

Their reply was as merciless as any 'angel'.

'Because you let them.'

'Weakness.'

'Brush them away.'

'As you would any spark.'

'Douse them . . .'

'Swat them with reality . . .'

Their tolerance of his stumbling was brief, their willingness to linger limited. This chorus was eager for climax: a grand summation.

'They are . . . *ephemeral*.'

'With us comes end of their dominion.'

'A close of . . . silly play.'

'We are – were – human. A head start.'

'We shall be angels of the higher – proper – kind.'

Guy had gone along so far but this hurdle was high enough to snag his parts. He had to ask.

'How can you be so sure of that? Look about . . .'

For there were bodies here and there, and terrified slaves on the verge of hysteria. Directly above their conferencing heads sat Herald's head, transplanted.

'There's none so blind,' pronounced the boy-mage, 'as those who *will* not see.'

'Dream-stuff. Inconsequence,' expanded last-legger. 'At worst we have only inserted them back into the lattice dance. They were – and will be again. What loss then? No harm. Not of any *lasting* nature.'

'We play with the tail end of the dream. With our remnant passions. Half betwixt sleep and wake.'

'All desires must be indulged . . .'

'. . . For fear they might anchor us here . . .'

'. . . When we should be gone.'

'We have no fear as to our immortal fate,' summarised the ancient, snowy, mage, with more confidence than a human was entitled to. 'We have seen the effulgent light. However faintly. We cannot help but go to it and worship. God's gravity draws us.'

'Therefore, would you deprive her of *that* for *this*?'

Guy knew the boy-mage was dismissing this world in comparison to even a sniff of that 'effulgence'. He knew he meant Bathie, his other half. It was a big proportion of yourself to just give up, no matter how good the reason.

Till now, though in the ring, she hadn't spoken.

'*He* would not,' she said, as firmly as he'd ever heard her. 'But *I* might.'

It turned out that even wizards can be shocked. To suggest spurning the ineffable for the day-to-day put chins on chests. Bathie pressed the dagger home – and even waggled it about a bit.

'So . . . let me think about it.'

The mages sighed.

Between that one breath and another, husband and wife together were expelled into the desert.

They picked themselves up and dusted each other down. The sun was merciless and overhead. All things shimmered in the noonday heat as if perceived from wizard perspective. Already, their scalps prickled, the soles of their feet burned. It seemed the most sensible thing to head back, hand in hand, through the palms to New-new-Binscombe.

Yet, though their fingers clasped, there was a fissure dividing them. Its depths lay beyond their powers of sight.

Bathie was the braver. She addressed it first.

'Did you read?'

'What I could.'

'And?'

He let fall her hand.

'. . . And I cannot follow you. Or k-keep you here.'

He'd already fought against perception of her slackening pace. Now there was no more reason for denial. Any slower and she'd be in reverse.

'I will take your decision and' – Guy spread his arms and was never so defenceless since receiving his first seax – 'abide by it.'

Her decision was already made. He knew. He was in her hair. He'd heard so in her hesitation when she chose to 'think about it'. Hoping against hope (the words on the pyramid notwithstanding) he'd looked for more. Now it was done. One or the other or both had wielded the scissors.

Guy knew nothing between them could ever be better than just 99 per cent again. There was no point in trying to build it back up.

She knew too, but couldn't say so. Lips twitched but no sounds came forth. Her eyes tended back towards the pyramid.

So Guy said it for her:

'"*The pain of life no more*".' He could manage no more than a whisper. '"*Best of all is never to be born . . .*"'

Bathie hesitated but nodded, eyes downcast.

There was only one thing left outstanding.

'And are y-you still t-two?' he asked.

'No, but . . .'

Again, he kindly completed for her.

'But now it no longer s-seems so . . . important?'

It was another thing unsayable in her present halfway state, but she owed him that much.

'No.'

At the end of things, Guy proved the most loving of the two. He was willing to apply the needful knife.

Fore and index fingers touched first his lips and then hers. The tongue was no longer to be trusted. And therefore a hushed but eloquent and gentle farewell.

By then, Mr and Mrs Ambassador had come to a halt. Guy took one step onward but would not let her join him. Those two fond fingers, still outstretched, turned rigid, pinning her to the spot, final as any stiletto in the pillow.

'No,' he echoed, since she was silent. 'Thank you, but no.' His voice almost cracked and broke, yet Guy rode it. 'Go gild the stars instead . . .'

He looked away, not wishing to see pain or joy or relief – or anything. Least of all he wanted to see her smiling away into infinite distance.

His pinioning fingers were raised by two small hands and kissed again, fervidly.

And then she was gone. He – and his tear ducts – no longer held anything back.

Guy stood all alone in the desert and wept.

Strange to relate, Guy slept badly that night. Despite exhausting himself with concubines and milky drinks.

The bed was remade, the room cleared of strumpets and goblets, only for all to be wrecked again. In the quiet of the night he found even the lightest of coverlets intolerable, the gauzy bug-net an oppressive weight. He wrestled the bedclothes to sweaty rags in his tossing and turning. And, though he longed for peace, his mind repopulated the bed-chamber with chattering phantoms. Oblivion joined his list of ludicrous ambitions.

Yet all the same, he dreamed. Boy-mage came through the walls and smirked.

It seemed so wonderfully realistic. Guy actually felt the edge of the mattress against his ribs as he went for the Impasse gun. He found it where it should be, beneath the bed, ready to hand after just a little lunge. On the way he noted the pattern of the carpet and the china po stationed alongside – which was impressive detailing for just a dream.

The boy no more than noted the levelled weapon. Guy might just as well have waved the pisspot.

'We have your wife,' he lisped, though not in any mocking tone. 'She is well. Such generosity in giving deserves reward. We know your second dearest wish . . .'

'*Do* you now?' Guy's tone was drier than the sands he'd walked home over. 'And do you also know one good reason why I shouldn't use this?'

The boy briefly slitted his eyes in rapture. He leaned forward and actually placed his thin chest against the muzzle of the gun.

'Because that would be *my* dearest wish?' he ventured.

A good answer. Guy drew Impasse back.

'I want nothing of you.'

'But this you'll like!' The mage's voice was wheedling, as if he'd gone to trouble it was a shame to waste. 'Don't delude yourself that we *care* – although some warm sentiments still remain. Likewise, never fear to find yourself in our debt. We are creditors who do not collect. What need have we of reserves or stock? It is a trivial thing for us to pool remaining energies and stir the lattice . . .'

'Is it really? Answer me something instead.'

'As well,' the youth bestowed. 'As *well*, Guy.'

'Why are you here?'

'Tonight?'

'Egypt. At all.'

'You touch upon my heart's desires again, Guy Ambassador. Doomsday is coming. Here. To these especial nodes in the lattice.'

Guy fell back on the bed, resigned.

'Let joy abound . . .' Sarcasm didn't suit him. Supposedly,

Ambassadors were forbidden it.

'Our sentiments exactly. It would not be fitting for us – of all folk – to miss it. Or linger after.'

'Good night.' Guy's eyes closed with weariness.

'Rest well,' said the boy, smiling with apparent affection. He overlooked the dismissal and dared reach down to smooth a furrowed brow. 'Sleep deep. The Lady Bathie sends you a long night ahead . . .'

Guy had been here before; had been through this before. Here was a place he knew well. This was the 'vision' he'd been granted under the wall-guns of Fortress Horsham. Only now was better. Now was *real*.

The Downs were below him like feminine curves. New-Godalming was a boiling ant-heap. He bestrode all. He was become – he somehow knew – Guy Destroyer, if only for the space of an Egyptian night.

The angels certainly knew. Rumbled miscreants, they flocked together. The fallen variety were mustering in legions. The sanctimonious sort thought it would avail them to hug the sidelines and deplore.

False notions on every side – so Guy the titan decreed. False factions. False prophets swarming across the Downs and sky – realms not theirs by right. Trespassers. Usurpers. Interlopers. Make-believe landlords. A punishment was reserved for their pretensions.

Blades should have seen them off long ago. Presented with man's rightful claim, they would – could – not have stood against it. Not with the word of truth in his mouth. However, for his own reasons, Blades had chosen not to. Harems and pomp had possessed him instead. So choice now passed to Guy.

He chose. He mostly chose to notice that all the usual tedious barriers between want and have were lowered. The angels noticed it next.

Also as before, Guy ate what was set before him. It ate a treat, he reckoned. It went down handsomely. He feasted – and some intoxicant inside the food set veins afire.

Actually, the battle was already won. Although Guy must have been there to prevail, he'd also missed it. This was aftermath: pure pleasure time.

Guy had pistols in both hands and yet a bright sword also. Today that was possible because the arms that wielded them were multiple. They came kaleidoscoping in from different days and places, each Guy's own but combining to a blur. Likewise, every suppressed ambition arrived at once, all prosaic padlocks torn away. Guy Destroyer was arrived, a myriad limbed vice-regent of the Almighty, judgement-dealer without pity.

But he was also still Guy Ambassador enough to wonder where his abundant mercy was gone: that inner quality he'd hitherto valued so much. Then he drowned the dreary cavil, violently forcing it under wild oceans of joy till it stopped moving. This chance was too wonderful, too real, not to leap into bed with wholeheartedly. This was no day for 'yes, but . . .'!

Neither were these his guns, nor any guns available from earthly armouries. They were better than Horsham's great wall-weapons but light as a lawyer's promise. They spat like bombards or dragons, issuing a great spout of yellow light which burned angels into atoms.

The angelic vanguard – those that still survived – tried to flee, to fly, but Guy sought them out, plucking them from the sky; dragging them back to earth in a plumage of flames. Their burned feather smell was glorious perfume all over Wessex.

With an excess of zeal, he tracked some right the way down, pointlessly keeping the trigger depressed and beam blaring, till all that reached ground was cinders. Others he merely blackened so that they hit hard, twitching their final moments without dignity. Glorious lips parted to scream only to find both words and throat all burned away.

Guy had an army with him, far below and far smaller than he: mere spear-bearers. Guy felt no need to even look upon them as they chittered round his mighty ankles, admiring. Alone of himself, Guy Destroyer sufficed. Blithe, untroubled, he walked on with huge strides, straddling the North Downs in a single step.

Over the Hog's Back, by New-Ash and New-Wanborough, he found the angelic reserve regiments in serried ranks – and he incinerated them. They danced a last jig in his rain of undying fire.

Then he was smaller, by his own desire. He could measure himself against individual enemies. Crashed athwart New-Wanborough's ancient tithe-barn was a semi-stunned angel. Its wings flapped and stirred, further scattering the sundered oak beams.

Guy wished for his sword – and it answered the call. Then he stood over the stricken cherub, legs and groin and parts thrust forward, dishonouring it. There was still sense in those unbearably beautiful golden eyes. So, Guy belaboured the aggressor for a long while, grunting, chopping, raining down blows. The blade scorched, turning white flesh brown wherever it slit. Only when the creature was like autumn leaves did he desist.

Afterwards, Guy exulted, raising arms and swords and guns to the Downs' sheltering sky. His ululation blew away the clouds. It brought down fleeing angels. The pygmy army around his feet, humanity triumphant, clapped hands to ears in uncomplaining pain.

Guy grew wings: great white, feathered, augmentations in satire of his intended prey, and followed the remnant enemy. If need be, he'd pursue them to Heaven and Hell and burn them out of there also.

Thus he went too far, to the borders of blasphemy. All good things must come to an end. The miscreants were fled elsewhere, unlikely to return. Aside from some still smoking bits, the world was left in as much peace as it was ever going to get.

Guy's eyes blinked – or were blinked for him – and now he was amongst the other vision: the one granted amidst the fleshpots of Frith Hill. It had not been the opiates imbibed there, after all, but a foretaste. Guy tasted and found that it was good.

'Tear it all down! Tear it all down!'

That clinched it. This was no dream. Not even his wildest nightmare would place him in New-Godalming Cathedral's Holy of Holies – whilst profaning it. His words had been predicted atop Frith Hill. He had to believe.

So, Guy knew what to do and say. His miraculous sword could sunder doors, even the thick-skinned and iron-studded doors of cathedrals. It did so repeatedly. His acolytes flooded in using the gashes he made. They were implausibly little, like imps or ants; teeming, tumbling through the breached hymen. Everywhere they alighted they ravaged like a plague of locusts.

Then Guy their gang leader was beside the High Altar. First he heaved over it, then heaved it over. Beneath was bare earth, leached bone-pale over the course of its half-millennium white-marble night. Guy Destroyer wanted light on it, the kiss of the sun after so long a famine. He thrust his hand – which could somehow reach – high up into the roof and tore down great timbers like twigs, punching his way into the cleansing air.

'Burn it all down! Burn it all down!'

His swarming assistants, all black as sin and swift as wrens, could produce sparks from their tiny fingertips. Similarly, his own sword was now a blazing torch, dripping globules of molten heat. Swept round his titanic form it soon had all that he required in flames. Even stone walls took light at Guy's behest, old granite and bargate melting down like honeycomb to puddle on the floor.

Conveniently man-sized again, there was just time to defile the Holy of Holies – entered as if by a rapist and left debased, its angel-guardian diced, its sacred glow snuffed out – before the whole edifice tumbled into ruin round Guy's ears. The destruction was so complete it would never rise again.

Outside, in the smoke darkened day, the Imperial family and regiments of priests were being massacred. They waited patiently in line for the executioners' garrotting wires. Racehorses, the pride of Guy's own stable, galloped by on fire, unregarded, unmourned.

Guy no longer cared for anything save that matters should be set right. Whilst waiting for further opportunity, he scourged some of the fallen with his reappeared blade. He carved slices off the bulge-eyed dead and spoke his opinion of the way things were. Guy harshly reviewed the hard-heartedness of the world.

All New-Wessex heard him, right from Thames to Wight, down and round to the dependencies of Kernow and Guernsey. Gaul's fortress vineyards heard, and Gibraltar and New-Sicily too. The current King of the Null paused in what and who he was doing. Unsuspected Null and shaggymen in Australasia harkened. Even the dark catacombs under Egypt reverberated with what Guy had to say.

Then the scene shifted to a glade. In the period he'd just skipped, Guy's wake had carved a road through forest, edging it with blistered trees. Nor had his sword slept in his hands, as blameless trunks bore grievous witness. On the contrary, it still fidgeted in his palm with plans of its own, urgently wanting *more*.

Unlike on the Downs, time and place were indeterminate. This too was Frith-foretold – but less exactly. Something in the air made Guy suspect events might not be actual. Yet. It could conceivably be happening – or was to be – outside of the normal range of things. However, given that high weirdness was the norm of late, such thoughts didn't take him far forward.

So something else did. A lone figure glided towards him.

It was Blades the first god-king – a perfect Blades – coming at him, serene and shiny as a statue, even absolving the sword from the bother of bearing him.

Suddenly, Guy was no longer so wonderfully sure. His resolution died on him just when he needed it. He'd been confident about *God* – but now here was *a* god, confusing the picture.

Nevertheless, he travelled towards Blades to meet him, intending to ask some pretty pressing questions. But beyond that even Guy Destroyer could not see. He was conscious of both his sword and his knees, sensing potential use of either.

Then Blades opened his mouth and in loving tones said :

'Die . . .'

Guy screamed and woke to a new day to deal with.

'Our own little Utopia. Anti-Babylon!'

Sea-captain was as proud of Alexandria-Jerusalem's harbour and shipyard as Hunter had been of his dead Egypt display.

And it *was* impressive, even to Guy's unwilling-to-be-engaged eyes. Not only functional (though certainly that as well), but blessed with white dressed stone where there was no strict need, plus shapes pleasing as well as practical. Graceful oceanic lines had been grafted on to the yeoman sturdiness of Wessex. Even more vitally, accountants and costers had been put in their proper place for this project, as useful servants rather than masters. So now it was both a hive of activity and not downcasting to look on. What more could you reasonably ask of architecture?

Of course, it required some selective viewing. Only turn about and there were fresh-built slums that hoved into sight. Which were barracks and which were homes? It had been easy to tell initially, but now ... Town planners proposed but occupants disposed. The ground plan of Guy's prescription for an ideal society had soon been modified by the rougher sort of tenant to suit *their* tastes. Multiple occupancies were knocked into one, neighbours bought out and little castles constructed. Spiders' webs of walkways spoilt the skylines; the 'Long Man' emblem, depicted by inexpert hands, abounded. Accordingly, the plain-people's dormitories no longer looked quite so plain. Neatness had gone to the wall(s) and Wessex-baroque, thought safely left behind at home, had come along as a stowaway hidden in the humbler baggage.

Amidst so many other plans going down in flames, Guy was speedily reconciled. Granted, he had won one great victory – even here the air felt cleaner and clearer for it – but other struggles continued. Guy remained in revolt against himself and the way the world was. Building Utopia from pirates, exiles and burrow-fresh shaggymen was always going to be a tall-order task. If you discounted prevailing over armies of angels, then Guy had a lukewarm record regarding miracles.

As viceroy of Alexandria-Jerusalem – and, indeed all New-Egypt – in Guy's absence, Sea-captain had neither time nor inclination to scold the lower ranks. He didn't care what the riffraff wrapped round themselves. If they wanted to customise their hovels, then fine; so long as it didn't let the Null in. All he asked and expected of them was that they didn't riot whilst he was busy making warships. *And*, of course, speaking of Null, the small matter of their city-wall construction shifts. And mandatory volunteering for patrols and sweeps of the desert and Delta. And taxes. And conscription. And so on. But surely they were but small prices to pay for signing up to Guy's 'New-Jerusalem' scheme? Whatever *that* was.

Sea-captain had shown willing. Though his head was full of plans for quinqueremes, he'd endeavoured to humour Guy and raise the tone. In letters one Null high, the 'Commandments' (all ten of them, which took up a lot of good marble) confronted all but the blind who ventured into Alexandria. Hitherto, they'd been dusty, only scholar-known things, neglected in favour of Blade's later, lighter, yoke. Now though, they had some currency again, particularly since all the Bibles under Guy's say-so had the Blades bits plucked out. Any day now, as soon as Alexandria-Jerusalem's printing presses found their feet, there'd be a new edition. Pending that, surviving scriptures only loosely occupied their purged bindings, as if hinting at fuller things to come.

All that was down to Sea-captain – sometimes personally. He'd suffered many a nasty paper-cut in the cause of Guy's will, tearing out pages deemed blasphemous, superfluous, useless . . . *And* he'd built the hoi polloi a stupendous church whose glinting sky-blue dome – when finished – would have made even the pyramid people gasp. Never mind that it was materials and effort equivalent to umpteen quinqueremes: ships with solid brass rams and puckle-gun capacity. Sea-captain had overlooked that and all sorts of sloppiness and sentiment from those who slept late into the morning in beds beyond the harbour. He sympathised with Guy and the cause – whatever it might be. Whilst he'd been left in charge, as befitted his none-nobler line, Viscount Sea-captain XIII had *endeavoured*.

If the events over Wanborough had been common knowledge yet, he'd have endeavoured a damn site harder – but still bridled at Guy's faint praise. The great Ambassador had done nothing but nod and stretch his lips at all the wonders shown him. Ever since returning from that Nile cruise he'd been as much inspiration as a wet washday. So what if the skinny witch had left him to mix – and mate, probably – with her own kind? He'd had weeks to get over that. There were plenty more mermaids left in the sea. It wasn't the end of the world!

He needed jolting out of it – that was the solution. A roll on the ocean waves – or on a soft-palmed and full-bottomed houri. Anything. Even conversation!

'So, my lord, what do you reckon?' Sea-captain gestured expansively, beaming in a manner not at all his, to take in the whole harbour complex and workforce, the bonded-rubble *Cobb* and sheltering fleet, all flying the open (or throttling) hands banner of the Ambassadors.

'Very nice . . .' said Guy – which was massively worse than 'rubbish!'.

'Do you mean to say,' exploded Sea-captain, who, for all he might be as smooth as an unplaned deck, really wouldn't have spoken that way had he known of Wanborough, 'that I sacrificed irreplaceable hours – no, *months* – at sea to get marked "very nice"? Lost all that time out of the only life I'll ever have? Have you any idea how many diver and slave bones are down there with the foundations? And all that scaffolding could have been ships, you know! Sending good men up into Null – and worse – heaving Palestine for your "cedars of Lebanon" timbers? So, all right, they were there exactly where you said they'd be . . .'

'Not I,' said Guy, who was enjoying this. The lash of a quite justified but harmless tongue was more cathartic than his experiment with the vice for real, at the hands of an actual dominatrix. 'Not I. Scripture.'

'Whoever. I ask you, did my huscarls hew biblical trees and hellish monsters for "very nice"? I think *not*!'

Suddenly, the outspread hands were brought home and inverted for Guy's inspection.

'And just look at all these paper-cuts! Agony . . . at the time!'

Guy's sense of humour might be in bed resting, having taken some razor-stripes of its own of late, but an appreciation of the ridiculous was with him still. He bowed under the proffered palms.

'For your wounded paws and feelings alike, I seek pardon,' he said, mock grovelling. It was judged nicely, with Ambassador precision; overdoing it enough to appease but not offend.

Sea-captain backtracked too, because Polly and Prudence (whom life or someone had robbed of 'humour') were stiffening. Without movement or outward alteration, the mirror-image ghosts were that much nearer doing what they did best.

'All I meant was . . .'

'Say no more, Thirteen. I entirely understand.'

Guy had sensed it too and trudged back to proper order – which was a pity, for he'd had few enough holidays from gloom since the pyramids.

'So, tell me,' he asked, in expected 'I'm above you and this' tones, but also as a bright new start, 'has all this that you've set yourself to – which is all and without exception utterly wonderful – been rewarded with recognition?'

'No. Not till just now when you said "nice" and—'

'That's not what I meant.'

Events had put a new edge on Guy. Nowadays, he turned on people. He could become as cold as one of Blades's decrees quicker than a huscarl snapping to attention.

But Sea-captain had his pride, lineage and achievements too; Polly and Prudence or no.

'Well then,' he snapped, 'what *do* you mean?'

'Visitors.'

Sea-captain considered more than he ought.

'The occasional famished Null comes to look. Penile wyrms sniff from a distance. We blow their bloody heads off.'

Guy's brow creased.

'I experience deep joy to hear it, but what I referred to was—'

'Was *Bladian* visitors,' said Sea-captain, for him. 'Those as who I've built against.'

'Precisely.'

Sea-captain pondered. A professional sort of pursing of the lips, prefacing whatever might follow with 'buyer beware'.

'A few sails on the horizon. Nothing we could catch. Nothing definite.'

'Scouts?'

'Possibly. Or shaggy fishermen maybe. Who knows?'

'You should.'

'Well, I don't. Nor can I converse with the dead. We've had a few of them washed up.'

Guy wouldn't let go.

'Describe them to me.'

'Before or after the little fishies had their fill?'

'The former. If you like.'

'I don't like. The sea's in my blood. That's the way I'll probably go.'

'It will be. In these very harbour waters in the next two minutes if you don't spit it out.'

The grand opening wasn't going as planned. Love and gratitude were on starvation rations. In his innocence, Sea-captain had thought he and Guy were friends.

'Pale men, like us. Not shaggies.'

'Tall? Impressive?'

What Guy meant was huscarls and Sea-captain knew full well – but wouldn't play.

'Once upon a time.'

Then Sea-captain looked Guy up and down, very coolly, and Polly and Prudence and all the assorted huscarls, cousins, flunkies and hangers-on also.

'There again,' he asked, 'what's "us"? It makes you wonder.'

And with that the old campaigner took his hurt look and feelings away to build on and embellish elsewhere. Apparently, another part of the thriving dockyard had just become irresistibly fascinating. Some of his own retinue went with him – not all but some, a bad sign whichever way you looked at it.

Again, Polly and Prudence had to be reined in, this time from pursuit. The dear departing had not been formally dismissed.

Guy signalled sufficient to calm them, letting both offence and offender go – just as he had another important person recently.

One actor's exit is another's opportunity. The space and chance cleared made room for one of the waiting gaggles. They simultaneously surged forward – and yet didn't, making themselves known and yet pretending not to. That was the trouble with not-long-since shaggies: they lacked depth of confidence in their upright gait.

Hunter approved of the experiment and gave them a helping hand.

'Guy – my lord Guy,' (this hurriedly and for form's sake since they were overheard), 'the city senate requests an audience.'

Actually, they hadn't – not yet – but were working their way up to it, if ignored.

And thus Guy learned how it was he recognised some of the shaved, shiny, faces. *That's* who they were. He inclined the sun of his visage to beam upon them.

Some bowed the knee, most just nodded. In response, core-huscarl and cousin lips curled. Born and bred Wessex folk didn't understand this thing at all. Guy was sowing seeds of Leveller notions and raising a crop of thorns to walk on. It wasn't that long ago this rabble were fouling their burrow at the sniff of a Null. Now they had the nerve to take their betters at their word and were acting like equals!

What with one thing and another, there was more poison in the air than sunshine – which was saying something in

Egypt. Most was of Guy's own, inadvertent, brewing. Be that as it may, whether made to his recipe or no, it left a bitter taste in Guy's mouth. Which must have been why it hurt to smile.

'And what can I do for *you*?' he asked, casting apart his hands like Sea-captain displaying his paper-cut stigmata. It was meant to be an *'ask and ye shall receive'* style gesture, but came out looking like an opening gambit at wrestling. Somewhere along the line he'd lost the knack of fake sincerity. In his present condition Guy could have recited love sonnets and made them sound like declarations of war.

Still, it was better than they were used to getting from viceroy Sea-captain. He'd not bothered pantomiming through their supposed 'rights and privileges' whilst the throne was his.

The spokesman was a Sicilian, a brimstone-mine beast of burden before, but now nominal lord of Alexandria-Jerusalem. He wore a chain of office and, truth to tell, it looked well on his filled-out chest. From within that cavity came tones suggesting lively hopes of even better days. Guy got back, with interest, the charge he'd laid upon him. It came garnished with flowery language.

'Master, we have met – as you decreed. And consulted – and listened, also as you would have us do. And in all we did we were mindful of your plea that we disown ourselves, owning only our authority, improving it to curb the proud and insolent; such as would disturb the tranquillity of this land, under whatever specious premises; that we relieve the oppressed, hear the groans of prisoners and widows and be pleased to reform the abuses of the professions. Further, that if there be anyone that makes many poor to make a few rich, then that suits not a commonwealth. In this same light we return to you . . .'

Till then, he'd been doing fine, revisiting the speech Guy had got from Blades and Blades had got from Cromwell. But now, venturing into unrehearsed waters, the ex-slave faltered. 'That is, we . . .'

'No,' stated Guy, quite gently really. 'That's mynah bird

stuff. Tell me what you've *actually* done.'

The Sicilian was not offended. He who'd raised him up at rocket pace had earned the right to bring him down – in moderation. There could only be momentary injustice in it.

'Well, lord,' he answered, in more normal voice, 'just that, to be honest. To tell the truth. Exactly what you asked. We've passed ordinances for the common good.'

Guy could almost believe him – it being the Achilles' heel of all Ambassadors to think no man really honest or honourable for its own sake – save themselves, naturally.

'Good. I'm very happy for you . . .'

He half turned and saw that at the commencement of the Cobb Sea-captain was getting it off his chest at some stevedores. They were hang-dog under the tirade's fiery blast – whilst also yearning to show the mighty mouth just what a baling hook might do.

Guy saw. Ambassadors ought to be able to read men almost as well as mages, but right then he wondered how many times had *he* merited such a response and never noticed. He'd find out. The proof of the pudding . . .

'Gracious, you're still here,' he told the senators. 'And? *And?*'

His sudden swivel took senate and snowy sisters alike by surprise.

And yes, there it was, if you took the trouble to see. The reflection of bile produced in the stomach flashed in the windows that were men's eyes. It was as Sir Tusker Ambassador had always told his children. '*My dear, dear, dear ones,*' he'd say, '*remember that you can never truly love that which you fear. But, all things considered, I'd sooner you* feared *me.*'

So here was proof, if needed. The pudding tasted disgusting . . .

Pathetically, the Sicilian held out a scroll, as though it might absorb the blame.

'Our words require your assent to be enacted. Otherwise, they remain merely words . . .'

'Albeit sound words, I'm sure,' Hunter butted in, not wanting them to be left with nothing. As former Prince-Bishop of his own little castle-cum-experiment, he was all too familiar with the games that went with democratic gestures.

Guy expelled what air he had left.

'Well, how many are there?'

Counting the decrees seemed to require an awful lot of Sicilian fingers, making Guy fear for the succeeding half hour. Or day. Or year. Or rest of his life.

Guy looked out to sea. The Blades books said that this was once Alexandria, 'Queen of Ports', that he'd decided to refound and rename. Through here had flowed all the fleets and trade of Paradise. Guy had advisedly chosen it for a glorious new beginning – only now it felt equally suitable for inglorious end. Just like every other place. The horizon looked more like a snapped trap of blue and lighter blue than a wide blue yonder. He had just a moment left to decide and then it would be for ever closed against him.

Had he anyone to do it for, Guy would have persevered and made things better. But he hadn't (not being a selfish man who'd include himself in the equation). Trained out of any general and broad affections, he'd focused what he'd got on one object. And now she was gone – or rather, she lived nearby, not wanting him.

So, when you looked at it, there was no sound cause to strive. Guy glared at the far distance again, trying to pierce it, as if ardour alone might spark the flame. Nothing came. He was firing blanks and could hurt no one, not even himself.

In other words, he was free.

Guy gave a roar, such as none had ever heard from him; a noise that turned the two P's whiter still and brought Sea-captain back at the double, expecting need of his expertise in 'trouble'.

It was only 'trouble' after a fashion, and even then not for him. Now the yoke was lifted, Guy was riding high above them all, though mortal eyes might not see it, higher even than he'd been above Wanborough barn.

'I tell you what,' he said to the senators, 'you have *this*! Which is what you want! I wish you joy with it.'

And with an inkstick which had once belonged to Blades, he inscribed a giant

G

on the reverse of their petition.

'One signature for all,' Guy explained. 'Retrospective and prospective. In advance. In perpetuity. Everlasting.'

The Senate took it back and looked and couldn't quite believe it yet. All the same, some more quick-off-the-mark ideas were already tapping at their doors.

'And *you*' – this to Sea-captain – 'to you I give this: a grovelling apology, for all past and future affronts . . .'

'King' Guy actually mimed a shrivelling down to utter abasement on the dockside – even if swiftly rewound and recovered from.

'. . . which is what you want. And not only that, but this too: a striking off of your shackles – to let you heed the call of the sea!'

The fulsomeness of it disarmed. Sea-captain's surliness slipped down to the paving quicker than Guy. His mouth opened – but was pre-empted.

'No, lovely Thirteen, don't deny it. You hear her summons and long to obey. Don't you dare call me a liar. It is what you want. So, I freely give it to you. Take your beloved Lady Bridget; take whatever galley escort you see fit. Go see . . .'

Guy genuinely appeared lost for words – which was hard to credit.

'. . . Go see . . . the sea!'

It had never occurred to Sea-captain, and one or two others there that day as well, to look at life in that manner. To just . . . ask yourself what you really wanted and then *do* it. Revolutionary! And yet so simple! Why hadn't they ever thought of it? The answer came to them immediately. Because, unlike Guy, they hadn't got the divine spark within, that's why.

Suddenly, all eyes were on Guy as the audience waited for more gems.

Alas, he was no longer communing with higher powers and again trod the same hard earth as they. His face was once more as fixed as fate.

Still, there was hope. With Ambassadors, who knew what went on beneath the steel veneer?

Sea-captain had no business disputing. It *was* exactly what he wanted, had he but paused to ask himself and stopped for an answer audible above duty's incessant nagging.

'But why?'

There, it was said. He'd blurted it out. Sea-captain had to check. You never got just what you wanted, not the way you wanted it. It was an iron law of life. But if this turned out to be true then all Sea-captain's certainties were going base over tip.

Therefore, he almost found it comforting, in a dull, despairing sort of way, to find nothing had really changed.

'Simple,' answered Guy in what, had Sea-captain only known it, was perfect recollection of Guy-over-Wanborough. 'Selfish reasons. I can hardly deal with Doomsday *and* sail the *Lady B* simultaneously. Well, can I?'

'Go on, tuck in!' said Sea-captain, relishing his revenge. 'Eat the meal that's set before you! This is what *you* wanted. I heard it from your own lips.'

Actually, as is so often the case, it both was and it wasn't. Guy still hadn't found what he was looking for – and never would, not here. He said as much and Sea-captain harrumphed disapproval.

It ought to have sufficed. Guy had asked for 'islands, interest and beauty' and they'd got him all three. Even Hunter agreed. It was dreadful the things that life did with people, even the best of them. Guy Ambassador had turned topsy-turvy. From being a pleasure to do business with, he'd become a business to do pleasure with.

The Middle Sea was millpond still and blue. It sparkled like a starscape under the noonday sun. Guy was under shade and under no pressure. His time was his own. It was sheer sourness not to just live and be glad. A curled lip was uncalled for.

Set amongst such perfect azure, the islands were white like a dazzling smile. The ruins thereon gleamed; even the long-lost fields were parched pale. Only the inhabitants provided any variant shades – but Guy didn't much care for purple.

Silently bidden, Polly refilled his cup. Undiluted wine at midday attracted some disapproving stares.

'A tasty paradox!' said Hunter, smacking his lips; for he too wanted to indulge but oughtn't. All the same, his archaeological erogenous zones were roused. '*This* we've not found before!'

You could tell he thirsted to land and celebrate. Pursuing their own agenda, the Null ashore were of like mind, urging him and all the other meat on to a visit.

Guy queried that with a frown. He was aware Egypt had been a bitter blow to the ex-bishop: a bathful of cold water over his imaginings once he'd wrenched its secrets up from the depths and dark. It ought to have cured him of the itch to make past ages walk again and clothe them in his own assumptions. And so it was probably for his own good that someone should tell him, 'Not so . . .'

Sea-captain was of like mind – or just mean.

'Cack! It's exactly what we've found all over. Long-lost people and successor Null. Let's hose the vermin down!'

He'd been looking for an opportunity to try out the newly refitted *Lady Bridget* and shake her guns and sails and crew from torpor. Even the flimsiest of excuses had been seized on to date: a shoal of dolphins, a raft of driftwood and weed – only to be slapped down by Guy who'd had his fill of fuss. But this was meatier stuff: meaty indeed, for the cavorting, copulating Null looked well on whatever it was they did all day.

Hunter took on Guy's killjoy mantle.

'No!' He flapped bony hands at the crumbling domes and whitewashed relics. 'We've not glimpsed island cultures before! This is unique: advanced. What was here wasn't shaggies! These were full human. This must have been paradise!'

Even as he spoke, Hunter knew it was a dead give-away, revealing the real reason for his search. No longer confident of a better place to come, he sought for signs that it might once have been. He couldn't help himself, not in general and certainly not now. Mariners bored into volunteering by the brazen calm were already heading cannonwards. Guy only had to give the word and Hunter would lose the evidence he craved to shoehorn.

The Ambassador-arbiter considered. Paradise? Perhaps once, in these overlooked little rocks, clawless man had been able to stand aloft. Maybe, maybe even for a long while, they'd been untroubled. But then, one fine day, the serpent entered their garden.

It was delicious, in a chilly way, to visualise that first stray Null which swam ashore. Perhaps it had dined upon an innocent and then gone back to fetch reinforcements. Or perhaps a whole troop had landed and poured into the white village like purple acid. From that it was a natural progression to wonder who the last human here had been, and what their thoughts were before the end. Like the final Egyptian waiting in his ready-made tomb, they must have reckoned themselves the last people in existence. Even centuries on and second hand, the image had the power to chill.

Guy raised his face from cup to sky in gratitude. This was occupying stuff: just what he'd ordered and hoped for. Complete minutes of life were going by without him brooding. The present question elbowed its way to the head of the queue, past and over other more patient petitioners – and good riddance too. A gulp of wine reinforced Guy's conclusion that the other queries couldn't have been all that important after all: not if they suffered in silence – the milksops.

So, did he want the scene preserved for others to find, for them to have their flesh creep in turn? It was in his nature to be indulgent – but to who and what? To Hunter's antiquarian twitches? To Sea-captain's lust for action? To the memory of the fortunate – and then not so fortunate – islanders? Or were all his obligations to today? There were living monsters within range. He had gunpowder going begging.

A windless day was no problem to a galley. They just deployed oars and carried on, the master of all Middle Sea eventualities. The quinquereme and brace of triremes escort had never ceased to function, unlike the becalmed *Bridget*, circling the inhabited isle like confident predators and sending the Null into a frenzy. Very probably, a sprinkle of seasoning on that was the scent wafting over intervening brine. They could detect the tang of their captive brethren.

It was Sea-captain's brilliant brainwave to recruit Null crew, aided by clever artisans who made it possible. Between them they'd come up with the subtle chain web which kept reluctant Null on rowing benches and throttled with exquisite agony the slightest contrary move. Then, supplying the rowers' motivation, was thrown in an idea Sea-captain stole from a secret Bladian torture chamber deep beneath New-Heathrow. Each bench sat sandwiched, front and back, between rows of spikes at eye and heart level. A gearing system shifted these in time with the oars, but always with a *slightly* more generous motion. The snarling Null either kow-towed before the skewers or got the point of Sea-captain's genius. Consequently, his new model navy moved at a sprightly, never flagging pace, – especially with a hold chock-full of spare monsters to replace the impaled.

Guy imagined them now, toiling away unseen below deck, pricked to sterling work for meat masters. It was a topic for many post-supper conversations, when the jug was passed and silly subjects seemed important, whether it was consoling shanties that the condemned Null sang, or hymns of hate.

Perchance the purple islanders heard them now or could sniff the cologne of sweat and sorrow across a gulf and through a hull.

Guy latched on to that disparity in destinies. Two sets of identical creatures had fared differently in the lottery of life. Two wyrds. One was worse than death and the other entailed sodomy in the sun and shelter from rain in murdered men's houses. It didn't seem fair really.

Also, Guy saw that no matter how low he'd sunk it was within his power to redress the injustice. Given that Blades had cosmically abdicated from doing the right thing, duty now devolved on poor old Guy. What a disaster! What a fate!

'W-wipe it clean,' he told Sea-captain, firmly, 'as though it had never been.'

Within seconds the *Bridget*'s gunports rattled open, drowning Hunter's whinges

Justice soon spoke loudly over the water.

Dusk drew on. Lunar light was already at work, supplying the sparkle on the sea. Guy couldn't sleep. Hunter wasn't speaking to him and Polly and Prudence weren't able to. Sea-captain was busy. Consequently, Guy Ambassador contemplated alone.

All the Middle Sea was vast before him: no land in sight and each point of the compass holding equal promise – or lack if it. Even the cleansing fire raised on the Null island was now out of sight and largely forgotten (save for one almighty sulk). The wide blue yonder was undifferentiated and bland potential – bar straight ahead. There, before the nose of aimless voyage, a storm was brewing. Not the end-of-days variety Guy instinctively sought, but the inconvenient, rain-containing kind.

If any direction was as good as another, Sea-captain had, not unreasonably, asked, why then must they steer straight for problems? Guy had no answer – but no countermand either. It just seemed fit.

The approaching clouds took on an ominous wolf's-head face, like Fimbulwinter, the storm that heralded Doomsday in legend. Appropriately, a rumbling growl preceded the grey and black. How apt, Guy thought.

Yes. Quite. Just *how* apt! His hopes rose and with them his eyes. He saw it at the same time as lookout. They acclaimed as one.

'*Sail! Sail! Sail ahoy!*'

On the horizon, under the wolf's maw: a triangle of white in contrast to the gloom, emerging from the dusk.

A vent in cloud cover, one beam of the moon, had betrayed its confidence. Like an adulteress revealed, one glimpse said enough to last for ever. Too late now! Let her about turn for obscurity and out of the limelight, but they had her measure. Any ship on an empty ocean holds more fascination than a long-lost brother. She promised purpose and they would never abandon her.

The crew must have been sleeping light, victims of undemanding days. They barely needed bells or cries to be hoisting full sail. Even the galleys, whose low gunwales demanded that they be wary of storm and wave, joined in. When the waters grew too choppy for oar-strokes and even willing Null were getting pierced, then the flapping poles could be stowed away. Long-Man-emblazoned canvas would take up the strain, granting the purple slaves a rare holiday.

The lone sail was not in the mood for company, commencing to tack round even during the brief interlude of that moonbeam. Sea-captain required no orders. This was his world and his time. Though too late to be on deck to see himself, he acted as if he had been. One look at the *Bridget*'s sails, one apiece for both storm and target, and then he was at ease.

'It'll be a long courtship,' he told Guy, bootless and bare-headed, still fastening his flies whilst watching everything aboard, gimlet-eyed. 'But never you fear. We'll have her . . .'

Guy looked into the grey wolf's eyes and experienced doubt like a cold shower. Quite who was 'having' whom, for instance? By then though, it was far too late to change his mind. Second thoughts would mean loss of face. Far better to drown and die.

The game was afoot, the immediate future settled. For the first time since Bathie went Guy was half content. Whilst the rigging above him writhed with life, he went down below to doze.

'She's closer,' said Sea-captain. 'We have our hooks in her and she knows it, bless her.'

Guy was glad 'she' did, because he couldn't see it. Dawn still showed the fugitive sail in sight but not noticeably larger than last night's recollection. He peered exaggeratedly hard in order to say so without saying.

'I know, I know,' responded Sea-captain, beside him at the rail. 'I warned you it'd be a long wooing.'

Actually, Sea-captain had played an artful hand through all the rough night, tacking round the penumbra of the storm the same as their quarry did – only better. With every enforced manoeuvre the *Bridget* gained a portion and sightings grew more frequent. In between whiles, her master's expertise sustained faith during the long intervals of solitude. Since Guy's tame seadog seemed to know the other ship's path as though he was steering her himself, all they need do was dog her heels till their paths crossed. Meanwhile, just in case the foe was granted a flash of inspiration, he also carefully hove into land, far out enough not to worry about fouling but sufficient to kill any clever ideas of doubling back and slipping betwixt ship and shore.

So, hour by hour, Sea-captain closed down the options, leaving only unpalatable things in the larder of possibilities. Either they could continue this undignified flight, merely postponing the inevitable, or else chance their arm (and lives) in the eye of the storm. Since it looked a grim one, something even the ship-sized wyrms would dive from, Sea-captain rightly guessed they wouldn't fancy that. Looming equally large as the squall was one remaining – sensible – option: to strike sails and stop for a chat.

Meanwhile, lighter winds circulating round the growing tempest kept the show on the road long enough for Guy to be unimpressed beside Sea-captain as they bit their breakfast bread next morning. All the crew were worn ragged with scraping up every scrap of breeze, a marked contrast to the ambassadorial retinue's sleek restedness. Most other eyes were red-rimmed and no pleasure to connect with. Guy took no notice, believing it his duty to be a cut above.

'Another' – Sea-captain sniffed the salt breeze – 'hour and we can address a shot to her. It'll fall short but not far. She'll get the picture.'

Guy liked the sound of that and smiled – until his companion spoke again.

'And then you'll say . . . ?'

The snap question took Guy by surprise. He'd failed already. Even on their death bed, Ambassadors were meant to have ripostes-in-depth ready to roll.

'Um . . . How about "Hello? What's *your* name? Are you, as I suspect, golden huscarls and lackeys of the arch-fiend Blades? He who is a false prophet, an impotent molester of slave-girls, a pathetic, salivating, scraggy-necked assassin of faithful servants and true religion? Do you have a *problem* with that? Would you like one?" Something along those lines, Thirteen. Will that do, do you think?'

Sea-captain nodded sagely. His eyes never left the relevant slice of horizon even as he answered.

'Yes. Should break the ice, I reckon . . .'

First light wasn't far off. The same, sadly, could be said of the storm. Otherwise, things were running as smoothly as the sea was not, till Guy's Jonah-style presence derailed them. Suddenly, despairing of that day's programme, the fugitive surprised and impressed Sea-captain by opting for his least likely outcome. She changed course and headed for the heart of darkness.

Happily, the *Bridget* didn't have to agonise over following suit. Other matters intervened.

Naturally, they'd hitherto shunned the climatic aberration, just as long as it returned the compliment and left them alone too. That had seemed the cheeriest and most polite course to take. Mother Nature might have her foul moods and tantrums but there was no need to gawp at such showing off. She'd probably be all sunny contriteness tomorrow – a morrow they'd now probably never see.

The mother of all thunderclaps plus sheet lightning to match, broke almost beside the *Bridget*. The world hung in unnatural suspension. Sails and rigging turned incandescent white against the angry sky so that, for a second, all aboard feared they were afire.

Such micro-panics were the least of their problems. For an equal space the surrounds stood clear as noon. The enraged sea was revealed with blinding clarity.

And there, not 3 miles off to windward, steamed the *Saucy Sailor*.

A vessel like an island, a Kraken of grey risen from inky depths. A once American but now Wessex dreadnought beholding them as they beheld it.

Darkness returned, save in the encore song-and-dance act on their retinas. Scintillating sunlets circled round the after-image of a behemoth man o' war.

Thunderbolts boomed overhead – or possibly guns the size of oaks.

Sea-captain turned to Guy, not to demand but to supply explanation. It was hardly needed – but wonderful good form.

'Do you know,' he said, in 'why deny it?' tones, 'I do suspect that might have been a trap. Goodbye, Guy . . .'

'I'll deal with him later, the obedient bastard!'

Sea-captain bared his teeth at the only galley to heed his signal to turn tail. The others had flouted it and him, staying in close to their charge and thus, illogically, earned his blessing.

Guy didn't think so. Days of reckoning definitely belonged to the opposite camp. The boot was on the other foot, the worm turned – and all the other metaphors of little comfort. Lionheart had done the right thing.

The *Lady Bridget* had put about, if only for form's sake, but the outcome could be calculated even by the slow of understanding. Now that Guy and Sea-captain came to think about it, now it was too late, a better strategy occurred to them. It would have been a glorious conclusion to go in guns blazing. Far better that than to be harried, deprived of dignity like a man with a goose at his heels, to the exact same conclusion.

Great minds thought alike at the same moment. With Polly and Prudence and Hunter following, Guy and Sea-captain tested their sea legs in the swell all the way to the *Bridget*'s stern. There was one gun there, a 'Parthian cannon' as Blades christened them for some reason. Barked commands secured it some servitors.

'Do you really think we should?'

Hunter indicated the closing distance between them and the *Saucy Sailor*. The rumble of her engines was now audible above anything the thunder produced. Her forward guns had them square in their sights. She did indeed look a dragon it would be unwise to rouse.

'Why not?' answered Guy, pointing to precisely the same hard facts. 'It makes no difference – save we'll feel better. And besides, if we offload a few cannonballs then we'll sink slower. Think of it: whole extra seconds of life!'

Hunter's lips compressed before they parted to speak.

'I now see the deep wisdom of your policy,' he said dryly. 'Pray proceed.'

'Ready, my lords . . .' The cannonmaster held up a glowing cord to prove it.

''Bout time too,' commented Sea-captain, mock-gruff. 'Now, off you go, if you please, sirrah. Present Mistress Iron-Corsets with our calling card.'

The party delicately shuffled out of recoil-range harm and, veterans all nowadays, waited open-mouthed like a comic collection of village idiots, as prescribed for eardrums' sake whilst awaiting explosions.

It came and was impressive, filling their little world with light and sound and peppery amusement for their nostrils.

It was also blessed with fortune, unlike the rest of their day.

From afar the dying resonance was prolonged by a metallic coda of impact. They could hardly hope to have done harm, but the spoiling of some perfect paintwork was a nice thought to take with you.

'You know,' said Sea-captain, wistfully (if one can be wistful at the bellow), 'I've half a mind – with your indulgence, Guy – to turn and try for a broadside. It'd be sweet to hear Bridget sing one last time.'

Alas, today was a solo show, for one star performer only. She proved to be a prima donna, unwilling to share the stage for amateur-hour. The very air in their ears 'whooomped' in sympathy with what must have been ten times worse aboard the *Saucy Sailor*.

A projectile seared and separated the space between them and the adjacent quinquereme. It ended in remote cataclysm, Blades knew where, but probably halfway back to Egypt.

Had it been rowing weather, the galley would have been stripped to splinters all along her port side and become proud possessor of half its Null rowers mounted like a butterfly collection. Thereafter, she'd have been condemned to just go round in circles: an imposition in fact of the metaphoric fate facing all of them.

And that was only a ranging shoot. If all of the *Saucy Sailor*'s weaponry had been fit and facing, then even that wouldn't have been necessary. She could have rained down careless shot and surely one would hit, sooner or later.

Of the happenstance (or bait) sail sighting there was now no sign or need. Unaided, the dreadnought was worth a gross of *Bridgets*, a Middle Sea coated with galleys. Even now, when it wouldn't be his worry for much longer, Guy wondered what would have happened if a fleet of these had come over the Atlantic.

Fortunately, the Professor and his American cohorts had been a timid lot, nervous about chancing their arm or tipping life on her back. Otherwise, Wessex might be worshipping a portly academic by now, instead of . . . something not a lot better, to be honest.

Right now however, Guy felt some sympathy with the American way. Life was casting a cold eye over him of late, never mind hinting at a romp in the hay. Shells were raining down like large lumps of the sky and the *Lady Bridget* was being stalked remorselessly, the unmistakable focus of uncharitable intentions. Try as he might, Guy just couldn't see scope for detecting a bright side in any of it.

For Polly and Prudence it was worse. Left with no practical means of protecting Guy, they found themselves at a loose end. The Devil then found work for their idle hands in the shape of thoughts of self – not guests they'd ever normally entertain. Now though, the past passed in review before their eyes and, all in all, it was a mournful show. Things hadn't been a barrel of laughs and shortly it was going to end. They didn't know whether to be sad or glad.

Hunter was saying his prayers, manly style, unbowed, prompting Guy to ponder whether he should do the same. On balance he thought not. He'd led a full rather than good life, and last-minute changes in direction struck him as slightly tacky – not to mention insincere. If it seemed so to him, then what on earth would an all-knowing judge make of it? No. Far better to leave be. That judge, being all-knowing, would understand and make . . . allowances.

Not before time, the *Saucy Sailor*'s unimpressive gunners got some return for their expenditure. A charge fell short of the quinquereme but still packed enough oomph to tilt all five decks of her prow-first into the water, shaking each and every line of caulking loose. She disintegrated as she sank and sank as she disintegrated. Mere minutes elapsed between her tail being raised and it sinking beneath the waves with bubbles as farewell. Guy idly wondered if acting captain Beelzebub could swim.

Then he saw proof of the maxim that it's an ill wind indeed that blows no good. Down in the drink were some liberated Null, clutching oars transformed in a flash from cruel captor to kind life-saver. He almost wished the odds-defiers well.

Where Sea-captain was gone Guy couldn't tell, but the

Bridget's crew were left free to form their own opinion. They proved of the opinion that all was lost. Every square inch of sail was up, the broadsides pointed uselessly port and starboard. All that remained to them was to eye the ship's boats with longing but aim to linger with honour.

Guy had huscarls with him, and Polly and Prudence too, to ensure that there be no distasteful scenes to mar journey's end. More surprisingly, it transpired he also had pity with and in him – still. Which pleased Guy greatly. He'd thought it all gone.

'Go!' he told the throng, and like greased lightning most did. That the *Bridget* was the primary target was plain beyond disputing. The remaining trireme had already perceived that and pointed her sharp bronze nose away from lethal company. The wisdom of it was proved by her survival and non-molestation. No one blamed her in the least. So, if enough small craft scattered in enough directions, and the storm was as merciful as Guy, then surely *some* of them might survive to rue the day.

Not if the *Saucy Sailor* had any input. It said so with puckle guns or even worse American equivalents. No sooner did a longboat hit the water than a lead hail hit it. Only emptied, leaky, vessels limped away.

Their nemesis then had contemptuous capacity enough to repeat the process on the *Bridget*'s rigging. For a spell it rained mariners and canvas shreds around Guy's head, in addition to fat droplets of the real thing: saliva from the wolf's head above. Guy recognised Bosun plummet past, now legless as well as tongueless. Pity failed to surge. Going to God in instalments would serve him right for interrupting in Yarmouth.

Sea-captain reappeared from below, rolling and wrestling the biggest powder barrel his hawser-arms could manage. It left him gasping, but not without that reserve of air required for explanation. This was his defining moment. He needed to speak.

Guy indulged him. It was not as though he had much else to do.

'She's going to ram,' Sea-captain wheezed, as he rolled out the barrel. 'Must be. Could have sunk us way back. Doesn't want to. Wants to plough us under. We'll see about that. *I'll* see! Punch a hole. Take her with me!'

Guy didn't wish to be a wet blanket – he was wet enough already – but couldn't transcend his doubts. He'd been aboard the *Saucy Sailor* and observed the breadth of steel between her and harm from romantic gestures such as Sea-captain proposed. All the same, he said nothing.

Unfortunately, some scepticism must have leaked from eyebrow angle or tilt of mouth.

'I know, I know . . .' said Sea-captain, as he struggled to the relevant rail. 'But I might as well. Seeing as I can't swim . . .'

Wessex sailors rarely could. Professional wisdom held it that such knowledge tended only to prolong the agony of shipwreck.

Put like that, Guy saw the sense of it. He nodded approvingly.

'No thrashing about gagging and spewing for *me*,' pronounced Sea-captain, now he was almost ready. 'I prefer to go out with a ban—'

What he sought came from an alternative supplier. A puckle spray impacted against him, head to toe. By some miracle the powder cask failed to explode – unlike Sea-captain. He and it went through the wreckage of the rail, into the sea that had been his mistress and livelihood.

The deck twanged and erupted in linear patterns beside Guy's boots but he spared time and control enough to say goodbye to Viscount Sea-captain XIII. The man had been . . . useful: undeserving of a comic end.

Instinctively, if vainly, Polly and Prudence moved closer. They arrived just in time to intercept something unpleasant. A portion of Polly's left foot was flicked away in a spray of sandal and scarlet. It was odd to see a soundless scream.

On the plus side, at least Guy now had something between him and the chill breeze driven forward by the metal colossus.

Prudence formed a handy windbreak as she kissed her companion and counselled courage. Guy meanwhile took shelter behind them. He'd worked all his life towards outfacing this moment. God forbid cold should make him shiver and people misinterpret it as cowardice . . .

The *Saucy Sailor* was now huge and horrible, horizon-hogging and inescapable, framed in dramatic fashion by Fimbulwinter formations. For it not to command your undivided attention was merely the purest of posing.

On the other hand, Guy rather applauded certain poses struck before death's door. At best, they seemed a transforming of the human condition, so subject to mortality and embarrassing predicaments, into something . . . finer. Therefore, he now admired the play of raindrops on the wounded deck instead of worrying. There was grace in their ephemeral impacts. And timeless pleasures.

So, as the metallic mountain bore down, klaxons blaring like a hydra in triumph, he cut it dead. Only when speeding grey steel encroached on peripheral vision did Guy condescend to pay heed. He addressed his eyes ahead. The beast towered above him.

Guy stood up straight and languidly flicked his fingers – at both it and life. It was all either deserved. Neither seemed to care.

Free – or soon to be – from the cage of flesh, Guy Ambassador felt happy that he'd done the right thing. Even if only at the last moment. His finest and final moment. If only it weren't so lonely.

Steel tore into wood. Men and material screamed. Water leaped up to swallow the world and all light.

Life had her revenge for Guy's disrespect. She served up a humiliating loss of balance and tangle of limbs. Hard objects won arguments with his head and softer parts. He was in the boundless sea but still not at liberty. Those parts of the *Lady Bridget* retaining a little afterlife of wholeness held him bound. Guy felt sure it was the ship's wheel repeatedly jabbing him in the back. A floor now promoted to ceiling cracked him on his brow. Tables turned, it had vengeance for hard pounding all its life.

Guy also experienced internal agony and disappointment. Someone, a self-deluding idiot sailor he'd bumped into somewhere, had told Guy drowning was an easy way to die – *'like slipping away in y'bed – so long as you doesn't struggle . . .'*

Rubbish. Guy *hadn't* struggled. He'd said his piece and played his part and let wyrd have the final say. Then, for all that, his reward was to find that lungfuls of salt water were about as soothing as Null-love. In a striking parallel, it stretched and stung organs designed for gentler treatment. Exasperated by his brain's stupid stoicism, Guy's body seized the helm and mutinied.

He'd no idea what degree of self-possession was required to just relax and drift down, but clearly he didn't possess it. Whilst breath remained, Guy reached for the life he'd so recently slighted. It showed she never took offence.

Debris and dead men bashed against him. Then a net. It swallowed him whole, along with many other items, and drew him from under the heavy sea, out of the *Bridget*'s ghostly gaol. Guy returned to the light of day.

He found friends there. Prudence was treading water, torn between support of her fainting other half and further dives for Guy. Their black tresses hung like seaweed, their eye and face paint had all run. Revealed to true scale by clinging gowns, they looked more human than ever before. The joyous smiles which greeted Guy crowned it.

He warmed to them in their vulnerability, even more than he had when they were strange and dangerous. Their gladness at his survival pierced Guy to the bone. He hadn't realised there was any unconditional love left in the world. He repented of his exploitation of it. Of his use of them.

Any emotion, even such pleasurable pain, was welcomed in. In fact, every sensation arrived as novelty and a new beginning, making Guy glad. He'd assumed the water was the end.

Not so. Guy left the twins and sea behind to rise above

both. He travelled in the sodden company of bits of body and splintery things. Empathising now with cod and lobsters, but unable to increase by one iota the dignity quotient, he awaited developments.

They came in the form of Wessex-folk at dreadnought deck level. High, high above the waves, teams hauled on the net like fishermen – or fishers of men. Their archetypal faces were cherished like a second chance.

They recognised him too, even in present drowned-rat disguise. They recognised him so well he almost went back down to the drink. Some of them, manners overcoming commonsense, loosened their grip to bow the knee. An officer swore at them and then apologised – to Guy.

He was still soaked and netted: covered in seaweed and snot and worse; but every sign said his rescuers wished to remedy that. Their co-ordinator's broad Downs-country features and accent radiated concern. He looked at Guy and Guy looked at him.

Then, though tilted at an odd angle and his countenance criss-crossed by mesh, Guy was respectfully addressed through the netting.

'My lord Guy! Blades be praised! Blades be *praised*!'

The sentiment was mumble-echoed by the rest. All along the rail that chorus was taken up as Guy was.

Team-leader leaned close to confide.

'We should have had faith. He *said* you couldn't be killed . . .'

Guy was woken by gunfire like the crack of doom, almost shaking him out of the sheets. The whole ship lifted with every giant's roar and discharge. The walls of his stateroom trembled. No slumber could survive it.

All the same, they sent a summoner, out of courtesy. A golden huscarl who nearly had to have the door down to make his presence known.

'Beloved master,' he shouted, bowing over his axe. 'You are required.'

'Who by? I'm sleepy.'

Obviously not authorised to say, the huscarl smiled instead. A bizarre sight.

'Please?' the man ventured, as experiment.

Stranger still. It was of a piece with the rest of Guy's treatment since being hauled aboard. Nothing but consideration and respect whilst he continually expected the needle stiletto or red-hot poker.

Guy swung out of his opulent cot, rested, refreshed, patched up and minded to oblige. It was odd, he reflected as he composed himself, how things got stood on their head: the *Lady Bridget*, himself in the water, smiles from should-be assassins. Whatever next?

A well-stocked wardrobe flung open, that was what. Guy refused to show surprise.

'I see. Pass me that frockcoat. No, the military red. Lace collar, silver buttons. Oh, is there now? Then the heavier of the two. Thank you.'

Again, there was the fear of fear. He had no notion about the climes outside or reception waiting. It might be freezing fog round a scaffold. Down below, thanks to the churning engines, it was perpetually armpit ambience.

The coat fitted like it was made to measure. A trifle old-fashioned, just like his own favourites, and out of season maybe – but no matter. Better to swelter than shiver. A man's execution was a vital, defining, day in his life. Even at the end of things you had to consider carefully.

Someone else had. It was as if they'd been expecting him as honoured guest. Here was a whole ensemble created for him – come to think of it, perhaps even tailored to the measurements he'd left behind. How else to account for the perfect boots, the Locks of St James's cocked hat? The latter in particular was irresistible, landing on his perfumed locks like an old friend. It could almost be the one the Null knocked off and probably ate or shat in. It begged to be worn, even in the unsuitable confines of below deck. Guy just couldn't say no and added 8 inches to his stature.

As they left his home and prison of the last day and night, Guy might well have been mistaken for the dapper aristo who'd first trodden the *Saucy Sailor* several years and a whole lifetime ago. Unless, that is, a perceptive person stared into his eyes.

There was no one aboard to take on the task and be so rude. There was no one at all. Though the *Saucy Sailor*'s ways and corridors were spacious, veritable cricket pitches compared to the *Bridget*'s, they went wasted. Perhaps all spare hands were attending to the drumroll of the guns, or possibly this was an area in quarantine.

Guy had no way of telling. Or whether it meant they feared or revered him.

Certainly they trusted him. Though Guy had been stripped and bathed by gentle hands upon boarding, the invasive process stopped short of disarmament. A stiletto still stiffened his blindingly polished boots. His revolver, cleaned and dried, was set on the dresser alongside his Bathie cameo-pendant. Guy checked and collected them all.

Therefore, as the huscarl guided Guy through the maze, it was always an option for the poor man to 'get the point' or develop lethal lead poisoning. It would be far from a 'stab in the dark', brightly bathed as they were by the Professor's ill-understood 'lectric fluid'. Guy could then guess for himself the general way up, and vault over the side, rather than meekly report for removal.

However, something restrained his hand; perhaps that very trust displayed by the huscarl's turned back. Taking advantage of it would be just too . . . Bladian for Guy's delicate stomach. Better to let this misled adonis live on and first see how Polly and the rest had fared before departing. Afterwards, with six shells at your hip, any ending could still be self-determined.

Guy's mercy was straight away rewarded. At a junction below a stairwell, another gaggle came into view. Familiar forms. Guy asked – for the moment – whether he might catch up.

Polly, Prudence and Hunter had the honour of a huscarl each, though not held under any particular detention. It did all seem only a showing of the way, an exceptionally courteous captivity, rather than escort to nemesis.

Guy and the girls kissed, shaken as much by emotion as the guns. Polly in particular, her demi-foot swathed in white but still more vivid than her face, seized him as though she wanted to merge. Only then could Guy and Hunter nod at each other and shake hands.

'I found a dead Null,' said his friend, almost apologetic, as if needing to excuse survival. 'They're surprisingly buoyant.'

The huscarls waited patiently through all the sentiment before one coughed politely. Then they split to top and tail the ascent of the stairs. Arrival revealed the party stood just one door away from open air and glorious morning – and the full benefit of the bombardment.

First they covered their ears, and then Guy wished for an extra pair of hands to cut out the sights.

Like them, Alexandria-Jerusalem was also being honoured. Nemesis had come to it. Guy saw now, through vision he had to force to the task, that wyrd had been kind to Sea-captain in cutting his thread before he could witness this.

The laboriously laid stones of the harbour were already laid low, sliding into the sea in monstrous splashes. The quinqueremes were afire. All that effort and sacrifice, the death of cedars in Lebanon, all wasted.

A few ships had cleared the Cobb; maybe too many for the

Saucy Sailor's lethality to deal with – but not for want of trying. Already the creeping barrage, having done its work downtown, was moving on to the marble halls and hovels where Guy had hoped to bake Utopia. The 'Strangling Hands' and 'Long Man' banners still fluttered from high points, a few puckles and cannon returned fire from on shore, but it and everything was hopeless. The shells like barrels would come and mix matter: men and marble alike, back into the atomic pool of possibilities they'd come from. And the same with the ideas they carried.

Guy made himself look, and saw clearly. The *Saucy Sailor* wasn't just pasting a town: it was cauterising possibilities. There mustn't be even a trace left of any other way of doing things.

Then, just when nothing could stop it, it stopped. The silence was like that before creation: profound, sacred. Even the defenders didn't wish to break it. Their gallant but futile efforts faltered down to rest. It was a moment like prayer – and certainly an answer to Guy's.

Thinking deeply but not cheerfully, the companions let themselves be led out of sunlight back into the Professor's poor substitute. A few paces along deck the huscarls ushered them inside again. Vast double doors gave them entry to the throne of God himself – or so they formerly believed.

Decks had been cut away right down into the hold. The blue world-egg sat secure in a network of beams and hawsers, hastily welded but then gloried with gilt.

Behind them, the huscarls genuflected. Below, more of their brethren than could be readily counted looked up. A gong was sounded with the flat of an axe.

Null in treadmills fastened to the ship's sides scampered obediently. Shining chains took up the strain. The world-egg cracked open.

'Worship me!'
  'No. Shan't.'

Hunter was subdued but resolved. Blades-the-god looked down from his high throne. He'd been fed full of stimulants for this audience – or perhaps that was normal practice. They'd seen the liquids supplied and clysters applied. Then his voice ceased to quaver and beanstick arms were up to lifting themselves from repose. Blades showed them what he was capable of. He rose, as if from the grave.

'Good. *Right* answer! You shall not die but live. You're the man I'm looking for – or one of them. I consecrate you Archbishop of all New-Wessex. So, approach for the laying on of hands . . .'

Blades deputised some acolytes at floor level and one tried to anoint Hunter's brow with chrism from a silver salver. Both appointment and sacrament got declined, graciously at first but then more forcibly. In the end though, with two golden huscarls pinning him, the daub was got on. Hunter was then briefly borne up to be flicked with withered hands.

'Congratulations, Archbishop!' said Blades.

'I . . . I . . .'

Hunter was absolutely lost for words, but should any deign to come it didn't look as if they'd be kind ones. Apparently, his vocabulary didn't contain anything even approaching the level of apostasy required. Powerful emotions shook both Hunter's frame and the burly types restraining it.

'There is no God but *God*!' he finally spat out, settling for the safe if not scorching. 'And-you-are-*not*-he! I . . . I . . .'

Paradoxically, it had to be admitted that Blades was godlike in his unconcern.

'I would love to chat,' he replied. 'Alas, time is short and your statements obvious – and, might I say, appallingly self-centred. Shut the Archbishop up, please.'

One huscarl moved smoothly from kindly custodian to 'sweet goodnight' merchant. He hit Hunter one mighty blow bang in the face and the new Lord Spiritual of all Wessex left the scene behind. Some skivvies then physically removed him, feet first, head scraping.

Meanwhile, Blades had turned to Guy.

'Do you want to keep these?' he asked, most solicitous, meaning Polly and Prudence standing at Guy's side. 'Only I see one of them is spoilt. I'm at your disposal. Would you like me to dispose of one or both?'

The two shrank into Guy like children. There are some situations beyond bravery. All their sad lives the being before them had been the Almighty. He'd proved to be not very nice. It was still a shock.

Guy lifted his head and voice. Of course, it could all be bluff and double-bluff, designed to find out his wishes and then deny them. However, he'd tired of textual analysis of every damned conversation. Let things signify their plain meaning just for once. That would be a joy snatched from the brink. A last little victory.

'If you're willing to give me one thing before I go, then promise me they'll be saved.'

Blades was perplexed.

'Theologically?' he asked,

'Actually.'

The god-king seemed relieved.

'Now, that I *can* arrange. Someone stow these scrumptious aberrations away somewhere. Somewhere safe. For later. And Guy, *dear* Guy, you have my word on it . . .'

The Ambassador was too slow in aborting his wry smile: a freakish expression in this most unsmiling of places.

Yet Blades matched it; arranging his cavernous wrinkles to ten-to-two. He even showed forth a spray of peg teeth.

'Which *does* mean something, I assure you, Guy; oh ye of little faith. They'll be spared to see . . .' he flapped one hand and creased his brow trying to remember. 'You know . . . chatty chap: self-centred. Came with you to bring me back from exile all those years ago. Just ordained him . . .'

'Hunter,' Guy supplied.

'Yes, him. They'll live to see Archbishop Hunter enthroned in New-Godalming. If so minded, of course. Assuming that's their sort of thing . . .'

'Your w-word?' Guy asked. 'Regardless?'

'Come what may.' Then Blades threw (or edged) back his head. 'Hear O Wessex,' he declaimed, 'my will and decree. The whey-faced wenches shall live!'

And then Blades looked at them, and it was surely not imagination that made Guy think the ancient rascal licked his lips. A last flicker of the energies that had engineered an empire.

'Now make them go away. Go on. Shoo! Shoo!'

Guy had got the best he was going to get, even if it concluded in senile lust and coughs. Polly and Prudence were made to go, albeit with many a kiss and trailing embrace. It came down in the end to orders and banishment, demeaning their last words together and making them harsh ones.

Finally, Guy had to turn his back, lest he weep as they did. It was hard to do so and miss out on a proper parting. However, there were matters outstanding.

'God sees,' Guy said, admonishing Blades in advance, 'and will hold you to it.'

Blades seemed content, once the hacking fit was passed.

'Anything else? Today's a reckoning up of all dues: a give-away sale. Today's the day to be bold!'

So Guy thought he might as well go for it.

'A quick death?'

Blades smiled again. The best dentists in Wessex really had worked wonders for him. The hardwood false fangs gleamed – albeit brown – like those of a merely middle-aged man.

'A quick death? Is that it? You really should be more greedy, Guy. Such was always my intention. Of course, I shall give you that.'

Guy considered, and took a last look at the light. What a pity it was the man-made variety.

'Alternatively,' Guy announced, 'I can give *you* that . . .'

The pistol was out of his pocket, unimpeded, free of snags, swifter than reaction. Then levelled and squeezed. Six times in the space of one short in-breath. Six shots, employing overwhelming generosity, not even saving one for himself to thwart the golden huscarls' revenge. And surely that would be long and tortuous . . .

Guy learned it from those same huscarls' unconcern. He was saying it aloud before the futile exercise was halfway through.

'Blanks. Blanks. *Blanks* . . .'

The click upon an empty chamber came as blessed relief.

'You really do think of everything, don't you?' Guy's voice was bitter rather than appreciative.

Blades wafted away some of the powder smoke.

'Gods are meant to, I believe. Which brings me to the crux of the matter – if you're quite finished . . .'

'Well, I still have my stiletto,' Guy admitted, wishing to circumvent further humiliation. They'd probably swapped it for a mild steel copy, a toy that would fold comically, even against geriatric hide.

'I know. Of course, you have. One didn't wish to unman you entirely – or at all, come to that. It's just that we need a while in which to talk naturally. You would have behaved differently without your little comforts and myriad options. An Ambassador can't change his spots – or some such metaphor. Unfortunately for them, poor, blind, wretches – oh, sorry, no offence.'

'None taken, I'm sure.' Guy smiled like the dead man he was. Blades nodded acknowledgement.

'But now, Guy, if you've got it off your chest – or finished trying to put it into mine, I'd like a word. And after, when we've done . . .'

'An easy death.' Guy would rather he said it first.

'Exactly.'

'Good.'

'Right then: to work! The teeny-weeny matter of judgement. Judgement for me, for you, the world – and just about everyone. Doomsday in short, I believe it's called. Come closer, child, stiletto and all.'

There were steps up to the throne of glory, blocked by huscarls of the maddest sort. Their eyes were tormented by insupportable devotion, made bearable solely by Bladian decree. He so decreed now and they cleared the way – *just* and slowly.

Guy arrived at the level of the Imperial feet. Scarlet slippers could not conceal the ravages wrought by corns and calluses

'Things slip away,' said Blades, addressing the top of Guy's head. 'Time, places, people. Especially people.'

Within the vaulting egg there was room for many mansions – or leastways, cupboards and containers. Visibly tiring, Blades pointed.

'That one, I think. Would you be so kind?'

A blind chamberlain groped his way to Guy and gave him a golden key.

Though it was hardly the moment, Guy had to wonder about him. Was it Blades's cruelty that left the man so, or his charity that employed a man whose sight was dimmed? It wasn't easy guessing where no rules applied.

So Guy simply took the proffered hand and key and went to the ranks of cabinets. The lock obliged readily, the door even more – for it was kicked open from within. Sounds of agony hit Guy's ears only marginally in advance of the door-edge slamming against him.

Two prisoners were pinned like insects inside, held by a most intricate display of elegant jewellers' chain embedded into their very flesh. That thrust for liberation had cost one of them dear.

'Hard to credit, I know,' said the antique voice above and behind Guy, 'but what you see here is all that I – *I*, Blades the Great, Null-bane and etc. – have left of the Imperial Corps of Wizards. Laughable, I agree. That which once marched through New-Godalming in battalions now fits comfortably – well, you know what I mean – into a box. This sole survivor wants to slip away, the shyster, as his brethren did. But I won't let him.'

Blades wagged an accusing finger in that direction.

'You signed up and shall serve your term, you wicked welsher. No merging with the universal matrix for you just yet!' Then, almost as a throwaway: 'Oh, pardon me, Guy. I digress. Where was I? Ah yes, meet my – that's right; hear and weep: *singular* – wizard, plus a scraping from what little you left alive at Wanborough.'

Introduced, the captive angel flapped its clipped and pinioned wings, opening golden eyes to pour distilled venom. Myriad links led into its body too, interwoven in such a way as to mean departure must involve spectacular suicide.

'Hearing of that . . . escapade,' Blades mused on, 'convinced me I must seek you. We've spent the ensuing period doing little else. Also, I now recall I ought to thank you too. May one ask how you managed it?'

Guy backed away from the horrible container, wondering what further use such a glacier-cool god-king could have for either its contents or him.

'Only if,' he ventured, 'I can ask you a few things likewise . . .'

'Done.'

Guy turned to face.

'The mages made it possible. As a present. Revealed in a dream.'

'It's me that's been "done", I see,' said Blades, dryly. 'Thank you for being so candid and crystal-clear.'

'That's how it was,' countered Guy, indifferent to rebukes. 'I swear. The angelic yoke on us was only ever there by our consent. A dream. Now it's over.'

Blades could have gone either way, but ultimately he sucked in his thin breath and went with Guy. Not that he let him off scot-free. The god-king mimicked peering round and about.

'And Mrs Ambassador . . .?'

'Is not here. I was given *them*,' he pointed at the wounded angel, 'for her. A p-poor exchange.'

Blades leaned back and steepled his fingers.

'There, I think, we must agree to disagree. Nor do I believe departing mages have such . . . adventures in their gift. No, *I* suspect a more almighty – and there's a clue – donor. However, we had a bargain and you've complied – just. Your turn.'

Guy inspected the ranks of questions, from pressing to piddling. Though they collectively looked at him with hope, he really couldn't be all that bothered. One or two of the closest would suffice. Then he wouldn't die still wondering. He'd heard it said that spirits in that condition came back to haunt for answers. Guy had no wish to return.

'Why the bombardment? Why do ill when you *needn't*? And then why stop?'

If it hadn't required so much energy Blades might have laughed.

'Such an easy one. Honestly! The poverty of your aspirations, Guy! Simple. I want to leave no love of me here – or anywhere. I require to be hated. And for that you don't need to annihilate. In fact, best not to. All that's required is to cause sorrow . . .'

An Ambassador could hardly deny the truth of it. Rather than collude Guy pressed on.

'And why these two tortured things?'

A dismissive click of the tongue.

'Don't act so prim, my boy. You've had occasion to apply the stick too. It's because they retain *relevance*. Both their sort deal in dreams – as you well know – and shall shortly hear . . .'

'Spare me. Forget I asked. But one other thing: *are* you a god?'

Blades smiled the smile that simultaneously replied and said '*Do you* really *need to ask that?*'

Unspoken query or no, Guy answered it.

'I want to hear you say so – in front of everyone.'

'Everyone' was the surprising number of huscarls, flunkies and assorted females still here in this stripped-down Imperial entourage. That they all believed went without saying. Guy wanted Blades to tell them the truth and tear them apart – just as he had once been torn. It was for their own good. And Blades's.

'That I can't do,' said the god-king, almost as if he longed to nevertheless. 'For reasons which will become apparent. Those same "dreams", you see . . .'

He turned a tiring head to the cupboarded captives.

'You two: pay attention! Sing from the same songsheet or I will play on your chains. Now, Guy, hear this. As the learned Hebrew once said: *"Gather together and I will tell you what will happen to you in the end of days . . ."*'

Something the human mage had experienced before made him readily compliant. So, though the words were by now familiar to him, he looked into another place and saw the story anew. Then he recounted it for them.

'My people will depart. My people will increase. And we shall be *millions*! I see burrows for those who are not my people: those who cannot soar. Null will hunt in the ruins of cities and dig again for tasty meat . . .'

Blades didn't insult Guy with interpretation – and besides he wearied.

'You know it, Guy. Having lost someone you know it more than most. The mages have discovered what they should not. They skip ahead of the human story, returning gleefully to God and higher things. That will put ideas in the heads of many more. Multitudes will be convinced that the dream is over – because that's the truth. The impulse to dissolution is irresistible for pilgrim creatures once they're made confident of what comes after. Who would not be the equal of angels – and more – given the choice? This example,' he moved a finger angel-wards, 'this outer-orbit of the kind, might disagree but, broadly speaking, I'm right. Believe me, Guy, knowledge of the lattice is subversive stuff! Spin it on a few generations and the only ones left will be the severely earth-bound. The timid and tunnel-visioned. Which, upon reflection, is an inadvertent pun – for that's where they'll be living! If you can call it "living" . . .'

Blades erupted into a clamour of dry coughs which postponed the *coup de grâce*, much to his pained annoyance.

'There won't be enough to man the walls,' he finally spat out. 'But the Null won't suffer. This world is enough for them: more than enough! *They*'ll still be here in strength to stalk our descendants, as they did before. You don't need visions to see that – though they help the slow. Once one mage pierces the flesh and finds all shapes are arbitrary – well, then it's inevitable! Our friend here in bondage confirms it. With or without his assistance I can see an empty world: a world like the Wessex I first walked on fifty – no, nearer sixty – years ago. Green and clean and pocked with burrows. Plus a few shaggymen waiting for the Null to find them. Little burrows, little lives: short lives! No need for Ambassadors there, Guy! It will be fresh, it will be quiet, but,' this in sudden and exhausting fury, '*it is NOT what I fought for!*'

The soliloquy drained him even as it pumped blood to his face. Blades conformed to the uncomfortable shape of the throne.

Guy *could* see it. His thoughts had been tending that way, despite all the gross diversions. He couldn't argue – but would still protest.

'Which,' he asked, almost casually, 'was *what* incidentally?'

Blades nodded feebly, not relishing something.

'You're right. I didn't come all this way to improve your understanding. I tormented my old age, I shifted my little world – at great pain and expense I might add – for higher things. Therefore, Guy, hear me: I came to Egypt to save my soul! Tell him, sister . . .'

The angel would not speak until a huscarl composed upon her chains.

'Into every world,' she part said, part screamed, 'comes revelation. Until then it is our playground, or even the Null's! And when, dread day, the word arrives, then, even then, it can still fail to speak through *COWARDICE!*' She hurled the accusation at Blades. 'Or wallowing in *fleshy* pits. Then woe and joy betide! Woe to that world and joy to us! Where the *word* is not said, there we may make a garden . . . ! A world without guidance? Tasty indeed!'

'Shut it!' said the voice of a Blades departed decades before, and circumstances rendered the command quite feasible. One huscarl boot applied to a cabinet door sealed the angel away. No more was heard.

There must have been something other than wood to supply silence, for it fell too absolute. Guy never learned what, but discovered instead that the blind chamberlain knew the way unaided. He shuffled over and turned the key.

'I've no more need of it or them,' said Blades, gladly. 'Take that thing and hurl it overboard.'

He'd been unaware that Guy now *saw* and was encompassing him in his stare. When Blades realised, it shook him.

'Coward indeed!' said Guy, with deceptive calm. 'Coward of all the ages! You were the *word* and you failed to say it . . .'

'I know, I know,' pleaded Blades, 'but look at the weather we've been having . . .'

The quip died a death, impaled on Guy's gaze. The god-king retreated back to seriousness.

'I thought I'd done so well,' he quavered. 'I was first to charge, last to retreat . . . usually. I built. Castles! Cathedrals! Everything!'

Guy shook his head and hat.

'Nothing! You were for yourself. Sham priest. Phoney prophet. I see all now. I don't want to stay. Give me my quick death.'

Already hosed down with acid words, Blades was brought up short. He could only nod.

'Leave us,' he announced, at the price of pain.

A lot of huscarls had already gone with the angel and mage cabinet: a tall order to manhandle from a moving ship. Those left behind never dreamed of defying. The remaining courtiers flowed away in a river of chainmail and silk, till only Blades and Guy were left facing each other.

The god-king held the Ambassador's eye, with a look unlike any other exchanged so far. What he said was equally conversation and his own long-brewed inmost thoughts unfolding.

'I can still save the day. I tried to cheat the all-seeing eye and remove you from the game. To leave him with no alternative but to use me, useless though I am. To maybe even forgive me. In that sense, I was a foolish little curate . . .'

And, in all their acquaintance, Guy had never heard him so unassailably sincere. It was disarming.

'But a curate still . . .' Blades meandered. 'Significantly enough. Not strict apostolic succession, but that same all-seeing eye is also kind. It can choose to turn a blind eye . . .'

This was not what Guy had anticipated. There was no visible threat from whence short shrift could come. Perhaps a cunning device within the walls? Spring-loaded spears? Or a trapdoor down to sharks below? Nothing manifested itself. No hinge or eyelet could be seen. It became confusing to be still around and breathing.

'I . . .' Guy started. A flash of the old, old, man's eyes stopped him.

'You're as bad as that Hunter fellow. Nothing but I, I, I. Everything revolves round you. Only it turns out that it actually *does*. I knew you couldn't be harmed. Eventually I knew, anyway' – this added in the interests of honesty. 'Plough your ship, puckle your heels: not a scratch, not a hair of your head harmed! No. You must be given your chance. Which also happens to be mine. Only do it gently – otherwise you'll break 'em of any theology. In my land they had a "Reformation" – ho-ho. Nothing survived. Only desert. You'll be kinder, I reckon . . .'

'This is not death!' Guy accused.

'Ah, Guy, but it *will* be. Patience. Hear me out. Then I can pass the mantle on. Knowingly. If you accept . . . Then what I *should* have done can be bequeathed to you.'

Guy felt not the slightest compulsion to assist. He was even willing to endure more of life in order to see Blades suffer.

'Why should I?'

The god-king was now stricken and spent on his rose-quartz throne, the stimulants expired or taking their revenge. His voice was down to a whisper.

'Because otherwise I *shall* have failed. I suspect I will be punished.'

'Good.'

'Therefore, let it happen in this life, not the next. Please . . .'

Guy was unmoved.

'All right then,' Blades gasped, 'heed *duty* instead. Save me and the world together. Don't let there be burrows again.'

Guy had never known those days but felt for the ancestors as if he had. Now it looked like his descendants might get to experience them for real. He tried an ambassadorial side-shuffle.

'So what if the world goes quiet and the Null have their little day? The portal from Paradise persists. There will be another Blades – and surely a better one . . .'

The god-king had already thought of that. He rallied his reserves as he had at the 'Great Defeat' on Epsom Downs (before abandoning them to the Null).

'Yes, the clock I came through remains in the original Godalming. My last mage sees – saw – it in the town museum. It glimmers in a dark corner still. Perchance some successor me will wonder at the light of dawn within its case and explore. But that's the thing: another *me*. They may succeed where I was negligent – or may not. Either way, centuries are lost. Whereas *we've* walked along a long old road. It's under our belts. I *know* – as do you now . . .'

Blades reckoned he saw a chink of weakness and metaphorically leaped for it, as best a prostrate ancient can.

'It may even have all happened before. Think, Guy: I found a quiet world – but with a hillside "Long Man" already carved and old. An earlier me, maybe. And remember the deep ruins? It makes you wonder . . . Failure's not just my personal preserve, you know.'

Like a condemned man at a rigged trial, Guy saw the way things were heading. He cursed Duty from the bottom of his heart – and the heart of his bottom, come to that.

'But *how*?' A shotgun-spray of a question. With it Guy realised he'd conceded, abandoned the line; exposed his back to the killing blow.

Blades would have shrugged had it not been too much to ask of his shoulders. His easy answer proved he'd done a spot of shrugging-off already.

'Well, surely I'm the *last* person you should ask, aren't I?'

At the end, the truth was becoming more and more natural: refreshing even. Blades wished he'd done it earlier.

Guy grimaced.

'And that "easy death"?' he asked.

Blades sighed in almost erotic anticipation.

'I beg you to give it me . . .'

And, as though it fled fast down a corridor, Guy saw the sunny life of liberty and lightheartedness he was meant to lead receding from him. The life he was made and yet not destined for. Left behind was a future grey and gruelling.

He stepped right up to the throne.

'I *will* h-have my revenge . . .'

'But?'

Guy bowed his head – within reach of two raised, wrinkled, hands. They struggled up to encompass his brow. There were tears of joy in the god-king's eyes.

'I bless you, Guy,' croaked Blades. 'And I ordain you. A priest for ever!'

Accepted like a curse, Guy drew in the bitter breath which would accept. Then he placed a pillow over Blades's face and pressed.

Two fresh openings in two pyramids.

Into one, gunpowder blown, went Emperor Blades with full honours, down to his eternal rest in Pharaoh Cheops's tomb.

From the other, born of decay, flew mages, already semi-angelic. Their scintillating pyramid was ceasing to. It sagged, sad and abandoned. These were almost the last away.

Yet some still paused to inspect the nearby ceremony. Guy would have looked up for one in particular, but duty called.

'There is no God but *God*!' Emperor Guy intoned, as loud he could. 'And Christ is his son! Hear the hidden truth of Blades who is gone! May he rest in peace having conveyed it.'

This time round Guy wanted to build on rock, not sand – even if it happened to be sand his audience below stood upon. That irony was just God's sense of humour. Probably.

Masons were already sealing the entrance they'd blasted, bringing darkness to aid that 'rest'. The dear departed certainly ought to have peace with all that weight of stone above him. Millennia worth of wear and tear now stood between Blades and Null scavengers – and anyone else who might try to resurrect him.

So much for his carcass. As for Blades's spirit and eternal fate, Guy declined to speculate. His thoughts might be uncharitable towards the man (and *only* a man) who'd placed him on high.

The select few on the lofty platform against the pyramid's side were turning to go. At its edges, cantors were passing the message to the throng.

'Oh ye men: know that the great Blades is dead – but God lives!'

Transmitted in their distinctive and unearthly style, the call travelled far out into the desert to enlighten scorpions and lizards, before dying for lack of force.

Nearer in, everyone heard. No one disagreed, no one rioted. The prior-convinced moved vapour-like amongst them to deal with disquiets, but weren't needed. Guy saw grounds for hope. The hoi polloi had been well prepared, their imaginations fertilised with a steady drip, drip, drip of propaganda. An Ambassador could arrange that sort of thing in his sleep. Today was harvest day. The first mass baptism had already taken place in the Nile.

Guy had concocted prime ambassadorial lies about why 'the great Blades', 'the *prophet* Blades', saw fit to chastise Alexandria-Jerusalem, or why mage-angels might attend his requiem. He'd waded up to his hocks in shameless deceit for him. And now it was done. No more Ambassador trickery. Guy never wanted to tell anything but the unalloyed truth ever again. The years ahead would be honest – and then he could lay his head to rest as well. Speed the day.

The way down was by means of an exceedingly long ladder. Polly and Prudence helped Archbishop Hunter over the brink before standing ready either side to do the same for beloved Guy. But then there was a third figure between them, also white but . . . glittering.

Guy thought it was his eyes playing tricks, the victims of heat haze or ophthalmia. Then he saw he wasn't cursed but blessed.

Their time was not human time. Bathie was full angel now; her raiment no longer crimson or, worse still, black. Now she wore a suit of stars.

Some saw, some heard, but only Guy did both. She came to him, forging a way by presence alone. People parted like the Red Sea, unable to detect the Moses giving them a shove.

Her eyes were fire, her fingertips likewise.

'*Dear* Guy,' she said – and mended everything. A single tear made its way down his rapt face.

She flew right to him and spoke again.

'Endure "duty" for just a little space. A while. Then there *shall* be joy!'

And she kissed him.

All the people, whether on high platform or down in the desert, saw that.

'Meanwhile . . . *Read!*'

Words conducted through her – not hers, but *via*. Statements straight from the structure of the universe. They shot along Guy's – but no longer *just* Guy's – arm, into heart and mind and mouth.

'*Recite!*' she said – and Guy could only follow.

'"*In the name of God, the beneficent, the merciful. Owner of the Day of Judgement . . .*"'

Guy recited and the people listened.

EPILOGUE

Notes on Godalming Clockmakers
  Godalming Museum Occasional Papers no. 37
  Based on late twentieth-century research by Freddy Hill.
  Copy-edited for reprint by Cult. Comm. D. Tang, Fall, 2024.
  With statute-required thanks to Cultural Funding Unit 2332 (Wessex-East, Sussex, SW Kent and Pas d'Calais) of the Pan-Euro-Union.
  Nihil Obstat: Cult. Comm. Diedre Tang

'*Eight-day English* **[as was – D.T.]** *trunk dial timepiece.*

This rustically handsome clock was made around 1680, most probably by Melchizedek Stedman, the first of four known generations of Godhelmian clockmakers. He resided at Brentinghams, the double-gabled house with ornate brick facade on the north side of the High Street, next to W. H. Smith's **[Former stationer's. Trading licence rescinded 2013 – D.T.]**. *The black dial is painted with yellow Roman and Arabic numerals, plus homely motifs of local wild flowers.*

[N.B. Not for publication.
Save for its early date and local provenance, this provincial piece holds little interest save for the hard-core horologist of possible reactionary and/or Little Englander tendencies. Transfer item to reserve store forthwith – D. T.]

THE END